HAVEN

KATE ROSHON

Haven by Kate Roshon
© 2017 Kate Roshon
All rights reserved.

978-1-935751-33-5 Paperback
978-1-935751-34-2 eBook

Published by
Scribbulations LLC
Kennett Square
Pennsylvania, USA

Acknowledgments

To my family: Deb, Andy, Emma, Jake, Martha, Riess, Tyler, Abby, Jamie, Jim, Irene, Dan, Heidi, Stella, Zoë, and Ruby. Mom and Dad, I really wouldn't be here without you!! Thanks for always believing in me. Kit Green, my comma and punctuation queen. I never could have done it without you; you are a true lifesaver. Thank you for not yelling at me TOO loud at all the thans and not thens and the lost commas before ands as well as the other punctuation no-no's!!
Most of all to Walt: you are the light of my life and my anchor. Thank you for your never-ending belief and faith in me. Without your love, life wouldn't be as bright. I'll always be your soft-shelled crab and you will always be my one and only love!

CHAPTER 1

Waking up one chilly March morning, Kala knew something was going to happen. It was the same feeling she had the day her parents died, leaving her on her own.

Officially, one of her older brothers was caring for her; he let her live in his house, yes, but that was all. As long as she didn't do anything that reflected badly on him and she followed his house rules, he didn't care where she was or what she was doing. He was a rich man who lived on a large estate, and for the most part, she was free to come and go as she pleased. Sometimes, at meal times mostly, she wished someone would ask her how her day had been or what was going on in her life. But, as a family, only she and her brother lived on the estate. House staff outnumbered them almost four to one.

As she showered, she tried to put a finger on what it was that was bothering her, but she couldn't quite pinpoint what it was. When she came out of the bathroom wrapped in a towel, her brother was sitting on her bed.

"Well, Casio, isn't this a surprise," she said. "Is the lord of the manor here to speak with his bastard sister?"

"Must you always have this attitude?" he retorted. "I have let you stay here, haven't I?"

She nodded her head once to acknowledge the point and then waited for him to continue. She had learned quickly when she had first come not to push her brother too hard. Kala and her brothers had always been told that Kala had been the product of an affair her mother had had, but Kala at least, always believed that there was more to the story. She had expected her parents to tell them the truth someday, but then their parents died. Their mother had doted on her, though, given that Kala had been the child of her older years, so her brothers might have looked upon Kala as the child who stole their mother from them. Older brother Shawan never acted this way, only Casio.

"You turn sixteen next week, Kala. It is the age of Ascension."

Kala gasped. She had forgotten about the Rite of Ascension. What would she do? She should have been better prepared, but that was a parent's job, and she had no parents. She knew that she would pass and pass well, but she wondered who would be her advocate, since she had no living parents, and Casio wasn't likely to take the time.

"And who is to advocate for me at my Rite of Ascension? You've never taken any interest in anything I do, or did."

"I've talked to Shawan. He'll do it. However, you will have to study hard. I'll want you out of this house at the end of the school year, and you can only be on your own if you can prove yourself."

"Don't worry, brother; I won't let you down. I can't wait to get out myself. Shall I move in with Shawan until my Rite of Ascension?"

"That won't be necessary. When we spoke, it was agreed that he would stay here while he works with you, and then, when it's over, you can both leave and let me be. I never wanted anything to do with either of you, and once this is over with, I can finally have my wish. Mother never should have had any children other than me."

"But you're not the oldest, Casio. If she hadn't had children after Shawan, you wouldn't have been born either."

"Maybe that would have been better," he said quietly, rising and turning to leave. "Kala, it's not that I don't love you and Shawan, because I do in my own way. It's just that I prefer my own kind of people."

With that, he left the room, closing the door behind him. His kind of people meant the rich TechNets who kept the world running. If it weren't for them, things would be very bad indeed.

Kala sighed heavily. It was not a pleasant way to start her day.

CHAPTER 2

As Kala walked to the estate's gate, she regarded the world that Casio had created for himself. Even with the land allotment from TechNet, Casio had done better for himself. He had bargained the four acres he had gotten automatically when he signed with TechNet into ten.

The estate was on part of what used to be Central Park in Old New York City. There were many gardens with exotic flowers, there were trees, and there was space. The house itself was small considering her brother's importance, but he had wanted it that way. What her brother truly loved and prized were the grounds, because the space guarded and insulated him from the outside world he seemed to hate so much. In some ways, she and Casio were more alike than either of them cared to admit.

When she got to the gate, she turned to look back at the grounds. The lawns were bordered with flowers of all kinds from around the world: roses, daisies, lilies, irises, and they bloomed in all the colors of the rainbow. The trees were large and old; some city elders had said some were trees from the early days of the park. What Kala loved most were the minigardens with the benches. She would sit in a different garden every day to do her homework. Her brother had even planted ancient boxwood plants to create a maze. Two of the gardens were created around working waterfalls. Because of Earth's water shortages, Casio had adapted the waterfalls so that they recirculated the water, only needing to refill them once every couple of years.

She breathed deeply and turned to go. Shawan would probably be at the house when she got home after school. It would be nice to see him again. She wondered if he would let her move in with him and Janna at the end of the school year. She would have passed her tests at school; she would have gone through the Ascension Rite and passed (surely with Shawan's help she would pass); and she would be able, at sixteen, to be on her own.

She opened the smaller, more manageable gate on the right side of the massive main gate and stepped out into another world. She was suddenly surrounded by the hustle and bustle of the crowded city. Years ago, its name had changed from New York City to Eastern City, when it had consolidated with other nearby old cities like Philadelphia to the south and Boston to the north. From history she had learned that, right after the Great War, cities around the world started to consolidate. The entire East Coast of the old United States was now Eastern City from the tip of Old Maine down to the tip of Old Florida and the United States were now just one United State, made up of the consolidated cities in the East Coast, Midwest, Northwest, Southwest, and West Coast.

Open spaces and parks still existed, but those would soon be gone. What the Earth needed was some population relief. The World consolidated government had put limits on the number of children each family could have, like old China did, but many couples didn't pay attention and kept having as many kids as they wanted. Kala knew that the government was sending manned missions into space to find suitable planets where humans could survive without too much expensive adaptation.

That's what I want to do, Kala thought to herself as she reached the subway station. *Go into space and help this overcrowded planet.*

She took out her ID badge and ran it under the scanner. She heard the usual beep as the light changed from red to green, and she passed through the turnstile. She hurried through night workers on their way home and day workers on their way to work. Then she spotted her friend Lindsey from her Teaching section and waved. They entered the waiting subway car and both moved toward the center.

"Were you able to figure out the math homework?" Lindsey asked as they met in the middle.

"Most of it. Want to go over it at school?"

Lindsey nodded. They sat in silence as the train pulled out of the station. Kala thought about her Rite of Ascension. Would Casio make her take the test on her birthing day in the middle of the week or would he at least give her until the weekend? She would have to ask him tonight.

"Lindsey, I need to talk to you after school today."

"Do you want to go to the library or ice cream shop?"

"I think today the ice cream shop will be a good choice. I'm rather

4

fed up with school at the moment."

Lindsey had already passed her Rite of Ascension tests. She had found an apartment, had a lead on a job, and was just waiting to pass her end-of-year finals before moving on in her life.

"How much history do you remember?" Kala asked suddenly.

"It's one of my favorite subjects, so I guess retain quite a bit," Lindsey grinned.

"Was there a reason that sixteen was chosen as the age of Ascension?"

Lindsey thought about it before answering.

"From what I remember, in the middle part of the last millennium, sixteen was the minimum age for a person to operate a motor vehicle. You know, the old gas-powered vehicles in the museum?"

Kala nodded.

At that moment, the train pulled into their stop. Lindsey waited until they were off the train and heading toward the exit before continuing.

"Well, in 2145, the government decided that they needed more people in the workforce. There were debates about what age to start conscripting workers, and from what I remember, they decided that younger would be better. So, at that point, since the kids were already taking the test to start operating a vehicle, they decided to change the test a bit and make it the precursor of what we now call the Ascension."

"Okay, got it. Now explain to me about the advocate thing. From what I remember from history class, when the kids started driving, they had to have an adult...any adult...in the vehicle for the first six months, or so. But that person wasn't necessarily a parent or guardian, was it?"

"Right, that was one of the things the government changed. They decided they wanted to be a bit more choosy. They needed the workers, but they wanted to be able to place the workers in the proper jobs, that way everyone would be happy and productive." Lindsey smiled, "What's up with all the Ascension questions?"

"Mine is next week. I was just making sure I had the history correct."

Throughout her classes that day, Kala thought about what she wanted to do. She knew that she had the option of stating her opinion of what she wanted to do with her life on the Rite of Ascension paperwork, but she wasn't sure what to put. She wanted to teach, but she also wanted to be part of the space program. Her studies at school had considered both interests, and if she did well on the final Rite of Ascension exam, she would get to make the choice herself.

CHAPTER 3

When the school day ended, she met Lindsey at their usual place.

"Still in the mood for a sundae?" Lindsey grinned.

"Will the rest of the gang be there?"

"As far as I know they should be."

"That's fine as long as we can talk privately first."

"Okay."

As they started to leave, Kala heard her name being called. Turning, she saw Mr. Alston, her school advisor, standing in the doorway.

"I'll catch up with you there," she told Lindsey as she turned back.

"I'll save you a seat."

Kala returned to the building that housed the school and counseling center. She met Mr. Alston just inside the front door. Without saying a word, he led the way down the hall to his office. When they arrived, he motioned for her enter and sit as he closed the door. She noticed that two men were already in the room, sitting in two extra chairs.

"Kala, these men are from the World Air and Space Administration and they are here to see you."

"Why would anyone from WASA want to see me?" Her eyes widened a bit in surprise.

Mr. Alston nodded to the older of the two men, who replied.

"Well, as you know, we keep track of all students who take an interest in space. After they take their Ascension Rite and apply to us for work, they are tested again in-house and then given jobs within the organization that fit their personalities. Following me so far?"

Kala nodded.

"Well, during a person's school years, we also keep track of those who have tested highly in the sciences. Of those, we look for the ones who have the tendency to lead. You have both of those qualities and more. We don't need to go into everything now, but let's just say you are just the kind of person we're looking for. We know you will be taking the Rite of Ascension test next week, and we wanted to be the first to offer you a position when you finish school."

The men were silent as Kala tried to comprehend what she had just been told. WASA was offering her a job to start the day after she finished school if she wanted it. Casio would spit nails. No matter what his position was with the TechNet's, this was sure to be a step above that. Even if she were to start at the bottom in the organization and work her way up, she would still be doing better than Casio.

"What kind of position are we talking about?"

"With your background you could go for almost anything. Shuttle pilot...after the required flight training, of course...mission specialist, ground crew, mission control. Name your interest, and there is a job for it."

"Why come to me now? Why not wait until I've gone through the Rite of Ascension and passed my final school exams? Aren't you being a bit premature? What if I choose something else?"

There was silence again while the three men looked at each other. Finally, the other, younger WASA man looked at her and spoke.

"I asked the same questions when they came to me two years ago," he replied. "I wasn't sure I would really get what they promised me, and I wasn't sure I wanted to be locked into a position before I got a chance to scope things out. So they let me think about it. About a week after my finals in school and my Rite of Ascension, I called and took the job. What I realized was this: no matter what I told myself I wanted, and no matter what other jobs I looked at, a space-related job was what really interested me. We feel it will be the same for you. We don't want you to sign any contracts now, but we want to give you something to think about."

"And I will have time to think about your proposition even after my Rite of Ascension and final exams?"

"Of course," Mr. Alston replied, looking at the two men for assurance. "The student is always given the option."

Kala noticed that Mr. Alston placed a strong emphasis on the word "student."

"I'll think about it, then, and I'll make my decision by the end of school next month."

The two men from WASA nodded.

"Just make sure Mr. Alston knows when you have made your decision, or if you have any questions, and he'll get in touch with us. Trust me, you won't be sorry if you decide to work with us."

Kala nodded at the three men, then picked up her book sack and headed for the door. Suddenly she stopped.

Turning back to the three men, she asked, "By chance, did someone recommend me?"

They looked at each other again.

"Well, actually," replied Mr. Alston, "someone did...your brother Casio."

Kala stared at them in disbelief. She was amazed that Casio would do this for her. She could see him recommending one of his TechNet cronies, but certainly not his own sister. What had possessed him to recommend her? She would find out when she got home.

Kala smiled, "Thanks. It certainly is something I will consider."

She walked out of Mr. Alston's office and stood in the hall, collecting her thoughts. Just wait until Lindsey heard! Suddenly she gulped. What was she going to tell Lindsey? Kala was smart enough to know that no such offer would be or had been made to Lindsey. Smart as her friend was, there would be no offers from WASA for her.

Kala was not sure what to do. Then, she began to walk with a purpose. She would go to the ice cream shop and tell her friend. Maybe they would be able to go to WASA together, because Kala was almost certain she would take the job.

What kind of a job had been offered to Lindsey? Had she accepted the offer? Were all students offered a position right before their Rite of Ascension and final exams? She pondered these questions on her way to the ice cream shop.

Entering the shop, she looked around. She saw Lindsey sitting at the usual corner table, and the rest of the crowd around the old-fashioned jukebox.

"What'd Mr. Alston want?"

"Did anyone come to see you about a job after finals?" Kala asked in return.

"No one came in person. I had the usual forms to fill out on what my interests might be. That's not unusual, not everyone gets a personal invite. Who was there to meet you?"

"A couple of guys from the recruitment section of WASA."

"WHAT? Are you serious? Casio's head will spin!"

"He's the one who recommended me."

Lindsey sat in stunned silence as she digested Kala's words. Kala realized, in that moment, that her friend wouldn't be mad at or jealous of her, one of the reasons Lindsey was such a good friend.

"You're kidding me, right?"

"Nope, I made a point to ask if someone had recommended me. They told me it was Casio," Kala shrugged. "What was your Rite of Ascension like?"

"General knowledge in the computer test and, of course, the family history. For me, the computer test seemed to be geared mainly toward the business and English side of things. The personal family history stuff was done in front of the board, but it's nothing you need to worry about. If WASA came to see you, they must have a lot of confidence that you'll pass with the numbers they require. I think the Ascension Rite is more of an aptitude test on what kind of job to place you in after school than anything else."

Thinking of others, Kala didn't know anyone who had failed. She wondered how and why the testing had first started and been used. Maybe the Rite of Ascension began when they had done away with the formal colleges and gone back to apprenticeships.

"Do you think my computer test will be geared more toward the sciences? I mean if WASA is interested in me..."

"Maybe, but then you have always been good in engineering. You really don't have to worry about the education side of it, you know. Since they follow a student's progress in school, they tend to gear the computer bit toward our strengths, with a little technical testing on our interests... from what I remember. Just concentrate on your family history and you will be fine."

"But what's the deal with family history?"

"I think it comes from the last war when so many families were separated. They want to make sure separations don't happen again. Or, if they do, there won't be mutations from the blood marriages that happened once families were separated and people didn't know they were marrying a close blood relative."

"I hadn't thought of that. Thanks, Lindsey. It really helps when I have someone to talk to!"

"You know I don't mind. You would do the same for me," Lindsey replied smiling. "And we'd better let the guys come over and sit down before they spend all their credits in that dratted old jukebox!"

"I think I'd like to spend a few credits in there myself," Kala said laughing. "It's been too long since I've just let go!"

"Hey, didn't you say that Shawan was coming today to stay with you and Casio to help you study?"

"Oh damn, I forgot! Sorry about the split, but I need to get home. I'll see you at school tomorrow!"

Kala grabbed her things and ran across the street to the nearby subway stop. Luckily, the train was just coming as she arrived on the platform. On the ride home, she thought about seeing Shawan again. It had been almost six months since she had seen her oldest brother and his family. Casio didn't believe much in family get-togethers, and even though she didn't have any curfews, Casio usually wouldn't let her off the property long enough after school, or on the weekends, to go see them. Once she was on her own, she planned to see them as often as she could. She loved her niece and nephew, and she missed them.

As the train pulled into her stop, she considered what it would be like to be on her own. She would be about the same age her mother had been when she had moved out of her grandparents' house. Kala couldn't wait to be free of Casio. She felt a bit sad. Why had Casio turned out the way he had? Her parents certainly hadn't given him any less love then they had given her or Shawan. They say that a person's personality is a combination of nature and nurture. She wondered if there were any relatives like Casio back in their line.

CHAPTER 4

Kala arrived at the back door of the estate just as Shawan pulled up to the front.

At least I'm not late, she thought.

She dropped her book sack by the stairs and went into the front hallway. She watched from the windows next to the door as her brother climbed off his motorbike, took off his helmet, and looked around. He was almost a full head taller than she was, but they both had their mother's features. Their eyes were close together, and they had small noses and their mother's full lips. In coloring, they resembled their father, with dark brown eyes and hair that matched and olive skin. Standing just over six feet, Shawan took after his mother's side of the family, while Kala, at five feet exactly, took after her father's side. They also had very similar personalities, laid back with street smarts and almost perfect memories. Happy to see Shawan, she opened the door and walked onto the porch. Shawan turned at the sound of the door, and the siblings smiled at each other.

"You know, this may be the one time I am actually taller than you are," she giggled.

"This is true," he laughed back. "He sure knows how to keep things pretty, doesn't he?" Shawan swept his arm round, indicating the estate.

"His property, if not his personal life," she replied.

Shawan just snorted, hanging his helmet on the handlebars and slinging his bag from the back of his bike to his shoulder, before bounding up the stairs to the porch. He gave his younger sister a quick hug and a kiss on the top of her head as he passed her on his way to the front door.

11

"I assume he wants you out as soon as you take your Rite of Ascension?"

"No. He's graciously allowing me to finish my final exams before he kicks me to the curb," she laughed, as she led the way into the house.

"Well, that's nice of him. You know that you are more than welcome to stay with us until you get an apartment, if you need to."

"I know, and I'll let you know. To tell you the truth, I haven't even started looking yet. There are the youth hotels, so I'll be able to stay there if I need to. And Lindsey also has an apartment, so I may be able to stay with her."

"You'll land on your feet yet! You know that we would love to have you, and the kids would love to spend some time with their auntie! They don't get to see you enough."

"There isn't a leash short enough to keep me away."

Shawan didn't respond to the last comment; they had arrived at his suite of rooms. He tossed his bag onto the bed and walked to the windows to view his younger brother's property.

"What are you thinking, brother?" Kala asked quietly.

"I was wondering why Casio turned out the way he did, and we turned out the way we did."

Kala laughed aloud when he said that.

"What's so funny?"

"It's just that I've been wondering that myself today. Mother and Father didn't raise him any differently than they did either of us. If anything, Mom favored me because of her age when I was born. But I don't think I was a preferred child, was I?"

Shawan continued looking out the window as he thought about her question.

"No, you weren't preferred and neither were Casio or I. I think that Casio is just part of a group that is very selective, and he prefers to be alone with those of his choosing. Since neither of us have quite the technical adeptness that he does, he prefers not to have the family connection."

"That makes sense. So... What do we do to get ready for the Ascension Rite? I think I want this over as much as he does, although not necessarily for the same reasons."

"No worries, sister. I think the only thing I will be needed for is to be advocate at the testing center. You will pass with flying colors."

"As advocate, what is your role in the Ascension Rite? I know my role is to pass the tests given and then decide on a career. But what exactly does an advocate do?"

"I fill out and sign all the paperwork. I go with you to the testing center, sign you in, and then wait for you to finish. When it's all over and you have passed...and I know you will...I certify that all the family history is correct and sign the paperwork again to certify that, as the family advocate, everything is correct. As soon as I sign that final time, you are on your own."

Kala inhaled and sighed. She walked over to the window and stood next to Shawan. Together, they were silent, gazing at their brother's estate. Finally, Kala turned and faced Shawan.

"I got a visit from WASA at school today."

"You did? Do tell."

"They want me to join up after my Ascension Rite and graduation. And you will never guess who nominated me."

"If you tell me 'Casio,' I think I'll faint."

"Well, then, sit down on the bed so you don't hit your head when you fall."

"What on earth possessed him to do that?"

"I don't know and I don't really care. I've been thinking about it, and I'll probably accept their offer. I want to explore other worlds. See what's out there for the human race. This isn't the only planet that we can live on without domes, you know."

"I can see you floating around in a shuttle as you hurtle toward other worlds," Shawan replied laughing.

Just then there was a knock on the door.

"Come in," Shawan called, still laughing.

"Well, isn't this the nice family reunion," said Casio, opening the door and coming in.

Kala and Shawan looked at each other and smiled before greeting Casio.

"The place hasn't changed a bit since I was here three years ago," said Shawan, walking over to his younger brother with an outstretched hand.

"I should hope not," replied Casio, ignoring Shawan's hand. "Once I got it set up the way I liked it, I wanted it to stay that way. It took me long enough to get the right staff combination who understood that."

Shawan stood in front of Casio with his hand out for a moment longer before he dropped it to his side.

"What purpose does a handshake serve, big brother? You know I don't believe in pretense. Honestly, you should know that about me by now, Shawan. You are here because Kala needs an advocate, and I don't have the time or the inclination to do it. When everything is over, I will expect you both to leave me alone in peace with the people of my own choosing."

"That won't be hard, Casio," Shawan replied. "It's about time that Kala got away from both of us and went out on her own. One thing I am curious about, though. What on earth possessed you to recommend her to WASA?"

Casio regarded them intently before answering.

"I know Kala has the ability to be in a technical field somewhere. I also know that she doesn't have what it takes to be in the TechNet group. I do have a few friends at WASA, so I called them and put in a word. Regardless of how I may act, I do want my family to do well."

"Not that I doubt your knowledge, Casio," Kala was puzzled, "but how do you know I don't have what it takes to be a TechNet? I'm not offended, because you're right. I don't want to be one. I'm just curious."

"Because you are more compassionate than most of us in TechNet. You know how I am with just you and Shawan; imagine a whole group of people like me in one place at one time. You'd never last. And don't jump down my throat. I'm not in the group at TechNet who want to blow the planet up and end the human race forever. It's just that we are what people used to refer to as computer geeks, the group of people who were always a breed apart from society, and we've tended to keep that tradition alive. We keep to ourselves, in a place where we feel safe, and we know that we will be protected. We also know that we are, for the most part, smarter than the general population, and we prefer to stick to our own where we know we will be understood."

Rarely had Kala and Shawan ever heard Casio give such a long speech. They didn't speak while they digested what he had said.

"Okay," replied Kala, "that's all I wanted to know."

Casio continued, "I have no doubt that you will pass your Ascension Rite next week, and then I expect you to be out of this house after your final exams at school. If you don't have a place to stay, I can arrange for an apartment. If you do decide to take the job with WASA, they have housing for all their employees. Anyway, I believe that Cook should have dinner ready by now, so why don't we go down and eat. Then I can get back to work. I'll be fairly busy for the next few weeks, so I'll probably be staying over at Main Complex while Shawan is here."

After dinner, Casio packed a bag for his stay in the apartment complex at TechNet. When he was ready to leave, he stopped by the study where Kala and Shawan were working.

"I'll be on my way now. Kala, I'll see you in a couple of weeks. Good luck on the Ascension Rite next week. Shawan, I'll see you when I see you. Maybe I'll come to Kala's graduation from school in May, but I don't know yet. The staff knows what to do to keep the place running, but I will have them check with you on what you want for meals. Good-bye for now." Instructions given, Casio turned and walked from the room.

Kala and Shawan sat in silence until they heard the front door close and Casio's scooter start up and drive away. Kala got up with a sigh and went to the window.

"What is it that makes him so different?" she asked.

"I don't know. I can't remember anyone in the family being so antisocial. If there was a family member like him, we could say there was precedence, but I just don't know."

Kala turned away from the window. "Yes, Mother and Father didn't treat any of us differently from each other, but as far back as I can remember, Casio has been different. I remember one time, when I was about eight or nine, I brought a few friends home from school. We were still living in K District at the time, I think. When my friends and I got home, Mother sat us down at the table and gave us a snack of milk and cookies. We were talking and laughing as we ate, while Mother watched us from the other room. Casio stood there looking at us. If I was eight then, he must have been twelve. When we were about done, he looked at me and asked me who these people were, what right did I think I had not only to bring these people into the house but also to be in the house myself. Then, he looked at Mother, turned, and stomped off to his room. To this day, I'll never forget the look on his face when he said those things. It was like I was a bug to be squashed for his amusement."

"I guess I never thought about what it was like for you as the youngest," Shawan paused, calculating. "Casio is four years older than you are and I am five years older than him, so between you and me there are nine years. When you were eight, I was seventeen and had already passed the Ascension Rite and was out of the house." He studied Kala, "Do you know why Mother and Father wanted you to live with Casio instead of me in their wills?"

"I think they hoped I would be able to pull him out of his shell and help him to be happier. I don't think they ever really realized what he was like and how tied up he is in having two separate societies, the TechNets...and the rest of us."

"Enough of this," Shawan said suddenly, "Shall we continue with your lesson or end for the night?"

"I think I'm done for the night. Why don't we pick up after school tomorrow?"

"Sounds good to me. In fact, I don't think you'll need much study at all. Just some daily review and you'll be fine. What we really need to do is decide when you are going to take the test."

"I thought it had to be on my birthday... At least that's what Casio always led me to believe."

"Well, that is the tradition, but it's not actually a requirement. I guess your birthday would probably be the best thing since Casio wants you out of here so quickly. Tomorrow, I'll go to the Center and register you for next Wednesday. Then, I'll go to the school and get you signed out for that day. We'll be a step ahead of things. What time are you done for the day? I'll plan on meeting you there when I'm done and bring you home."

"I'm finished at two-thirty. By the time I get all my stuff together and talk to my friends, I'm usually leaving by three o'clock."

"Okay! I'll wait for you out front and see you at three o'clock, if that's all right with you."

"Sounds perfect."

Shawan slapped his knees as he stood up and stretched. He joined Kala at the window and, once again, regarded his younger brother's property. For the hundredth time, he wished he had the allotments for a place even half this size. His children would love all the open space.

"I don't know about you," he said finally, turning away from the window, "but I'm ready for something sweet to eat! Where does Cook hide the desserts?"

"Follow me, brother. I've learned many of Cook's secrets over the years and she has learned many of mine. Right about now, she is putting out a plate of fruit and a plate of cookies and brownies along with milk, juice, and soda for the staff. Over the years I've gotten into the habit of joining them. I'm sure she will include some for you, and if she hasn't, she will! Follow me."

"I'm right behind you!"

Chapter 5

By the time Kala's birthday rolled around the following Wednesday, she had family history and Rite of Ascension studying coming out of her ears. Getting up early that morning with Shawan, she ate the large breakfast that Cook had fixed her and, for the thousandth time, thought about how much easier things ran when Casio wasn't around. After breakfast, Shawan drove her down to the Testing Center at Center City Square. They were the first to arrive for the testing, so after signing in, she was happy to have her choice of seats. The first part of the test, the computer part, was general knowledge and basic day-to-day living information that would point her toward her final job in life. Then, when she finished the computer part, she would be taken in front of the Board for the oral tests on her family history. By the time she was done with that, her written test would be graded and the results would be known.

By five o'clock, she would not only be sixteen but also free and legally on her own—after high school graduation. She knew that Shawan would be waiting for her when she was done, and she knew that Casio would be home tomorrow. As far as she was concerned, it was a given that he would know she had passed the Rite of Ascension. TechNet had people working everywhere and knew everything, so she had no doubt that Casio would know the results before she did or, at least, at the same time. Casio would probably take tonight to celebrate the independence he so desperately wanted.

Looking around, she noticed that while she had been planning her life, the room had filled up with other eager students. At precisely eight o'clock, the proctor came in with a basket of memory sticks for the computers.

Each stick matched a student and fit into a slot in the computer screen directly in front of them; the council individualized each test to make the testing easier. There could be no cheating of any kind, as the sticks were tamperproof, created to accept only the data specified.

"My name is Mrs. Simerson and this is the Rite of Ascension test for Wednesday, March 15, 2554. Did everyone sign in out front?"

Everyone nodded.

"Is everyone sixteen as of today?"

Everyone nodded.

"Okay, then, let's get started. In this basket are your tests. There is a memory stick for each of you. If, for some reason, you don't have a memory stick when I am done handing them out, please indicate so by turning on the red problem light next to your computer. If there is an error on our part, you will get extra time at the end to make up for starting late. If the mistake is on your part, you will be quietly escorted from the room so you won't disturb the other students.

"This test is designed to last four hours. It can take you less time, but it will not take you more. If you are not done with the test at the end of four hours, you must stop. Your grade will be based on what you have accomplished. If you are one of the three students with a special time dispensation, your memory stick has been coded to allow for an extra hour.

"Everyone is allotted two restroom breaks and will be escorted from your desk to the restroom and back. Please indicate your need for a break by turning on your red light, and a monitor will come to your desk. You will be given a one and a half hour break that will include your lunch after the written exam is over and before the oral exam begins. If you are done in less than the four hours, please indicate so by turning on the green light on your computer. One of the monitors will come over to collect your memory stick and escort you from the room.

"Your break with lunch will begin at the end of four hours or when you turn on the green light. You will be escorted to the cafeteria in this building. You will be given your oral exam after the allotted lunch break ends.

"No one will be able to begin their test until all the sticks have been handed out and the signal to begin has been given. Good luck, everyone."

With the final three words, the computer screens rose from their slot in the desks and turned on. The slot for the memory sticks blinked so that, when the students got their sticks, the access port could be easily identified. Once all the sticks had been handed out and properly inserted into each computer, Mrs. Simerson took one last look around the room.

"Okay, the time is now 8:35. The test will be over at 12:35. Good luck and begin."

The room went silent except for the clicking of the computer keys as the students worked. As Kala worked through her exam, she realized that Shawan had been right; she was more than ready for this. She got into a rhythm and tried not to work too fast or too slow. She kept an eye on the clock. After two hours, she needed a bathroom break. Finding a good stopping point, she turned on the red light. A proctor came over to her desk.

"I need a bathroom break," she whispered.

"Your work saved to this point?" the proctor whispered back.

She nodded once to show that it was. No sooner had she done so, her computer turned off. She assumed it would turn back on when she got back to her desk. Going through the exit door, Kala was surprised to see the proctor lock the door behind them. He pointed to the women's room and stood waiting. He was in the same place when she came out of the restroom. He unlocked the door and escorted her back to her desk. She sat down, made herself comfortable, and her computer came back on. She took a deep breath and began working herself back to her previous pace. But, as she worked this time, she lost track of the time and let the test guide her.

With no sense of time, Kala was surprised when she found herself suddenly at the end of the test. She looked up and saw that she was done with thirty minutes to spare. Knowing that she couldn't go back and change anything, she saved her work and turned on the green light. While she was waiting for a proctor to come to her desk, she looked around the room and realized that she was the first one to finish.

"You're all done?" the proctor quietly asked when she arrived at Kala's desk. "Have you saved your work?"

"Yes, ma'am." Kala replied in the same soft voice.

The proctor made a signal to the main proctor at the front desk and Kala's memory key was ejected into the proctor's hand. With a quick nod of her head, the proctor indicated that Kala should go to the front desk.

"Congratulations, my dear," the proctor smiled, speaking softly, as Kala reached her desk. "You have passed with flying colors."

Kala was slightly surprised to hear this information. She didn't realize she was being graded as she worked.

"Thank you, ma'am," she replied quietly.

"It is now five minutes past twelve, you have until 1:35 before your oral exam begins. Ms. Johansen will escort you to the cafeteria where you will be able to order whatever you like. You will not be required to pay as this is considered part of your Ascension Rite. Good luck on your oral exam and congratulations again."

"Thank you very much."

Kala turned and followed the woman indicated to be Ms. Johansen. When they were out of the testing room, Ms. Johansen smiled.

"So you are Casio's little sister. He never said you were so beautiful; he just said you were as smart as he was."

Kala was flabbergasted.

"You know Casio?"

"It's the reason I'm moderating today. He asked me, as a special favor to him, that I watch over his baby sister and make sure she gets through the day all right. If you didn't already know, he really does love you and he is very proud of you."

"I didn't know. He doesn't talk to me very much, and I always thought I was a burden to him. I suppose it would embarrass him if I were to say that you told me this information?"

"You're probably right. It would!" Ms. Johansen replied laughing.

"If I can be so bold and ask... How do you know Casio?"

"My brother works in his section at TechNet and he's eaten dinner at our house before. If you don't mind my saying, he is an odd duck!"

"Oh, I don't mind. In fact, I agree with you totally!"

The two walked in silence as they made their way to the cafeteria. When they were almost there, Kala stopped.

"Can I ask you a question?"

"Go ahead."

"I know this may seem odd coming from me, but what is my brother really like? He's never shown our older brother or me anything but contempt. If he really does care about me, at least I'd like to know what he's like."

Ms. Johansen paused before answering.

"He is a very smart man, but you know that already. He has a wicked sense of humor and is a very talented cook, although he doesn't like to cook that often. He has an innate sense of fairness that makes him one of the best team leaders that TechNet has seen in years. He's kind and he's always making sure that everyone on his team has what they need to be comfortable."

Kala looked at Ms. Johansen as she described a man she had never known existed. She must have had a strange look on her face because Ms. Johansen just laughed when she saw it.

"Did I just describe someone you've never met?"

"Yes. I never knew that man was real. Thank you."

"You're welcome. Just never tell him that I was the one to rat him out!"

"Your secret is safe with me."

"Well, here we are at the cafeteria. Remember to keep your badge visible. You can order anything you want and it will be charged to the Center. Just make sure you eat enough. The proctors tend to run people ragged during the oral exam!"

"Thanks for the warning and all the information on Casio. It really was helpful."

"You're welcome and good luck this afternoon. Someone will come in and get you when it's time to go over to your assigned oral exam room."

Kala hesitated at the entrance to the cafeteria before entering. She wasn't expecting the food to be up to Cook's caliber at home, but it did smell good. With a tray filled with a plate of pasta, a salad, fresh fruit for dessert, and water to drink, she found a corner to sit where she could be alone to look out the window at the city view.

She started going over her family history in her mind, but then decided to stop because, she realized, either she knew it or she didn't. She decided not to think about anything at all and just let her mind wander. As she sat and looked out over the city, she wondered what it was like in the early twenty-first century when people still drove cars, ate meat, and carried guns. In a way, she always wanted to be able to go back and live in a time when the world wasn't so populated. Then she realized that she would be giving up much of what she was accustomed to in everyday life. It would probably be the same if someone from that time tried to go back to the early nineteen hundreds.

The one thing she really did envy from those times was the open space. If it weren't for the time she had spent on Casio's property, she would be very depressed. She loved open space, with trees and flowers and being able to hear the birds sing in the morning. She hoped that when she did join WASA, she would be able to go on an exploratory mission in space. She wanted to be able to go to a planet and colonize it. If that were to happen, she would make sure that they wouldn't muddle that one up.

She was just finishing her lunch when a woman came up to her.

"Are you Kala Melina?" she asked.

"Yes, I am."

"I'm Mrs. Peterson. I'm here to take you to your oral presentation."

"Okay. Let me clean up my stuff here and I'm ready."

On the way out of the cafeteria, they stopped by a disposal unit. Kala inserted her trash and placed her tray on the conveyor belt next to it for recycling.

"Do you need to use the ladies room before you get started?"

"That would probably be a good idea, thank you."

"Let's go this way then. It's no longer and it does go by a restroom."

As Kala followed Mrs. Peterson, she began to feel a few butterflies in her stomach. She breathed deeply and willed herself back to calm. After using the restroom, she and Mrs. Peterson walked down the hall to a moving walkway leading to a small building to the left of the larger main building. When they entered the building, it took a moment for her eyes to adjust, but she soon realized that this part of the Central City Complex was what used to be the New York Metropolitan Museum of Art. Ancient art still hung on the walls. Next to nature, Kala liked art. She stared at the pictures and statues as they passed by.

"You like art?" Mrs. Peterson asked.

"Yes, I do, almost as much as I love nature." Kala replied.

"That's why I brought you this way. I could tell by the wistful look on your face when I came to get you at lunch."

"My friends always tell me that I shouldn't go into a line of work that requires me to lie because I can't do it. I always give myself away by the look on my face. I've never learned to mask my feelings."

"That isn't always a bad thing. We still need honest people in the world."

"I guess we do."

Mrs. Peterson looked at Kala and smiled.

"Don't be nervous, dear. This part of the test is no problem. The rumors are just that, rumors. The Board of Testers wants people to be nervous and scared because they believe that it makes them more important than they really are. In truth, it's just a formality. The decision of where a person is going to be assigned is made after the written test, which, as you now know, is scored as you take it. The oral exam doesn't even have any bearing on the family history anymore. Just be yourself and you'll be fine."

"Thank you for the advice. It's very helpful."

"Well, here we are, dear." Mrs. Peterson said as they arrived at a plain wooden door.

The older woman knocked twice before opening the door. When they entered, Kala again noticed all the ancient artwork on the walls. She forced herself to focus as Mrs. Peterson led the way over to a row of adults facing her. Mrs. Peterson motioned for Kala to stand at the designated place while she went over to the woman on the right end of the table. She took the memory chip containing Kala's morning written test and handed it to the woman. Kala watched as the older woman placed the chip in a slot in her computer. There was silence as the results of Kala's morning test posted on each computer screen. Kala stood with her arms at her side looking closely, trying to read the faces of the board members. Finally, the man in the middle of the table, the Board chairman, looked up and nodded to Mrs. Peterson, who turned and headed toward the door. Kala watched Mrs. Peterson go and didn't turn back to the Board until the door had closed behind her.

When Kala turned back to the Board, she saw them all watching her. She squared her shoulders and stood up straight with her arms at her sides, indicating her readiness to move forward with the test.

"Congratulations, Ms. Melina. You have the highest score ever recorded in the history of the Ascension Rite. They were even higher than your brother Casio's scores."

Kala didn't know what to say. She couldn't believe that she had done something better than Casio. She nodded once, with a slight smile on her lips, to indicate her acceptance of this knowledge and her readiness to move forward with the test.

"As I am sure you have heard, this portion of your Rite of Ascension is based on family history. You will be required to give us a brief family tree back two generations as well as answer some brief questions. Are you ready to move forward?"

"Yes, sir, I am."

"Okay, let's begin. If you could please start by giving us your family history going back two generations; this is to include brothers, sisters, mother, father, aunts, uncles, grandparents with their siblings, and great-grandparents with their siblings."

This had been the one thing that Shawan had really worked with her on and she still didn't feel very confident. She was sure if she did it in the rote style she had practiced, and they didn't interrupt her too much, she would be fine. When she got to the end, she realized that she had gotten it all right without stopping and without pausing. She had known, of course, that the Board had a copy of the list in front of them, and they would have known if there had been any mistakes. There was a brief break as the board pulled up the list of questions written just for her.

"Would you like a drink of water before we continue?" the chairman asked.

"That would be very nice, sir."

The board member on the end got up and went to a speaker in the wall. Kala saw the woman press a button and heard her ask for ice water to be brought to Testing Room One.

"Why don't you take a minute to rest while we wait for the water? It should be here shortly."

"Thank you, but I'd rather continue if you don't mind. No offense, but I'd like to get this over with so I can relax."

The board members laughed.

"No offense taken. Whether you believe it or not, we do know how hard it is for you to be on that side of the table. We were there once too!" The woman smiled.

Just as she finished speaking, a side door opened and a young man appeared carrying Kala's glass of water. Once her thirst was quenched, she looked at the board and indicated she was ready to continue.

This time the questioning didn't last as long. When they were done, the head of the board asked Kala to step through the door on the far side of the room where she would find Mrs. Peterson waiting for her. Mrs. Peterson would take her back to the cafeteria for refreshment while she waited for her results.

On their way to the cafeteria, Kala asked if they could walk more slowly so she could look at the art they had passed on their way in. Mrs. Peterson agreed.

"Do you have plans when you graduate at the end of the school year?" Mrs. Peterson asked as they walked.

Kala hesitated before replying, gazing at the reproduction of the Mona Lisa on the wall in front of her.

"I think space is the place for me," she replied. "While I would miss the art, there would be new art to create on the planets I could explore. In addition, there'd be plenty of space and nature in which to get lost. Not to mention the quiet."

"That's just the response I would have expected from a Melina," Mrs. Peterson replied laughing. "Your answer just combined the answers both your brothers gave at their Ascension Rites."

"Leave it to me to fall somewhere between my brothers," Kala laughed. "Were you my brothers' guide when they came in for their tests?"

"As a matter of fact, I was. I had been here five years when Shawan came through. Five years later I saw Casio, and now, four years later, here you are. One of the reasons I love this job so much is that I get a chance to meet whole families. I am now starting to see children of people who took their Rite of Ascension when I first started. I really enjoy seeing the full circle of a family unit."

When they got back to the cafeteria, Shawan was waiting for her.

"They didn't tell me you would be here waiting," Kala exclaimed, giving her brother a hug.

"I had stopped back to check on your progress and was told you were on your way back here to wait for your results. I was told that if I wanted to wait and go with you to get your results, I could."

"I'm glad you're here. It would have been unbearable waiting alone!"

"Well, I'll leave you two to your waiting," Mrs. Peterson said. "I know you will do fine, and I'm sure we'll be hearing about all your great deeds in the future."

"Thank you for your vote of confidence. It was very nice to meet you."

Kala and Shawan silently watched Mrs. Peterson leave. Sitting down at a table, they looked out the window at the view. In the distance was the park where Casio's house was, and closer was the old Art Museum and the old Library. Kala was excited at the thought of all the books inside the library building.

"What are you thinking, sister?"

"Just thinking about what my next step is going to be. Will I take the job with WASA, or will I do something else?"

"I thought you were set on WASA."

"I guess for the most part I am, but there is still a small voice that is questioning that decision. I mean, why should I be so quick to decide? If I really am that marketable, then why limit myself so quickly?"

"Maybe you're trying to talk yourself out of success. I don't want to influence your decision, but I think that WASA really is the right place for you. I think whether they give you a job here on Earth or send you into space, you will be where you belong."

Kala sat back in her chair and looked out the window toward the green trees of the park.

"I think you're right. It's probably just a case of nerves and I'll get over of it. What does scare me is that if I went into space at this point, it would probably be a one-way trip and I'd miss you, Janna, and the kids. I think I'd even miss Casio and his standoffishness."

"That would only be natural. Why do you think it would be one-way?"

"You know that even though they have a list of planets that are available for human habitation, many of them are too far away for back and forth travel. The trips that would be undertaken, for the most part, would be one-way." Thinking of more pleasant possibilities, Kala added, "I'd hope I'd get a world that is well-balanced between land and water with mostly warm weather!"

"You were always a sun lover!" Shawan replied laughing.

"I almost forgot to tell you, Shawan, I scored higher than Casio did on the written part of the exam! I don't think by much, but I did."

Shawan's mouth fell open at that bit of news. Then, he burst out laughing.

"I can't believe it! Casio isn't the smartest one in the family! He'll be impossible after hearing that. Are you sure you don't want to come live with us until you graduate?"

"I'm sure. The place is big enough that we never have to see each other. Anyway, Casio usually avoids me at all costs, even at meals. Sometimes I'm alone with the staff for weeks on end. I don't think I'm more than another staff member to him anyway. I'm sure he's already gotten my scores over at TechNet, so he may decide not to come home until I've moved out after graduation. I'll be fine. Really, I will."

"Are you sure?"

"I am. I would love to come and live with you and Janna, but I know as well as you do that you don't have the room. I know you mean well, Shawan, and I love you too, but I'll be fine. After I graduate, I'll get a big place of my own and you all can come and visit me. How does that sound?"

"That sounds perfect. I am very proud of you. I know that Mom and Dad would be proud as well."

As they talked, a man in a dark suit walked up to them.

"Kala Melina?" he asked looking at them.

"That would be me," she replied.

"The Board has finished going over your oral and written tests and are ready for you and your brother to sign the final papers of Ascension. If you'll gather your things and follow me, please."

He waited patiently while they tidied up and then led the way back to Testing Room One. They walked without speaking, and Shawan gave Kala an encouraging look.

"You'll be fine, little sister," he whispered as they arrived at the door.

She only had time to give him a brief smile and nod of her head as their guide opened the door and led them in front of the Board. The same people who had interrogated her earlier were still there. As she moved forward to the indicated spot on the floor, she looked closely at the faces of the people in front of her. She tried to gauge the disposition of the people about to put her on her way to independence. They all wore solemn expressions except the chairman who gave her a small smile.

"Who stands as Advocate for Kala Melina?" he asked solemnly.

"I do," replied Shawan as he stepped forward. "I am Shawan Melina, older brother to Kala Melina."

"And where are your parents, Mr. Melina?"

"Our parents are both dead, Mr. Chairman. They were killed two years ago in the derailment of the last of the old-fashioned trains."

"And you are her current guardian?"

"No, our middle brother Casio Melina is, but his job at TechNet didn't leave him time to act as proper advocate. He signed the papers for me to act as advocate in his stead."

"You have those papers with you, Mr. Melina?"

"Yes, sir, I do. I gave a copy to the front desk when we checked in this morning and have another copy here for you this afternoon. May I step forward?"

"Please."

Shawan walked up to the chairman and handed him the second copy of the required documents. Everyone was silent as he walked back to his place beside Kala.

"Well, it looks like all is in order here," the chairman started. Then he addressed Kala directly. "As you were told earlier, you have the highest scores ever recorded by this center. Higher even, then your previously mentioned brother Casio. That, in itself, should give you reason to smile."

At that comment, most of the board members grinned and chuckled. Kala and Shawan grinned back.

"All that is left now is for me to certify the results, give you the oath and have your brother here countersign indicating that a family member was here as witness. After that, you only need to wait until graduation, and you will be able to move forward in the world. Are you ready to proceed?"

"Yes, sir, I am most certainly ready!"

There were a few smiles from the board at her emphatic reply.

"Then with your right hand over your heart, please raise your left hand and repeat after me."

With that, Kala took the oath of Ascension. When she was done, the chairman indicated that both she and Shawan should come forward and sign the documents. When they had finished, she felt it was almost anticlimactic. All the studying, the hard work, and the worry were finished. She just had to graduate in May and she would be on her own. She wondered again, as she watched Shawan sign on the Advocate's line, what the future would hold for her.

CHAPTER 6

As they left the building, Kala looked up at the sunset and wondered what it would be like in space. She wondered if she would even make it into space.

"What are you thinking, sister?" Shawan asked as they descended into the subway.

"Just wondering what it's like in space."

"I'm sure that you'll find out soon enough. I think that's where you'll end up. I mean, you're already a space case."

Kala laughed and playfully slapped him on the shoulder as they boarded the waiting train. She wondered about the future as they looked for empty seats on the crowded train. Finally, they found two seats together.

"Do you really think I'll get a chance to go into space?"

"I think with your scores, you'll be able to do whatever you want. While I don't think they would want to lose you, I think WASA would be stupid to try to hold you back. You'll be able to write your own ticket."

"What do you think Casio will do when he finds out?"

"You mean you don't think he knows already?"

"Well, there is that. Sometimes I think he knows at least one person in every government office in the world."

"I don't think you're far off. If he doesn't know someone personally, he probably knows someone who knows someone, if you know what I mean."

"I do. I wonder if Mom and Dad would be proud of me."

"I believe Mom and Dad would be over the moon."

They rode the rest of the way in silence and watched the city speed by.

When they arrived back at the house, they found that Shawan's wife Janna was there with their kids, Lanna and Trace.

"What are you guys doing here?" Kala asked after a round of hugs.

"Casio called and let us know that he would let us celebrate your Ascension Rite here tonight, and we can spend the night. He even sent a car for us."

"Wow," said Kala, "he never lets anyone have car privileges if he can help it. I wonder what made him do that. Maybe he's finally realizing that he'll be on his own soon and he's decided to spread the happiness. Did he say if he was going to be home for this family gathering?"

"He left the message with Cook, who said that he wasn't going to be home until this weekend, by which time all the people who don't normally live here should be gone. And I can hear him saying that in those words exactly." Janna smiled.

"Who's up for a swim in the pool?" Kala asked.

The children clapped, the adults laughed, and everyone was happy to stop thinking about Casio.

That night over dinner, Kala and Shawan told his family and the house staff what had happened during the day. They held the best part for dessert. When Cook came out with the dessert, Kala had her call out the rest of the staff.

"Now, before I tell this best part, the staff has to swear to me that they will never say anything to my brother about what we have talked about tonight or what I am about to say. Can you do that for me?"

All the staff nodded in agreement. She knew that she could count on them never to say anything to Casio. She knew that they all loved her and respected her kindnesses toward them over the years, and they considered her as much of a boss as Casio.

"Okay, here is the best part of the whole day. I have the highest score ever recorded on the Rite of Ascension test."

"You mean next to Casio, of course," replied Janna.

"No, Jan, I mean the highest test score ever recorded. I scored higher than Casio."

There was silence before the room erupted in excited chatter. The family gathered around Kala to offer congratulations, and the staff, after congratulating Kala, quietly resumed their work. After calm returned, they heard a car pull up to the front door. They knew that Casio had taken the company limo to the city and wasn't expected back, so they couldn't think who this visitor might be. They heard the voice of Joro, Casio's butler, as he opened the door. Soon Joro led a tall good-looking woman into the room.

"Casio hasn't made it home yet?" she asked.

"We aren't expecting him until the weekend." Shawan replied in a manner that indicated he knew the woman. "He's not much into family gatherings, and he knew that my family would want to celebrate my sister's Rite of Ascension before going home tomorrow. We'll be taking Kala to school on our way home in the morning. Do you have a reason for being here?"

"He told me to meet him here, Shawan, but he didn't say why. You know how he can be. Are you going to introduce me to the rest of your family?"

"I suppose, if I must."

With that, Shawan grudgingly introduced the family to Lillia Thomason, a distant cousin on their father's side.

"So, you're Dad's cousin. How come you never told me about her, Shawan?"

"There was no reason to. It was more of a business partnership then a family one."

"I seem to remember hearing your name around the house when Dad would talk about business. I guess that's why it sounds familiar. But why didn't they ever mention that you were family?"

"Like Shawan said, there was no reason to. We were business partners, and our families were never that close. To be honest, I don't know why Casio wants me here. All he said was that I was to meet him here for a surprise that could only be reveled on the occasion of your Rite of Ascension."

"Why don't you have a seat, Lillia? I'm sure we'll find out why you're here soon enough. Would you like something to eat or drink while we wait for Casio and his surprise to get home?"

"Nothing to eat, but I will take a drink. Whatever diet soda you have cold would be fine."

Kala got up and went into the kitchen.

"Doesn't Casio have staff to do that?" Lillia asked after Kala had left the room.

"Yes, but Kala doesn't like to bother them for something like a soda. The staff just finished cleaning up after dinner and setting up dessert. If Casio were here, I'm sure he would have the staff do it, but Kala isn't Casio. You're sure you don't know why Casio wanted you here tonight?"

"No idea whatsoever. We've stayed in contact after your parents died and we've even done business together. Ever since you closed up your Dad's company after the accident, he has made sure that TechNet has given us enough contracts to stay afloat. I'm assuming that my visit has something to do with Kala's Ascension Rite and her job opportunities after graduation."

"I think Kala may have gotten a job offer already."

"From what Casio has told me about her, it doesn't surprise me. I'm not one hundred percent sure of his reason. It's just a guess."

As Kala came back into the room with the soda, they heard a motorbike pull up in the front driveway.

"That must be Casio now," said Kala.

The engine of the motorbike went silent. They heard the front door open and close and followed the footsteps as they went from the front door to the room where they waited. The door opened. Casio faced the silent group seated round the table.

CHAPTER 7

"Well, it's nice to see that everyone is here. I didn't want to have to wait or repeat myself."

"So, what's the big surprise, Casio?" Kala asked as Casio rang the bell for the maid to bring him a drink.

"By now, we all know that you passed...and with flying colors. Congratulations are in order, little sister. My score has stood for years, and if anyone was going to beat it, I'm glad that it was family. However, we're not here to talk about your score. We're here to talk about your future. I know that WASA has already been to school to see you, and I assume you know that if you join them, they will provide for you in the same way that TechNet provides for their employees."

Everyone at the table agreed with his assumption. But what Casio spoke of next surprised them. He told them about a part of their parents' will that hadn't been revealed at the time of their death. This part described pieces of land in Old New York and Old Philadelphia that no one in the family had known about.

"The will stipulates that Kala gets one piece of land and Shawan gets the other. The will also stipulates that Kala and Shawan are to decide between them who got which piece."

Casio went on to explain that both pieces of land had houses already built on them and that trust funds had been established to take care of the monetary needs of running large estates.

"If you take the offer from WASA, Kala, you won't need either property. Assuming you will join WASA, I was thinking that Shawan and Janna should get the property of their choice and Lillia should get the other. Each property has five acres of land. Each is protected in trust as long as there is a descendant living, either on the property or not, unless that family member chooses to sell, in which case they would get the money."

The room was silent as everyone digested the startling news.

"But what if I don't join WASA? What about Lillia then? Was it really fair to bring her here and let her know about this if I decide to do something else?"

"Would you really turn WASA down?"

"I don't know. I haven't seen any other options yet. You're making a large assumption that I am going to join up. And... What if they find out I have the option of having my own land and house already? What if they want to make use of that and not what they offer me? You really have jumped the gun here, brother."

Casio stared at his sister as if she had two heads. No one had ever dared speak to him in this manner, especially not his younger sister.

"You dare to speak to me this way? After everything I've done for you?"

"And who asked you to do these things for me, Casio? I never did, and I can't imagine that Mother and Father ever did. So, where did you get the idea that I needed my big brother to stick up for me? Are you so stuck on social standing that you need to worry about what your brother and sister do with their lives so they don't bring you down? Please explain the need you have to meddle in our lives. Or is it just my life?"

Casio looked downcast. "I guess I just wanted to try and do something nice for my little sister. By the time I had the opportunity to help Shawan, he was already well-established in a job and married to Janna with a child on the way. When Mother and Father died and you came to live with me, I thought I would try to help you if I could. You know how I am, Kala. I don't show emotion that well, so I tried to help the best I could. When I saw where your interests lay, I tried to lead you in that direction. Then I talked to the people at WASA and asked them to watch you. What they said to you at your school is true. If you don't want to work for them, that will be okay, but I know they would be happy to have you."

Kala softened. "Casio, I know you mean well, but I would really appreciate being able to make my own decisions." She turned to her newfound cousin. "Lillia, I am sorry to meet you and have you hear a family squabble. I'd like to be able to spend some time with you in the future and get to know you as a friend and a member of the family."

"I'd like that too, Kala. You seem like a wonderful young lady, and if it helps any, I work for WASA."

"You do? Can we sit down and talk sometime? Maybe that will help me make up my mind."

"I'd love to. Why don't we meet after school someday and I'll take you to dinner."

"Thank you, that sounds wonderful. For now, I think I'm going to take a walk in the gardens to think about everything. I'll be back in a while."

After she left, Shawan looked at Casio.

"Do you really think you were doing the right thing for Kala by meddling, or was it for your own means so you could have another contact at WASA?"

Casio hesitated, considering his answer. When he finally spoke, it was in a quieter, humbler voice than Shawan or anyone else in the room had ever heard him use.

"I was truly doing this for her. Yes, of course, it crossed my mind on how it would benefit me, but that wasn't the reason when I first started. I truly wanted to make her life better. I know how hard it's been for her since Mother and Father died, and I wanted to try to ease that pain for her a bit. I know that I can be pushy and overbearing, but I was doing what I thought she would want. It never occurred to me that she would want to do anything else. I know how much she loves science and space."

"But you also know how much she loves classical art, books, and music. Do you know how much she loves to read the classic novels from the nineteenth century? Classics like Dickens and the Bronte sisters. Did you know any of this about your sister?"

"No, I didn't know that."

"Why didn't you take the time to find out?"

"Shawan, you know how I feel about the family."

"I know you feel that you should have been the only child and you are embarrassed by us. But I have a feeling that if you were to try...and I mean really try...you would find that we have more in common than you might think."

Casio didn't respond.

"Come on, Janna, kids. I think it's time we packed our things to leave tomorrow. If you ever want to be in touch with us, Casio, you know where we live. Even if we move to one of the new estates, you'll know how to get in touch with us. We'll be leaving early tomorrow to get Kala and the kids to school so don't worry about having to see us."

Almost immediately, Casio and Lillia were alone in the dining room. They sat in silence until Lillia spoke.

"Are all your family gatherings so fun-filled?"

"We usually don't get together, so I guess when we do all the bad feelings come up."

"Thank you for including me, though. It was nice to finally meet more people in my family and know who they are. Do you think Kala will go with WASA or not?"

"After her little speech earlier, I'm not sure. I hope so, because I think she would be good at whatever they give her, but I'm not sure now."

"I'm sure that, whatever she decides, it will all work out in the end. She has a good head on her shoulders."

"I will admit that she did get the Melina self-awareness. We always know what is best for ourselves, even if it takes us a while to get there."

Just then, Joro came into the room. He looked at Casio and waited for instructions.

"Call the staff to clear away the last of the dishes, and then you can all go for the night. We're going into the study and I'll make drinks in there, if we want anything else. Just make sure to have the staff check the room for dirty glasses in the morning."

"Yes, sir."

"Joro, wait a minute." Casio called as the butler turned to exit the room.

"Yes, sir?"

"Has my sister said anything to you or anyone else on the staff about her plans for the future?"

"Ms. Melina hasn't said anything to me, and I'm not aware of her having talked to anyone on the staff."

"You'd tell me if she had?"

"Of course I would, sir. She doesn't talk to us much anymore since the end of last summer. She's been working very hard at school and on her Rite of Ascension studies."

"Okay, thank you, Joro."

Casio turned toward his cousin. "Care to join me in the study?"

Lillia nodded her head in ascent. Together, they walked in cordial silence to the large sitting room. On the left, there was a closed door. Casio walked to the door and opened it. Inside was a room that Lillia wasn't quite expecting from a man like Casio. She had thought his private study would be a dark room with lots of mahogany shelving, a large desk in the corner and many books on the shelves. What she saw was a bright room with lots of computers and technology. The bookshelves were highly polished steel and the desk was modern. She wasn't quite sure why this surprised her, but it did. Maybe it was such a contrast to the rest of the house, and she felt that, at heart, Casio was a very old-fashioned man.

She watched him walk over to the small built-in bar in the corner.

"Would you like something to drink? I hate to drink alone."

"Do you have any scotch?"

He opened a cabinet above the sink and pulled out a bottle of Chivas Regal.

"Wow, that's the good stuff."

"Would I have anything else?"

"This is true."

"Do you like it neat or on the rocks?"

"On the rocks with a splash of water, please." She didn't speak as Casio fixed the drinks.

Taking their drinks to a large, comfortable sofa in front of the fireplace, they watched the flames dance.

"Why do you put on the act of being so standoffish?" Lillia asked.

"It isn't really an act."

"But I've seen you outside of this house and you are two different people."

Casio hesitated before responding.

"It's a family thing, I guess. I've always felt more comfortable around people who aren't related to me. When I was younger, I wished I had been an only child, and I guess that, sometimes, I still do. I've spent years in therapy at TechNet, and I still don't have a reason for it. The therapist has tried to convince me to try hypnosis, but I've never really trusted it. Maybe someday I'll find out."

"Have you ever been in love?"

The question surprised Casio. His face reddened.

Then he answered, "Once, I guess, but I never did anything about it."

"Why?"

"I hate rejection, and I didn't want to take the chance that she wouldn't feel the same way. I've had a few flings, but nothing serious. What about you?"

"Only once, and it was more of a love from afar. I was hurt once, and I didn't want it to happen again."

When they had run out of things to say, Casio stood up.

"I think I'd better call it a night. I've got an early day tomorrow, so I'd better get some sleep. You can stay up if you want."

"No, that's okay. I've got an early day myself and I should get back to my apartment."

"You're not staying the night?"

"No. I'm being picked up at my apartment at 7:30, so I thought it best just to come out here for the meeting. Will I see you again soon?"

"I'm sure our paths will cross. At least to complete the paperwork if Kala decides to join WASA, and you get one of the properties."

"I hope so. I'll talk to you soon, Casio. Take care of yourself."

"You too, Lillia."

Casio saw her to the front door and watched her pull away before closing the door and heading upstairs to his room.

Chapter 8

The next morning when Casio came down for breakfast, Kala was the only one at the table.

"Where are Shawan and his family? I thought they were going to take you to school?"

"They left already. He told you he would be leaving early, and I decided not to make him go out of his way to take me to school."

"I thought he'd at least stay to say thank you for letting him stay here."

Kala had nothing to say to this and went back to her breakfast. They ate in their usual silence for a while, and then, Casio looked up.

"Do you really hate me that much, Kala?"

Kala thought about her answer before replying.

"I don't think 'hate' is the right word, Casio. I do puzzle about you and the way you are, but I don't hate you. I really do love you, but I also think you are a strange duck."

"I am sorry for not being more open to you and the rest of the family. I've been trying for years to understand why I am the way I am. I still haven't figured it out, but I am trying."

"Thank you for sharing that with me. I think, for the first time, I realize that." Kala smiled at him. "I've got to leave for school now. I missed a couple of tests yesterday, and I've got to make them up today. Will you be home for dinner?"

"Unless something comes up at work, I plan to be."

"Do you think we could really talk then?"

"About what?"

"About anything, I just want to be able to have a conversation with you. Maybe we could talk about my plans for the future, what we did today, or trivial things. If I do join WASA and go into space, we might not have that much time left together as a family, and I don't want to leave not knowing my brother."

"I think that can be managed."

"I'm glad. I'll see you tonight."

Kala grabbed her books and left. When she arrived at school, Mr. Alston was waiting for her.

"I hear congratulations are in order. From what we see of your scores, you did very well yesterday. I'm sure you will keep your grades up so you will be graduating with the school's highest honors."

"Thank you, Mr. Alston. I did my best."

Mr. Alston smiled.

"Have you thought any more about the job offer from WASA?"

"I have, and I am leaning that way, but I still haven't totally made up my mind. I'd like to see what else might be out there for me. Could I meet with you sometime to look at other prospects?"

"Since you passed your Ascension Rite so resoundingly and are a self-paced student at this point, why don't you get your tests today out of the way and come to my office afterward. I don't have any appointments today. I'll have some information for you on fields I think you might be interested in waiting for you."

"Thank you. I should be done sometime around lunch."

Once settled in the self-paced classroom, she only had to sign into a computer; she wasn't required to meet with a teacher. She completed her tests more quickly than she anticipated, and ensuring her ID card and her books were safely stowed away in her book sack, she headed back to Mr. Alston's office. As she neared the office door, she noticed that it was open. Approaching, she gently tapped on the glass. Mr. Alston glanced up and motioned her into the room.

"Close the door behind you, Kala, that way we won't be disturbed unless it's important."

"Thanks, Mr. Alston!"

"I've come up with quite a few options that you would be both interested in and be qualified for."

He pulled a small pile of papers from a basket on the side of his desk.

"You printed them out?" Kala asked, surprised.

In the world she lived in, not much was printed. With the low resources for papermaking and no reliable substitute available, printing was kept to a minimum.

"I searched online and found documents we already had here in the office. For anything that wasn't up-to-date, I printed out the new material. Why does that surprise you? Schools have always been exempt from printing restrictions."

Kala shrugged. "I don't know why it surprised me. I guess I just never really thought about it, that's all. What did you find?"

"Why don't you take these to the table and see," Mr. Alston replied, handing her the small stack of papers and brochures.

At the table, Kala spread the brochures and papers out in front of her and started reading them. As she went through them, she sorted them into two piles: the "no" pile and the "maybe" pile. Once she had made the first go through, she took the "no" pile back to Mr. Alston.

"None of these sound interesting to me," she said as she handed them back to him.

"Okay, how about the others?"

"I'm going to go through them again more thoroughly. Is it possible for me to take them home and review them there?"

"Sure. In fact, I think that is a good idea. It will give you time to think carefully about each option."

"I'll bring them back tomorrow."

"Whenever." He smiled. "I trust you to get them back to me when you're ready. How are things going otherwise?"

"Fine, I guess. I need to start thinking about moving out of Casio's house as soon as I've graduated, and I need to decide on a life career, but other than that I think things are going well."

Mr. Alston laughed as she stated her future so matter-of-factly.

"What's so funny?"

"Just the way you've stated things. I guess living with Casio for the past couple of years hasn't been easy."

Kala thought a moment before answering.

"It took some getting used to in the beginning, but once I got used to how he liked things done, there weren't any problems."

"Casio isn't an easy person to get along with."

"You're not telling me anything I don't know. He is my brother, though, and whatever his quirks, I do love him."

Mr. Alston smiled again. "Since today is Thursday, why don't you keep those brochures and printouts until Monday? That way you have at least an extra day or two to go over your choices."

"Thank you, I appreciate it. I won't mess them up or anything."

"I know you won't, Kala. If it were any other student, I wouldn't be letting them out of my sight, but since it's you, I don't have a problem with it. Why don't we set up an appointment for Monday at ten o'clock?"

Kala pulled out her vid-phone and opened the calendar, scrolling to Monday. After checking her schedule, she said, "Can you do 10:30?"

"I can. I'll see you then."

"Thank you for everything, Mr. Alston."

"My pleasure, Kala. You are delight to work with and I hope you find what you are looking for in that pile."

"I do too. I'll see you Monday."

Kala gathered up her things and, glancing at the wall clock, saw that it was lunchtime and headed to the cafeteria. She saw Lindsey and their gang of friends sitting at their usual table. Lindsey looked up, saw her, and waved. Kala waved back and, at the table, dropped her stuff by the one empty chair.

"I'm going to get some food and I'll be right back. Does anyone want anything while I'm over there?"

Acknowledging their negative response, Kala went to the food line. As she stood in line, she noticed that many people were looking at her and smiling. Not just students but also faculty and staff as well. Finally, one of her fellow seniors came over to her.

"Is it true you got the highest score ever recorded in the Ascension Rite?" she asked.

"I guess it is," Kala replied smiling back at the girl, whose face she recognized but whose name she didn't know.

"Wow, that's great! Congratulations!"

"Thank you."

Kala picked up her food without further comment or interruption. Returning to the table, her friends were all smiling at her.

"Okay, so who ate what canary?" she asked the group in general.

They all started laughing.

"Was that girl asking about your test score?" Tonio Freeman asked.

"How'd you know?"

"Just the look on your face when she asked. You looked surprised and embarrassed."

Kala's face reddened. "How else am I supposed to look, Tonio? How did word get out so quickly? How am I supposed to feel at beating my own brother's score?"

She sat down in her seat and stared at her food without really seeing it.

"Kala, what's wrong?" Lindsey asked, suddenly concerned for her friend.

"I think it just really hit me that, for once, Casio isn't the best at something, and not only did someone beat him but that someone was me, his own sister. How am I supposed to live with that?"

"Take it in stride, Kala," replied Chase Carpenter, "I mean what if Casio wasn't your brother. Would it still be weird to have bested him?"

"Of course not," Kala shot back immediately. "Well, not really." She amended quickly.

"Just because he wasn't related to you? That makes no sense whatsoever," chimed in Chantal Freeman, Tonio's twin sister.

"And how would you be if you bested Tonio?"

"Would never happen," Chantal replied, "We got the exact same score. I don't think one of us would outdo the other on something like that."

"Is that the twin thing again?"

"Probably," they replied in unison.

Kala shook her head. "I don't know. It's probably because I'm so used to Casio being the top of the food chain in the family that when someone else does something better than him, it feels strange."

No one answered but, having met her older brother, they all knew what she meant. Lindsey glanced at the clock and noticed the time.

"We've got to fly, guys. Those of us who aren't in self-paced study need to get back to class."

She stood up, looking at Kala.

"Want to meet after school today?" Lindsey asked.

"Not today. I have a few things I need to go over tonight. Will you be here for a full day tomorrow?"

"I'll probably only spend half a day. Afternoon is the job fair for those who haven't decided, so I'm free after math class."

"I don't have to be here tomorrow, but I'll probably come in for a while in the morning to work on an English paper. Why don't we meet at my house at 12:30? When I get home from the library I'll ask Cook to make us lunch and you can help me go through some of these brochures Mr. Alston gave me today."

"Good plan! I'll see you about 12:30 tomorrow then," Lindsey said, waving as she headed off to her afternoon classes.

Kala sat in the silence. Finally, she shook her head and got up, gathered her things, and started for home.

She had one last paper due for her English class and she needed at least one more source, so the next morning, she left early for school to use the library. When she arrived, she was surprised at how empty it was. Usually at this time of the semester, instructors and students milled about trying to get last-minute work done on projects. She found an open computer in a secluded corner and sat down to work. Getting into the rhythm of her work, she soon lost track of time. At eleven-thirty, the computer began to beep at her and she jumped, then she realized she had set the clock on the computer so she would get home before Lindsey got there. Quickly saving her work, she gathered her things and made for the exit that was closest to the subway station.

On the quick ride home, she thought about the job information sheets that Mr. Alston had given her.

Is there something better than WASA? she thought as she got off at her stop.

Glancing at her watch on her way out, she saw it was almost twelve-fifteen. She'd need to hurry in order to make it home before Lindsey. Walking in the kitchen door, she saw that Cook had set the kitchen table for her and Lindsey to use, so she dropped her bag by the table. As she was leaving the room, she noticed Cook moving to pick the bag up and put it away.

"Don't worry about it," she said, "I'll need some things from there during lunch, so it's okay where it is."

"No problem, Miss," Cook responded.

She was hurrying to the front door when she heard a knock. She looked through the glass and saw Lindsey standing there.

"Hello there," Lindsey said as Kala opened the door.

"Hello. Are you hungry? It looks like Cook made a feast for lunch!"

"I'm starved! Do you have the brochures Mr. Alston gave you?"

"Got them right here."

When the girls reached the kitchen, Cook had food and drinks laid out.

Kala reached into her bag and brought out the pile of papers and brochures that Mr. Alston had given her. During the meal, Kala and Lindsey went through them and split them into two piles: the "no" pile and the "maybe or yes" pile. Once that was done the "no" pile went back into her bag.

Then they put the "maybe or yes" back between them. One by one, they went through this pile. They didn't even notice when Cook took their lunch dishes away and put dessert and more drinks in front of them. In the end, they had the pile whittled down to one: WASA.

"Well, I guess that decides that, doesn't it?" Kala said sitting back in her chair. "After considering everything, it still comes down to WASA."

"Does that upset you?"

"Not really," Kala replied after a moment's thought. "I just wanted to make sure."

"I really do envy you," Lindsey said.

"You do?"

"Yes. I mean, you have a nice place to live, another house with land waiting for you if you stay on Earth, a great job prospect, and a great life ahead."

"I never really thought about it that way. You don't hate me because of any of that, do you?"

"Of course not! Why would I?"

"Because I have so many things that you don't have."

"And that makes a difference...why? Kala, you are the most down-to-earth person I know. You don't let any of this stuff go to your head, and you truly care about your friends. I won't lie and tell you I'm not jealous sometimes, but I wouldn't change anything about you."

There was silence as Kala considered what Lindsey had told her.

"Thank you, Lindsey. I'm very lucky to have a friend like you."

"We're both lucky, Kala. Hey, look at the time! I need to get home for dinner. Thank you for lunch! Will I see you at school on Monday?"

"I don't see why not. I have some final work to do on my projects for English and science, and I'll need web access I can only get at the library, so I'll probably be there most of the day."

"You are so lucky being in self-paced study!"

"You want to take my place? It really is a pain in the butt sometimes. I'd like to be back in a classroom with you guys."

"Want to trade places?"

Kala just laughed. This conversation was often repeated between the two, and each knew they were right where they needed to be. After Kala closed the door behind Lindsey, she went back into the kitchen.

"After that wonderful lunch, I don't think I'm going to want more than a salad for dinner, if that's okay."

"Mr. Melina ordered a large dinner for this evening, Miss," Cook replied, looking nervous.

"Just make a salad to go with whatever he ordered and I'll eat that. I'll tell him I ate late at school."

Cook nodded and smiled. She knew that Kala wouldn't let her get into trouble with Casio. She watched Kala with affection, as she picked up her things from the kitchen table and headed up to her suite of rooms.

As Cook got back to work, she wished, as she often did, that Kala had been her daughter. Kala's life would have been much simpler and she was sure that Kala's life would have been much happier. She felt Kala shouldn't have been forced to live here with Mr. Melina. Her parents should have left her in custody with the older brother; she would have been better off. With a shake of her head, Cook quickly stopped that line of thinking. Mr. Melina would fire her for thinking that way.

CHAPTER 9

As Cook was thinking about Kala's life with Casio, Kala's thoughts were exactly the same. She wondered how things would have been different if she had lived with Shawan. Would she have still gotten the offer from WASA, or would she be looking for a job elsewhere? She sighed as she put her books next to her desk. She didn't feel like studying. Instead, she sat on her balcony and enjoyed the beauty of the grounds.

Soon, she found her thoughts drifting to the property in Old Philadelphia. She hoped she'd be able to take a trip to see it when she got out of school. She'd have to remember to ask Casio at dinner tonight. Maybe she would take part of her allotted vacation after school to go there. Maybe she would ask Lindsey to go with her. It would be fun to have a girls' only vacation.

Dinner turned out to be a very relaxed affair that night. Casio had taken the time to change out of his work clothes and tried very hard to be congenial. For the first time in years, Kala felt she was really learning things about her brother and thought there might be a chance for him to be okay and move forward in his relationships. At the end of the meal, over coffee and tea, she decided to ask about the property in Old Philadelphia.

"Do you think I could use some of my vacation after graduation to go see the house in Old Philadelphia?" she asked.

"I don't see why not," he replied. "Would you want to go alone or would you want me to go with you?"

"Well... I'd like to take Lindsey, if you think that's okay."

He thought about her choice of companion before replying.

"It would be fine with me as your guardian. Just make sure it's okay with Lindsey's parents."

"Of course. Once I decide when I'm going, how do I arrange for transportation?"

"Just let me know and I'll show you. You'll probably want to take the bullet train." Casio paused and, then, continued. "On another subject, have you decided what you're going to do after you graduate?"

"I've pretty much decided that WASA is my choice. My guidance counselor gave me brochures about other jobs, and I reviewed them today. There was nothing else that interested me."

"I'm glad to hear that you've decided. I think you'll really enjoy working there."

"I do have one request though, Casio."

"What's that?"

"Please let me do this on my own. I know that you love me and want to help, but I really think it would be best for me if I tried and even failed sometimes."

Casio's smile was lopsided and he laughed softly before replying.

"I think that, after the other night, I wouldn't have it any other way!"

Kala just laughed as Casio rang the bell for the rest of the dishes to be cleared.

"How are things going in school?"

"I'm just about done with everything. I have final projects due in English and science, but after that, I'll be done until graduation."

"How much do you have left on your projects?"

"For the English project, I have the research and rough draft done; I just need to type the final draft. For the science project, I'm doing the topography of the eastern coastline of the country from before the Great Tsunami of 2122, and I want to add a few final cosmetic touches. They should both be done by mid-to-late April."

"So, you'll be done with everything about two weeks before graduation."

"That sounds about right."

"Have you told your counselor about your decision to go with WASA?"

"We're meeting on Monday. He only gave me the brochures today, and we agreed that I'd take the weekend to go over them."

Casio gave her a look.

"I know... It's only Friday. But I invited Lindsey for lunch, and we went through them together. It was good for her to see some of the things that are available as well. It didn't really take all that long."

"I guess, then, you had already made your decision?"

"I suppose so, but I did want to see what else was out there."

"I understand."

"Thank you for spending this evening with me, Casio. I'm glad we were able to just talk."

"You're welcome. It was a nice way to spend the evening. I'm sorry we didn't do it sooner. I guess I was spending too much time being the big-shot older brother."

"I think I know you well enough to understand you were only doing your best. You were never expecting to have to take in your little sister. Especially a sister you never wanted to have in the first place, and before you get mad at me, Casio, you've admitted it more than once. I've heard you say many times that you wished you had been Mother and Father's only child."

"I wish that we had done this a long time ago...sat down and talked, I mean. Have I been a terrible brother?"

Kala hesitated before answering.

"I wouldn't say terrible. It's just that you were into your own thing and didn't have time for much else. You've treated me and Shawan the same, so I can't say that you were that way with just me."

They sat in silence.

"I feel like going outside to one of the gardens," Kala suddenly said. "Would you like to join me?"

"I'd love to. Would you like to continue our conversation?" Casio smiled.

"Of course I would!" Kala headed to the door.

Casio rang the bell again for Joro and let him know they were going for a walk. Catching up to Kala, he found her outside the back door, trying to decide where to go and sit.

"Would you like to see my favorite place to sit when I take a walk around the grounds?" he asked.

Kala nodded and Casio led her off to the right. They walked almost to the edge of the property before turning sharply to the left. To the right was a small Japanese-inspired rock garden with a waterfall that Kala had never seen before.

"I thought I knew all the gardens on the property. When did you have this put in?"

"I added it about eight years ago."

"How could I have missed it?"

"I don't know. I never tried to hide it."

She studied the exquisite garden. The rocks were small white stones raked into a circular pattern. On the left side, a waterfall cascaded down jet-black lava rock. The water from the waterfall traveled in a small river along the property fence to a pond where it was recirculated back through the system. Around the waterfall and pond, Casio had landscaped very rare plants, including ones that had been in the Central American rain forests. She stared in amazement and tried to process all the new things she was seeing.

"This is wonderful, Casio. Do you come out here often?"

"Not often enough. It's a wonderful place to relax and let troubles slip away. I've actually contemplated having Mom and Dad's ashes moved here."

"Oh, Casio, that would be wonderful! They would have loved this little sanctuary!"

They sat in silence, simply listening to the nature around them. Kala walked to a bench by the waterfall and sat down. She let the nature surrounding her take her away, and she imagined the Earth, as it had been millennia ago, before humans had ruined it.

"You and I are more alike than I think either of us would like to admit sometimes," Casio said quietly.

"No doubt about that," Kala replied, laughing. "I think that's why we rub each other the wrong way so often."

Casio laughed his agreement as he walked to the bench on the other side of the waterfall and sat down. They stayed by the waterfall late into the night talking and getting to know each other. Feeling confident in his new relationship with Kala, Casio amended his request that she be out of the house right after graduation and told her she could stay as long as she needed.

For Kala, the next month seemed to fly by. And, then, it was time for graduation. She had signed a general contract with WASA, which said she would work there but didn't lock her into a position until she had worked there for at least a month and was able to see what interested her. With Casio's help, she had booked a trip to Old Philadelphia with Lindsey and was scheduled to spend two weeks at the house. WASA had learned of the house in Old Philadelphia and offered her an opportunity to work in the WASA office in the area. Grateful for the offer, Kala decided to wait on her answer until after she had seen the house. WASA agreed and made arrangements for her go to the office while she was in Old Philadelphia.

On the day of graduation, the whole family was there. She thought she almost heard Casio cheering louder than anyone else when her name was called. Since Lindsey and she were scheduled to leave two days after graduation, a big party had been planned for the two families at the estate. Surprisingly, Casio spared no expense and even hired extra staff to help. Counting the two families and their friends, almost a hundred people filled the house. Tents were set up on the main lawn with tables and chairs, along with smaller tents with benches and tables throughout the property. Casio had arranged a buffet to be set up along one side of the big tent, with smaller food stations at the other tents. Food and drink flowed freely, and no one was denied anything.

"This must be costing him a small fortune," Kala whispered to Shawan during the festivities.

"Whatever you said to him when you talked must have really made an impact," Shawan replied. "I think he's doing this because he's genuinely happy for you, not because he's happy to see you go."

"I have a feeling you may be right. He certainly has changed since our talk last month."

After the last guest had left, Casio gathered the family for one last surprise.

"I've been trying to decide what to give our sister for her graduation," he started by saying. "Since she already has a place to live and a job, I knew I couldn't help with either one of those. Also, knowing that, when she decides on a job with WASA, there is a possibility she may be leaving Earth, I didn't want to give her anything too big or bulky. I've finally decided on something I thought she might like."

Smiling, he pulled out a small box and handed it to Kala. Ripping off the wrapping, she pulled the lid off. She stared in the box before she took the contents out. As she examined the pack of holo-disks, she started to smile. Without a word, she walked over to Casio and gave him a hug and kiss.

"This is the best gift ever, even if I never leave Earth!"

"What is it?" asked Janna.

"It's all my favorite books, music, and art, plus photos of family and all my friends on holo-disk!"

"Wow, Casio! That's pretty impressive," said Shawan.

"I felt that our sister should start her life with some of what she likes. There's always the chance to add more."

Then, Casio pulled out a bottle of champagne that he had been saving for the occasion. As he showed the bottle around, everyone raised his or her eyebrows.

"You really are going all out aren't you, Casio? Are you sure you're doing this for Kala and not because you'll finally be on your own again soon?" Shawan asked.

"After my talk with Kala last month, I realized that celebrating my 'independence' with the family would be a bit crass. That celebration will happen but with my friends, not my family. Don't worry, Shawan, I may have changed, but not that much. I still can't wait to be back on my own, but I have now realized that family is important too."

With glasses filled with champagne, and sparkling cider for the younger folk, everyone raised their glasses in a toast to the graduates.

Chapter 10

The next day, everyone slept in. Shawan and his family had stayed the night, and lingering over breakfast, they all enjoyed chatting and telling stories. After her brother and family left, Kala packed for her trip. While she was deciding what clothes to take, Lindsey called.

"What are you taking with you to wear?" Lindsey sounded frantic.

"I was just working on that when you called. Mostly casual, I guess, with a few going-out outfits. Casio says there are a lot of nice places to eat there. We'll also have to go to the local WASA office at least once to check it out, so I'm taking a couple of business outfits."

"I still can't believe I got that job offer from them! I wanted to thank you again."

"For what? Recognizing your administrative talents? You deserve it."

"My parents are upset that I'm thinking about moving, though."

"It's not that far of a bullet ride, and with the credits we'll be making, you can visit them as often as you like."

"I know, but they were looking forward to me getting married and settling nearby and having lots of grandchildren."

Kala just laughed.

"All right... Now I know what kind of clothes to bring. Did you say there was a pool at this house as well?"

"I don't remember what Casio said, but bring a suit or two just in case. Better safe than sorry and swimming suits are small."

"Sounds like a plan to me. What time are we supposed to be at the station tomorrow?"

"The train leaves at 8:45, and Casio's letting us use his TechNet limo. You're on my way to the station, so let's say we pick you up at 7:30? That way we'll be sure to be there on time. Casio said he got us seats in the front on the upper level of the observation car, so we should have a good trip."

"Sounds good to me, I'll see you tomorrow at 7:30 then. Bye."

"Bye."

Kala smiled as she went back to packing. Starting a new job with a friend was nice; it meant she wouldn't be totally alone. Once they decided which office to work in, they would be set. Kala wondered if she would be sent into space or not and, if she was, what Lindsey would do.

Neither girl ate breakfast the next morning because Casio had told them they would be served food on the train. When they got to the station, a personal guide that Casio had arranged met them. She called a porter to take their bags and led them to the first class waiting and boarding area, where beverages awaited them. When boarding started, their guide reappeared and took them to the first class platform. After boarding, they quickly found their seats in the observation car and gave their breakfast order to an attentive waiter.

The trip was uneventful, and when they arrived, Kala and Lindsey were happy to see a WASA car waiting for them. The car brought them to the house and waited while they settled their cases and prepared for a meeting with the head of the local WASA office. Even though they had been assured their job offers were good for whichever office they chose, seeing this office and meeting a few of the people there would help with the decision-making.

Meeting over, they were on their way home when Kala thought of something.

"What will you do with your apartment in Old New York if we move here?" she asked Lindsey.

"It was a company apartment, so now that I've given up the other job I don't get the apartment even if we do stay in Old New York. I figured since we'd be working for WASA, we'd get an apartment from them."

"I hadn't thought of that. You know, I hadn't even looked for a place to live up there."

Back at the house, they changed into bathing suits and shorts to spend the rest of the afternoon relaxing, sunbathing, and swimming at the pool. Soon, Eva, one of the house staff, came out to ask them about dinner.

"Ma'am, it's almost 4:30 and the cook wanted to know what you might want for dinner and what time you might want it."

"I didn't realize it was so late. It's such a beautiful night, is there any way we can eat outside?"

"We can set up the side porch over there," Eva replied, pointing.

"That would be wonderful, Eva. Why don't we eat around 7:30?"

"Very good, ma'am," Eva replied. "Is there anything special you would like for dinner?"

Kala and Lindsey looked at each other. Knowing what Lindsey liked to eat, Kala spoke for both of them.

"Well, since we don't know the cook all that well yet, let's say chicken, rice, and a green salad. If there's any nice fruit, we'll have a fruit salad for dessert."

"I know the cook has several very good chicken dishes. Would you like spicy or mild?"

Kala considered the question.

"Spicy," she said finally.

"For the dessert, I know that there are fresh blackberries and raspberries on the property that are ready for picking and the cook makes a wonderful cobbler. Is that okay?"

"Even better! Vanilla ice cream to go with that would be perfect."

"If there's no ice cream, I know there's fresh whipped cream."

"Thank you for all your help today, Eva! I think if we move here, we'll all get along just fine!"

Eva smiled a noncommittal response.

"Don't worry," Kala said, "I know that my brother Casio has stayed here. I'm nothing like him, so there won't be the same demands made on the staff as those he might have made. We couldn't be more different."

Eva's smile broadened, telling Kala that she had read the initial response correctly.

"Dinner will be ready on the side porch at 7:30," she said. "Is there anything you would like to drink?"

"I think water will be fine for me," answered Kala, "What about you, Lindsey?"

"Water is fine."

Lindsey smiled and shook her head as she watched Eva walk away.

"I could get used to this very quickly," she said quietly.

Kala laughed in response.

The next morning, the girls got up early and played a set of tennis before getting ready for their second appointment at the local WASA office. After showering and dressing, they met in the small dining room off the kitchen for breakfast. This would be the day that would decide where they would work—the Philadelphia office or the New York office.

At lunch, the girls sat in a corner of the cafeteria discussing the morning.

"What did you think of Flight Operations?" Kala asked.

"I think I liked that the best. There doesn't seem to be much downtime, and the work is interesting. What did Mr. Paulson want to talk to you about?"

"He wanted to talk about the possibility of my going on a manned mission."

"Really, do tell!"

"Well, from what he said, there are a few planets that look promising to support life with minimal to no domes needed, and little to no work needed to make them ready for humans."

"Sounds interesting, when would you know more?"

"It depends on what office we decide to work for. If we decide to work in the New York office, he'll send his recommendations to whoever we work for there, and if we decide to work in the Philadelphia office, he'll get his recommendations to whoever we work for here, assuming it isn't him."

As they gathered up their lunch remains, Mr. Paulson approached them.

"How do you ladies like the office so far?"

"We like it very much, sir," Kala replied. "You've certainly given us some food for thought as far as working here."

"Well, I think that WASA will be better off for having you, no matter what office you choose to work in. Are you ready to continue with your day?"

"We were just finishing up."

Following the director, they returned to the control room where they spent their afternoon. At the end of the day, the girls were invited to the local pub for the Friday night happy hour.

"We'd love to go," said Lindsey, "but we're not old enough to drink alcohol yet. Does that make a difference?"

"Not at all," replied chief controller Peter Johanson, "lots of people are not of drinking age. We usually take over one of the local restaurants that have happy hours. Believe me, restaurants are more than willing to accommodate a large group like ours!"

"Where are we going this week?" Johanson asked the man sitting next to him.

"La Plat," was the reply.

"No problem, then," Johanson said, "They always take care of us. They even run a tab for us and send it over to Mr. Paulson to pay. Looks like you're in for a good party!"

"You are incorrigible, Pete!" Mr. Paulson grumbled and everyone laughed.

"That's why you love me, sir!"

Mr. Paulson harrumphed and motioned the girls to follow him back to his office.

"I'll bring the girls over when we're done our meeting," he told Peter.

"We may be awhile."

"Don't keep them too long," Peter warned, "I want to get to know my two new hires!"

"You wish!" Kala shot back at him with a smile.

Gathering their things, Kala and Lindsey followed Mr. Paulson into his office. He closed the door behind them and motioned them to sit in chairs in front of his desk. He observed them intently after he sat down.

"So, what do you ladies think of our little operation here?" he asked finally.

"Nice little joint you have here, sir," replied Kala.

Lindsey shot her a look for her flip response, but Kala ignored her as Mr. Paulson laughed.

"If you decide to work here, and I sincerely hope you do, you will fit in just perfectly. I try to run an organization where people feel comfortable with each other."

"Seems to me, sir, you succeed," Kala said.

"Thank you, Kala. When do you think you'll make up your minds?"

Kala and Lindsey looked at each other, and Kala nodded.

"We've made our decision, sir."

He looked at them expectantly, but they took their time in answering.

"Well?" he asked.

"We've decided to work at this office," Lindsey replied.

"What made up your minds?" Mr. Paulson asked, smiling.

"The atmosphere." Kala replied. "The work ethic and standard is just as high as the New York office, but the work atmosphere is much more relaxed and easygoing. In New York, they take themselves too seriously."

"When do you think you'll be able to start?"

"We need to let the New York office know...and our families. Once that's done, we'll need some time to move here. Is three weeks okay?"

"That will be fine. Why don't we say June 15th? That gives you a few extra days to get settled. We'll have the paperwork ready for you to sign when you start. Now, let's go join the fun over at La Plat and tell everyone the good news."

CHAPTER 11

Kala and Lindsey didn't tell their families of their decision right away. Their plan was to gather each family at the same time and then break the news as though both families were together. Kala's family took the news very well, as expected. Lindsey's family, more accurately her mother, did not take the news quite as well.

"Why do you need to move away from us?" cried Mrs. Johnson.

"Mother, it's only Old Philadelphia, and it's not like I'm leaving the planet or anything! Kala's the one they would want for that type of duty, not me!"

"Small consolation for stealing a woman's daughter," Mrs. Johnson wailed.

"Was she like this when Tim and Laura left home?" she asked her father.

"It's because you're the youngest," her father said quietly.

"Old Philadelphia is just a short train ride away, Mother. You can visit me any time you like, and I'll get lots of chances to come and visit you! Why are you so upset?"

"You'll forget about us the minute you leave this house! Who's going to take care of you? Who's going to do your laundry, cook your meals, make your lunch?"

"Mom, there is staff in the house for that. You and Dad could even come and live on the grounds in one of the guesthouses there! I'm sure Kala wouldn't mind."

Mrs. Johnson glared at Lindsey. How could she explain her feelings to her daughter? At the beginning of Lindsey and Kala's friendship, Mrs. Johnson had liked Kala very much. But when she found out who Kala's parents were, her attitude suddenly changed. She didn't hate Kala, but she intensely disapproved of Kala and her family.

"Okay, Mother, I've had enough! I want to know once and for all, why you don't like Kala and her family. As far as I know, they've never done anything to you or this family. They have never been anything but gracious to us!"

Total silence filled the room. Lindsey had never before spoken to her mother in this way, and everyone was shocked. Finally, Mrs. Johnson stopped crying. She wiped her eyes and face before speaking.

"It's just that she has things that we don't," she said, looking at Lindsey.

"That's not it, Mother, and you know it." Lindsey almost spat back. "There's something more, and you are afraid to tell me."

Lindsey's parents locked eyes before her father took Lindsey's arm and led her to the nearest chair. He looked back at his wife again before taking a deep breath.

"Years ago, before we had you kids and before Kala and her brothers were born, we became very close friends with the Melinas. The four of us did everything together. The four of us remained best friends right up until the time you and Kala were born."

"What happened?" Lindsey asked, almost afraid to know the answer.

Her parents looked at each other again.

"Must we really do this, George?"

"I think it's about time the girls knew the truth, Paulette, don't you? Lindsey, being ours, will tell Kala, and Kala will then be able to tell her family the truth."

Paulette Johnson hesitated before slowly nodding her ascent. Mr. Johnson looked at the floor and paused, carefully choosing his words. When he was ready, he looked at Lindsey.

"Kala isn't Johanna and Petrio Melina's natural daughter, she's ours."

Lindsey's eyes opened wide.

"When we found out we were pregnant again, we were thrilled. We were doing well and we were happy. When the doctor told us twins we were even happier."

"Twins! Lindsey exclaimed, jumping out of her chair, "Kala and I don't have the same birthday. How can we be twins?"

"Let me tell you my way, Lindsey, please. I'll get to that part."

Lindsey stared at her parents before moving to a chair on the other side of the room and sitting down.

"After the doctors had done some tests, they told us that both of you wouldn't survive if we left you both in utero, so we had to make a dreadful choice. We couldn't decide between our children and we wouldn't. However, the doctors pushed and said that if we didn't make a choice, both of you would die. We were talking about it with Kala's parents one night, and that's when Kala's mother came up with the idea. I think two ideas occurred to her at the same time, but she only told us the one. She knew that doctors had been working on a way to separate twins in utero, and then removing one and implanting the fetus into another mother. She said she would be willing to carry the twin they took from your mother. She would carry the baby to term and when she delivered, she would give the baby back to us. Only, as you now know, that's not quite what happened. Petrio agreed, although he wasn't happy with his wife's plan, and after a discussion that night on our own, your mother and I agreed if it meant saving both of our children, we would do it."

Mr. Johnson paused and sipped his drink. He looked at Lindsey's face and saw the shock there.

"Kala is my sister?" Her voice quivered.

Mrs. Johnson sobbed quietly and quickly turned her face. Mr. Johnson gave her hand a quick squeeze.

"Yes. After the doctors successfully performed the transplant, the Melinas suddenly disappeared from our lives. We had all been living on the South Tip...the old state of Florida...and didn't know what happened to them, but we could guess. We tried repeatedly to contact them, but they had moved and left a restriction on the forwarding address. We searched unsuccessfully to find them and our baby after you had been born, but found that there was no record of the birth in any hospital on the Eastern seaboard. We later found out that after Johanna had recovered from the transplant, Petrio had accepted a temporary reassignment to the Mid-Continent area and wouldn't return for a few years. When they did return, we had moved to Old New York for the company, and we heard that Petrio had been assigned to the Old New York Central City District. Petrio had made quite the life for them by then, and Kala was a happy, healthy child. We learned that, because of the transplant, her development in the womb had been delayed, so she was born a few weeks after you."

Paulette suddenly spoke.

"We tried again to contact them, but they wouldn't take our calls. They blocked our email addresses and sent our handwritten mail back unopened. We tried to go to the authorities, but because of Petrio's position, they wouldn't listen to us. Finally, we just gave up hope of ever getting our baby back and resigned ourselves to watch from a distance. Because of the credits we had used trying to find Kala, we found ourselves in a debit with the company, so our status changed and we moved in here.

"When you came home from school and told us you'd made a new friend we were elated. We didn't know who Kala or her parents were at first because we didn't know her last name. But when we saw her parents at a school function, we knew. I was frightened when they saw us that they would move again or put Kala into another school, but they didn't. They never had any contact with us, but they didn't stop you and Kala from being friends. I guess I was selfish in having you play here so much; I wanted to spend some time with her as well."

"When Petrio and Johanna died," Mr. Johnson resumed the story, "we almost told you everything then, but we knew the first thing you'd do would be to tell Kala, and we thought she was going through enough already."

Lindsey absorbed the news in silence. Finally, she got up and went to the window.

"I have a twin sister," she whispered to herself before turning back to her parents. "I always had a feeling that there was something missing from my life. When I was with Kala, it was like something was filled in, and now I know why. If you were so happy that we found each other, how did that turn to dislike and not wanting us to be friends?" Lindsey was suddenly angry. "And, you never told me? All the while you were you harping on honesty in the family, you were hiding this."

"It's because of this secret that we harped on honesty," her mother replied. "We always felt we should have told you and your brother and sister the truth, but the time never seemed to be right. We never discouraged you from being friends. I think you can see that. And as for disliking Kala's parents, they stole our daughter away from us. Isn't that enough of a reason to dislike someone?"

"That's the easy way out, Mother. You never told me because the older I got, and the closer I got to Kala, the harder it got. You just wanted to save yourself the trouble."

"You see, George, I told you she'd hate us,"

"Oh, shut up, Mother! I do not hate you. I could never hate you. Disillusioned with you, yes. Disappointed with you, yes. Saddened by your lack of faith in me, yes. But, no, I don't hate you. I will be moving to Old Philadelphia with Kala, and I don't know what to tell her." Lindsey pointed at her parents. "I think you should be the ones to tell Kala, but I know that will never happen, so in the end I'll probably be the one who'll have to do it."

She continued in a flat tone, "I'm going to start packing. Kala and I begin work on June 15th, but we're going to move before then. The company moving van will be here on Monday; Kala and I plan on leaving

Tuesday. After the moving truck leaves, I'm going to Kala's house to spend the night so we can leave early Tuesday morning."

With a touch of sadness in her voice, Lindsey ended, "We can celebrate my new job or not, but I hope you can be happy for me. Now... I need to be alone."

The first thing Lindsey did when got to her room was call Kala.

"How did it go with your family?"

"It went well. They're all happy for me and would have liked to have a going-away party but I said no. Told them we just wanted to pack up and be quietly on our way. How about you, did everything go okay?"

"Not really. My mother pulled her usual stunt about her baby moving so far away. They laid a bunch of stuff on me that I'll tell you about some other time, but the sooner we leave the better."

"Was it really that bad?"

"Yes."

"I'm sorry, Lin! You're not going to change your mind, are you?"

"After what my parents told me today, I don't know if I can wait until Monday to leave!"

"You want to spend the rest of the weekend here?"

"No," she answered, reluctantly, "no matter what is going on, I need to tough it out. It'll be hard, but I think things will straighten themselves out, and I need them to be straight before we leave. Then I can tell you the whole story. What time should I expect the movers Monday?"

"They're going to be here at about nine, so you can probably expect them by noon at the latest."

"Okay. I'll come Monday after they leave."

"Later 'gator." Kala replied and disconnected.

Lindsey sat still, recalling the conversation with her parents. Finally, determined to move forward, she started packing. She packed all her clothes except what she needed for the next couple of days. As she worked her way around the room, she realized how much stuff she had. She started sorting things, making two piles: one to take with her and the other to give away. She didn't realize how much time had passed until she heard a knock on her door. She turned around and saw her mother standing at the door with a wooden box in her hands.

"Come in, Mother" she said quietly, clearing off a space on the bed for them to sit.

"I'm not bothering you, am I?" Paulette asked, "Because I can come back later."

"Don't be silly," Lindsey replied softly. "You never bother me."

Her mother entered the room and sat next to her on the bed. She looked down at the box in her hands, gathering her thoughts. Looking up at Lindsey, she sighed.

"These are some things I got for you over the years. I've been saving them for when you got married, but I thought I might give them to you now. It seems like the right time."

Lindsey took the box and opened it. Inside there were letters and pictures from when she was little. Looking through the box, she noticed a small square of folded tissue in the corner. She glanced at her mother, who smiled, as Lindsey gingerly picked up the small square. As she peeled the paper away from the object, she wondered what it was and was surprised by the small diamond ring that she saw.

"What's this?" she asked.

"It's your grandmother's wedding band. When she was preparing her estate, she specifically stated she wanted you to have this. She left similar items for Timmy and Laura but she wanted this to be saved for you. I am sorry for the way I acted earlier. I know that Old Philadelphia isn't that far away and we can visit any time we want. I just always assumed that you would be living near us here in Old New York."

Lindsey leaned over and hugged her.

"You will always be in my heart and thoughts. We can talk every day by vid-phone if you want, and if you ever need anything you know you can come to me."

"I have your brother and sister as well, my dear! It's just that you're all so grown up now. After losing Kala, I always wanted to stay close to my children because I thought that would mean I'd never lose you. I put the fact that children grow up out of my mind. Until now, that is, because you've all grown up into wonderful adults. It's just hard for a mother to let go."

"I know, Mom. I would like to stay here in Old New York, but this opportunity is just too good to pass up."

They sat in silence holding hands.

"Let me ask you this," Lindsey said finally. "Would you prefer I didn't tell Kala about what happened?"

Her mother got up and went to the window. She stared out without really seeing what was outside as she thought about her answer.

"If you think it will hurt your friendship, then no, I don't want you to tell her. If you think she'll be hurt at first and then eventually get over it, then I would be okay with it. I think your father would be too. For once, it's going to have to be your choice, and it's going to have to be your choice how you tell her, if you decide that's best."

The clock chimed and Lindsey realized that she needed to finish packing. Her mother helped, and they talked about Lindsey's hopes and dreams for the future.

Finally, Lindsey sat down with a loud sigh and smiled, "That's about all I'm up for today! I can finish up tomorrow. Do you and Dad want to do anything special for dinner tonight?"

"We thought we'd meet Timmy and Laura and their families at Milacron for dinner."

"Wow! Isn't that a bit expensive?"

Milacron was one of the best restaurants in the Old Times Square section of the city. It had an assortment of Italian, Japanese, Chinese, Thai, and Middle Eastern cuisines. Old Times Square was the best place to go for people with varied food tastes, like her family.

"Nothing is too good for this meal," her mother replied, hugging Lindsey and laughing. "Timmy and Laura are probably already on their way there now. So we'd best get changed and be on our way."

As Lindsey got dressed, she thought about her brother and sister. She was going to miss them when she went to Old Philadelphia. Laura, the oldest in the family, lived just a mile away from her parents with her husband and two children. Timmy was the middle child. Unmarried, he lived in the same complex that Laura did. She was happy they were a very close family.

Monday morning finally arrived, and both girls were ready for the move to be over.

When the time came for Lindsey to leave, she realized just how much she was going to miss her parents. She gave them both big hugs and promised to call every week. As her father loaded her overnight bag into the cab, she pulled her mother aside.

"I am going to tell Kala, but not right away. I need time so I can understand what happened myself. I just want you to know that, eventually, I will tell her."

"I know, sweetheart," her mother replied, "just make sure when you do tell her that she understands how much we really did want her."

"I will."

The cabbie honked the horn. Lindsey hugged her parents again and got in. She watched her parents grow smaller as the cab pulled away into the distance. Finally, when they were out of sight, she turned around and looked ahead.

The girls hardly slept at all that night. They stayed in Kala's room and sat up talking most of the night. They knew that, after today, their lives would be full of new responsibilities. They decided to have fun on this night, one of their last just being carefree girls, before beginning their exciting careers.

The next morning, when they rolled out of bed, they almost regretted the fun of the night before. The car WASA had insisted on to take them to the Philadelphia office was arriving early.

"Get used to it," Mr. Johanson had said, "we always have a car take our people on midrange trips."

The minute the girls finished their breakfast with Casio and Shawan and his family, the car drove up the driveway. As they made their way to the front door, the entire staff came out to say good-bye. There were hugs for everyone, and Kala hugged Casio longer then she would have thought just a couple of months ago.

"I will miss you, brother. Despite our differences, I will miss you."

"I go to Old Philadelphia a lot for TechNet, so we'll see each other. I'll also make sure that Shawan and his family visit here every now and then, but only if you promise to visit us here every now and then."

"It's a deal!"

With a final look around, Kala got into the car and closed the door. She was on her way to a new chapter of her life.

CHAPTER 12

The first two weeks in Old Philadelphia flew by. Kala and Lindsey used the time to explore the house and grounds and their new urban setting. They learned the different routes to and from work every day, and which was the best at what time. They also spent a day at the office taking care of paperwork so they could start working immediately on their first official day.

They were deliberate in getting to know the house staff. They discussed food likes and dislikes with the cook, butler duties with the butler, cleaning and laundry schedules with the maids, and gardening duties with gardener.

WASA had already given them a hefty sign-on bonus, so they had lots of credits to play with. Because a trust had been set up to pay for all the expenses associated with the upkeep of the house and grounds, and to pay the staff, the girls could spend their personal credits however they wanted.

By Monday, June 15th, they were raring to get started. Their work schedule was seven-thirty to four-thirty with an hour lunch every day. When they arrived at the office, they went directly to Mr. Paulson.

"Good morning, ladies! You're going start out as runners so you can get a feeling for the business as a whole. Your base will be in the control room. If you find something in the control room that you don't like, you need to speak up and we can try to get it fixed or move you to another area within the complex."

Now that WASA was preparing more than one manned shuttle for deep space missions, everyone in the control room was multitasking to major extremes. Talking their responsibilities over, the girls decided to split the control room in half with each taking a half.

When it was lunchtime, Pete Johanson took his break and ate with them. "Thanks for the great coordination on the running this morning," he said when he sat down with his food.

"Not a problem," replied Kala. "Splitting the control room seemed the best way to get the most coverage without doubling up on things. This afternoon we're going to switch sides so we can get to know the people on the other side."

"Pete, can I ask you a question?" asked Lindsey.

"You just did, but go ahead and ask me another one," replied Pete with a smile.

Lindsey and Kala both rolled their eyes.

"What's up with Lorna in accounting?"

"Why do you ask?"

"She gave me a bunch of flack when I went over with your paperwork right before lunch."

"Don't mind her. She pulls something with all the new employees. She needs to know everything, but while her knowledge has come in handy on occasion, she can be quite annoying. But she's harmless."

As the weeks went on, Kala and Lindsey did less running and more work in the control room. They slowly evolved into unique positions: Kala as a researcher and Lindsey as a general office assistant, going where she was needed every day. One Friday afternoon, after they'd been there three months, Kala was called into Mr. Paulson's office.

"Have a seat, Kala," Mr. Paulson said as he closed the door.

Kala settled in the chair, curious about why he wanted to see her.

"So, how do you like working here so far?"

"I like it a lot. It's very challenging, and I like a good challenge."

"That's good to know," Mr. Paulson replied, "Because I have a very big one for you."

Kala waited expectantly.

"As you know, we have a few missions going up in the next couple of months. We'd like you to be on one of them."

"Me?" Kala asked, shocked. "What would I be doing? And aren't these missions supposed to be one-way? I mean, they're going out not only to find suitable planets but also to get them ready for human habitation. I thought WASA didn't want a repeat of the X Mission."

Each was silent as they remembered the failed one-way mission to a planet thought to be hospitable to human life. But when the landing team had arrived on the planet, they had all died within minutes of opening the shuttle's hatches. The final investigation report had concluded that the readings they had gotten of a clean, clear, breathable atmosphere were the result of faulty data and that equipment had probably been sabotaged. The families had only memorial services to remember and plaques to commemorate their loved ones. There had been no way to bury the X Mission team.

"You're right on all counts. As you know, we've developed a reliable long-range communication system that will reach out to fifty million light years. Right now, we're not planning any trips further than that. What we need is someone who can be a diplomatic go-between to communicate between a new settlement and Earth."

"And you want me to be the go-between? Do you have a team you want me to join?"

"Two mission teams have put in a request for you. We've decided that if you accept this offer, we'll let you decide which team you want to join."

"May I ask which teams requested me?"

"You may and, although I shouldn't, I will tell you that you were requested by Bill Johnson for his Foxtrot team and Charlie Hudson for his Sierra team."

She thought about each. She knew both Bill Johnson and Charlie Hudson and was confident that she would be able to work for and with either one. Then, it hit her that she was actually being asked to go off-world and probably would not come back.

"How much time do I have to think about this?"

"Well, Foxtrot is leaving in nine weeks, and Sierra is leaving in six months. If you decide you want to go with Foxtrot, we'll need to know immediately. I'd say that since today is Friday, you have at least until Monday to think about it. Just to make sure you understand, if you go on one of these missions, it means leaving Earth forever. As long as the communications systems hold up, missions will be able to get messages back, but when and if we ever lose contact, each mission will be on its own."

"I understand that, sir. I'll give you my answer on Monday."

"Great! Now get back to work and remember you can talk about being asked on a mission, but not which mission."

"I understand that, sir. I'd better get back, I see Lindsey waiting to go to lunch."

"I'll be waiting for your answer."

"Kala, is everything okay?" Lindsey asked when Kala got back to her desk.
"I'll tell you over lunch."

Once they were seated in the most isolated corner of the cafeteria, Lindsey looked at Kala expectantly.

"I've been offered a place on a mission," Kala blurted out.

"Which one?"

"I can't say exactly, but there were two offers."

"Are you going to take one of them?"

"I don't know. I have to look into the planets that the missions I've been offered are going to. Once I've done that I'll make my decision."

They were silent as they both ate. Kala looked out the window at the small garden outside of the lunchroom. She hoped that one of the missions was going to a world that had plant life as well as bodies of water. Would there be life forms? Would those life forms be intelligent? Kala sighed before turning back to her food.

"What are you thinking?" Lindsey asked quietly.

"About what I'd miss if I go. You top the list, you know. Over the years that we've known each other, you've become like a sister to me." Kala suddenly noticed Lindsey's face. "What is that look for?"

"Nothing that we have time to talk about now, but when we get home tonight, I want to have a serious chat. It may help in your decision about whether or not to go off-planet, and if you do, maybe even which team to go with."

"Okay, as long as you're sure I didn't say or do something to make you mad at me."

"No, I'm not mad at you. It's just that your news has hit close to what my parents told me before we came here. I should have told you before, but I was scared. We'll talk about it tonight."

That night, over dinner, Lindsey told Kala what her parents had revealed. When she was done, they sat in silence while Kala absorbed the news.

"My parents always told us that I was the result of an affair," Kala finally said.

"Probably so you wouldn't say anything if we ever met each other."

"I always wondered why my parents acted so strange when we became friends."

"My parents were the same at first too."

"And they were so formal when they saw each other. This explains so much."

The girls stopped talking as Eva came in to clear the table. Kala stared out the window and was lost in thought.

"Ma'am, did you want dessert," she heard Eva asking.

"Not right now, Eva, thank you. Maybe we'll have something later."

"Very good, Miss. Is it okay if we left it in the main refrigerator for you? We're having the celebration for Mr. Johann's birthday tonight."

"That's fine, Eva. I hope you ordered the food and drink for it on the house account like I told you to."

"Yes, ma'am, we did. Thank you again for doing that for us."

"It's my pleasure! Have fun tonight and leave whatever dishes we might use later on until the morning."

Eva nodded and left the room whistling. Kala and Lindsey sat and listened to the sounds of the house around them.

"Are you mad at me, Kala?" Lindsey asked quietly.

"Not at you, Lindsey, not ever at you. You didn't do this to us. My parents did. I'm the one who should be asking if you're mad at me. It's just that we're now left with the consequences of their actions. At some point, I am going to have to decide what and when I'm going to tell Shawan and Casio."

"Wouldn't it be better to tell them sooner rather than later?"

"I'm not so sure about that," Kala said getting up from the table and walking toward the door that led to the back gardens. "I'm going for a walk. I'll be back in a little bit."

During the rest of the weekend, Kala thought about both the job opportunity and what Lindsey had told her. At lunch on Sunday, Kala brought up the subject again.

"Would you be upset if I took one of the missions to space?" she asked Lindsey.

"Why should I be upset? I think I'd be more upset if you didn't."

"Would you stay on here if I go?"

"I don't see why not. It's a great place to work and I really like the people. What are you going to do with the house if you go?"

"Well, the will stipulated that if I didn't want it, or if I take a job where I don't need it, then Shawan would get it if he wasn't living in the house in Old New York. If Shawan didn't need or want it, then Lillia would be next in line to take possession."

Kala paused before continuing.

"Well, Shawan and his family are happily ensconced in the house in Old New York, and Lillia has signed documents giving up all rights to both houses. I think I'll have the lawyers draw up the documents for you to get this house."

Lindsey was stunned.

"But that would mean telling Shawan and Casio. Besides, doesn't the house belong to your family?"

"Well, as far as I'm concerned, you are part of my family, even if we didn't know it until recently. I've thought about it the past two days, and the way I figure it is this: it's my house and I can do with it as I please."

"But the will..."

"The will states that I get a house in either Old New York or Old Philadelphia and Shawan gets the other one. If one of the houses is left vacant, then Lillia gets it. Well, I've taken possession of this house, and Shawan has taken possession of the New York house. Lillia signed away any rights to either house, even knowing that I might be leaving Earth to go into space. It seems only fitting that my newfound family should get in on the action. I'm sure my parents didn't dream of this when they set up the arrangement, but this is the way it's going to be."

Lindsey tried to get her mind around her windfall. She was sure that her parents wouldn't know what to do with her new fortunes. And her mother had been worried about Kala's reaction!

"Let's go for a walk. If I'm really going to leave Earth, I'd better get my fill of it now." Kala said, changing the topic.

The girls went into the gardens. They walked in silence for a while, each in their own thoughts.

"Do you know anything about the missions you've been asked to join?" Lindsey asked finally.

"I do." Kala replied. "I'm not supposed to say anything about the specific missions, but I think I can talk generally. Both planets have breathable air, and they both have a mixture of ocean and landmasses. One of the two, the one I'm leaning toward joining, has more of a temperate climate. Most of the landmasses are around the equator and seem to be tropical. There are sandy waterfronts that lead into more densely forested areas. There are a couple of landmasses at either pole, but they are much like the poles here on Earth. I don't think there are any Inuits going on the mission," she said, smiling. "We'll scout the poles, obviously, and place monitoring stations, but even when humans do totally colonize the planet, I don't think there will be much going on there."

"What about sentient life? From what I understand, the probes weren't too good about picking up that kind of stuff."

"If you think about it, anything that would be aware of one of our probes would probably stay away from it. We did lose contact with the probes, but from what the experts have said, that wasn't necessarily from being tampered with once they got there."

"Are you scared at the prospect at being on another world with no way to get back to Earth?"

"Terrified, but if we don't do something soon, the whole human race will kill itself by overpopulation and depleted resources. Besides, we'll be in contact with Earth for at least a limited amount of time, and we can always ask for backup."

"If nothing goes wrong..."

"That's true, but I'm trying to be optimistic," Kala said with a slight smile.

Their conversation lulled, and the girls listened to the sounds of nature around them. The birds were lively, talking back and forth; they could hear two of the nearby waterfalls; and they could faintly hear the sounds of the party in the main house.

"What do you think about coming to space with me?" Kala asked suddenly.

"I couldn't, Kala, and I think you know why. My mother already lost one child and even with two left, I don't think she'd handle it very well. Besides, I'm not much for long trips in enclosed spaces, remember?"

They both remembered the seventh grade class trip to the western part of the country. They had taken the bullet train, and Lindsey had been miserable for most of the trip.

"Maybe if they send sleeper ships in the future, but right now, I don't think it would be a good idea."

"You're right. It was just a thought."

Kala got up and looked around the grounds she now called home. The set-up of the house and grounds was very similar to that of the house in Old New York, but the selection of plants was different. Kala had made some changes when she had first arrived to suit her own tastes. With the help of the gardener, she had chosen plants, bushes, and trees to complement the gardens that were already there. Now, there were paths lined with flowers, bushes, and trees that would have color on them year round.

The property also had greenhouses that grew much of the fruits, vegetables, and herbs that were used in the cooking. Whatever the estate didn't use was either dried or canned and then given away to shelters. When she had first moved to the house, Kala found out that much of the surplus food was simply thrown away. She took it upon herself to find places that could use the surplus. The need for fresh food was so great that she was adding two more greenhouses to the property to help alleviate some of the hunger in her neighborhood.

She was also searching for suitable storefront space in the more urban parts to begin a food distribution site. Once she had found a site and converted it, she would set up a shop open to all shelters in the area. She planned to not only use the food from her own gardens and greenhouses but also import whatever was needed from local farms in the outlying areas. A counselor from her high school had recently retired from teaching and had bought an organic farm in Old Philadelphia to be closer to his family. Kala intended to use as much of his production as possible.

"What are you thinking?" Lindsey saw the faraway look on Kala's face.

"About all the plans I had for this place and the things I wanted to do for the people who can't afford to do for themselves."

"You can still do it. I'll be here to watch over everything you start, and you can leave Earth knowing that you did what you could. You will know that you did many good things for a lot of people."

"I know, and I guess it's my ego that wants to be able to see the things that I could bring about."

"For a while you will be able to see it. I'll be able to send you updates as long as the communications hold up. I'm sure, as a WASA employee, I'll be able to send messages, and I'm sure that your brothers will be allowed to as well, so you'll be kept up-to-date."

"I hadn't thought of it that way." Kala sat back down, happier.

They stayed up later than normal that night talking about the future, making plans for the future businesses on Earth and for Kala's future in space.

CHAPTER 13

At work Monday morning, the control room was abuzz with major activity.
"What's going on?" Lindsey whispered to Pete.

"There was a major incident on the launch pad over the weekend that was incited by the World Pure section of TechNet. The only clue we have is the ID they used to get into the complex. Unfortunately, that ID belonged to a high level official and both the official and his ID have been missing for three weeks."

"Have your contacts at TechNet been any use at all?" Kala asked.

"Not really," Pete replied, slightly dismayed.

"How did this not leak to the media?" Lindsey asked.

"We're very good at keeping things quiet if we need to. This is one of those times when going public would be extremely harmful to all future missions. You know that the public already feels that we shouldn't be leaving Earth; they don't want us to ruin any other planets."

Lindsey turned to say something to Kala and noticed that she wasn't there. She looked around the room and saw her on the phone at her desk. Lindsey assumed that Kala was probably calling Casio to see if his TechNet connection would be helpful.

She turned back to Pete. "What happened?"

"They ruined some of the delicate communications equipment needed to build the satellites that were going to orbit the upcoming mission planets. Luckily, they didn't get to the backups before Security caught up with them. We still have the parts needed, but we will be pushing it to get backup equipment put together before Foxtrot leaves in six weeks.

Hopefully, we can do it."

Kala rejoined them.

"I just called my brother at TechNet. He's going to look into it on his end. He'll call me back as soon as he has something for us."

"Thank you, Kala. I'm sure that will help us." Pete replied, relieved. "We were going to ask if you would call him. I wasn't sure if you'd be willing to."

They saw Mr. Paulson come out of his office. He walked to the front of the control room and rapped on a desk to get everyone's attention.

"I assume that everyone has been brought up to speed about what happened this weekend. I now need to ask for everyone's help. I know that we've been working very hard to get Foxtrot, and then Sierra, up and running, but we're going to need to work a little harder to make sure that Foxtrot can get off in six weeks. I'm not going to let this hinder or change our schedule. Kala and Lindsey are going to be put into full work rotation. We are going into twenty-four hour shifts starting now. I will post an updated schedule as soon as I'm done here. If you are on a swing or overnight shift, you can go home and get ready for that shift. You are all good people, and I'm sure that we can get through this and make both missions total successes.

"The authorities will be coming and interviewing everyone in the office. We ask that you cooperate fully and answer all questions to the best of your ability. If you have information that you feel needs to be known by management, please tell Pete or myself, and we'll investigate it, if necessary. We will also ensure that, if you need counsel in the room with you, we will arrange for that. Remember to check the updated schedule after I post it, and keep up your excellent work. Thank you, everyone."

Kala and Lindsey returned to their desks to await their new assignments. After posting the schedule, Mr. Paulson walked over to Kala's desk.

"Have you made a decision, Kala?" he asked bluntly.

"Yes, sir, I have. I'd like to discuss it in your office."

Mr. Paulson pointed to his office door and Kala followed him.

"What else is on your mind, Kala?" Mr. Paulson asked as he settled into his chair.

"I've made the decision to sign on with Sierra team, but I wanted to ask, after this, do you think it's still safe to continue with the missions?"

"Yes, I do. You know that no matter what might happen to equipment here, no one will ever be able to get to the ships."

"Even if WASA finds that an employee is involved?"

Mr. Paulson didn't reply right away. He knew that Kala was right, and admitting that might mean admitting that they might have to delay one, if not both, of the missions. And delaying either of the missions would seriously hurt WASA's credibility with the public.

"Kala," he said finally, "we have military guards around the ships. There is absolutely no way anyone who isn't authorized can get near them."

"What if the person is authorized?"

"You know authorized personnel changes daily. There isn't much a person could do in one day."

"Sir, you know as well as I do that a person who is qualified can do a lot in one day. It won't stop me from going on the mission, but I think someone needs to realize, or at least admit, there is a serious threat here."

"We know that, Kala, and we also know that we can only do so much. If someone really wants to sabotage these missions, they will find a way. They may damage the communications satellites. Even with no communication, we could still get a mission to the planet, but there would probably be no follow-up missions to that particular planet. They could do damage to a small circuit in the ship that would make it blow up on the pad or shortly after takeoff. But, then again, they could try and we would thwart them at every turn, and we would be successful. We have to try. For the human race and for Earth, we have to try. If we don't at least try, it will mean admitting defeat and consigning Earth and the human race to a slow, painful death. Maybe Earth could renew itself after the human race is dead, but do you really want to take that chance?"

Kala thought about what he said then sighed in consent. She stood up to leave but stopped halfway to the door and turned back to Mr. Paulson.

"When will the paperwork be ready for me to sign?"

"By the end of the week. I'm not going to let it hold up your training, though. I'm going to contact Charlie and have him get you into the schedule starting tomorrow. You might want to contact family tonight to let them know. You'll be a very busy lady from now on."

"When will the announcement be made to them?" She asked indicating her coworkers in the control room.

"Well, considering today will be your last day in there, I might as well make the announcement as soon as I contact Charlie. Please tell anyone on other shifts that haven't left yet to wait; tell them I have one more announcement for them."

Kala left the office and did as Mr. Paulson asked. Lindsey was on the phone but looked over at her quizzically. Kala gave a small nod.

When Mr. Paulson came out of his office everyone sensed something big was about to happen; the room grew silent as he strode toward the big windows in front. He surveyed the room and studied the faces of his team members. Finally, he gestured to Kala.

"Kala, would you come up here and join me, please." He paused as she walked from her desk. "As many of you know, Kala and Lindsey are the most recent additions to our little team. When Kala was first offered the position at WASA, it was thought that she would eventually be the person who would be put in charge of the new office being built on the West Coast in the Bay Area District. When she arrived in this office to work, my job was to train her for that task, but I soon saw that her skills would be better suited elsewhere. I asked the top brass for permission to include her in one of the off-world missions. Then, I asked the leaders of the next four missions if they would want her on their team. Two leaders expressed an interest. I made the offers to Kala, and she has decided to join Charlie Hudson's Sierra team. She will begin her training with them tomorrow. I'd like to thank Kala for her hard work for us here and wish her luck on her new mission!"

Everyone in the room cheered and gathered around Kala, offering congratulations. Finally, when the hubbub had died away, Mr. Paulson raised his hands for attention again.

"I know with all that's happened, there's a lot to catch up on, but I'm going to close the office down for the rest of the day shift and send everyone out to lunch. I've already made arrangements with Mariello's for WASA to cover all the food and drink for the afternoon. Just remember, we have a tough road ahead of us, so don't overdo it! Enjoy this time off, gang. It's going to be the last for a while!"

Everyone cheered again and grabbed their things. Kala went to her desk and sat down.

"Aren't you coming to the party, Kala?" someone called from the door.

"I'll be there in a few minutes. I've got a few things to clear up before I leave."

Once everyone had gone, Kala looked to Lindsey's desk and saw her friend, and newfound sister, still sitting there.

"Aren't you going to the party?" Kala asked.

"When you go, I go," was the reply.

They both laughed.

Kala gathered the papers that were piled on her desk. Going through them, she sorted them into smaller piles. Finally finished, she took one of the piles over to Lindsey.

"This is the stuff we've been working on for Paula. You should be able to figure out what I've done to complement your work. If you have any questions, you'll know where to find me...for the next six months anyhow!"

They laughed again. Kala went back to her desk and looked at the piles of paper she had left there. She put them into folders and labeled them. Just as she finished up, Mr. Paulson came out of his office.

"What are you still doing here?"

"I wanted to get my desk cleared off before I left." Kala replied.

Mr. Paulson waited expectantly.

"I've gotten everything organized and into folders. The folders are all labeled, and I'll leave them here on my desk where they can be found and easily given to whoever takes over my position."

"Thank you. Now go to your farewell party! That's an order. I'll be right behind you. I'm just getting the final paperwork ready for the signature process."

The girls left for Mariello's.

The afternoon was filled with good food and stories. As people were preparing to leave, Pete pulled Kala to the front of the room and called for everyone's attention.

"Kala, I know you haven't worked with us for long but we wanted to let you know how much we appreciated everything you've done for us."

He handed Kala a small, blue box with the WASA emblem on the top. She opened it slowly to reveal a coin about the size of the old fifty-cent piece. On one side was etched the shuttle from the twenty-first century that was the predecessor of the present ships. On the other side was the current ship being used in space exploration. On the side with the current ship were the words, "To Seek and Explore," and on the flip side with the old ship were the words, "In the Path of Heroes."

Kala knew that these coins were usually reserved for commanders and other leaders who were retiring from WASA or those leaders who were going off on a dangerous mission. She looked at the coin and then at the people who had been her coworkers for the past few months. She never thought that she could become so close with people so quickly, but realized that people who worked for places like WASA probably got closer quicker because of the inherent dangers of the job.

"Thank you, all, for this. I will treasure it forever. This medallion will go with me when I leave on my mission. It really has been a pleasure working with you all, and I'm going to leave it at that before I start crying!"

Then she wove her way through the crowd toward Lindsey and the door.

They walked in silence together, listening to the sounds of the city as they headed to the subway stop. On the train, Lindsey turned to Kala.

"Are you sure you're ready for this?"

"I'm not sure of anything, Lin. I just know that I need to feel like I'm making a difference, and if this is my way of doing that, then so be it. I just wish you could come with me."

"Someone needs to stay here and remind you of your roots!"

Laughing, they got off the train.

When they got to the house, they saw cars in the driveway.

"Who's here to visit us, do you think?" Lindsey wondered aloud.

"We'll find out soon enough, I suppose."

As they walked up the front steps, the front door opened and Eva came out to meet them.

"I'm sorry, Miss. I couldn't stop them from coming in."

"Who are you talking about, Eva?"

"The people from TechNet. They showed up about half an hour ago and barged past me when I answered the doorbell."

"Eva, slow down. Did they say why they were here?"

"No. They just came in, asked to be directed to the study, and told me to tell you to join them there as soon as you got home."

"Did you make sure they got food and drink?"

"I asked, ma'am, but they refused. I showed them the wet bar, and let them know if they changed their minds and wanted any food, they should let me know. They only said to leave the room, telling me again to send you there as soon as you got home. Then they shut the door."

"It's okay, Eva, you did the right thing."

"What do you think they want?" Lindsey asked as they went to the study.

"I have no clue." Kala shook her head.

When they got to the study door, Kala realized that Eva was still following them.

"Eva, please have chef make some of her wonderful finger food...you know, the minisandwiches we like...and her lovely iced tea with sugar and fresh mint from the garden. Bring them here when everything is ready. I have a feeling we'll need it."

"Yes, ma'am. Is there anything else?" Eva asked wanting to do anything she could to help Kala.

"Yes, stop worrying. You did everything you could in the situation, and you aren't in any trouble. There is no way to stop TechNet when they want something."

Eva smiled gratefully as she left for the kitchen with Kala's request. Kala and Lindsey looked at each other for assurance before Kala opened the study door.

Three men from TechNet were gathered around the fireplace looking at one of the books Kala kept by the couch. The first thing Kala noticed about them was how much they looked alike. They were all around five foot five with short brown hair, brown eyes, and very pale skin. The clothes they wore were also remarkable in their sameness: black suits, white button-down shirts, and the red TechNet tie. Their eyes were cold and hard as they looked at Kala and Lindsey; they almost looked like criminals who had just been woken up from deep sleep imprisonment.

"How may we help you gentlemen?" Kala asked after she and Lindsay had entered the room and shut the door.

"Casio will be very mad if something happens to her," said a quiet female voice from the corner.

Kala and Lindsey almost jumped out of their skins as they turned toward the speaker.

"Well, we'll just have to make sure that nothing happens to her then," replied one of the men at the fireplace.

The woman simply looked back at them through hooded eyes. She was the female version of the men: short, dark hair, brown eyes, and pale skin. Instead of pants, she wore a skirt, but otherwise, her clothes were just the same.

"You haven't answered my question," Kala said, trying to sound calmer than she felt.

"You can get WASA to stop sending out exploratory manned missions," replied one of the men.

"What makes you think they'll listen to us?" Lindsey asked.

"Your friend's family is what makes us think that," replied the woman.

"Like my friend asked," Kala said, "what makes you think they'll listen to a couple of young, green fly girls like us? We haven't been with them long enough to have any pull."

"But just look at your family connections, Ms. Melina, your parents being who they were, and your brother being so high up on the TechNet corporate ladder."

"What do my parents or my brother have to do with my life choices? I have graduated school and passed my Rite of Ascension. I am now considered an adult and should be treated as such. If you want to ask me to do something for you, or think like you do, I suggest you come and speak directly to me about it."

"That is what we are doing now, Ms. Melina."

"By threatening my friends and my family? How far do you think that's going to get you?"

The TechNets stared at her. They clearly hadn't realized that the two years of living with Casio had taught her a thing or two about dealing with people from their offices. Kala could see the silent communication going on between the four of them. Finally, the woman stood up and turned toward the window.

"Obviously, Casio has told you more about our organization then we realized," she said.

"Not as much as you might think, but more than you probably realize." Kala responded.

"You know about the faction of TechNet that wants to end the human race?"

Kala and Lindsey nodded.

"You know the main group wants to let the Earth continue its space exploration to save the human race on off-world planets?"

Again the girls nodded.

"Well, there is a group in between that wants the human race to continue, but it should only continue on Earth. We don't feel we should be going out to other planets and destroying them like we destroyed Earth. If the human race can't change its ways, then it should be forced to deal with the mess it made here instead of making one on other planets."

"Let me ask *you* a question," Kala, said. "What if the human race has learned the error of its ways, and the only way to fix the problem is to give the Earth a rest and time to heal? Did you ever think of that?"

"Explain" was the response she got from one of the men.

"Okay, I'm not going to argue the fact that the human race has done great harm to the planet. That is an obvious fact and I would lose that argument. But I do feel that we have finally learned from our past and realized that the only way we can save Earth is to get humans off the planet and give it some kind of respite. We need to thin out the population here and start colonizing other planets so we can survive as a race."

"How do you plan on keeping up the lines of communication?" asked one of the men.

"If the vandals would stop destroying the communication equipment, there would be many years of communication between Earth and the colonies WASA is planning. As TechNet has created many of the components for the long distance communication devices, I'm sure you know the distances we can traverse and still have decent communication. Well, WASA is planning on staying within that range for now. Once the first new colonies are up functioning, WASA can create communication relay stations or something similar. But, for now, baby steps are needed, or the branch of TechNet that wants to destroy the human race will get its wish and not have to lift a finger."

While the TechNets considered what she had said, Kala went to the wall unit and called Eva in the kitchen. She told her to bring in the prepared tray of food and drink. When she turned back to the TechNets, they were standing in a group by the fireplace talking quietly. Kala walked over to Lindsey.

"Do you think they're coming to you because of Casio?" Lindsey whispered.

"I'd bet on it." Kala whispered back. "I'm pretty sure he isn't directly involved, but I think they're here because of my relationship to him. I'd also bet they didn't think I'd stand up for myself. I'm not sure if they thought Casio had worn me down or beaten me into a pliable little thing. But one thing I am sure of... They're not getting what they expected."

Just then, there was a soft rap on the door and Eva entered. The woman went over to the sideboard and laid out the food and iced tea, placing napkins and six plates next to the tray along with serving utensils and glasses.

"Will there be anything else, Miss?"

"Not right now, Eva. I'll let you know when you can clear away."

Eva nodded and left the room, pulling the door quietly closed behind her. Kala walked over to the sideboard and poured herself some tea.

"Would anyone like a drink with their food?"

"I'll have some tea," replied Lindsey.

The four TechNets went over to liquor cabinet to see what was in there.

"No liquor?" asked one of the men.

"We don't drink," replied Lindsey, "so we see no point of keeping it in the house. We only get enough if we're having a party or someone who likes to drink is coming over. Otherwise, there is no point keeping alcohol in the house."

"What about unexpected guests?" asked the woman.

"Anyone who knows us knows that we don't keep it in the house and either brings what they want or does without." Then Kala poured tea for herself and Lindsey, while Lindsey went to the sideboard for the minisandwiches.

"Since you were comfortable enough to let yourselves into my house, I think you can get your own drinks and food. You can also tell me why you are really here. If the real reason is that you want to bully me into getting WASA to stop the missions, I can tell you now that you have failed. If my brother sent you to find out how I am doing, let him know I am fine and will be going into space as planned."

When Kala finished speaking, the TechNets said nothing.

"I know the announcement was only made today, but knowing my brother, I'm sure he knew about it before I even left the office for the day. If there is nothing else for you to say to me, then have a nice little snack and be on your way. I have lots of work to do, and I would appreciate it if you would leave me to it."

Once again, there was silence as the TechNets looked at each other and then at Kala, who could see they weren't used to being spoken to in such a manner. Finally, the woman addressed Kala.

"Thank you for speaking so plainly with us, Ms. Melina. As I'm sure you know, not many people do. We just want to make sure that WASA is doing the right thing by sending people into space."

"Are you sure that's really it?" Kala asked. "Or are you trying to protect your jobs by keeping humans here on Earth?"

"Our group at TechNet is sure that's really it. There may be outside Earth-only groups that have ulterior motives; our TechNet group only wants the best for the human race. Don't forget, we lost people on the X Mission as well. We don't want any more unnecessary loss of life. We have interviewed all the people who are intending to go on the next two missions, and we are satisfied that they have the right belief in what they are doing. We'll go and leave you in peace now. Is there any message you'd like to send to Casio?"

"No thank you. I'll be speaking to him in a few days."

The woman nodded and then motioned for the men to follow her. As Kala and Lindsey watched them drive away, Kala thought again how glad she was that she didn't work for TechNet. Casio had been right when he told her she wouldn't fit in with that group.

CHAPTER 14

Between catching up on the mission and getting the house ready for her departure, Kala barely had time to breath during the following months. No one in the family, including Lillia, disagreed with her signing the Old Philadelphia house over to Lindsey. By the girls' seventeenth birthdays, Kala and Lindsey were both well-established at WASA and in their lives in Old Philadelphia.

Lindsey had made arrangements for her parents to move to Old Philadelphia and live with her after Kala left. Her brother and sister had also gotten job transfers to locations nearer the rest of the family. Kala felt better about leaving her friend, and newly found sister, now that everything was going so well for them both.

For the month before the mission, Kala and her crewmates would be moving to the WASA Houston base in Mid-Continent, in what used to be Texas. About a week before the move, Kala used vacation days to spend time with family. Lindsey's family, Casio, and Shawan and his family all came to Old Philadelphia.

The night before she left, Kala held a big party not only for her family but also for those from WASA who didn't have any family. Kala knew that most of her crewmates were also having parties, so she made sure all her guests knew they were free to come and go to attend the other parties. After the guests left, Kala stood in a corner and noted everyone in the room.

Even though she had pictures, she wanted to make sure that she remembered everyone. She studied her brothers, niece and nephew, her sister-in-law. She wanted to remember them laughing as they were now.

She looked around and found Lindsey sitting off to one side with her family. She wanted to remember them, too, as they were also her family. When all were committed to memory, she walked to the middle of the room and clinked her glass.

"Well, I guess it's time to say good-bye. Tomorrow morning I leave for Old Houston, and my life will never be the same. I've had a wonderful life here on Earth, and I hope I'll have a wonderful life where I'm going. I couldn't have asked for a better family or friends. If you want to get in touch with me, I've left envelopes in your rooms with the information needed to contact me while I'm at the Houston base and after we've left Earth. There will be a brief communications blackout when we reach the planet while we're getting the communications satellite in orbit. After that, we'll be building the relay station on the ground. I expect the blackout won't last long, and I will be in contact once communications are back up again. They won't be great, once we are on the planet, but we will be able to send messages. Please remember how much I love you and how much I will miss you."

There was a snort from Casio's direction.

"Yes, I love you and will miss you, Casio! You always made me think on my feet, and I'll always be grateful to you for that! You are all my family and nothing can ever take that away from us. Please talk about me to your children and make sure they all know that what we are doing at WASA is for the good of the planet."

Everyone surrounded Kala with hugs and love for the last time.

The next morning, Kala left quietly before anyone got up to avoid a big, emotional scene.

When she arrived in at the Houston base, she noticed that she was the only one there other than Charlie Hudson. Stowing her bags in the shared sleeping area, she wandered out to the control room. She stood in the back of the room and looked out at the ship that would be her home in a month. They would be on board for seven weeks before reaching their destination. While the ship was bigger than the ships of the past, Kala expected quarters to be cramped.

She knew that their destination was a planet near the failed X Mission planet, and she wondered if WASA planned to go past that planet to put a marker in orbit commemorating the people they had lost. Thinking of X Mission, Kala knew their mission was carrying DNA samples for many different species, including humans, so that if something happened and no other mission was sent, there might be a possibility of making the their mission viable.

Just then, she heard footsteps behind her and she turned to see Charlie walking down the hall. He saw her standing in the door and waved.

"When did you arrive?" he asked, heading toward her.

"About thirty minutes ago. What about you?"

"I've been here for about a week. There's always more work a commander has to take care of before a mission. Everyone should be here by tomorrow afternoon and, then, the real fun can start."

Kala rolled her eyes before turning her attention back to the ship.

"It's amazing, isn't it," Charlie said softly.

"It really is. No matter how often I've seen a launch site, I never get enough of it."

"You've been seeing the video feed in Old Philly. It's a whole other thing to be seeing it live. This makes it more real, doesn't it?"

Kala nodded her head. She sighed and stepped away.

"Where's the cafeteria in this building? I haven't eaten since I left this morning and I'm starving."

"Why don't you join me? I was headed there myself to get a snack, so we can sit and get to know each other a bit. I think I know you least of all the crew."

They had been chatting for about an hour and a half when Kala sat back in her chair and looked Charlie straight in the eye.

"Tell me the truth, Commander. What are they not telling us about this mission?"

"Excuse me?" Charlie asked, surprised.

"You know as well as I do that feed in the control room isn't live. It's a very good loop, but a loop is what it is. So tell me, what are they trying to hide?"

Charlie was silent, staring at her. Then, he got up from his chair and motioned Kala to follow him. They went from the cafeteria to one of the ultra-private training rooms in the complex. Charlie entered the code and they went in. The door silently closed behind them. Charlie motioned her to sit at the end of the table closest to the monitor and controls. He entered something into the computer, and a schematic of a ship appeared on the monitor.

The ship was almost three times bigger than the one that was supposedly sitting on the launch pad. Kala could see that there was room for many more passengers and much more equipment. She could also see that there was an entire section just for the scientific equipment and samples they would be taking with them. She let the image sink in before turning back to Charlie and cocking her head quizzically at him.

"Because of the troubles we've had with TechNet and other Earth-only groups, we've decided that the truth needed to be hidden. To be honest, what the ship will hold isn't even the full extent of what will be going on this trip. We'll be rendezvousing with a ship that's been built in orbit about twice the size of this ship. This ship you see is an exact duplicate of what went off for Foxtrot."

"I still don't understand. Why all the secrecy?"

"After this mission there will be no more secrecy. But, for the moment, we still fear sabotage, so precautions are being taken. When we are safely away, WASA administration will have a worldwide vid-conference. They will announce the true dimensions of this ship and the Foxtrot ship, the true scope of the number of crew involved, both awake and in deep sleep, the human and animal DNA samples taken, the animal life taken in deep sleep, and the plants and seedlings taken."

"Does the core crew know the full dimensions of the real mission?"

"You mean other than the command staff?"

"Who else is there? Since we thought this was going to be a trip of ten to fifteen people, who else would there be?"

"Technically, the command staff is only myself; my second-in-command, Danielle Chang; and Bill Chow, the security chief."

"You sit there talking technicalities! How can not telling people about that," she said, jumping up and indicating the screen, "be considered a technicality! By all that's holy, Charlie, how are we supposed to trust our command structure if we're not told the truth? What about the controls and all the details?"

"Nothing has changed, Kala. All the controls will be the same, just on a bigger scale. Besides, when everyone gets here and we start the training, they will learn what's real, and everyone will be trained on the actual ship."

"I don't believe this," she said pacing. "Since the day I started at WASA, someone has been preaching to me about spreading the truth. No more lies, I've been told. We've been perpetuating the biggest lie of all, and we didn't even know it!" She slapped her hand on the table.

"Just how do you think the public would react to knowing that we're taking even more people and resources than we initially told them?" Charlie replied.

"What about knowing that even more families were going to be split up forever on what might be a trip to a doomed planet? We can't be sure of the surveillance from the satellites. All the planets we're going to might be like X's, and what then? All this time and credits wasted just to prove that we would only be able to live on domed worlds if we leave Earth? How have you been recruiting people if you haven't been telling them the truth?" Kala still was angry.

"If you think about it, we haven't been outright lying to them either. We've just been careful not to have them in the same room at the same time. Think about your training over the last few weeks. Did you ever meet anyone other than the command staff?"

Kala thought about it and then shook her head.

"The recruits have been training with their work section only. Most of them will be loaded onto the ship in deep sleep and won't know the difference until we reach our destination. Once we're there and we've off-loaded everyone, they'll find out the truth. That also saves some headaches if there are problems."

"But what if we need the help of these people because we run into problems along the way?"

"All the team leaders will be awake. If we need other team members to be awakened, they will be. Trust me, Kala, everything will work out." He looked deep into her eyes.

"Okay, I'll trust you." She said, accepting him at his word. "But I still don't understand what my job will be."

"You're going to be the onsite administrative assistant for the mission. You'll be coordinating supplies, helping keep track of man-hours, and helping the command staff with the daily paperwork. You'll have training in a little bit of everything, and you will be the 'go to' person as far as paperwork goes."

"So I'll be a glorified space secretary?"

Charlie rolled his eyes. "Are you always this way?"

"One thing I learned from my brother Casio is to always speak the truth. Don't worry, though. I'm usually calmer when I know what's going on and I'm more sure about what I'm getting myself into. I have one more question. Since I am going to be the admin, will I at least know the full personnel compliment before we lift off?"

"Yes. Other than the command staff, you will be the only person at the start of the trip who knows the full complement of people and supplies."

After her initial shock, Kala buckled down and got to work. She learned the ship's systems and exactly what paperwork she would be responsible for. Once she felt comfortable with what was needed, she created her own more efficient forms. She was working at a computer one day when Charlie approached her.

"What's up?" She asked when he came into the room.

"We've just gotten a message from Foxtrot. They want the full command team in the ready room to hear it, and I want you there as well."

Kala didn't question the news; she grabbed a recording pad and followed Charlie to the secondary ready room. As she was headed toward a corner to watch, Charlie motioned her to the front and had her sit with the command team.

"You are a valued member of this team and I will not have you forever hiding in corners," he whispered in her ear.

She snapped him a salute just as the view screen cleared to show a beautiful view of what looked to be a rain forest. The colors were quite shocking and different from what the rain forest looked like on Earth. There were shades of blue, pink, red, yellow, and green. The river running in the distance looked to be crystal clear with a hint of purple. The sky was blue like Earth's and the distant sun was yellow with a twinge of green.

After a minute of gazing at this scene, Commander Bill Johnson came into view. He looked slightly haggard but seemed to be doing well. At least the fresh air seemed to be agreeing with him.

"Just sending the regularly scheduled report," he started. "So far, the indigenous life seems to be staying away from us. We've heard some noises in the distance that sound almost like big cats, and at dusk and dawn, there's some kind of flying predator, but nothing has bothered us. We've gotten the feeling we're being watched, but we expected that. We've gotten the ship totally stripped except for the communications relay, and the main square of buildings has really taken shape. There have been the usual run-ins with indigenous plants, but nothing serious, and we've found that there is some kind of mineral in the water that has affected us, but we think we've found a way to filter it out. The only serious problem we appear to be having is that there is something on the surface that seems to be draining our power packs; it's probably the reason we haven't been able to establish a live feed. We may not be able to send many more communications. But I see no reason why more people can't be sent here to establish a more permanent settlement."

There was a pause as they heard a loud roar in the background. Then they saw two immense winged creatures take off in the distance.

"Those are two of the flying creatures I've told you about. That seems to be some kind of mating ritual. We have a group on their way to explore and try to capture some close-up footage. If we don't get a chance to send any more communications, just know that things are going well here, and we have all agreed that this would be a wonderful place for a community.

It is definitely one-way and will definitely be low-tech if we can't figure out what is draining the battery packs. Hope all is well and we will continue to transmit to the ship as long as we're able. The ship will continue to transmit to Earth at regular intervals and is programmed to transmit a final message and go offline to conserve its own resources if it doesn't get communication from us for more than one month. This is Bill Johnson signing off for now."

They watched Bill walk out of the frame. Instead of turning off the camera as he usually did, he panned around to capture distant and close-up images of the foliage that surrounded him. Then he shut the camera off. The room was silent as everyone absorbed what they had just seen.

Kala spoke.

"Does this power drain worry anyone else?" she asked.

"I think it bothers all of us," replied John Lister, head of the Houston base. "But I think we also need to take into account that Bill seems to feel it won't be a problem if the colonists don't mind a low-tech society."

"When was this message sent?" asked Karri Pasternak, one of the mission specialists assigned to the Sierra mission.

"Yesterday afternoon," replied John. "We got the warning that another message was coming in, flagged urgent, so we thought we'd catch you up before it came in."

There was a beep from the COM unit next to John, and he depressed the button.

"The message has come through and we've begun the decoding process," the communications technician advised.

"Put what you have up on the screen," replied John.

"I think you'd better view it in private first, sir. It's pretty graphic."

John looked at the COM unit like it was going to explain the last statement. Then, he pushed back from the console and left the room. The group that remained in the ready room glanced nervously at each other while they waited for him to come back. After ten minutes, John came back into the room; the first thing everyone noticed was his white complexion.

"There has been a change of status of the planet. We will be classifying it unsuitable. Your questions will all be answered by this video."

He depressed the "play" button and a scene very similar to the one they had seen earlier appeared. After a moment a still haggard, but now defeated-looking, Bill Johnson came on the screen. There was a pause as he looked at the camera. He looked as if he were trying to remember where he was and what he was doing. Finally, he took a deep breath and began to speak.

"Well, we finally solved the power drain problem as well as finding out more about our flying friends. They seem to be a dragon creature of some kind. They don't breathe fire, but they do look a lot like the ancient Chinese creatures from the writings and drawings from thousands of years ago. They were unconcerned with the presence of our group when we arrived to shoot footage. We're sending this footage now since I don't know how much longer we'll be able to last here."

Bill paused again and looked around, as if to see if he was being followed. He took another deep breath and started speaking again.

"We have found that the source of the power drain seems to be a natural phenomenon due to the strange minerals on the planet. We've also discovered creatures that live in consort with the dragons. They are as violent as the dragons are docile, and when they caught the expedition team's smell, they hunted the team. There was only one member left alive to get footage of the dragons and these creatures to us. The rest of the expedition were killed and eaten by the creatures. They look like they are related to the dragons. However, unlike the dragons, they are highly aggressive and they like their meat fresh.

"We were able to kill the ones that followed the surviving team member back to base camp, but we believe that more of these creatures are on the way. This has made it necessary for us to abandon the base camp and move toward the ocean. We are taking as much food as we can carry, along with all the rafts, and heading for the Southern continent. We're unsure if we'll be able to make contact with the ship, so this may be our last transmission. We still think this would make a good planet for colonization, but we feel we need to warn anyone coming here of the dangers and to make sure they bring protection.

"I am sending all our logs, along with the set of intended coordinates of where we plan on going in the South. If another ship comes to this area, the South would be the place to start looking for us. Once we get to our new location, we will try making contact, and if we can, you will start hearing from us again. May whatever gods you pray to be kind to us and, hopefully, one day we will meet up with other humans from Earth."

Again, there was stunned silence in the ready room as everyone tried to digest this new information.

"The logs and all the other information are still being downloaded and decoded. Once everything has been reviewed, we will have another meeting." John instructed.

"Will our mission be changing?" Kala asked quietly.

"Not at this point. We're still waiting for all the information and the other videos to be viewed and deciphered. Once that happens, we'll make a decision. We believe that your mission will go on as planned and another mission will be sent to Omicron, the name Bill gave the planet. We still need planets. Only now we'll have to rely on the first settlers for the final ruling. You are all aware that this is a one-way trip. Bill and his team knew that as well. If anyone feels they can't go on with the mission now that they've seen this, see Charlie. We won't think less of anyone if they decide they want to stay here on Earth. This briefing is concluded for now but stay close so we can meet again when all input is ready for viewing."

Everyone silently left the room. Kala went back to her cubical to work on the forms and databases she was designing for the mission. Even though she had been given fairly wide latitude, everything she designed and created needed to be approved before liftoff. In the back of her mind, though, she was now wondering if she really wanted to go. She knew it would be dangerous and she knew it would be one-way; only now, with these transmissions from Bill, the real truth about the dangers was being exposed.

After working three hours, she looked up at the clock and stretched. She decided it was time for a break and wandered toward the cafeteria.

If I keep eating this way, she thought, *I'll be too fat to go on the mission, and I'll have to stay home.*

It was then she realized that no matter the danger, she very much wanted to go on the mission. The Earth was slowly dying and she wanted a chance, no matter how slim it might be, for it to live. When she got to the cafeteria, she noticed a group of xenobiologists from the mission sitting in a corner. They knew she was an admin to the command team and they waved her over to the table. She pointed to the food station and nodded.

"Is it true what we're hearing about the latest transmission from Bill Johnson?" one ashen-faced young girl asked.

"It's true there was another transmission," Kala replied, "but you know I can't discuss anything until all the data has been analyzed. You know the importance of making sure you have all the data before making conclusions. Because there are so many lives at stake, WASA wants to make absolutely sure we will be able to have a fighting chance out there."

There was quiet grumbling at her answer.

"Let me put it another way, would you want the command team to pressure you into describing what attacked the group without seeing the data?"

They looked at her totally incensed.

"Well, there you have it, then. How can you expect WASA to make a decision like this before all the data is in and has been analyzed? You can't because you won't, so just give them the time they need. We still have three weeks before we are scheduled to lift off. If they need to, WASA will delay the mission until they can make sure."

"They haven't so far," someone in the corner said very quietly.

"Do you know that for a fact?" Kala snapped. "How do you know for sure that X Mission and Foxtrot weren't delayed? How can you all be so sure that WASA doesn't have our best interests at heart? I think you all need to think about the real reasons you signed up for this mission. Are you going because of your love of your planet and your field of study, or are you going to get a higher position and your family more credits? Think long and hard about that before you make any decisions. Whatever your reason might be, it is your business, but the safety of the crew and the mission is WASA's while we are on Earth, and Charlie Hudson's once we leave, and I'll be damned if anyone is going to put that in jeopardy because they are too scared or too unwilling to learn new things."

She picked up her tray of food and walked out of the room. She barely heard the sound of clapping coming from the room over the pounding of her heart in her ears. When she got back to her cubical and had sat down, she suddenly burst into tears. She had been feeling like pot that was boiling over and the tears were a needed release. Now calm, she blew her nose, ate her lunch, and got back to work.

After a while, she went to the vending machine to get a drink. When she got back to her desk, she found Charlie and a man she didn't know waiting for her.

"Just tell me I'm not in trouble and I'll be happy."

"What would you be in trouble for?" asked Charlie. "All you did was show a slight case of nerves while defending your employer and your supervisor. We're here because we're concerned about your outburst, not because it got you into trouble."

She raised her eyebrows at him in curiosity.

"I don't know if you've ever met Thom Bradley, the administrator in charge of mission personnel," Charlie said pointing at the man next to him. "He happened to be in the cafeteria and overheard your little tirade. He asked me what your exact position was with the mission. When I told him, he suggested that we change your status and give you an upgrade."

"To what, head bean counter instead of junior bean counter?" Kala asked in a slightly sarcastic manner.

"I know you were being sarcastic but, in a nutshell, yes," replied Mr. Bradley, laughing.

"Excuse me?"

"We want to expand your duties and upgrade your position to an

Alpha-1 clearance," said Mr. Bradley. "We were just going to make do with the Alpha-1s that we had, but when I went to see Charlie wanting to give you more opportunities, he suggested that having a backup might be a good idea. Whether you believe it or not, standing up to a bunch of WASA scientists like you did today takes guts. That's why we need you in this position. You have the ability to stand up for yourself, and for those who needed it, while still being fair to both parties."

"Not to mention," said Charlie "you've not spent years mired in WASA politics, so you don't feel the need to placate anyone."

"What exactly does Alpha-1 mean? What does it entail?"

"Alpha-1 is the highest security clearance we have here at WASA. It means you would have the ability to vet people going on the mission; you would be able to perform full background checks. You wouldn't need to be directly in charge of hiring or firing, but your feelings and recommendations on personnel and other administrative activities would be listened to very closely.

Kala mulled over the idea.

"You'd also get extra credits," Charlie added.

"Tell me what I'm supposed to do with the credits I'm already getting," Kala snorted. "I've finally found an even way of divvying out what I'm getting already, and now you want to add more?"

"It's only fair to pay you what the position is supposed to be paid. You could put it into the management of the food stores you've set up for the Old Philadelphia city shelters."

"Well, you've twisted my arm. I don't see any reason not to take the position, and without sounding stuck up, I think I would be good at it."

"Good," said Mr. Bradley. "I'll get the paperwork drawn up for you to sign. Charlie can get you up to speed on any extra duties he wants you to take over, and we'll be good to go."

Just like that, Kala found herself a full part of the command staff.

CHAPTER 15

In the afternoon, after she had finished with Charlie, Kala informed her family of her new status and then went to Thom Bradley's office to sign the official paperwork. Once she knew what her new credit balance would be, she called her attorney and had him revise the paperwork for the division of the credits. When she was finished, she was famished.

She took files with her to the cafeteria and sat in a corner reviewing the staff positions that Charlie wanted her to look at. She was surprised at how much he wanted her to be involved in the day-to-day running of the mission. Knowing that she would be an important part of such a difficult mission increased her confidence. As she was checking the division of the scientists' deep sleep wake-up schedule, she felt a tap on her shoulder. She looked around to see one of the biologists from earlier in the day. She pointed to a seat and the woman sat down.

"Charlie made an announcement to all the divisions that we should come to you with any issues we may have concerning the mission. He said you would be able to get things handled."

"I'll certainly do my best, Doctor...?"

"Haverton. Wasilla Haverton."

"Dr. Haverton, how may I help you?"

"After your speech earlier today, I realized that we were speaking out of ignorance. We have been told next to nothing about our mission, and we know even less of the planet where we will be making our new home. If you could give the teams of scientists more information, that would help us a great deal."

Kala sat back in her chair and looked at the small woman seated across from her. Dr. Haverton was one of the few people shorter than Kala. Barely five feet tall and probably not weighing more than one hundred pounds, Dr. Haverton was small and compact, with a dark complexion that emphasized her Middle Eastern heritage. Any vocal accent identifying her country of birth had long ago disappeared with her years in America.

"Are you telling me that the teams have gotten no information at all about the mission, even regarding their own discipline?"

Dr. Haverton nodded solemnly. Kala sighed deeply and gathered her papers.

"I will talk to Charlie right now," she said, "and I will try to get each team something to work with for their specific concentration. I know that isn't much, but I will try to get something. Will that work?"

"Anything will be helpful at this point. I think most of our worry is that we're going in blind. We know how the ship works, we know what we are taking with us for our concentration, but we don't know anything about what to expect when we get there. We do understand there isn't much available info, but like I said before, anything you can get us would help to allay our fears."

"I can't guarantee information, Doctor, but I will do my best."

"Thank you, Ms. Melina. The heads of the scientific teams had a meeting after you spoke earlier, and we decided that you are someone who can be trusted to be fair to both sides of a discussion."

"Like I said, Doctor, I'll do my best. Where can I meet you later?"

"You know where Science Wing Four is?"

Kala nodded.

"The department heads will be meeting and working in the main lab this evening. We'll wait there."

"I will meet you there later," Kala replied.

On her way to Charlie's office Kala thought about how to phrase the request for information. She finally decided on the truth. When she got to his office, the door was open and Charlie was sitting at his desk. She rapped twice on the doorframe.

"Come on in and have a seat," Charlie smiled, seeing it was Kala. "What's up?"

"I just got a visit from Wasilla Haverton."

"Wasilla, really? That's interesting."

"She wanted to know if the scientists could get any information about where we were going. I explained we didn't have much, but that I would talk to you about it and see what you said."

Charlie turned and looked out the window overlooking the field behind the complex. He sighed as he turned back to Kala.

"We knew this would come up sooner or later, so we have packets being put together now with what information we have. Each team leader will get one packet for each of their team members. You can let the team leaders know they will have the packets in the next day or so and apologize for the delay in getting the information to them. No other explanation is to be given."

"Care to give me the explanation for my reference so I can give a response that sounds halfway credible?"

"You know the basic things we've kept hidden from the teams...the true size of the ship, the true numbers of people and livestock going with us. What we haven't gotten a chance to brief you on is the real reason for the push to find a suitable planet for us to live on. Our deep space probes have found an object headed toward Earth. We've been able to determine that it's very large...a ship of some sort. A decision has been made at the highest levels to get as many humans off Earth as possible, just in case the ship carries hostile and warlike beings. We want humans to survive somewhere."

Kala said nothing and nodded her head.

Then she smiled appreciatively at Charlie. "It'll take me a while to fully absorb what you've just said, but knowing the logic behind our mission, I believe I can more honestly put off our scientists."

"Thank you, Kala. Whatever you can do will be a big help."

Later, Kala found her way to Science Wing Four. When she arrived at the main science lab, she found all but one of the department heads there.

"Who's missing?"

"Dr. Marring had to go deal with a problem in the xexo lab, but said to get started without him. We can fill him in on whatever he misses," replied Dr. Haverton.

Kala told them the bare minimum. She mentioned that something had shown up on the long-range scanners, that the world government and WASA felt it necessary to get as many people off the planet as possible, just in case. She also told them what she could about the planet they were going to. She ended by telling them information packets would be given to each department head in the next twenty-four to forty-eight hours.

"Are there any questions?"

Dr. Haverton answered for all, "We'll wait for the packets and see what we are given. We appreciate your meeting with us and are glad to have you aboard."

Kala returned to her cubicle, feeling drained. Looking at the huge pile on her desk made her even more exhausted, so she decided to check her email and vid-phone messages one final time and shut down for the day. Whatever was there could wait until tomorrow.

Not ready to eat, she went to the crew quarters and decided to write letters home. She enjoyed the old-fashioned art of calligraphy and knew she wouldn't have much longer to practice. She had been writing for some time when a couple of crewmembers who shared her quarters came in. It was dinnertime. Now feeling hunger pangs, she put away her writing and made for the cafeteria. As she was walking, she heard someone calling her name. When she turned around she saw Dr. Haverton. She waited for the woman, and they walked together to the cafeteria.

"What can I do for you, Doctor?"

"I just wanted to thank you for what you shared with us earlier. We can now focus our work and be more prepared."

Kala knew there was more and waited. After a moment, Dr. Haverton dropped her eyes.

"Dr. Haverton, whatever it is, just say it. Nothing can be that bad."

"It's just that a few of our people have decided to leave the project. They said they don't feel safe and they've decided that the credits aren't enough to leave their families."

"How many?"

Dr. Haverton handed her a PDA. Kala read the resignation letter and the names that had signed and looked back at the scientist.

"Come with me," Kala said, turning around. She led the way to the conference room. Once there, she called Charlie and asked him to join them. While they were waiting, she spoke plainly to Dr. Haverton.

"From the information I gave you earlier today, I'm sure you realize what is at stake for Earth. Do you know what this will mean for the mission? I'm sure you tried to talk these people out of leaving...didn't you?"

Kala's questions were met by silence.

"Doctor, do you realize leaving now could be considered sabotage? And do you know what they do with saboteurs? The penalties conspirators will be subject to? Do you have any idea what the loss of these people dooms Earth to?" With the last question Kala stood and slapped the table with all her might.

Then Charlie walked in and closed the door behind him.

"What's going on?" he asked, looking between Kala and the doctor.

"Show him."

"Ms. Melina, please," the doctor pleaded.

"Show him," she said in an icy tone, one she had never thought she was capable of using before now.

Slowly Dr. Haverton held the PDA toward Charlie. He looked at the scientist and looked at Kala. When he saw the look on Kala's face, he took the unit and read. Kala saw his eyes reach the end of the document and go back to the beginning again. She watched him read the document at least twice more before looking back up.

"Can this be serious?" he asked, looking at Kala.

"Ask Dr. Haverton."

Charlie looked at the scientist for confirmation.

"We cannot, in good conscience, condone these trips off-world. We will be condemning other worlds and planets to the same fate as Earth."

"How can you be so sure?" Charlie asked.

"Because, despite protestations to the contrary, humans will never change. We are the only known species, on Earth or otherwise, that makes war and kills its own. We believe that, in another thousand years, maybe we'd be ready, but not now."

Charlie looked again at the PDA in his hand. Then he stood and went to the old-fashioned phone on the wall. After speaking into it quietly for a moment, he came back and sat down. He placed the PDA on the table in front of him and leaned back in his chair. The silence dragged on as he looked across the table, then out the window. Kala took his lead and leaned back in her chair, looking noncommital, all the while her insides quivering with nerves.

CHAPTER 16

Assuming an ease she didn't feel, Kala looked up at the ceiling and thought about what would happen. She now understood Charlie well enough, to know that he had probably called the director who would call security before coming to the conference room. She wondered if they had backup scientists to replace those they were about to lose. She suddenly realized that she was already thinking like a member of command and smiled. Just as she was about to access the computer in front of her, the door opened and Dr. Jim Jackson walked in followed by a security officer.

Dr. Jackson held his hand out to Charlie, who silently handed over the PDA. After scanning the document, he sat down at the head of the table and motioned for the security officer to wait outside. After the man had left the room, closing the door, he leaned back in his chair and looked at Dr. Haverton.

"It seems that you and your cronies have taken great pains to ruin Earth's chances of survival."

For the first time that afternoon, Wasilla Haverton looked a bit unsure of herself. She sat forward in her chair and directed her comments directly to Dr. Jackson.

"I assume you are aware of the mission of Free Earth."

"You assume correctly."

"We feel that the inhabitants of Earth need to correct their mistakes before we go gallivanting into the galaxy."

"But colonizing the moon was okay?"

"It's close enough to Earth for help to arrive quickly, if needed. What we are doing now is nothing more than putting people in danger."

Dr. Jackson leaned forward and crossed his arms on the table in front of him. He considered his next words very carefully before speaking.

"So... as long as we are destroying a planet close enough to get our people out of danger, that's okay. But if we send them out farther, that's wrong. Explosions on the moon twenty years ago killed three hundred people. Another forty-five died before we could get help to them. We're not sending more than that on these trips. I'm sure you know that much of the cargo is embryos so that, if something does go wrong, we won't lose living people."

Dr. Haverton didn't answer immediately. She looked at Dr. Jackson and then slowly looked from him to Charlie and, lastly, let her gaze move to Kala. She looked the longest and hardest at Kala.

"No, it wasn't right, but this team is the youngest and least tried. What happened to sending seasoned teams into space?"

"We send the people we feel are most qualified," Charlie replied. "If these people happen to be young, then that's what we send. Young people can be just as qualified, if not more so, than older people. More often than not, being young means being tech-savvy and more up to date with the most current versions of software and hardware as well as knowing the latest in management techniques. Being young doesn't always mean "least" in anything."

"But being young means being less tried!"

"Doctor, who is it you are trying to protect?" Dr. Jackson asked suddenly.

Dr. Haverton looked surprised at the question. When she didn't respond immediately, Kala leaned forward.

"I don't think that's the real question, Dr. Jackson. I think the question is who did you lose on a past mission."

As soon as Kala asked the question she knew she had exposed the scientist's motivation. She reached across the table and took her hand.

"Don't you think it would be a better tribute to the memory of this person that we keep trying to save the human race? If it was someone who was important to you or someone else on your team, don't you think they died doing what they believed in? Do you really think they would want us to let them die in vain?"

Kala watched a tear roll down Dr. Haverton's cheek and fall onto the table. Looking into Kala's eyes, she seemed defeated. She sighed, stood, and walked over to the window. She waited before turning back to the group to answer the questions.

"Every scientist for this mission lost someone they care about on the X Mission...a friend, spouse, child...someone. We don't want to lose anyone else from the scientific community, and we don't feel it is right for other families to have to go through what we went through. The movement that started to stop the missions is based on this conviction. But if we give the word, we can stop the sabotage. Give us a good reason to tell our people to stop, and we will."

Kala and Charlie turned to Dr. Jackson, a question in their eyes. He hesitated, then nodded.

Accessing the computer, Charlie brought up the long-range satellite images up on the main viewer.

After a moment, one image appeared on the viewer. Dr. Haverton gasped as she realized what the image was and what it meant. After studying the image, she turned to Charlie and Dr. Jackson.

"Why haven't you made this public?" she asked in an accusatory tone.

"And cause the entire world to panic? That would be worse than what we're doing now. Believe it or not, Doctor, there are times to reveal the whole truth and there are times not to. This is one of those times. We're telling people that it is important to find another planet to colonize, but we're not telling them entirely why. Our planet is dying. This ship may destroy the Earth faster if...and I stress 'if'...that is its intention."

"How do we know that the ship won't follow us to our new planet?"

"They haven't yet," replied Charlie. "Our last two ships traveled past this alien ship and they didn't seem to take notice. We think something about Earth itself interests them. It may be the Earth's current condition is perfect for them to colonize; it may be they want to help us. We won't know until they get here, and if it is their intention to kill us off, we don't want to wait. We will send as many people as possible away before this ship arrives so that, if these beings do come here to do damage, at least some of the human race have survived elsewhere."

"Aren't you discriminating by only taking the best of the human race?"

"What makes you say that?" asked Charlie. "We have DNA samples from every person on Earth stored in computers. We are making sure that each ship is taking a wide variety of in-vitro babies. As long as the planets we land on are viable, we will know that we will survive."

Dr. Haverton mulled this over for a few moments. She eyed those sitting at the table, breathing deeply.

"I understand why you are doing this, but for myself, I still don't think that I can work for WASA on this project anymore. I would like to remove myself from any off-planet missions and...I know it may not be possible...

Is there any way I could continue to help WASA in another capacity?"

"We'll have to think about your continued role with WASA after this... if you have a future with us, that is," replied Dr. Jackson. "You and the other scientists on this list stand to be accused of sabotage, and I'm not sure there will be much a future for you in this organization...or any other."

"What do you think the other scientists will do with information we've told you?" asked Charlie.

"I'm sure some of them will decide to stay on, but I'm equally certain that others will still leave. I don't know who will do what, but if you were going to get rid of all of us, I would still consider doing it. Because I am certain that some of those who choose to stay will only do so to cause trouble."

"Doctor, since your decision is to leave, we will accompany you to lab area so you can remove personal items and then escort you from the building."

"Thank you."

"We have assembled the other scientists and are bringing them here. We will keep you separate from the others for now to be sure that the others hear this information only from us. Your communications will be restricted. Lines of communication will be reopened after we have sorted out everyone's wishes. Do you understand these precautions?"

The doctor nodded.

Charlie spoke up. "Doctor, I would like to continue to use you as a consultant, if nothing else. You have a wonderful mind for working out problems in exobiology."

"I would like that, Charlie. I'm sure you will know how to get in touch with me afterward."

She turned to Kala and Dr. Jackson, "I am sorry this had to happen. I was terribly torn, but I think the way things are working out are for the best." She continued, her voice resolute. "If you need any information about the scientists who are looking to cause real trouble, please let me know. I have never wanted to cause harm to people and always hated that part of the movement. Don't get me wrong. I still believe in the movement, but I'm no longer so gung ho about it. I will do what I can to help the Earth, but I think I'd be a bigger help if I were to stay on it."

She turned to Kala and indicated she was ready to go.

"Take her through the old Beta Tunnel," said Charlie. "It dead-ends right below the scientists' wing. Once Dr. Haverton has finished cleaning out her desk, the guards will have their orders on where to take and hold her. I expect you to be back while the other scientists are still here to corroborate their information with Dr. Haverton's."

Kala nodded and she and Dr. Haverton rose from the table.

"Go that way," Charlie said pointing toward a door in the corner. "It leads right to the tunnel."

As soon as the door closed behind them, Kala heard the main door to the conference room opening and the other scientists walking into the room.

Kala and Dr. Haverton didn't speak as they traveled through the tunnel to the elevator. When they arrived at the lab area, Dr. Haverton went to work silently removing all personal items from her desk. Under the watchful eyes of the guards, she placed all WASA-related material on top of her desk. Finally, she stepped back and indicated she was done and for a guard to check her box. He quickly found three memory chips and handed them to Kala. Kala looked hard at the doctor before going to the nearest computer to check out the chips. Finding that the first chip contained classified material, Kala immediately put all three into her pocket.

"We'll return these chips once they have been fully checked and wiped clean. We'll also keep the box and thoroughly check everything you've placed into it."

"Those chips aren't what you think..." Dr. Haverton began.

"Doctor, do you really think we'd be that lax not to do a thorough check?" Kala interrupted, angered at the doctor's actions. "I found classified files on one chip already, and I am guessing there are more on the other two. You have items in this box that would be good hiding places for even more chips." Kala glared at the woman. "I do believe you are trying to see how far you can push the new employee. You won't get far. I will not be put in the middle of your little ideological war against WASA. You and your fellow insurgents will be given your choice of service, I'm sure. But be assured the other scientists who decide to leave will be subject to the same scrutiny as you. Now I will inform Charlie and Dr. Jackson of your deception. Have a seat while I find out what Charlie wants me to do."

Dr. Haverton sat in her desk chair as Kala walked to a house phone and dialed the conference room. Kala quietly brought Charlie up-to-date on what had happened and waited for instructions. A few silent minutes passed. She could hear Charlie talking to Dr. Jackson. Then Charlie was back and asked for the sergeant who was in charge of the guards. They spoke briefly. Kala heard the sergeant respond "Yes" and watched him hang up the phone. Then she and the sergeant returned to Dr. Haverton.

Pointing to one of the guards, the sergeant said, "You will go with Ms. Melina and carry this box back to the conference room." Pointing to the other three guards in the room, he said, "You, and the good doctor here, will come with me. We will take her to one of the holding cells and wait there until Dr. Jackson and Commander Hudson arrive with new orders."

Kala's guard picked up the box. Just as they turned to go, Dr. Haverton called after Kala.

"Kala, I truly didn't want you to get in the middle of this," she said. "I was hoping they'd reconsider promoting someone so young and untried. I hoped to play on your nerves and fear. I never realized you'd be so strong."

Kala glared at her, then asked, "Do you know anyone at TechNet?"

"A few people. Why do you ask?"

"Does the name Casio Melina ring a bell?"

Kala watched as the color drained from the doctor's face.

"I see you recognize the name. I also see that you are making the connection you should have made before now. You wonder how I can be so tough at such a young age? Well, try growing up with Casio Melina as an older brother and guardian. He was, and is, a tough taskmaster, but he is also a wonderful brother. He taught me well during my time with him, and I will always do well by remembering what he taught me." Kala turned and, with the guard following close behind, left the room.

Nearing the conference room, she could hear loud, angry voices coming through the door. The guard posted outside the door was about to open it, but she motioned him not to. She stood, listening to what was being said.

"And what good would kidnapping people do?" she heard Charlie ask. "Yes, we would try to find these people, but if they weren't available to go on a specific mission, we would just send someone else. Why can't you understand that what we're doing is for the good of the people of Earth?"

"How do you know that this ship isn't coming for the good of the Earth?" she heard someone ask. "Are you sure that this ship isn't being sent to help us save the planet?"

"You saw the pictures of the planets in this thing's wake. They were all destroyed."

The discussion dissolved and she heard many voices talking over each other. The talking stopped as soon as she opened the door and entered the room. The scientists looked at her with something akin to hatred in their eyes; Charlie looked distracted. Kala took in the scene and noticed that Dr. Jackson was no longer there. She motioned for the guard carrying Dr. Haverton's box to place it on a table in the corner and then sent him to wait outside with the other guard.

"Don't let me interrupt you," she said, taking an empty seat next to Charlie.

"This is entirely your fault," said one of the scientists maliciously.

"How do you figure that?" she asked, raising her eyebrows.

"You're too damn smart for your own good. You come in here asking questions and acting like you own the place. Giving speeches to people twice your age and with twice your experience..."

"Oh, get off your high horse for once," Kala interrupted. "Just because I don't have the five degrees you have and decided to go to work instead of staying in school, like a scared rabbit hiding from the world! Remember how you were young once yourself. I'm sure that there are things I could tell you that would make your ears burn. Yes, I'm barely seventeen, but I have learned a thing or two in my life."

"And you're sure that you can lead people as experienced as us..." one of the scientists spat.

"I can't lead you and give you orders in the way you seem to expect, but I can work *with* you and lead in that way. It won't be what you are used to, but I will be doing my job. I have a feeling, though, that even if I were to lead in the way you would want, you wouldn't consider me the right person for the job, regardless of my age." She eyed the man. "So, Doctor, what is the real issue here?"

The doctors looked at each other in silent conference.

Then the scientist spoke, "Casio led us to believe you would be more... how should I put it...pliable than you have shown to be."

"My brother has always underestimated me," Kala said. "He seems to always have my best intentions at heart, but he never really did get to know me. I believe, Doctor, you would be best served, in the future, to come to your own conclusions about people." Her eyes swept the room. "I can tell you, now, that your comrade, Dr. Haverton, is being held in a detention cell for trying to steal WASA classified material. Commander Hudson and Dr. Jackson will make the determination of what to do with the rest of you, but," she pointed at the box, "it is now my job to search the rest of her items and her desk for any more chips that she might have hidden. If you'll all excuse me, I'll get that taken care of." She turned to Charlie. "When you're done here, I'll be either next door or at Dr. Haverton's desk."

Kala stood and pulled out the three chips in her pocket and handed them to Charlie. She motioned to a guard to take the box and follow her. She was still going through the items when Charlie joined her about forty-five minutes later, sighing heavily as he sat down at the table beside her.

"So, what do you think?" he asked.

"I don't know," she replied, leaning back and stretching. "They were certainly well-prepared. But until we get a chance to check the data on the chips, I don't think we'll really know what they're up to."

"Jim has teams going over every inch of the ship, inside and out, to see if they can find anything wrong. We found at least one 'unofficial' chip in the desk of each scientist. The chips are being examined, but so far, we've found nothing. What surprises us is their animosity toward you. Is there anything you can think of that might cause that?"

"Well, they mentioned Casio. They seem to think that he beat me down and made me docile. They believed that, because of my age and family connection, I would fall in line with their movement and quietly follow them. When I was promoted to the command staff, I guess they were ecstatic and speeded up whatever they had planned."

Charlie got up and wandered around the table looking at the items that Kala had laid out. He glanced at items here and there, but walked around the table without really seeing them.

"We need to find a space to check out all the other items we confiscated. We can't use the lab space because the new teams need to use the space to get up to speed."

"Is there a room off the lower level tunnels that we can use?"

Charlie looked up, surprised by the question.

"I hadn't thought of that. I believe there may be a few large rooms down there we can use. Let me look into it. I can transfer all the items from the scientists' desks down there. I want you to take the rest of the night off, and if you haven't already, I am ordering you to get something to eat and then relax for what's left of the evening."

"I'll just finish up with this stuff before I go."

"You'll go now. The last thing I need is for you to collapse from exhaustion. You have already proven yourself a valuable member of this team. There is no need to kill yourself; the majority of the crew has accepted you as part of the command staff. You are going to be a fine leader, so don't give yourself such a hard time. Now, go and get some rest. In the morning, I'll let you know where we moved everything."

Kala wanted to argue, but she finally admitted she was tired and would be able to think better in the morning. She stood up, stretched, and headed for the cafeteria.

CHAPTER 17

The next few weeks were busy for the entire crew. Kala had contacted Casio, and through his contacts, WASA was able to find the damage, limited though it was, that had been done to the ship. All the crew, including the command staff, went through another round of background investigations. One more conspirator was found and removed from the mission. When it came time to lift off, the mission was only two weeks later than originally scheduled.

The last day before takeoff, the crew manning the ship was allowed to spend time with their families. The crew who were going into cold sleep had spent time with their families the week before. After final preparations, they were then put into the cold sleep stations and loaded onto the ship. Shawan and his family, Casio, and Lindsey came to see Kala, and she spent the afternoon giving them the penny tour. WASA spared no expense on a luncheon for all the families and made sure they had uninterrupted time to spend together before the crew left the Earth for the last time. Finally, about forty-five minutes before the crew was to be sequestered, Dr. Jackson and a few of the top WASA brass joined the party.

They made the rounds of the tables, meeting the families, joining in small talk, and answering questions where they could. After their rounds were finished, Dr. Jackson walked to the front of the room, followed by the other WASA leaders. He rapped on the microphone for attention and the room gradually grew quiet.

"In a few minutes, we'll be asking you to say good-bye to your loved ones. Tomorrow, our team will be sending another talented group of professionals into space, to a place we've never imagined. They all know that there is danger involved in this mission, and they have all decided to face their fears and meet them head on. You can all be proud of them for being chosen for this mission. As you all know, contact will be limited for a period of time. We hope that we have updated our equipment enough to stay in touch once they reach their destination, but we won't know until they get there."

Someone behind Dr. Jackson stepped up and whispered in his ear. He nodded and turned back to the audience.

"You all should have received a packet that includes codes for direct email and vid-mail access to your family members. Your communications will be filtered through the WASA servers, but there will be no censorship; all communication that is private will remain so. If you have questions or concerns regarding your communications with the crew, you can talk to the WASA contact names included in your packet."

Dr. Jackson watched as everyone looked through the packets. After a few minutes, he rapped on the microphone again.

"Now that you've checked your packets, it is time to end the party. I am sorry to be rushing things, but our team needs to get their rest; tomorrow is a big day." He smiled solemnly at the group. "This is the time for good-byes. Afterward, you will be escorted to your rooms where you will have a view of the ship. In the morning, after breakfast, you will be taken to the family area to watch the liftoff. Again, remember, your family members are providing a service for this planet that no one can equal. They are heroes and will be treated as such." He smiled more warmly. "Have a good night, everyone."

There were hugs and kisses all around. Kala was surprised when Casio pulled her into a bear hug. She felt him place something in her pocket and assumed that since he was trying to be discrete, she pretended not to notice.

But Casio drew her attention to it. "This chip can replace a guidance chip if you feel there is a chance of sabotage," he spoke quietly in her ear. "If the saboteurs try to fly the ship with it installed, they won't be able to go anywhere. The ship will stay in whatever orbit it has been placed and communications with Earth will still be possible. Don't ask where I got it or who made it. Just know that Dr. Jackson and the other top WASA officials already know about it. The only person you need to tell will be Charlie."

"Thank you, Casio. I will miss you, and I promise not to embarrass you!"

"You could never do that, little sister!"

After another round of hugs, the families were led out of the room and the crew was alone. At Dr. Jackson's urging, they gathered at the front tables and sat down.

"This is it, gang. I want you to get the best sleep you can tonight because tomorrow is going to be a long day. We'll need the command staff in suit-up at five o'clock, and the rest of you by five-thirty. Once the command staff is loaded in the front, the rest of you will be loaded through the back. You all know your load-in crewmember and you all have a buddy. We expect a check-in once you've been loaded and your communications equipment has been hooked up. Good luck, everyone! We'll see you in the morning."

Kala pulled Charlie aside and gave him the chip from Casio.

"It's a false guidance chip," she explained. "Casio gave it to me and said if there are any problems...or any glimmer of problems...once installed, this chip will keep the ship in orbit around the planet."

Charlie looked at her with raised eyebrows.

"I've learned not to ask Casio many questions. He did tell me that this was done with Dr. Jackson's and the executive team's knowledge. It might be worthwhile to install it as the last thing we do before leaving the ship. One of us can keep the real chip for future use, if needed."

"I agree. Why don't you hold on to this in your stuff? I think it would be better out of sight that way. Go get some rest and I'll see you at suit-up."

Kala took the scenic route back to her quarters. She made one last check of her personal carry-on bag and put the chip in with her movie and book player. It looked enough like a book disk that unless someone knew what they were looking for, they wouldn't notice the difference.

That done, she slowly made her way to the bathroom for her final shower on Earth. During the day, she had found herself saying, "This is the last time I'll do this on Earth," several times. She smiled as she realized most of the other crew had probably been doing the same thing. She smiled and nodded to people as she returned to her quarters. As she settled herself into bed, she wondered if she'd be able to sleep.

CHAPTER 18

The final countdown started as soon as the shuttle door closed behind the last crewmember. The race between the pretakeoff checklist and the countdown began in earnest. At the five-minute mark, the crew completed the checklist. All that was needed was to wait for the ignition call.

For everyone on the ship, their families, and the personnel in the control center, those five minutes seemed to take forever. The excitement level rose as each minute went by, and at the last thirty seconds, the exhilaration was palpable. Everyone standing on the ground felt it tremble as the engines ignited and saw the bright orange glow under the fuel boosters quickly grow. As the ship rose upward, the crew locked eyes.

In five minutes, they were free in space and on their own. After ten minutes, Charlie gave the separation order to release the fuel tanks. Fuel tanks released, the navigation officer coded the destination into the piloting module. They would fly on full autopilot, but Charlie decided crew members would still monitor the controls to facilitate a quicker response if an emergency should arise. Once they were completely on their own and had been given the okay from Houston base control, Charlie gave the order to leave their seats and change out of their space suits. Internal air was on, and by the time they had changed, the gravity had been set to three quarters of Earth and they could get to work.

Since it would take six weeks to get to their destination, each team immediately began preparing what they'd need upon landing. Kala's job was to liaise between the teams and the command staff; in addition, she was in charge of creating the landing schedule. After changing, she went to the room that had been designated as her office. It was a small room with bare walls and a desk in the corner facing the door. She sat down at the desk, noting that her computer, like all the computers onboard, was the latest in both hardware and software. She carefully stored her personal disks, the fake guidance chip among them, in the top drawer. Turning her computer on, she quickly got to work creating all the forms she would need, starting with the disembarkation forms to the forms for the maintenance of their new world.

She didn't realize how long she'd been working until she heard a knock on the door. She glanced at the clock and saw that she'd been at it for almost forty-five minutes. When she looked up at the door, she saw Charlie leaning against the doorframe with a smile on his face.

"What's so funny?"

"All work and no play makes for a dull astronaut."

"What should I be doing?"

"Taking your last look at Earth; it really is quite the view from up here, and once we're out of range, there's no looking back. Come and join me on the bridge and take a look. Besides, you need to have a general knowledge of how things run around here anyway, and now's as good a time as any."

Kala first locked her desk then followed Charlie to the bridge. On the way, she noticed all the activity going on around them. She knew that once the Earth was out of range, activity would greatly increase. Many people were coming out of their sleeping cabins and heading toward the cafeteria. Fresh food wouldn't be ready, but nutrition packets would be available. More importantly, there was the large screen monitor with the view of a retreating Earth. She smiled to herself as she thought of the adventure ahead of them.

Turning the last corner to the bridge, she saw that the bridge was the true hub of activity on the ship. She followed Charlie to the command chair and stood slightly behind his left elbow, her eyes never leaving the forward screen with the picture of Earth. She never realized how beautiful it was from space, a blue ball with white clouds swirling over the ever-changing landmasses framed by the velvet black of space and stars looking like sparkling diamonds. Kala was totally entranced by the picture, and for a moment, she was flooded by a terrible homesickness. She let the feeling wash over her a little before clearing her head and turning to matters at hand.

Glancing at Charlie, she wondered what he was thinking. She knew that part of his reason for leaving was the tragic death of his wife and child three years before. In the WASA biography, it stated he had never really gotten over the deaths, and looking at him, Kala could almost hear him saying good-bye, leaving that piece of his life behind.

"It is beautiful isn't it," he said quietly.

"Very. Sad to know it's the last time we'll ever see it live like this. All we'll have in a few days is the video."

Charlie nodded his head. Without taking his eyes from the screen, Charlie started barking orders.

"Jansen, input the first set of coordinates."

"Aye, sir."

"Patterson, notify Houston we're inputting the first set of coordinates."

"Aye, sir."

Charlie continued to give orders, and when he was satisfied that everything would run as he wanted in his absence, he got up and motioned for Kala to follow him. He led her to the captain's galley off the bridge. The small, comfortable room was set up to quickly supply food to the bridge staff on duty. Upon entering, they smelled the cooked food. At the serving station, Charlie helped himself to pasta and a salad, motioning to Kala to help herself as well. As they settled down at the table with food and drink, the rest of the command crew came in and served themselves. Once everyone was seated, Charlie tapped the table for attention.

"Now that we're safely underway, it's time to get into full swing. During the next six weeks, we'll start seedlings so that we can plant gardens as soon as we land. We'll also put some of the animal eggs and sperm into incubation so that we can bring pregnant females down to the planet..."

"Aren't you rushing things a bit?" asked one of the scientists. "I mean, we aren't even sure this planet will support our kind of life."

"And what are we going to do if it doesn't?" countered Kala. "Remember, this is a one-way trip." She smiled. "But we do know the planet has an oxygen-based atmosphere that will support human life, and while we don't know about the soil, we can assume that we will be able to adapt our plants. If we need to, we can always work out a way to graft our plants with the indigenous plant life so that we can make a hybrid we can use."

"Won't we be doing to this planet what is forcing us to leave Earth?" Sergeant Yamamato, one of the mission specialists, asked.

"No," Charlie replied, "because we won't be using any air-polluting equipment. If there is harm, we aim to limit it."

"Let's say we do have to create hybrid plants," said Janet Albertson, "and they take over and destroy what's already there? Wouldn't that create an ecological disaster?"

"Yes, there may be some changes on the planet, but we will take precautions. We will make sure that we don't repeat the mistakes made on Earth. Why do you think we're meeting now?" Charlie looked intently round the room. "Because we want to make sure we have a viable plan when we get to our new home."

"Nice words, but how can we be sure you mean what you say?"

"If you're not sure, then watch us," said Kala. "See how we run the ship; watch how we treat our people. This is how we will treat our new home, with love and respect. If we all work together, we'll be able to make our new world one that will last."

They moved on to discuss an intermediate plan for scheduling of the labs, while Kala developed the permanent one. Teams would rotate the first couple of weeks and ramp up to a twenty-four hour schedule the week leading up to landing. They decided that, once on the planet surface, at least one lab for each team would be set up so they could get all their programs up and running. After these initial, basic decisions were made, the meeting ended and everyone headed back to their sections.

"Where you off to?" Kala asked Charlie, as they gathered up their paperwork.

"Back to the bridge for a while and then to my quarters. How about you?"

"Back to my quarters."

"Don't forget to actually rest when you get there."

"Yes, sir," Kala answered with a smile as she headed off.

The first few days in space were relatively peaceful. Everyone took turns watching as the Earth receded from view. And then they began looking forward; Charlie had turned the external cameras toward their destination. On the fourth day, there was some excitement when someone reported that some of the cryofreeze stations had been tampered with. But the report was erroneous; it turned out to be a false reading.

In one sense, Kala was almost disappointed that things were going so smoothly. It also scared her. Casio had always been fond of saying that when things were going too well, that's when you should worry. She was on her way to lunch, after the cryo incident, when she passed some of the engineers and overheard part of their conversation. It took a minute for what she had heard to sink in.

She paused to replay in her head what she had heard, then immediately went off in search of Charlie or Danielle Chang, his second-in-command.

Danielle was the first person she ran into, quite literally, when she got to the bridge.

"What's the big hurry?"

"I'm not really sure, but I've overheard something and felt I needed to bring it to you or Charlie."

Danielle looked at her expectantly.

"Not here, somewhere private. If I'm right, I don't want to start a panic."

Danielle nodded and led the way to Charlie's office off the bridge. She knocked twice on the door before opening it. Kala saw Charlie sitting at his desk. Across from him was Tom Cooke, the head of the engineering department.

"Come in," Charlie said, waiving them in. "We were just finishing up here. Thank you, Tom, I'll make sure to follow up on your concerns."

Kala and Danielle watched Tom leave the room. Once he had gone, Danielle closed the door behind them. Charlie leaned back in his chair and watched as they sat down on the couch Tom had just vacated.

"Would either of you like anything to drink?"

"Nothing for me," said Danielle.

"Lemon soda, if you have any, sir," Kala replied.

Charlie looked at her sharply at the use of "sir." She hadn't called him that since well before they left the facility on Earth.

"Well?"

"I don't know if this is for real or not, but on my way to lunch, I overheard some of the engineers talking. One of them asked the other if everything was all set. The reply was that the engines had been taken care of and all that was left was the communications array. The first one said that everything had better be ready, or they wouldn't get the rest of the money that TechNet had promised them."

Charlie sighed, a troubled look on his face.

"Tom was in here worried about the extra work some of his engineers were taking on. He was having their work double-checked by people he trusted, and they found some inconsistencies. Did you by chance hear the names of the men you heard talking?"

Kala nodded.

Charlie handed her a pad. "Please write down their names. I think you understand about listening devices."

Kala wrote the names on the pad and handed it back to Charlie. When Charlie saw the names she had written, his face seemed to pale a bit more and he looked even more troubled.

"Well, you are the second person to tell me about these people. I'll talk to Tom and find something for these guys to do that won't hurt anyone but, hopefully, not get them wondering. Not a word to anyone about this, even Tom. For now, it's best we keep this quiet."

"Yes, sir," the women replied in unison.

"Thanks. Remember to keep your eyes and ears open. We're too far away from Earth to turn back now or for help to get to us in time if we needed it. We're on our own. We need to be able to handle whatever is thrown at us and let Earth know about it after the fact."

Kala and Danielle quit the room, leaving Charlie to consider his next move. Before the door closed behind her, Kala looked back and saw him staring at his computer. She sighed and, no longer hungry, headed back to her office. Once back at her desk, she found she was having trouble concentrating. She decided she'd had enough and put away her work. Maybe now she could eat. She shut down her computer and turned off the desk light. Just as she was opening her door, she heard voices outside in the hall. Peering through a crack in the door, she saw a group of technicians walking toward her office. Hoping they hadn't seen her, she flattened herself against the door. The techs didn't notice the slightly ajar door; they stopped just outside her office, talking.

"Do you think she'll really help us?" one of the women in the group asked.

"Of the command staff, I think she's the most likely," replied the man who appeared to be the leader. "This young girl has connections at TechNet, but I don't really trust her, and the Commander, while trying to give the appearance otherwise, is more by the book then he'd like us to believe. I think the Second is our best bet."

They must be talking about Danielle, Kala thought.

"What if she goes straight to the Commander or the girl?"

"We deal with that when, and if, it happens. Right now, we need to find someone who will help our cause. We won't be able to get everything done and we need to find someone to help us. We all know the best thing for us would be a recruit from the command staff, and she's the only one I can think of that might help us."

"Why do you think the girl with the TechNet connection wouldn't help us? I don't understand why you don't trust her."

"It's not the TechNet connection I have the problem with. In fact, that would be the best thing for us. But I think she's too young and too idealistic. Too starry-eyed about the stars. We need someone who, while still young, has been around awhile and has a proven track record of being loyal to the leaders on Earth."

They moved away at that moment and Kala could no longer hear any more of the conversation. She stood frozen, her blood running cold and her heart beating fast. Her cheeks flushed and her body was flooded with a fear she had never known before. She tried to think where to go first to find Charlie. Moving back toward her computer, she booted up and waited the agonizing minute for it to be accessed. Then she opened the program used to locate workers on the ship and entered Charlie's name and ID. It seemed to take longer than normal to give her Charlie's location, but when she had it, she shut the computer down again and headed to the cafeteria.

Charlie rarely ate in the captain's galley, instead preferring to spend time with the members of the crew in the cafeteria. He would normally take whatever seat was available and eat with different people at every meal. By the time Kala arrived at the cafeteria, she could see that Charlie was sitting in the corner with Tom Cooke and a few of the engineers and that there was a seat available at the table. After getting food and drink, she walked over to the table.

"Got room for another person here?" Kala asked as she reached the table.

She saw the quick look of fear in one of the engineer's eyes before they repositioned themselves around the table to make room for her. She noticed that they positioned themselves so that she was sitting across from Charlie. She knew that they were trying to intimidate her, but she refused to be intimidated.

Charlie looked at her and she indicated that she wanted to speak with him privately. The conversation at the table went well, though a bit tense, and at the end, Kala knew she had won a bit of a victory; the engineers were the first to stand and exit the room. She was sure that one or two of the men had been in the group she had heard earlier. Once she was alone with Charlie, she moved to sit next to him.

"Is there a problem?" he asked broadly, pulling his dessert in front of him.

"More than just a few disgruntled engineers, I'm afraid," she replied, doing the same.

They attacked their desserts, appearing to the rest of the room like two friends enjoying each other's company.

"What's happened now?"

"Before I came here, a group of engineers stopped to talk outside my office. I'm pretty sure they didn't see me because the room was dark. They were talking about approaching someone in command, and it sounded like it could be Danielle. Some wanted to come to me because of my TechNet connection, but I was dismissed because of my age."

Charlie looked up at her sharply. "How do you know they were talking about you and Danielle?"

"They talked about people without using names, but I could tell by the descriptions who they were talking about. I was the girl with the TechNet connection, Danielle was the Second, and you, of course, were the Commander. I think we may need to do more than just keep an eye on them."

"I think you're right," Charlie said after a moment's thought. "I'll contact Tom and we'll figure out the best way to go about it. I'll keep you updated."

"Thanks."

And they left, each headed in a different direction.

The next morning on her way to her office after breakfast, she was detoured by a message from Charlie. As she made her way to his office on the bridge, she noticed a few engineers giving her dirty looks. She pulled up short as she entered the room and saw the people Charlie had assembled in the room. Along with five engineers, she quickly spotted Danielle and Tom Cooke.

"Now that all parties involved are here, we can begin," Charlie said. "The command staff has learned that plans are being made that would put our mission in danger. As commander, I cannot let this happen. Since you five are the primary people to be named, you will be placed in solitary confinement until we reach the planet. We will need you to help with the move to the planet, but if you refuse, you will be put into one of the vacant cold sleep stations and taken down in cold sleep. The command staff will decide what happens to you next after we reach the planet. Do you have any questions?"

He leaned back in his chair and looked around at the sullen faces in the room. He let the silence drag on. Finally, he stood up and walked in front of his desk.

"You all knew that this is a one-way trip and that any sabotage affects the entire crew. But it doesn't have to be this way..."

"So what's a few hundred lives compared to the billions on Earth," one of the men shouted standing up.

"The difference is that we're trying to save the human race," Charlie snapped. "As you all know, there is an alien ship headed toward Earth. If the aliens are hostile and bent on destruction, and we believe they are, nothing on Earth will survive. What you may not realize is that the teams who have already been sent off planet may be the only hope of survival for the human race. So think about that while you are sitting in confinement, and try to wrap your brains around it."

He turned to his desk and pressed the button to call in the guards. When the engineers had been led from the room, Charlie sat down and sighed. Kala, Danielle, and Tom remained silent.

"I don't think we got them all, but hopefully, the example we're making of these five will make the others think carefully about sabotage. Right now, I just want to make it to the planet surface safely. If we still have to keep our eyes on them on the planet, I think we can probably find a place to put them or, at least, keep them out of our hair. I hope it doesn't come to that, but if it does, I have plans under way to locate a space far from the landing and settlement sites, and I will use it if necessary."

Danielle and Tom nodded their agreement and left. Kala remained, still silent. She went to the wall where Charlie had hung pictures of his family. She studied the pictures of his wife and daughter before turning around.

"I agree that something needs to be done, but do you think that removal from the colony will be enough?"

"What else can we do? We won't have enough power to keep them in cold sleep forever, and there is a ban on the death penalty in the colony contract. What other choice do we have?"

"None really. I guess if you think about it in terms of the old-fashioned death penalty, separation is a mild punishment. I'm sure you'll choose a place where they can grow food and give them enough supplies to survive. They just won't be able to leave there." She shrugged her shoulders. "Let's hope the next couple of weeks are quiet. We don't need any more trouble as we approach the landing."

Charlie smiled as he stood up from his chair and stretched to his full height. Kala laughed outright when she heard his spine crack down its full length.

"I think you need a break, Commander! Would you join me in the gym for a workout?"

"Sounds like an excellent idea! I'll meet you there in about ten minutes."

CHAPTER 19

With the engineers in confinement, normal activity resumed. Privately, Kala decided that, somehow, they had gotten lucky and, without knowing it, had confined the leaders of the sabotage. A few people came forward to give new information on the plans and submitted themselves for disciplinary action. For those people, Charlie was lenient and gave them only extra duty to undo what the dissenters had done. They were mostly successful, and what they couldn't fix they were able to work around.

A week before arriving at the planet, they began to wake up the personnel needed for the landing. The shuttles were dusted off, pilot training updated, and cargo lists prepared. Kala never remembered being so busy or enjoying the work so much in her life.

I wonder how much longer we can go on like this, she thought as she collapsed on her bed the night before they reached the planet. *It'll be nice to get a vacation!*

All that week, Charlie had focused the exterior cameras on their new home, and when Kala arrived on the bridge in the morning, the planet was the dominant feature on the main viewer. For a moment, she simply stood and gazed at the planet they were approaching. Then, she went to her station to the left of Charlie's chair. She saw Danielle at her station on Charlie's right. Charlie was at the engineering station in deep conversation with Tom Cooke.

Kala sat down at her console and brought up the procedures needed to place them into orbit. Once they had chosen a landing site, they would move the ship to a geosynchronous orbit above that point, but for now, getting safely into orbit was the primary duty. Kala noticed her message board had a list of messages from different department heads and she scrolled through them. After she had answered the most urgent messages, she sent a message to all the department heads, as well as Danielle and Charlie, informing them there would be a full meeting after they had made orbit. Until the meeting, she would answer only those messages directly involved in achieving orbit.

She checked the main viewer and noticed the planet was getting bigger by the minute. Turning back to her duties, she felt that the forward motion of the ship was different. It took her a minute to recognize that the engines had been reduced, and they were all but coasting into orbit. Now, thinking about it, she realized that the engine speed had been slowly winding down for the past few days.

Kala got back to work. After what she thought was only a few minutes, she jumped when someone tapped her on the shoulder. She looked around and saw Charlie bending over her shoulder.

"We're home," he said in a low voice only she could hear. "Okay, everyone," he said in a louder voice as he stood up, "let's get busy. Engineering, engines to a full stop. Earth Sciences get the probes ready for launch the minute we hit orbit."

The bridge erupted into controlled chaos as the ship continued to slow and finally stop. Later, when they remembered that moment, they all agreed they were sure of the exact moment the ship stopped.

"Ladies and gentlemen," Charlie announced over the ship intercom, "we have arrived at our new home. The drop will commence once a landing site has been chosen. All team leaders please study the data as it becomes available and be ready to meet with the command staff with your recommendations."

He flicked off the intercom and began to give orders. Kala glanced up at the main viewer and saw the puffs of smoke as the surface probes were launched. Checking her monitors, she saw data flowing as the telemetry from the probes began to arrive. She knew that, during her watch, all five of the probes would reach their destinations and begin to send back the information needed to choose the landing site.

After each probe had landed and sent back its data, the probes would then go into holding mode until new orders could be sent or the probes were retrieved. On her monitors, Kala watched the team leaders access the data on the public drives and saw them place their own reports there. As each new report went on the drive, Kala opened it, identified the information it contained, and sent it on to the proper place. She tried to make Charlie's job easier by intercepting the "minor" issues as they arose.

She prioritized all the "emergencies" and gave Charlie only those that required his authorization codes. Looking up at one point, she found Charlie's eyes and they smiled at each other, both feeling the elation at making it this far. She also felt a little flutter in her stomach, but attributing it to hunger, she grabbed an energy bar and didn't think about it again.

Five hours later, the probes had sent back their final reports and, then, when into holding mode. Almost immediately, the team leaders started buzzing through to talk to Charlie. Kala took their requests and promised they would be addressed at the meeting. Sitting back in her chair, she watched as data from the probes again flicked across the screen.

Something from early telemetry from probe five caught her eye. She leaned into the screen and reviewed it again. She studied the information intently before looking around for one of the biologists. Seeing Dr. Leah Wilson sitting in a corner, Kala caught the woman's eye and beckoned her over.

"I noticed something from initial data from probe five you might find interesting," Kala told the woman.

Dr. Wilson looked at the picture and the data beside it before backing away from the monitor.

"Doctor, what is it?" Kala asked, alarmed by the look on the older woman's face.

When Dr. Wilson didn't reply, Kala moved away from her and searched for Charlie. She finally spotted him looking over the shoulder of one of the engineers. Crossing the room quickly, she put her hand on his back to get his attention. He peered down at her with a quizzical expression on his face.

"Probe five found something," she whispered, "I'm not quite sure of all the implications, but from Dr. Wilson's reaction, I think you need to come and look."

Charlie looked across the room toward Kala's station and saw the scientist's face. He hurried to Kala's station, Kala following closely behind. The doctor was still in the same place. Charlie sat down in Kala's chair and stared at the monitor. One look at the screen and he almost fell off the chair.

"Holy shit!" he exclaimed loudly. "Sorry," he quickly apologized after getting looks from some of the bridge crew. "Has anyone else seen this yet?" He directed the question at Kala.

"All the reports are being sent to the team leaders. I'm not sure if Bio has this yet or not."

"Damn. Okay, I'll talk to them. You take the doctor to her quarters to recover. Stay with her if you need to. Just make sure she doesn't talk to anyone. If you're not here on the bridge when I get back, I'll page you. Now go!"

With a nod, Kala took the doctor by the arm and led her off the bridge and down the hall toward her quarters. Kala hadn't really understood all the data she had seen, but she had understood enough.

"Doctor, does this really mean what I think it means?"

"If you think it means there are other forms of humanoid life on this planet, then you are correct. It seems that the initial surveys, mechanical and human, missed that information. The other four probes on the surface haven't found anything, so it is quite likely that whatever lives down there only lives, or lived, in the area surveyed by the probe."

"Were you able to ascertain if there is evidence of current humanoid life?"

"Not from what probe five sent up, but that doesn't mean anything. Whoever they are, or were, could have moved to this location. We just can't tell yet."

"And why didn't we see something as the probes got lower in the atmosphere?"

"There's no way to know. Maybe these creatures moved into the cave system we saw because the sounds of the probe rockets scared them into cover. Or maybe they've died out. We just can't tell at this point."

Suddenly a line from one of her childhood books popped into Kala's head. She couldn't remember it exactly, but a character was explaining to others why they were staying on a planet with the people there. He said something like they would stay where they had landed. Kala understood that this was going to be their situation; they were stuck with what they had and they would have to make the best of it.

Kala made Dr. Wilson comfortable in her quarters, then returned to the bridge. When she got there, Charlie was still sitting at her computer with all monitors showing the probe five data. She stood behind him, looking at all the data and pictures.

"What do you think we should do?" she asked quietly.

"I think this area needs to be our landing site. We have to see what happened to these beings."

"What if the same thing happens to us?"

"We need to change the landing schedule to send down Bill Chow and some of his men. They'll be able to assess the situation and get a perimeter established. Hopefully, nothing will come of it, and we'll be able to make some new friends, but we need to be sure. I'm going to call for a delay in the landing until we take care of this."

Switching on the COM unit, Charlie called for the security chief to come to the bridge. As they waited, Charlie pointed out a few things in the pictures that began to scare her.

"Take a minute to look here and here," he said pointing out two distinct features in the photos. "You should notice something similar in those features."

He got up and Kala sat in her chair to get a better view of the photos on her monitor. After a minute, she stared at Charlie with a look of horror on her face.

"How can that be?" she asked quietly. "This is nowhere near where that mission was supposed to end up."

"I don't know, but I intend to find out. While I'm in my office with Bill Chow, I want you to find out exactly who has seen this information outside the bridge crew, and I want them here immediately. It won't take me long to give Bill orders. We'll meet in the bridge conference room in case anything else comes up."

Kala nodded and was about to say something when Bill Chow arrived. At five foot seven inches and close to two hundred pounds, his physical presence reinforced his role. Not a scrap of fat was to be found on the man. He was solid muscle. When most people looked at Bill they assumed he would rather kill them than have lunch with them, but they couldn't have been more wrong.

Bill approached Charlie and snapped a quick salute before looking at the monitor.

"Holy Gods! What is that?" Bill exclaimed before he could stop himself.

"Let's go in the conference room."

Bill, seeing the concern on Charlie's face, immediately followed him to the conference room; Kala stayed at her station.

"Be honest with me, Charlie. Is that what I think it is?" Bill asked when the conference room door had closed.

"We think so, but we have to be sure before we send more people down there. We have found three other good sites for landing, but this is by far the best. But we need to make sure that our people will be safe."

"How many can I bring?"

"Five plus yourself and one command staff."

"Damn it, Charlie. I can't be protecting people on a mission like this!"

"And I need a member of my staff down there to see exactly what is going on! I don't want you to go anywhere but the ship. If there are people left alive, there will probably be some evidence of it. We have the records of all the space missions; we need to know which one this was."

"Can't you tell from the probe video?"

"It wasn't able to get close enough to see the name on the ship. We need people for that."

"And you're sure that the atmosphere is breathable?"

"Wear your suit to be sure, but from what all the probes say, it is within acceptable limits." Charlie put his hand on the security chief's shoulder, "Bill, we need this to be kept under wraps for the moment, so take only your most reliable people."

The security chief nodded without taking his eyes off the screen.

"When do you want us to leave?" he asked Charlie.

"As soon as possible, and remember to choose your team carefully. Discretion is paramount."

"Anything else?" Bill asked, taking his eyes off the monitors and looking at Charlie.

"No, I think that about does it. Remember, Bill, our choice of landing sites rides on this."

Bill nodded again before turning smartly and leaving the room. Charlie remained in silence, staring at the picture from probe five on the monitor in front of him, before walking over to the wet bar and getting the strongest drink he could find.

CHAPTER 20

After getting his drink, Charlie went to the door and motioned for Kala to join him.

"Wet your whistle?" he asked after she entered.

"Cold water would be fine," she replied, sitting in front of the monitor. "Do you really think it's a shuttle?"

"I don't know what to think," Charlie replied handing her a glass of cold water and sitting down. "No one had a destination in this quadrant; none of our missions had a course that brought them close enough to crash-land here. All our ships made it to the planets they were destined for. Not all of them were able to survive the landing, as we know, but they all made it to their destination."

"There's always been something about X that's bothered me. I've never been able to put my finger on it, but from everything I've read about the mission. That last transmission..."

Kala let her last thought fade away and looked at picture on the monitor. Suddenly, she gasped and sat forward punching a few keys; the X mission file appeared on a second monitor. She opened the last picture sent from the mission commander.

"Look at these two pictures."

Charlie sat down next to her and looked from one monitor to another for a few moments.

"Okay, I give up. What am I supposed to be looking at?"

"Look closely at the surrounding landscape. Doesn't it look slightly familiar?"

Charlie looked intently at scenery surrounding the lifeless bodies of the Mission X crew members. The probe at the landing site had continued to send data for almost a month after the disaster so all the picture data had contained their bodies. Suddenly Charlie saw what Kala was trying to point out to him. He accessed the controls for probe five and began to pan around the area, up and down as well as in, out, and around. It wasn't until he panned the ground closer to the ship that they saw the bones.

"Holy Gods," Charlie whispered, "how could this have happened?"

"I don't know, but we need to find out."

Charlie pushed the COM unit button and paged Bill Chow. After a moment, the intercom beeped.

"Your mission has changed a bit, Chief. Kala is going to be the command staff joining you. We will both join you at the shuttle shortly. I'll explain when we get there."

"Aye, aye, skipper. I've just finished prepping the team and the ship. We'll be ready by the time you get here."

"And make sure you have enough rebreathers with you. You may need them after all."

"Yes, sir."

Signing off, Charlie turned to Kala.

"Get yourself ready and meet me in the hanger. I'll brief Bill and his team."

Kala nodded and moved toward the door.

"Keep this under wraps for now," Charlie said as she reached the door. "We have to find out what is going on before we say anything to the crew."

Heading to her quarters, Kala thought about what they had seen and wondered what had really happened to the crew of the ill-fated Mission X. When she got to her quarters, she threw a bag together and, on impulse, threw in a handheld unit with their mission specs on them in case they met a sentient being capable of understanding. She hoped to explain their mission. After a quick check to make sure she had everything, she locked her trunk and made for the shuttle bay. When she got there, she saw that Charlie was just finishing up his briefing of Bill and his team.

"Kala knows what to look for, so if there are any questions once you get down there, go to her. Check in as soon as you can after you arrive and then hourly, or more often if needed. We'll wait for your first check-in. After that, if we don't hear from you after two hours we'll attempt to contact you. Any questions?"

There were no questions. Charlie wished them luck and turned to walk away. He got halfway to the shuttle-bay door, before he turned back and called Kala over.

"I want you to be careful down there," he said quietly, "I wouldn't want to have to train someone new."

Kala thought she heard something in his voice other than the usual concern for her as one of his command staff, but didn't question him. Instead, she smiled and gave him a thumbs-up before turning to the ship and boarding. She watched Bill Chow stow her gear, then she sat down in the last open seat. She listened with half an ear as the pilot performed the preflight checklist, but her mind was on what they might find on the planet.

She thought about the bones scattered around the ship. She couldn't imagine what it must have been like for the crew as they approached the planet thinking they had arrived at their new home. She wondered what it had been like for them as they debarked from the shuttle to, what they thought, would be their new home, only to collapse and die a painful death. She shuddered at the thought.

As they traveled toward the planet, Kala began to formulate a search plan. First, they needed to get into the Mission X shuttle and see if there was enough power to access the logs. Kala knew the logs would be their initial source of information needed for their survival on the planet. Leaning forward, she asked Bill if she could retrieve her notepad and pen. She needed to write down her thoughts. After receiving his "yes," she quickly unbuckled and reached into the compartment containing her bag. With paper and pen in hand, she buckled up and began jotting down notes.

"Okay, folks, we're on final approach to the planet. Please make sure your tray tables and seats are in their upright positions and your seat belt is securely fastened."

Kala and the others laughed nervously.

"Once we've landed and we're suited up, we'll do a mandatory check to make sure each suit's fit is right. Anyone who doesn't have a proper-fitting suit will be staying here in the shuttle."

Bill stopped giving instructions as the pilot went through the landing procedure check and put the shuttle on the ground. Once all motion had ceased, he resumed where he had had left off.

"The suits must be airtight...no leaks. After previous missions, we can't take any chances, people. Before we get suited up, I believe Ms. Melina has a quick briefing for us."

He made room for Kala up front. When she had taken her place, she paused to scan the faces of the team. What she saw five intelligent, hardworking people who wanted nothing more than to spend the rest of their lives living peacefully in their quiet corner of the galaxy. She inhaled deeply and let her breath out slowly before she started.

"I know that you came on this trip blind with no knowledge of what you're walking into, but you're about to find out. Probe five sent back pictures of what looked like a Mission X shuttle. We are here to either confirm or deny." One of the men raised his hand. "Yes, Mr. Soto?"

"From what I understand, this wasn't the planet Mission X was supposed to land on. Is that correct?"

"Yes."

"So why would one of their shuttles be here?"

"That's what we don't know and hope to find out. We do know that the last visual transmission showed the teams exiting the shuttle and almost immediately being overcome by something in the air. That's the reason for our suits. We have more than one problem here today. One, we don't know why they landed here instead of their intended planet. Two, we don't know what might be in the air that overtook the mission crew so quickly. Three, we don't know where the rest of the bodies are; this would have been a full shuttle. We also need to know if we must have domes in order to live here, so we can plan for them. We need answers to these questions before we can land more people. One more thing, until you are told otherwise, you are to keep your rebreathers on. Is that clear?"

She looked at them intently as they, one-by-one, accepted her orders.

"Do you have any more questions for me?"

There were none. Kala turned to Bill. "Okay, as long as there aren't any questions..."

"What kind of a mission is this really?" someone suddenly asked.

"I'm sorry," said Bill, "but what part of 'do you have any more questions' did you not understand?"

There was a hush before Bill continued.

"This is a *recon* mission, people. You are here under my command, and I am here under the command of Kala Melina, whether you like it or not, so get used to it. You need to put aside your personal feelings for the good of the entire mission and move on. Now, suit up. From what we've been able to establish, we don't have much daylight left, and I want to get this search over quickly."

Once suit checks were done and he was satisfied, Bill opened the door. They moved slowly down the shuttle ramp. Bill placed Kala in the middle and warned everyone that she had better not come to harm. They proceeded at a slow pace to the Mission X shuttle site, performing recon along the route. Once they reached the shuttle, the team searched the area thoroughly. After the immediate area was secured, Bill and Kala began working on the shuttle door, while the rest of the team found what was left of the bodies. One of the men sent the required message back to their ship. After forty-five minutes, Bill and Kala gained access to the interior of the shuttle. They were amazed at what they found inside.

For all the exterior damage, there was little damage on the inside. They could tell that whatever damage had occurred had been repaired a long time ago.

"This is very strange," Kala said aloud from where she was sitting in the pilot's seat.

"What's that?" Bill asked coming up beside her and sitting down in the copilot's chair.

"These readings are all wrong. No wonder they landed here instead of where they were supposed to."

Bill gave her a blank look.

"Okay, these readings here," she said pointing to the monitor between the two seats, "indicate where *this* planet is in the solar system and this reading over here," she said, pointing to a different dot on the same monitor, "indicates where they should have been."

Bill stared, stunned, at the distance before sitting up straight in his chair.

"Holy shit!" he exclaimed. "That's at least five light years off course!"

"Correct," she said softly, "and from what I've been able to tell so far, while watching the logs download, the only way they could have ended up here is through sabotage."

Bill looked at her sharply, not wanting to believe what she had just told him. After a moment, he looked back at the screen and muttered something in his native language before getting up from the chair.

"Does the commander know about this yet?"

"What's there to tell him? I haven't been able to analyze the data and I don't trust the power here to hold up that much longer..."

There was a sudden yelp from the back of the shuttle interrupting Kala's next words. Exchanging wild glances, Bill and Kala ran to the back of the craft.

CHAPTER 21

Kala and Bill found Crewman Johnson standing and Crewman Tomisetto lying on the floor. The men were two of Bill Chow's best men and had many years of space experience under their belts.

"What the hell happened here?" demanded Bill.

"I tell you there's something in there," Crewman Johnson insisted. "Those wires didn't chew themselves, did they?"

"What could fit into that space?" asked Crewman Tomisetto. "Our hands don't even fit in there."

"There are creatures that are smaller than the naked eye can see, Crewman!" Bill snapped. "Just because you can't see them with the naked eye doesn't mean they're not there. I expect you to remember that!"

"Yes, sir! What I meant, sir, was that I believed that whatever chewed the wiring had to be bigger than what just grabbed me."

"How can you be sure?"

"Because the marks made on wires and the interior of the housing were both made by the same creature, and that creature had to be about half a kilo. Whatever touched me must be about a quarter of that size."

"Could it have been a feeler? Another part of this creature?"

By the look on the two crewmen's faces and the silence that followed, Bill and Kala could tell that option hadn't occurred to them.

At least, Kala thought, *they have the decency to look embarrassed.*

"We didn't think of that, sir."

"Just keep in mind we're not on Earth anymore. You need to start thinking outside the box."

Both men nodded. Bill gave Crewman Johnson a cursory once over before sending him back to work. Putting his hand on Kala's elbow, he guided her back to the cockpit and to the captain's chair.

"Finish the download so we can get out of here quickly if we need to," he told her quietly. "I'm getting one of my feelings and I don't like it."

"The download probably finished while we were talking with Johnson and Tomisetto," she replied. "I need to run a few more checks and see if there's anything else I can get from the systems."

Bill grunted his agreement.

"How'd you get this command at such a young age?" he asked after watching her for a few minutes.

"Charlie had faith in me, I guess," she replied paying more attention to the displays in front of her then to the question.

"So you know, I agree with the decision. There aren't many seventeen-year-olds that are as in control of themselves as you are. God knows I wasn't at your age."

"Thank you," Kala said looking at the man beside her with a new respect.

"You're welcome. I just want you to know that I'll back whatever decisions you make unless they put us in danger, in which case I'm taking over." He smiled. "A good head at your age can't always make up for experience."

"I would hope you'd jump in if needed. I'm not going to pretend I know everything. I know that I lack experience and need to be shown what to do and to be led when necessary." Kala smiled back.

Kala checked the continuing download and felt much better about the mission than when they first arrived. Letting her mind wander a bit, she sat back in her seat. She thought about a book she had read years ago; a man landed on a planet and needed to get acclimated to its atmosphere before being able to breathe normally. She wondered if that was what they would have to do. Glancing back at the monitor, she suddenly sat up and stared at the screen. She turned for Bill and saw that he had gotten up and was with the men working on the wiring. Once she got his attention, she waited until he sat down in the copilot's seat before saying anything.

"I think I've figured out what killed them," she said quietly, pointing at the monitor.

Bill looked at the monitor and raised his eyebrows.

"Can this be right?"

Kala nodded.

"Are you telling me all we need to do is slowly fill this cabin with the air that's outside and we'll get acclimated and be able to breathe without keeling over?"

"Yes."

"Let's get back to our shuttle so you can contact the commander. I'll bring the rest of the team there and we'll try..."

"I'd rather know for sure before we put them in danger," Kala said quickly, getting up to swing the cockpit door closed. "We can easily try it on ourselves here. If it works, we can acclimate the others. If it doesn't work, then we're no worse off than we are now."

"Okay. I'll tell Johnson and Tomisetto not to bother us for a bit. While I'm doing that, you contact Charlie and let him know what you discovered and what we're going to do."

"Don't be long. I don't want to give either one of us the chance to chicken out of this!"

Bill chuckled as he went to the rear of the craft to talk to the crewmen.

"And you're sure this will work?" Charlie asked.

"Well, at least it will tell us if we'll need domes to survive or not."

"Agreed, but be careful, I can't afford to lose either you or Bill right now. Let me know what happens and let me know if I will need to effect a medical rescue."

"Understood. Bill's back now so I'm going to sign off and get this little experiment underway."

"Good luck! Hudson out."

"What did you tell them?" Kala asked as Bill sealed off the cockpit.

"That we are completing an experiment and we can't be disturbed for the next hour. I figure we should know one way or the other by then."

They both chuckled as they set up the experiment. Kala started working on the oxygen equipment and stopped suddenly.

"We haven't decided which one of us is going to try this," she said, turning to Bill.

Bill looked at her for a second like she had grown another head before laughing outright.

"I guess I assumed it was going to be me, and I'm guessing you assumed it was going to be you," he said, still laughing.

She nodded, laughing as well. But after calming down, they regarded each other with growing seriousness. Both were silent, and then, Kala spoke.

"Charlie can replace me easier then he can you, whether he wants to or not. I think it needs to be me."

"Unfortunately, I think you're right. I now understand why he has depended on you so much. For a young person, you do have a good head on your shoulders. You can see to the bottom of a problem, even if you find the outcome untenable. All right, you're our guinea pig for the day, as our ancestors used to say. What do you need me to do?"

"Just be ready with the oxygen. If I'm wrong about this, I'll need it."

"How long do I give you before I administer?"

"I guess when I motion for it, or I'm turning blue. You ready?"

Bill took the portable oxygen unit and got it ready. When he said "Ready," she sat down and put her hands on her helmet. Before she took it off, they locked eyes. Then, Kala took a quick breath and removed her helmet. For almost ten seconds nothing happened, then without warning, she felt like a rock had been dropped onto her chest. She struggled for each breath. Time seemed to slow and almost stop. When she was about to signal Bill for the oxygen, she suddenly could breathe freely again.

She inhaled deeply twice before she straightened up and looked around the cockpit. Without the helmet, the colors were more vivid, and the air, though a bit acidic, was fresh.

"I'm okay," she said to Bill.

"What's it like?" he asked, his voice, through his helmet, sounding like it was coming from a far distance.

"A bit acidic but okay. It's nice to breathe fresh air again. How long did it take me to get acclimated?"

"About forty-five seconds. I didn't start the stopwatch at the same time you took off your helmet."

She looked thoughtful before turning back to the computer. She did some quick calculations, all the while muttering to herself. When she finally turned back to Bill, she wasn't smiling.

"I won't be able to go back to our ship; this is a onetime only deal. I didn't understand until now, but once acclimated to the air down here, no one will be able to go back to the canned air of the ship. I think that might be what killed the people from the shuttle. They were acclimated to this air, went back to the Mission X ship and its air, probably felt ill, and when they returned here, their bodies couldn't deal with the change again."

"Okay, so we need to contact Charlie again and let him know what happened to you and what you think. It looks like we can't risk people taking off their helmets until they can stay here permanently."

"Some of the team has to stay down here. I don't fancy staying here by myself!"

"You're right. Let me think about who I want to stay with you before we contact Charlie."

Bill opened his PDA and examined the security schedule. After some rearranging, he had chosen those who would stay with Kala. He showed the names to her, and when she nodded, he went to find them.

Back at their shuttle, Kala contacted Charlie and went over the plan with him.

"Are you sure about this, Kala?" Charlie asked with real concern in his voice.

"No, but what else can we do? It doesn't mean we have to use this as the landing site; you can always send someone here to pick us up. But it does mean that we'll have to delay the landing."

"Hopefully not by much," Charlie said. "We're getting antsy up here."

"Unless you want to incapacitate everyone at once for forty-five seconds to a minute, we need to delay!" Kala said more vehemently then she intended.

Charlie was silent, then said, "You're right, of course. We'll get everything prepared up here and choose a landing site. Let us know what we need to do to make it quick and safe!"

"Will do," she replied in a softer voice, "and, Commander, I'm sorry for snapping. It's just that this news has made us a bit tense."

"No apology necessary," Charlie answered. "Just keep yourself safe."

Kala left the cockpit and walked into the main cabin of the Sierra shuttle. She hadn't really paid attention to her environs when they flew here. Suddenly, a thought struck her. She remembered the main cabin of the Mission X shuttle. All the seats were missing, along with as much usable material as possible. She wondered, again, what those people had gone through when they had first landed. She went back into the cockpit and contacted Charlie again.

"Have you tried looking for the Mission X ship in orbit?" she asked before he had a chance to say anything.

There was a long pause before Charlie responded.

"To be honest, it never crossed our minds. I'll get the search started now."

"Start with probes three and four on the planet," she suggested. "I don't know why, but with some of the stuff we've found here, I have this feeling they may have ended up crashing the ship. Those probes are close enough to here that they might show us something."

"Good idea. I've learned that your hunches are usually right on." Charlie's tone turned serious. "Don't worry, everything will work out okay."

"I know but something here still bothers me. I think the way we handle the acclimation will help, but I still don't know..."

She let the sentence trail off and they were silent, only hearing the crackle of space between them.

"I'd better sign off for now," Charlie said. "People will think there's something going on between us," he joked.

Kala responded with nervous laughter and signed off. She sat, thinking back to when her relationship with Charlie had begun to change. She realized that it had happened slowly, over the course of the journey.

Could it have happened even before we left? she asked herself. She got up and headed back into the main cabin.

Bill, Crewman Johnson, and Lt. Jerrium were waiting for her.

"Okay, you two," she said, acknowledging she was in charge, "I assume that Bill has told you the reason you are here?"

They both looked a little nervous and nodded.

"Okay. Getting acclimated will not be easy to go through. But," she smiled at them, "as you can see, I'm not wearing my helmet. I've already done it, so I know what it's like. It hurts like hell at first, but the good news is any pain doesn't last for long. It may seem like forever, but it really is less than a minute. How long to get acclimated may vary for each of you, but we're going to do this in stages. Bill won't be getting acclimated so he can return to the ship with the others to get supplies."

Kala paused a minute.

"You were both personally chosen by Bill because he has faith in your ability to go through this change and not be afraid to stay permanently on the planet now. If you don't want to do this, you can go back with him."

Neither one of them moved nor spoke.

"Okay... Who wants to go first?"

After a brief pause, Johnson raised his hand.

"Thank you, crewman."

"Before you go into the cockpit with Bill, I'll go over the procedure and what will happen. We're very interested in your reactions, since they may be different from mine. So, after you are done, I'll ask you to describe what happened and I'll record it."

Kala explained what had happened to her and the steps Bill would be taking to insure their personal safety. As she motioned to Johnson, he got nods of encouragement from Bill, Kala, and Lt. Jerrium.

Bill led Johnson into the shuttle's cockpit and closed the door. Kala and Lt. Jerrium listened, at first to silence, and then heard the sounds of Johnson falling to the floor. After five minutes, Bill came out of the cockpit with Johnson, a bit ashen-faced, a step behind.

"It wasn't too bad, was it?" Kala asked, smiling.

Johnson shook his head, placed his helmet on the storage rack, and proceeded to describe a similar reaction to Kala's. Next, Bill took Lt. Jerrium into the cockpit. Once acclimated, Johnson, Jerrium, and Kala went to the Mission X shuttle to search for clothes to wear until their belongings could be sent down from the ship.

Bill met them there and sent Johnson and Jerrium to take air readings and explore.

"Well, I guess it's time for the rest of us to go back up to the ship. You're sure you three will be all right down here tonight?"

"What choice do we have?"

Bill conceded the point with a nod of his head before saying, "It's just that I really hate leaving you here, that's all."

"I know you do, but once I breathed this air, the choice was made. If you trust the people you're leaving with me, then don't worry about it. We'll be fine."

"It's not the 'we' I'm worried about, Kala, it's the 'you.'"

Kala looked at him quizzically.

"Charlie told me especially to watch out for you," he grinned sheepishly, "I think you remind him of his wife."

Kala was surprised.

"Can you tell me what happened to Charlie's wife and daughter?"

Bill hesitated before he responded. He walked to the window and stared out at the strange world beyond his helmet.

"They were caught out during the last plague. Charlie was working at the Houston base and couldn't reach them when word came down about the severity. By the time he was able to get home, they were already dead. He never forgave himself for leaving them alone."

"It wasn't his fault!" Kala exclaimed.

"He knows that now, but at the time, he didn't. She was the light of his life and he was the light of hers. I've never seen two people so in love. And they adored their daughter. She was five when the plague struck. I guess she'd be seven or eight by now. It was a real shame, but in the end, Charlie knew that, had he gone, he would have gotten sick too...maybe even die... and he wouldn't have been any good to anyone. He was younger than Tabie and they weren't even sure they could have children, so when Cherie came along they both doted on her."

Bill paused, remembering a time when life wasn't good for any of them.

"How did you make it through the plague?" he asked Kala.

"My parents had just been killed in a car accident and I was living with my brother Casio. We were quarantined on his estate with the staff and a doctor from TechNet."

"You were one of the lucky ones. Anyway, after Tabie and Cherie died, Charlie threw himself into his work to forget. He lived and breathed WASA for almost three years...until you came along, that is. Mind you, I've worked with Charlie Hudson for all our years at WASA...eight or nine years now... and I've never seen such a change in a man."

Bill whirled and looked intently at Kala before he continued speaking.

"I believe that Charlie Hudson is falling in love with you, whether he knows it yet or not. I will tell you this once, and then we will never speak of it again. If you do anything to hurt him, you will have to answer to me. He is a good man with a good heart, and I believe you are a good person as well. Please treat him with the respect and care he is due."

Kala's throat was tight. She hadn't known of Charlie's pain, but she knew now, deep in her heart, that she might be falling in love with him.

"Don't worry, Bill, I'll never do anything to hurt him," she reassured him, "I have to think about what I feel and want to do, but I won't hurt Charlie." She was resolute. "Now, get going. We'll need supplies as soon as possible. And Charlie will be expecting a full report. We need to begin acclimating people so we can start the drop."

Bill gave her a salute and a jaunty, "Yes, ma'am!" and headed back to the *Sierra* shuttle.

Kala sat in the pilot's chair for a long time after Bill left, thinking about their conversation. She realized she had never had a real boyfriend. At almost seventeen, she was on the command staff of a spaceship that had gone to another planet—and she had never had a boyfriend! She laughed aloud, and her laugh sounded harsh.

"I've left my family," she spoke aloud, "I've left my friends, and I've left everything I've ever known. And now I have the commander falling in love with me, and I've never had a boyfriend!"

She slapped her hands on the console in front of her and stood up. She started pacing angrily and almost ran into Johnson.

"I'm sorry, ma'am, but you're needed outside by one of the bodies."

"That's okay. I was headed outside. Do you know what the problem is?"

"No idea, ma'am. Lt. Jerrium sent me to get you."

"Okay... And cease and desist with this 'ma'am' business. Now that we're on the planet, I'm just Kala. Do you think you can do that?"

Johnson smiled and nodded, "I think I can try."

"That's all I can ask for. Now lead the way."

He led Kala to two of the bodies that were furthest from the shuttle; it was where Lt. Jerrium was working. Kala observed the woman first and, then, walked over to her.

"What's the problem, Lieutenant?"

"Some of the air readings we made earlier while we were in the suits don't seem to jibe with the readings I'm getting now. Also, there are some marks on the bones that worry me."

"Worry you? How?"

"Something has chewed on these bones."

"That doesn't surprise me," Kala replied. "There must be meat eaters here. Something must have come along and chewed on the bones after the meat eaters were done. That's all."

"That's not the only thing I wanted you to see," the lieutenant said, heading toward a nearby hill. "Look at this."

Kala followed Lt. Jerrium to where she had stopped just short of a major crater in the side of the hill.

"What am I looking at?" Kala asked.

"Look past the plants."

Kala squinted and looked around the crater trying to identify as many details as she could. Suddenly she saw something metallic under the brush to their left. She looked around the crater again and noticed more pieces.

"I have to tell Commander Hudson about this. Don't disturb anything other than the bodies. I'd like more experts down here before we do anything else with this discovery."

"Should Johnson and I mark off the area so it's more noticeable to the ship?"

"That's a good idea. Get as much marked off as possible to make it visible. This will be a surprise for Commander Hudson and Chief Chow!"

CHAPTER 22

After Lieutenant Jerrium left to find something to cordon off the crater area, Kala returned to their shuttle to contact Charlie. On her way there, she wondered if she should talk about what Bill had told her earlier but decided not to. Once back at the shuttle, she noticed that the COM unit was blinking with messages.

The first message was from Bill telling her that they had arrived safely at the ship and were getting the supplies together. The second was from Charlie requesting that she call him back at her leisure with an update. She knew, from his words, he trusted her to respond as soon as she was able, so she decided to change out of her space suit first. She went into the main cabin of the shuttle and started looking through the compartments. She finally found an old jumpsuit that looked like it would fit her. After she had changed, she relished the feeling of air on her bare arms before returning to the cockpit to contact Charlie. She was surprised to see Charlie answering her call.

"Answering your own calls now, Commander?" she joked.

"Only when I want to talk to the person on the other end," he replied with a half-smile on his face. "So...what's the news?"

Kala filled him in on what they had found so far, including the pieces of the Mission X ship.

"The crashed ship looks like it's been in the jungle a long time. I'm not sure why, but it gives me hope that someone is still alive here. Did Bill give you the PDA?"

"We're analyzing the data on it now." He looked over his shoulder and quizzed Danielle, who was standing behind him. After Danielle replied, Charlie turned back to Kala, "She said they're finding some interesting stuff on there. She'll contact you later with something more definite."

There was a brief silence as they stared at each other.

"Have you figured out the solar cycle yet?" Kala finally asked.

"Looks like its twenty-five hours so it's not too different from Earth..." Kala saw Danielle lean over and whisper into Charlie's ear.

"Looks like you were right about the difference in air elements. Once we're down and we take off our breathing gear, we'll be down to stay. We're sending all the data to the science teams now. I'm putting a top priority on the air situation to see if there's any way to tank some of the air on the planet to be analyzed up here. We'll let you know if it can be done." He paused. "What's it really like down there?" he asked wistfully.

"It's beautiful," she replied. "I think this area needs to be the landing site. We have too many questions to land and set up somewhere else and come back here to investigate. We need to understand what happened here. And, if there are people alive, they couldn't have gone too far. Have you been able to find a shuttle or any satellites they might have placed into orbit?"

"Not a thing. I'm wondering if that crater might be a portion of the ship or maybe a satellite that crashed into the planet."

"That's what I'm thinking, but I don't want to jump to any conclusions. I need people down here, Charlie."

"I know you do. I'm going to be sending down another team with Bill right away, and everyone will be staying this time so you three won't be alone down there tonight. They will land the shuttle, help unload, and only the pilot will lift off again, so if you need anything other than what was on Bill's list, you'd better tell me now."

"I can't think of anything. Food, water, and clothes are the most important essentials right now. Bill has a list of a few other items as well as the tools for excavation, so I think we'll be okay for now."

"Take care of yourself, Smiley," he said using the nickname he had given her. "If everything goes well, we should start the major move down in the next couple of days. Bill will be bringing down some of the communications equipment, so you'll be able to contact us from the field if you need anything. He'll see you soon."

"I'll listen for the shuttle and go to meet him. Thank you, Commander. Melina out."

After she broke the connection, she headed to the landing site. She passed the crater and saw that it had been roped off, and Johnson and Jerrium were back at their assigned jobs. Since she was waiting for Bill's shuttle, she decided to start working on clearing some of the overgrowth around the crash site. She had been working for about thirty minutes when she heard the roar of the shuttle overhead. Just as the three of them got to the landing site, the shuttle was coasting to a stop.

Kala noticed that the people who were going to be staying on the planet were wearing the minimal rebreathing masks, a helpful change that might make the acclimation to the planet's atmosphere less harsh. Once unloading was done, Kala wished the pilot a safe flight back.

"Wish I could stay now, ma'am," he said as he handed her a packet from Charlie. "Seems like a real nice place here."

"Let's hope so, it's our new home!" Kala replied. She gave him a packet and a container containing vials of sample materials. "Please make sure you give these to either Commander Hudson or SIC Chang."

"You got it. I'll see you on my next drop."

Kala waved good-bye and watched the door close before going back to the Mission X shuttle. When she got there, those in and out of breathing masks were already putting up temporary housing and getting the gear stowed, as well as erecting the communications array.

"Okay, those still in rebreathers come with me and Commander Chow, Johnson and Jerrium keep working out here while we get the new folks acclimated," she said leading the way to the shuttle. "And work on the housing first. I don't know about the rest of you, but I want to be sheltered for the night!"

Kala heard the nervous laughter as she entered the shuttle. They followed the same procedure as before except that Bill went first and by himself so that Kala didn't have to worry about watching more than one person. She sensed that watching Bill go first would also help relieve some of the tension. The acclimation went quickly and everyone began working after a brief rest. Before Kala knew it, the sun was beginning to set. She put down her tools and called for a halt to the work.

"I think we've done enough for one day, everyone," she said. "Why don't we take some time to wash up and meet back here for a bonfire and some dinner? Remember, you can wash in the water, but don't drink it!"

Everyone cheered, then stored their tools in the storage containers, and went off to get washed up. After everyone had cleaned up and changed, they gathered in the central square they had created. The bonfire in the center was burning brightly, and the crew surrounded it, eating their first meal on the planet surface.

Kala opened a video and audio feed to the ship so those still on the ship could participate with those experiencing the first night on the planet.

Charlie had called for all work to be stopped so that everyone on the ship and the planet could sit down to their meals at the same time. After the meal was over and cleanup done, and while everyone was relaxing, Kala and Bill went to a secluded area and narrowed the COM link so they could talk to Charlie privately.

"How's it going down there?"

"Well...," Kala said, glancing at Bill, "We believe people can start coming down. But don't send everyone down at once. I think one or two shuttles a day are probably okay. We badly need to have specialists and equipment, so they should be on the first shuttles. Have any tests been started based on the logs we sent up?"

"Lots. And all the science teams are going nuts. There are debates on whether or not any of the embryos will be viable based on the unknown elements in the air. They're running tests based on the samples you sent up today. Hopefully, they'll find answers quickly. I have Danielle working on a new landing schedule, so we'll send someone else from the command staff tomorrow to help you."

"I can handle it," Kala protested.

"I know you can handle it, but you need to rest sometime. And with another command member, you can take shifts." Charlie smiled. "Bill, do you mind if I talk to Kala alone for a few minutes? You have the assignment I gave you before you left this morning. I know it will keep you busy."

"Not a problem, Commander. I'll be in touch tomorrow."

Kala heard Bill bellowing orders for guard rotation for the night as he walked away. She turned back to the monitor. For the first time, her woman's intuition kicked in, and she felt she knew what Charlie wanted to talk about.

"What's up, Commander?"

"For this conversation, it's Charlie."

"Okay, so I ask again. What's up?"

Charlie hesitated and then blurted out, "I think I may be falling in love with you...and to be honest, it scares me."

"Why does it scare you?"

"I lost my family and I don't want to lose anyone else. There are other reasons too, but mostly because I haven't felt this way in a long time."

Kala watched him and, searching for words, wished she had had a boyfriend.

"You're not that much older than I am," she said finally. "You got married and had a child at a young age. You won't lose me suddenly, so there's no need to worry about that."

"But..."

She put up her hand to silence him. "I know what you're going to say. I can't be sure that one of us won't die, but somehow I do know it. Don't ask me how, but I do." She watched his expression change and locked eyes with him. "I want you to know I feel the same way and it scares me as well, but for different reasons. But let's just decide to take this slowly for now and see where it leads us, okay?"

Charlie nodded and smiled. "You are a wonder, you know that? I think you're right. We'll take it slow and we *will* make it here on this planet, no matter what!"

Kala giggled, "Well, I'd better go before there's talk that I'm the commander's favorite and I don't do my share of the work! We'll talk again tomorrow and start to get to know each other better."

And they signed off.

Kala sat for a few minutes listening to the sounds around her. She heard the laughter of the crew as they put the finishing touches on the housing and made sleeping arrangements. She heard the native wildlife responding to the invaders of their world. After a while, she decided to walk back to the main part of the camp, where she found the group reassembling around the remains of the fire.

"Everything okay?" Bill asked her.

"Everything is just fine. The commander had a few things he wanted to go over regarding the test results we sent up. We have some new tests to run in the morning so we can send something up when the shuttle comes down in the afternoon." She smiled at Bill, then clapped her hands and addressed the group. "I think it's time to hit the sack now, people. We have some rough work ahead of us in the morning. We'll wake at dawn for breakfast."

Some grumbled, but everyone got up and made their way to the housing. Kala had started walking to a housing unit when Bill caught her arm and steered her in the other direction to an out-of-the-way spot.

Pointing to two housing units, he grinned. "By order of our esteemed commander, we get our own!"

"Hallelujah!" Kala exclaimed, laughing. As Bill started to walk toward his unit, Kala grabbed his arm. "Are you up for a quick chat?"

"Sure, what's up?" Bill reached into his unit and pulled out a couple of stools for them to sit on.

"Charlie admitted his feelings about me earlier when we were talking, and I think I may be feeling the same way. I've never had a boyfriend and I don't want to do anything wrong. How do I show him I want to go slowly?"

"Keep telling him you want to make sure you're both ready. Go one step at a time."

"Like that's really going to be hard with him up there and me down here," she said, a little sarcastically.

"Just remember where he's coming from Kala," Bill replied with a sad smile.

"I've never really had a serious relationship, so I'm not sure how to handle this, Bill. I don't want to screw it up. We're stuck here, and if the relationship doesn't work out now, life would be only slightly uncomfortable. But you know that once we get settled down here, one of our biggest commodities will be babies, and I just... Hell, I don't know what I'm saying. I only know that I don't want to screw anything up for anyone, that's all."

"You won't screw anything up, Kala. We all want this place to work. We want to be able to survive here and let Earth know they can send more people. If you keep treating people the way you have been...in an honest, open manner...you'll be fine. Don't change, not for any person or any reason."

"Thanks, Bill. That's just what I needed to hear." She yawned. "See you in the morning."

Chapter 23

As the days went by, everyone on the surface developed a routine. In the morning, groups would reconnoiter a little farther from base camp to gather floral and mineral samples. They looked for the closest water sources as well as workable land for planting their crops. They were always on the lookout for life forms of any kind. In the afternoon, rotating teams would unload the daily shuttle and set up equipment brought down from the ship. One group worked solely to help the shuttle crew staying on the surface get acclimated to the air. Once the people on the ship got the satellite up and running and the ground equipment was set up, there was daily contact with Earth. Until the relay equipment was brought down, only short communication was permitted.

The labs were the first buildings to go up, and the biologists started growing animals and plants. Given their power supply was limited, they needed to reserve power for scientific and communication uses. Horses and pack animals were going to be grown and used for fieldwork and other low-tech needs. WASA had designed the mission not only to create a new home for humans, but also to colonize the planet using low-tech methods so that people who wanted to get back to basics would be able to do so.

Eventually, the time came when all who were left to come down to the planet were Charlie and the remaining command team. All necessary technology was operating, and the interior of the ship was stripped. With prudent handling, there was enough fuel to allow a shuttle to return to the ship for a few years, but they were there to stay. On the one-month anniversary of the landing, Charlie and the remaining command team finally stepped foot on the planet. Privately, Charlie had asked Bill to have Kala oversee his acclimation. Of course, Bill had told Kala about the request, and Kala did not mention it to Charlie.

One week after the entire mission crew was together again, they had a big blowout bonfire and dinner. Communal kitchens—one kitchen for every three housing units—had been set up, so each kitchen group prepared food or brought seating and tables. Everyone was ready for a grand celebration.

"Okay, gang, before we start this feast," Charlie addressed the crowd, "I declare we are officially landed on this lovely planet. WASA has been calling it Planet Z. So, until we have a new name... Welcome to our new home, Planet Z, everyone!"

Everyone cheered and the party began. Charlie had decreed the following day to be a rest day, so everyone made the most of the party. As the revelry went on, Charlie pulled Kala aside and led her away for a walk.

"So what do you think of our new world?" he asked.

"Well, it's very nice, and I like the space and all the green," she said and then paused. "The people aren't that bad either," she continued, smiling up at him.

They walked on a bit farther, with Charlie unobtrusively guiding Kala to a clearing he had found. He hadn't told anyone about it, and during his spare time he had set up his housing unit there. Kala gasped in astonishment.

"You've only been here a week! When did you have time to do all this?" she asked, her voice filled with amazement.

"During breaks and downtime mostly, but I did get some help from a few people. Look around and see if you like it. I built it partly for you too."

Kala walked slowly around the clearing, looking at the structure that Charlie had built. It was by far the largest of the housing units; it had four or five rooms and what looked like a common room with a kitchen area. All the foliage in a circle about twenty-five feet from the unit had been cleared, and a small fence had been erected to keep the native plants at bay. He'd also covered the ground with mulch made from the local trees, mixed with a small gravelly type material that Kala could only guess was part of the biodegradable packing material they had brought with them. Along one edge, Kala could see an area marked off that would one day, if everything went right, hold a vegetable garden. The trees and plants that rimmed the area seemed to be a multitude of color with rainbow-colored flowers and leaves of every shade of green and blue.

Charlie's effort took Kala's breath away, and the only thing she could think to do was to hug him. But, after a moment, the feeling of the hug changed from one of innocence to something much more. Kala looked up into Charlie's eyes, wondering if her own eyes were shining as much as his. On impulse, she pulled his face toward hers and kissed him. As the kiss lingered, she felt Charlie's hand move up her back to both steady her and pull her closer. At last, she pulled back a bit to stare into his eyes again.

"I've never..." she started to say, but he put his finger on her lips to quiet her.

"I know," he said quietly. "The time has to be right for that, but for now this is okay. I'll be living here and when you're ready, you can move in. We don't even have to sleep in the same room. There are four bedrooms."

They stood silently, clasped in each other's arms. Kala leaned her head against his chest and listened to the thump of Charlie's heart.

"Do you want to see the inside?" he asked.

"I'd love to."

Charlie took her hand, led her inside, and showed her all the rooms. He proudly spoke of what he had planned for decorations, adding that he looked forward to her own ideas.

"Are you sure you didn't have help doing all this?" she asked as they left to head back to her housing unit.

"Well..." he said, pausing for effect, "Bill did help some."

Kala laughed.

"You and he are two peas in a pod," she giggled. "You do realize," she said, turning serious, "that he is trying to play matchmaker for the two of us?"

"Of course I do! You think Bill would dare to assume to put himself into anyone's business without prior approval?"

Kala laughed again as they arrived back at the bonfire. Just outside of the firelight, Charlie grabbed her arm.

"This relationship will only go as far as you want it to, Kala Melina," Charlie whispered in her ear. "But let it be known that I *have* fallen in love with you and I *will* fight for you."

Declaration made, he let go of her arm and walked into the circle of light. Kala stood where she was for a moment, not afraid of what people would think, but feeling scared. Then, she shook her head and walked forward to a dessert table. Grabbing something to eat and drink, she found an open seat next to a few of the engineers.

"We've never gotten the chance to thank you for what you did during the trip," said one of them whose name she didn't know.

"And what was that?" she asked, nibbling on her food.

"Making sure the commander knew what was going on and making sure the dissenters were taken care of. They seemed to have changed, and thanks to you, the commander listens to us now. We just wanted to thank you for that."

"I was only doing my job, but I'm glad I was able to help."

"You helped out more then you know," said another engineer. "We didn't think that the commander would believe us and we were getting ready to come either to you or SIC Chang. You stepped in just in time."

Kala regarded the engineers coldly. "What do you mean? What do you really want?"

They looked at her, stunned.

"Don't look so surprised," she said. "If you weren't just totally kissing my ass, I'm in the wrong business."

There was a pause, then the same engineer spoke again.

"We want those you call dissenters to have the same rights the rest of us have. We want them to have the same freedoms the rest of us have."

"They are free to move about the camp. This is a small expedition and we can't afford to lose anyone, so we will keep an eye on them. But don't think that we're so stupid as to not protect ourselves."

When there was no reply, Kala continued more gently, but firmly.

"We need every person we have, but if we have to, we will move people to an isolated area, a quick ride away. Let your friends know we are keeping an eye on them, and they'd better behave themselves." Kala stood up and, with a quick glance, located Charlie and Bill. Looking at the engineers, she made to leave. "Continue to enjoy the evening, and enjoy your day off tomorrow, because I think you'll find that, after tonight, you'll be watched now as well."

She walked purposefully toward Charlie and Bill. Seeing Kala's face, the smiles faded from their faces. Bill got up to leave the two alone, but Kala motioned him to stay.

"Seems our engineer problem from the ship has followed us," she said as she sat down next to them.

"Explain," said Charlie.

"That group I was just sitting with," she said with a nod of her head in their direction, "would like us to pull our tail off the troublemakers from the ship. They insist that we leave off and let them be. I told them we don't want to lose anyone, but there is no chance of leaving off, and that they should expect to be watched as well."

"You did the right thing," Bill told her with a sigh. "I'll reset the duty roster. Do you want to sign off on it, sir?"

"No. I trust you. Give me the details tomorrow when you get a chance."

Kala and Charlie watched Bill walk away. They sat in companionable silence before Kala asked the question that had been in her mind since they had kissed earlier.

"Why me?"

"Why you what?" Charlie asked, confused.

"Why is it me that you think you're falling in love with? Am I like your wife or am I her opposite? I'm just curious."

Charlie hesitated, thinking about his answer.

"You're a strange combination of being exactly like her, and nothing like her," he said finally. "She never would have come on this mission. She would have wanted to stay on Earth and raise our daughter and any other children we might have had. No matter what the consequences, she would have stayed." Charlie looked determined. "But I couldn't stay. So when Tabie and Cherie died in the plague, I swore to them that I would live no matter how much I wanted to die and be with them. It seemed like the only way to honor their memories."

He stopped speaking and raised his glass to drink. Seeing the glass was empty, he leaned over and picked up the flask next to him. He held it up to Kala, silently asking if she wanted some. She raised her glass and Charlie filled both of their glasses.

"I know I'm being long-winded, but you need to understand where I'm coming from, and a little about Tabie, to understand why you. Can you understand that?"

Kala nodded.

"Okay." Charlie smiled at her. "After they died, I threw myself into my work at WASA. It became my life. When you arrived at the Houston base, I thought I was seeing Tabie again...the resemblance is amazing. I'll have to show you a picture sometime... Anyway, I began to realize that if I was going to lead this mission, I needed to be able to put the past in the past. The vacation I took right before we left was to go and say good-bye. I stayed at their graves for most of a day telling Tabie and Cherie all about you and the mission. I know that may sound silly, but it made leaving them behind a little easier. During the trip, as I observed your personality more and more, it became clear to me that the only real similarity between you and Tabie were your looks. So... Why you? What got me interested in the first place were your looks, but what kept me interested was your personality."

Charlie stared into Kala's eyes. "If you decide that you don't want to be involved with me, then we can part as friends. I believe we can do that. If you do want to be involved, we can go as quickly or as slowly as you want."

He paused. "Did I lay too much on you at once?"

"Not too much," Kala said, shaking her head, "I do need to think about what you've said, but in the meantime, what do you think about putting one of those extra bedrooms to use? I think we could be together to get to know each other and see where things go."

"You would be okay with that?"

"I suggested it, didn't I? What's the worst thing people can say about us? That we're shacking up together? Better they talk about that than trying to plan more sabotage." She looked down at her lap, her mood suddenly shifting. "It makes me sad to think that people don't change. This was meant to be a new beginning, a chance to be happy, and they're going to take that all away from us just because they think people shouldn't leave Earth."

Looking around the camp, she surveyed her companions. Charlie watched her face and saw a flurry of emotions cross it.

"We're here to start a new life," she said, agitated, "and all they can do is sit around and moan about the 'good life' they left behind. Don't they realize that their families are courting death?"

"Calm down, Kala! We'll get them sorted out," he said quietly. "You're right in thinking that we can't afford to lose people, but if we need to, we will deal with them and isolate them. We'll do what do what needs to be done."

Charlie looked at her with pleading eyes, and after a moment, Kala nodded, the fire going out of her eyes.

Later, Bill joined them once again and Danielle appeared. Together, all four made a plan for watching the dissenters. Satisfied, they each went separate ways to sleep.

It was a long time before Charlie could fall asleep. He thought about Kala and what might happen in the future. He wanted things to work out and to be able to start a new life with her, to create the life he never got the chance to have with Tabie. Then he wondered if that was really fair to Kala, to make her fill in for a dead wife and produce kids to replace a dead kid. He tossed and turned and, finally, at 5 a.m., he got up, dressed, and went to work at the command center in the old shuttle. He'd been working a couple of hours when Kala and Bill joined him.

"This is supposed to be a day of rest," he told them smiling.

"And you're here for what reason?" Bill shot back.

"Couldn't sleep," was the jaunty reply. "I hate leaving things undone."

"Make that four of us," was the reply from the door, and they turned to see Lieutenant Jamaar standing there. "I'm here on Chief Chow's order, Commander. He asked me to come and receive final orders for handling any traitors."

"They're not traitors yet, Lieutenant," admonished Charlie.

"I know that, sir, but there have been whispers, and we need to be ready."

"Just make sure you keep that in mind," said Bill.

The lieutenant nodded and Bill led him out. Danielle, Charlie, and Kala each went to a monitor and began work of their own. After working for a while, Kala decided it was time to take advantage of her day off. She rose from her chair.

To no one in particular, she announced, "Well, I'm going to take advantage of what looks to be a wonderful day and get some work done at my housing unit. I'll see you all later."

CHAPTER 24

Once at her housing unit, Kala went directly to the kitchen area. She felt a small breakfast was in order and, in a spur-of-the-moment decision, decided to cook enough for a second person. She made eggs with fresh vegetables, toast, and brewed a coffee substitute. The finishing touch was fruit juice from the refrigeration unit. Just as she was putting the omelets on the plates, she heard a knock at the door.

"Come in," she called.

She continued bringing food to the table as Charlie came in the door.

"Eating utensils?" he asked.

"Already on the table," she replied handing him a plate. "Sit and eat. I hope you like it."

Charlie devoured everything on his plate, plus two glasses of juice and a mug of coffee substitute. After they had finished, she put the dishes in the sink, refilled their coffee cups, and sat again at the table.

Charlie coughed.

"So... Do you have much to move over to my housing unit?"

"Not really. Just a few personal items. The dishes and household items stay with the unit, so unless you think we'll need more, there's no need to take them. Shouldn't take me more than a few minutes to pack up my clothes and personal..." she stopped suddenly as a new thought occurred to her. "Did you place the fake chip in the guidance system?"

Charlie stared at her with a blank look and, then, started laughing at the look on her face.

"Of course I did. The day Danielle went to your quarters to pack up your things, she found it. She came to me to ask what it was and, after explaining, I installed it. It's okay. Even if they get to the ship they won't be able to get anywhere."

Kala let out a sigh of relief and went to the sink to start washing the dishes.

"Why don't you pack and I'll take care of this," Charlie said. "We'll need to get used to splitting duties and now's as good a time as any to start."

"I do have one question. Can you cook?"

"Let's put it this way. Tabie never even went into the kitchen. But, with the way you cook, we'll be splitting cooking duties!"

"Sounds good to me." Kala laughed. "I'll get my things."

In the bedroom, she sat on the bed and looked around the room. It hadn't been home for long, but it had been home, and now she was going to a new home. She sighed, pulled out her carry sack, and started gathering her possessions. Her clothes, the items Casio had given her, the movies that Shawan and his family had given her, and all her family photos. She had just finished when she felt someone looking at her. She looked up at the door and saw Charlie standing there watching her.

"Is it interesting watching a person pack their clothes?"

He didn't answer, but walked over and sat down next to her on the bed.

"I know this isn't a question a person normally asks but have you ever..." He let the sentence fade away.

She blushed and looked down at the floor. Charlie placed his hand under her chin and forced her to look at him.

"I don't mean to embarrass you, Kala, it's just that I want our first time to be special and it's important to me to make your first time special as well. Have you ever even had a boyfriend?" he asked gently.

She shook her head; a tear rolled down her cheek.

"What's this?" Charlie asked, wiping the tear away.

"I don't know," she answered, standing up and walking to the window. "I was old-fashioned and saving myself for my husband. I didn't expect to be on another planet hoping I could have as many babies as possible to save the human race."

Charlie came up behind her, turning her around so he could look into her eyes. He didn't say anything. He took her face in his hands and gently kissed her forehead. He then kissed her eyes and, finally, kissed her tears away. Before he knew what he was doing, he found her lips. Slowly and gently to be sure, but it was a much different kiss than their first. After a moment, he opened his eyes and pulled back, feeling her sway slightly from the loss of contact. She opened her eyes and smiled at him before leaning into him and kissing him again. Then, pulling away, she took his hand and led him to the bed.

153

"Are you sure about this?" Charlie breathed huskily.

Instead of answering, she kissed him again. She pressed her hands against his chest and began to unzip his jumpsuit. He wriggled his arms out when she got the zipper to his waist. Slowly, he laid her back on the bed and unzipped her jumpsuit.

With a tenderness he didn't remember using with Tabie, he slowly undressed Kala before undressing himself. With all his self-control, he used every technique he could think of to marry her to him in spirit as well as body. When he entered her he took special care to be gentle, knowing it was her first time, and was relieved Kala showed no signs of feeling hurt or discomfort. He took that as a good sign. As she lay in his arms after, Charlie looked down at Kala's face trying to discover what she was feeling or thinking.

"I'm sorry. I didn't want it to be this way. I wanted... Hell, I don't know what I wanted, but it wasn't *this*."

"Why? Was this so wrong? If I hadn't wanted it to happen, trust me, it wouldn't have. You would probably be lying on the floor in a considerable amount of pain." She laughed softly.

She gently touched his cheek and, then, let her hand tenderly wander over his face, feeling every curve and line.

"You are much older than your years," she went on, her voice still soft. "Even so, you still have much to learn about women. Tabie would probably say the same thing if she were here. You loved her very much and she will always be a part of you, but I'm sure that, if she's looking down on you now, she would want you to move on with your life. You don't have to forget her, but you need to start living again."

Charlie was silent, then Kala noticed the tear on his cheek.

"Have you ever really mourned her?" Kala asked quietly

His answer was another tear. Kala pulled him toward her and held him tightly while he cried. At times he sobbed so deeply he could barely breathe, and other times he simply whimpered. After he had cried himself out, Charlie lifted his head and looked at her with red and swollen eyes.

"I guess this seals the deal then," Kala said with a smile.

"Seals the deal?"

"You cried on my shoulder, which must mean something. You wanted to know if I was ready for a bonding of some sort with you. Well, I think we just had our bonding. What do you think?"

"I think you're right. And I think it's time we moved your stuff."

She nodded her agreement. They sat up and found their clothes.

"I think I need a quick shower before getting dressed. Care to save some hot water and shower with me?" she asked, just a bit coyly.

This time his answer was a laugh and a lift into the shower stall. They soaped each other in spots they couldn't reach themselves and made love again while standing under the waterfall of hot water.

Once dressed, Charlie carried Kala's belongings to the clearing and his housing unit.

"Would you mind if I took a bedroom of my own?" Kala asked as they stepped inside.

"Not at all. We don't need to rush. We can be together whenever we want but still have our own space. My room is the one on the left of the common room. You can have your pick of the others."

Kala chose the one on the right, directly across the common room from Charlie's. After she had put away her belongings, she went back to the common room and examined her new surroundings. Charlie was unpacking the few dishes and silverware they had brought from her place and storing them with his.

"Would you like me to show you around again?

"I'd love that."

"Okay, let's go outside. I want to show you the gardens now that I've gotten things planted and things are starting to sprout."

He took his time showing her the vegetable garden along with the area he was planning to use for a shed and animal housing once the breeding animals had given birth to the first generation.

"I'll need help clearing the area and building the shed, but I think, if we work on it a little every day, it will go quickly."

They heard someone approaching and turned to see Danielle coming into the clearing with Bill right on her heels.

"We might have a problem, Commander," Danielle blurted out, without greeting or preamble.

Charlie raised his eyebrows.

"The men we've been watching have tried to take one of the shuttles back to the ship."

Kala and Charlie looked at each other.

"That isn't something that worries me too much. It's the loss of fuel that worries me more."

Bill looked slightly confused.

"I'm sorry, Bill, I forgot. You don't know. Kala's brother Casio had a chip manufactured that would totally blank out the guidance system. The chip is programmed to make the ship stay in orbit around the planet and not deviate. Danielle, it's the chip you found when you packed Kala's things. Now, radio the guards to round up these guys and put them in Kala's housing unit..."

"Kala's?" Bill and Danielle interrupted, incensed.

Charlie and Kala couldn't help but laugh at their reaction. After they calmed down, Kala and Charlie explained that Kala was now staying in her own room at Charlie's housing unit. Being centrally located, Kala's housing unit was a perfect place to keep the dissenters. The command staff would meet them there.

"Obviously you and Charlie have come to an agreement," Bill said quietly to Kala as they walked to the unit.

Kala smiled and barely nodded as they and the dissenters arrived together at the same moment. The guards stood them front of Kala's empty unit, surrounding them so there could be no surprises.

"Well, it looks like we've some traitors in our midst," Charlie said, his voice ringing with authority and a tinge of anger. "You know there is no going back to Earth. As you have heard your comrades say we're home now. If you don't like it, I'm sorry; you should have considered that before we took off. You were offered the chance to back out before we lifted off." His voice turned steely. "However, if you are here to commit a terror campaign to make us go home or be rescued, that isn't going to happen." Charlie sighed and his voice softened. "So, the next question is what do we do now? How do we deal with people who don't want to be here? Someone, please, tell me what you want to do."

There was silence before one of the men stepped forward.

"We want to form a separate colony," he said. "We don't want to go home because we do believe the danger on Earth is great, but we don't want to be part of a low-tech society. We want whatever tools you will give us to create a high-tech society..."

"Why did you come to this planet, then?" Charlie interrupted harshly. "You knew we were going to build a low-tech colony."

"We wanted off Earth. We understood the danger to be closer than people were led to believe. We have no desire to return there. We want a high-tech life apart and to be left to ourselves. We do understand that, because we're acclimated to the air of this planet, it is now impossible to leave it, so we want to go to another part of the planet and live there, if we cannot live separately from you here."

Charlie considered the man's demands.

"I'd like you to stay here while we discuss options. Do you agree?"

The leader turned to the group and saw their looks of consent before nodding to Charlie.

"You understand, of course, that you will be guarded."
The men and women nodded and went inside.

At Bill's housing unit, cold drinks and a tray of snacks provided a welcome relief for Charlie, Kala, and Danielle.

"So much for a quiet day off," Danielle said after sitting down at the kitchen table.

The others laughed.

"What *are* we going to do with them, Charlie?" asked Danielle. "You can't honestly be thinking about giving them what they ask for?"

"Actually, Danielle, I am thinking about it. We could each have the life we want. And, if they were nearby, it could be beneficial. We could write a contract between our two settlements letting them have the machines. At least we'd know the machines are being well-taken care of."

"Are you sure they won't try to get back to Earth?" Bill asked.

"What does it matter if they do try? They would die in any attempt to leave the planet and they know it. There is nothing they can use to create a homing device. I think separation works out best for us all. Think about it, and I believe you'll agree."

They sat in silence, thinking about what the dissenters wanted and Charlie's proposal. In the end, they all agreed that separation was the best option. They discussed different ways to split up equipment, and finally, Kala came up with a solution.

"Find an area equidistant between us and where you'll put the dissenters and build a place for creating embryos, both human and animal. Low-tech and high-tech people can live there to seed our colony and their colony. Once both colonies have created what they need, this place can be closed, with low-techs and high-techs taking what they've each created. Each colony could maintain contact with the other and help out when needed. We can grow food for them, and they can help keep the machines we absolutely need running. It's the perfect plan!"

Over the next hours, Kala, Bill, Danielle, and Charlie hammered out a possible contract. They sent for leader of the group. When he arrived Charlie explained the plan to them.

"I'll have to discuss this with the others, of course, but it sounds fair and reasonable."

"Take your time, and let us know if there's anything you'd like to change, but I have a feeling that the planet will be big enough for all of us. We can make this work; we have to make this work. If not, we're doomed." Charlie said with passion.

"I do have one question before I go. Has there been any sign of the people who landed the Mission X shuttle?"

Charlie shook his head. "No. We've had no sign other than the bones scattered around the shuttle and the crater. We're thinking that no one survived. If they did survive, they must have gone to another location and don't know we're here. We'll need to keep in contact about that as well."

"I'll show the contract to the others. We'll let you know our answer in the next day or so."

When he had gone, the four went out to the garden. Fresh air was what they needed.

"I'm going to try to get *some* relaxation out of this day," Bill said, finally, heading back inside. "Let me know when we hear something."

Danielle spoke up, "I have housework to do," and departed.

Left alone, Charlie and Kala went back to Charlie's place. Kala went to the sprouting vegetable garden and admired the new plants poking their heads above the alien earth. Her thoughts strayed to the gardens she'd had in Old New York and Old Philadelphia and she was suddenly homesick. She sighed and looked up at the sky wondering what Lindsey was doing right now. She thought about Casio and Shawan. The loneliness was briefly overwhelming. Closing her eyes, she could see them at the farewell in the Houston base. She felt a tear slide down her cheek. Charlie came up behind her and slipped his arms around her waist.

"Feeling a bit homesick?"

"A bit," she replied, leaning back against him. "How did you know?"

"Do you have any pictures of the gardens you left behind?"

Kala smiled, "I have loads of them. All I brought with me were pictures, movies, and books. There was no need to bring anything else. If I couldn't find something I wanted in the supplies we brought, I wanted be able to make it myself or trade for it."

"Sounds like you thought things out well." He kissed her cheek.

"Are you going to recommend that Earth send more people here?" she asked suddenly, turning toward him.

"I hadn't really decided yet," he answered, taken aback slightly by her sudden change in mood and letting her go.

He walked over to where the fence was holding back the natural flora and picked a flower. He stood there studying the flower, then, with a final sniff, he turned back to look at her. He studied her and was again amazed by how much she looked like Tabie.

She was just over five feet with brown hair down to her shoulders. Her eyes were bright blue, almost clear, and her skin was turning dark brown from all the outdoor work she had been doing. Her face was open and honest, and he could almost always tell what she was thinking. Charlie liked the clear open look she gave him. Unlike some people, it always put him at ease to know where he stood with her. Right now, though, her face was clouded, and her thoughts, other than missing home, were hidden from him. He didn't like that.

"Kala, what's bothering you?"

"I feel we're missing something. We didn't find enough bodies to account for the entire Mission X crew, and other than the shuttle, no ships are intact. There should be people around here somewhere. It scares me."

"Would it make you feel better if I sent out scouts?"

"Immensely. We need to know what we're dealing with if we're going to ask more people to come and settle here. Don't you think?"

He studied her again before nodding.

"You're right. I've already made out schedules for our three shuttles. They'll begin recon tomorrow morning. Pretty soon, we'll have mapped this whole continent."

"What about the other continents?"

"Kala, love, we have to start taking chances at some point! I know you're worried, but I believe that if we make sure this continent is safe, we can, at least, have another couple of ships join us. Once they arrive and we've increased our numbers, we'll be able to start on the other continents. If there are other people, and they have the technology, they'll come to us at some point, but we have to move forward."

Kala frowned.

"Nothing is safe all the time. Sometimes you just have to learn to let go and move ahead on faith. As long as we move forward and have strength, we will be fine. Life is going to be hard enough here without second-guessing ourselves or cowering in a corner!"

"I know you're right," Kala sighed. "I guess it's just that I feel kind of alone here without all the people I know from Earth. It's so quiet at night when I'm lying in bed. I miss the old noises. Even on Casio's estate, I could hear city sounds. I know I came here, in part, for the quiet, but it's still disconcerting at times."

They didn't speak and stood looking at the surrounding gardens, listening to the life of the planet. Eventually, Charlie turned toward the unit.

"You coming? It's going to be an early and long day tomorrow, so we'd better eat some dinner. I have a feeling we'll be starting to deal with the little things."

Kala followed him into the house making for the kitchen area.

"I'll get dinner tonight," Charlie told her. "Why don't you go and settle in."

"Yes, sir," she said with a laugh as she went to her room instead.

As Kala arranged her things, she realized how little of her past life she had really brought with her. The largest part of her weight allowance had been her pictures, book CDs, and movie CDs. She hadn't brought many clothes and, unlike the scientists, she didn't have a lifetime's worth of work that she wanted to continue.

She sat on her bed and studied the pictures of her family. Casio was serious, as usual, and Shawan and his brood were all smiles and happy. She found a picture of Lindsey and put it in the family section of her album, looking at it the longest. In her next letter, she would have to remember to tell her about Charlie. Lindsey, of all people, would be happy for her. Just then, she heard Charlie calling from the other room that dinner was ready.

CHAPTER 25

As Charlie predicted, the next day was hectic with new "emergencies" coming in from the outlying posts and news coming in from the recon flights. As they classified the land clear further out from the landing site, people were moving farther away to claim as much land as possible. In the colony contract they had signed, they had agreed to work as part of the landing unit for at least a year. The contract also laid out the responsibility of the command staff to lead the colony until a ruling council could be duly elected by the general population. In the meantime, a leadership committee composed of the heads of each group was set up to advise the command staff.

Toward the end of the workday, reports started coming in from the southernmost holding of possible sightings of other humans on their way to the settlement. In the main square, word spread like wildfire and adrenaline levels rose.

Not wanting first contact to be too overwhelming, Charlie asked everyone to stay inside their homes or work places. He instructed the security team, who would be making first contact, to bring the humans to the main square. Tensions rose as everyone waited for word. Finally, the command staff heard that the security team and a group of humans were on their way to the main square.

Fifteen minutes later, the group arrived in the main square. Charlie, Kala, Bill, and Danielle stood in the center of the square, while people watched from the surrounding buildings. Charlie had turned the cameras on to record the meeting for the next report to Earth. They watched the group come around the corner, with the unknowns in the middle and the security team in front and back.

The team escorted the visitors right up to the command staff and stopped smartly. The captain saluted Charlie and stepped forward.

"Sir, this is Anne Lasson Greene. She states she is the daughter of Commander Jon Lasson."

Charlie raised one eyebrow.

"It's very nice to meet you, Ms. Greene. Why don't we step in here and talk," Charlie said, indicating an unoccupied building on his left that had been prepared for the meeting.

After the command staff and the planet humans entered the building, the security team remained at attention by all the doors. The doors of the other buildings opened and people poured out. They milled about, waiting for some word on what was going on inside.

Inside, all were cordial, though Charlie didn't believe the group's claim they were the descendants of the failed Mission X. He believed the only way they could be descendants was if the ship and the shuttles had gone through a time vortex. And, in Charlie's mind, there was no way this could have happened.

"Would you like something to eat or drink?" Charlie offered, indicating a side table filled with different foods and drinks.

Anne Greene declined, but encouraged her people to partake if they wanted. Once they were all seated, Charlie started by asking the question that was bothering him the most.

"So... How is it that a child who was twelve years old when she left Earth two years ago on Mission X now seems to be older than twenty?"

Everyone, including his own people, turned to look at Anne. Kala glanced around the table and could see a different expression on each person's face. Her people were expecting a logical explanation, while Anne's people looked wary. After some seconds, Kala saw Anne's face change as she made a decision.

"You are correct. We are from Earth, but not from Mission X. We are, what your people call, the 'Taken.' We were taken from Earth and seeded on different planets to see how we would adapt. I and others were seeded on this planet to see how we would adapt to the atmosphere, and when our Takers...what we call them...felt humans would do well here, they wanted to seed more of us. Your Mission X was diverted here. Some of the crew were integrated into our society. Others wanted to leave and wouldn't believe us when we told them they couldn't. The shuttle and crash site you found are from their attempt to leave..." She paused.

"But we didn't bring them down."

Anne looked at Charlie to gauge his reaction, then continued, "When they tried leaving, the oxygen atmosphere of their ship made them go mad, and they returned to the planet. When they left the shuttle, they thought they were on a different planet and under attack. They died trying to defend themselves against an imaginary attack. We tried to explain, and in the frenzy, many good people on both sides were killed." She lowered her head and sighed. "We took the names of some of the Mission X crew to remember and honor them. Anne Lasson was one of the ones killed... along with all the children from Mission X who tried to leave. When the adults still alive came to their senses, they realized what had happened and took their own lives."

Anne stopped and got up. She walked over to the refreshments and poured herself a glass of fruit juice. Draining the glass, she refilled it and went back to her seat. She sat silently while Charlie and the rest of the command staff absorbed what she had told them. She watched Charlie's face intently, seeking clues for what he would say or do next.

"I know this is hard to believe, Commander, but it is the truth. I am not that Anne Lasson. She and her family are dead. There are a few people left from the mission, but we thought it best if we came to meet you without them. We want to be sure you believe they are still with us of their own accord and not being forced. If you want, we can take some of your people to meet with them."

"Why can't you bring them to us?" Danielle asked.

Anne hesitated and looked down at her glass.

"We thought it best," was all she said.

"You do realize," Kala said quietly, "that it doesn't look good for you that you won't allow them to come and see us. It's almost as if you think they'll tell us something you don't want us to hear."

Anne fidgeted with her glass.

"They would tell you things that you're not quite ready to hear, that is true. But this is only one of the reasons they aren't allowed to come. I will allow you to see them in our village, but until you've learned more about our life here, we can't...and won't...allow you to see them any other way."

"Okay," Charlie said, making a decision. "I want to send one of my command staff to see your village, meet with your people, and these Mission X survivors. Can that meeting be unsupervised?"

"I can agree to that. Trust me, Commander, I know we eventually can come to many agreements. This I can, and will, guarantee."

"I'm glad to hear it," Charlie replied. "Will you be our guests for the night?"

"We would love to stay, but we need to get back to our people and let them know you are friendly."

"One more question, then, if you don't mind," Charlie said. "How is it that you were able to hide not only your life signs, but an entire village from our probes?"

Everyone looked at Anne Greene, waiting to hear her answer.

"That's one of the many things you will learn when you come to our village."

"And you will guarantee that whomever I send will be allowed to return to us? I will not take any chances with my people."

"Your people will be allowed to return to you. We will send a guide to take your person to and from our village."

Anne rose and motioned for her people to follow. Charlie followed them out and instructed the security team to escort them back to the edge of the southern holding and to fix the time for a trip the next day. Those inside had all relaxed at the same time in a collective sigh of relief.

"That didn't go too badly," said Captain Joe Malabar, Bill's second-in-command, to no one in particular.

"I don't know about that," said Danielle. "The commander didn't get any of the answers he wanted, and we still need to send someone to their village."

The conversation continued, and Kala listened to different people's thoughts on what Charlie should do. None of their suggestions included his going to the Taken's village. She wondered whom he would send and decided it would probably be Danielle or Bill. She was just about to say something to Danielle when Charlie came back into the room.

He pointed Bill, Danielle, Kala, and Joe Malabar toward the furthest corner of the room.

Once they were huddled together, he said, "We need to decide who's going to their village tomorrow. I have a person in mind, but I want to make sure you all concur."

The four exchanged glances.

"I say Bill," Kala spoke up quietly. "He has both the security training to defend himself and the diplomacy skills to negotiate as needed."

Danielle and Joe nodded their heads in agreement.

"I agree," Charlie said. He turned to Bill.

"First thing tomorrow, you are to go to their village and scope out the situation. Get as much information as possible, and try to make visual recordings without them knowing. I want to know exactly what's going on there. I also want to know what kind of society they have created and if either the low-techs or high-techs among us will be able to blend in with, or at least work with, them in the future. Questions?"

"Not at the moment," Bill said shaking his head. "If I think of anything between now and when I leave, I'll let you know. I'll ready a small bag with some simple things we won't mind them seeing. If there really are aliens here, I'm betting there are Earth items they'd be interested in that won't matter if they're seen. I'll see you before I leave in the morning."

"You might want to take a change of clothes." Charlie said. "You never know if you'll want to...or be invited to...stay the night," he amended after getting curious looks from the others.

"Never thought of that," said Bill. "I'll run everything but the clothes by you in the morning before I leave."

After Bill left, Kala tried unsuccessfully to stifle a yawn before giving in.

"It's been a long day for all of us," Danielle said, smiling. "What do you say you order us to make it an early night, Commander?"

"I don't think I need to make it an order," he said smiling back, "but I will suggest it. We're in for a rough couple of days, and I think we need to grab our rest when we can. Malabar, I want you to spread the word there'll be a full meeting Friday night here in the main square. Bill should be back by then and we'll have had time to analyze what he's learned and examine any recordings. I want to make sure everyone is kept informed about what we know." He turned to the rest of the room and raised his voice to include everyone in his remarks. "If anyone in this room hears gossip or rumors about our visitors, I want you to send the person to one of the command staff, and we will set them straight. Is that clear to everyone?"

When he was satisfied with the response, he dismissed everyone to go about their business, suggesting they have an early night. He turned back to Joe Malabar for final orders.

But before he could speak to Joe, the leader of the dissenters approached Charlie, contract in hand.

"Commander, we were going to accept your proposal, but after what we've seen and heard today about the existence of this village and Mission X survivors, we have changed our minds. We want to stay and be a part of the settlement."

Charlie stared intently at the man, wondering if the change of heart was some ploy.

"You understand what staying here means?"

The man nodded and said, "We are willing to take care of the higher-tech machines and tools, if you let us."

"And are you willing to abide by our rules?"

"Yes."

Hoping he was making the right decision, Charlie made up his mind.

"Okay, you can stay."

The man handed Charlie the contract, shook his hand, and left.

Joe Malabar and Danielle had observed the exchange and were now grimly shaking their heads.

Charlie turned to Joe.

"You heard all this?"

Joe sighed and nodded.

"I was going to tell you to double the security team around the sensitive material because of our visitors. Now we have another reason. If you notice anything suspicious, I want it dealt with first and brought to my attention second."

"Yes, sir!"

"And I want no harm to come to anybody. Is that also clear?" He waited and Joe nodded.

"Good. Captain Malabar, one more thing...if you don't mind."

Charlie smiled and told Danielle to go. She already knew what Charlie was going to tell Joe; there was no reason to hear it again.

"Kala has moved into my quarters," he said softly. "If there is any need for either one of us, she will be in one of my guest rooms for the time being."

Joe nodded and looked at Charlie expectantly, to see if Charlie would say more. When he was silent, Joe nodded again and left. Charlie and Kala walked silently back to their housing unit. Once there, Kala dropped into the nearest chair.

"What a day," she sighed. "I guess we're not going to have many down days for a while."

"Would you rather be busy or bored?"

Kala laughed, rising to get a drink. Showing the bottle of fruit juice to Charlie, she poured two glasses. Settled down with their drinks, they reviewed the day's exciting events. Soon, Kala yawned again and stood up with a back-cracking stretch.

"Time to get some rest," she said. "I, for one, could use it."

She leaned over Charlie, who was still sitting in his chair, and kissed him on the head.

"I think for tonight, it would be best if we slept in separate rooms. What do you think, Prince Charming?"

"I think you're right," he replied, reaching around and pulling her into his lap. "This one time, I'm not going to argue the point. Rest well, my smiley one, and dream only good dreams."

He kissed her gently and released her, giving her a push off his lap. She laughed and tussled his hair on the way to her room. Once in her room, she sat down on her bed with a long sigh. She was so exhausted she couldn't move. But, after a minute, she got up and got ready for bed. Climbing into bed, she was convinced she wouldn't be able to fall asleep thinking about everything that had happened. The next thing she knew someone was knocking on the door and calling her name.

"Kala, it's time to get up," she heard through the door.

"Can't I have five more minutes, please?" she asked plaintively.

"Nope, I've given you all the time I can. I let you sleep in while I got ready, so it's your turn."

"Okay, okay, you slave driver. I'm up," she said swinging her feet onto the floor.

She sat, eyes closed, before pushing herself from the bed. She grabbed her clothes and headed to the bathroom. As she bathed and dressed, she heard Charlie in the kitchen preparing breakfast and she smiled to herself. By the time she entered the kitchen, she was more awake, and the smell of Charlie's cooking was making her stomach rumble. She saw that Charlie had set the table and laid out food, coffee, and fresh juice.

"This looks great," she said, sitting down.

After eating breakfast and cleaning up the kitchen, they grabbed their gear and headed to the command center. Bill was waiting for them in Charlie's office when they arrived.

"Any last minute instructions, Boss?"

"Nothing that I can think of. You're more than qualified to think on your feet, and you've worked long enough with me to know what kind of intel I want. I trust you'll also gather what we need to know about these Taken people and the Mission X survivors."

Bill nodded as he bent over to pick up his gear. He stopped in mid-action and stood back up again, looking at Charlie and Kala.

"How do I get in touch with you if I run into trouble?"

"Use your radio. If we don't hear from you by breakfast tomorrow morning, we'll send a recon and recovery team to get you and as many of the survivors as possible. However, we hope you gain their trust so they'll want to work with us. Just do your best, Bill. I'm sure that you will get us the intel we need, and you'll find out what they want from us. I need to decide if we should send for more people from Earth, and I need to decide quickly."

Bill nodded again, picked up his gear, and headed toward the door. Charlie and Kala followed him out into the square, where they met Danielle on her way to the office. Charlie, Kala, and Danielle as well as a small group, already at work for the day, stopped on the far edge of the square and watched Bill enter the woods. There was a sense of excitement as they saw some of yesterday's visitors greet him and watched Bill disappear into the woods with the Takens.

CHAPTER 26

Bill was still trying to think of a way to start conversation when the guide turned to him.

"What brought your ship to this particular planet? Surely you couldn't have known about the atmosphere and that it would eventually trap you here."

"You're correct. We only had cursory scans of the planet, and the early probes didn't get far enough into the atmosphere to give us truly good information. We came here because, after analysis, we believed the planet would support life without needing domes. It seemed like an ideal place for us to settle. Our scans didn't completely cover this area of landmass or we would have noticed your village as well."

Bill's last statement was met with silence, and they continued walking.

Clearly interested in what Bill had offered, the guide asked, "Do you think that if we hadn't wanted to be seen, we wouldn't have been, no matter how sophisticated your equipment?"

"I don't understand what you're getting at," Bill replied, puzzled. "Obviously, we didn't know you were here. Like I said, our probes didn't come far enough into the atmosphere. How would we have known you were here?"

"Let me ask this, then. Shouldn't your initial probes, or even the probes from your ship, have picked up a civilization no matter how small? Surely buildings grouped together and the ambient body heat would have been noticed?"

"What if your society were living in a cave system of some sort? Many

169

societies do live that way. Our probes wouldn't have picked up people living in caves. Any life signs would have been chalked up to indigenous life. If we *had* found humanoid life, we would have either moved on or landed and settled in a place that was far enough away to avoid contact for a few years until we were ready."

"But you won't even consider that we might have the technology to hide ourselves from your sensors?"

"I didn't say that. I'm just trying to throw other options out there."

The guide nodded and walked on in silence. Bill knew there was something the guide wanted from him, but he couldn't tell exactly what it was. He'd have to make sure to mention these questions in his report. As they neared their destination, Bill heard the daily industry of many people. When they came out of the woods and the village came into view, Bill stopped dead in his tracks and stared in astonishment. His guide had gone a few more steps before he realized that Bill had stopped. For some reason, the first thing that came to Bill's mind was that he didn't even know his guide's name.

"You do realize I don't even know your name."

"I am Chalara Dow," he replied, smiling at the incongruity of the statement. "Is that all you can say at your first sight of our little village?"

"Little village?" Bill asked, a bit incensed. "Now I know why you kept pushing me with your questions. What do you have? An invisibility field? A force field? Or is it a cloak...or whatever you want to call it. We should have seen this place! We should have known you were here!"

"It is proof to us that our shield works. We were given the schematics and the materials to build it from our Takers, but we weren't sure it would really work. It's nice to know that it does. Does it worry you?"

"A bit, yes. It makes me wonder...if something bad were to happen... would you help us protect ourselves."

"You don't have to worry about that," Chalara said after a pause. "The Takers tend to hide the entire planet and only show it to those they want to reveal it to. Because of their previous encounters with humans, they feel the race is worth saving, so they have shown humans the way here."

By now, they had entered the village proper, and Bill was trying to absorb as much as he could. He could see right off that it wasn't very high-tech. There was some technology, but only basic street lighting and, from what he could see through the windows of buildings, basic low-tech computers, like the ones that would have been used on Earth in the late twentieth and early twenty-first century. He saw a few people had handheld units of some kind and assumed that these people were part of the ruling body.

Looking around, Bill noticed the most common form of transportation was an eight-legged beast that looked like a combination of an ox and a horse. As he stopped to watch, he realized the beasts were elegant despite the extra legs. He saw other animals that bore a strong resemblance to those on Earth, but had very visible differences. The chickens and roosters had fewer feathers, but the feathers they did have were a strange confluence of colors, like bright orange and pink.

The buildings, on the other hand, were almost identical to ones in pictures he had seen of ancient American Indian cliff dwellings, maybe even old Mexican dwellings. He would decide later for his report which they reminded of him more. The buildings had many windows and the exteriors were made of what looked to be a mud mixture. The mixture was probably smoothed over a thatch of some sort, but there were no cracks. They seemed very well-built.

The clothing the people wore looked sturdy and was loose-fitting and airy, appropriate for tropical weather. Most of the cloth was cut in a plain style but brightly colored with geometric shapes. Briefly, Bill wondered if he would be able to learn their secret for making the dyes; he knew some of the people in the colony would love the colors.

As they continued to walk along, Bill saw the village wasn't quite as big as it first appeared. It was larger than he had expected, yes, but not as large as his first impression. It appeared the architecture and gardening layouts were used to the residents' advantage, and Bill began to wonder if these people had actually built the village. He turned to ask his guide but, seeing the intent look on the man's face, decided to remain silent. There would be time later for questions. Instead, he followed the man's gaze and saw he was looking at Anne Greene. Chalara led him over to the woman.

She motioned for them to follow her into a building that appeared to be in the village's center. If the room they entered was any indication to Bill of how the residents lived, he thought they lived well but not overly well. The interior was furnished with beautifully carved wooden tables, chairs, and benches. The walls were painted with earthy tones, and the furniture had been left its natural color. Before sitting down, Anne turned to one of the women in the room and whispered to her. When she was done, she sat down across from her guest.

"We're glad your group decided to send a representative to visit us," she started. "We don't want to change the way you are setting up your colony, but we do feel that certain things have to be worked out in order for us to live together in harmony."

"I agree."

"We realize that you are here to find a new home for humans, but there are a few things you need to understand about us. We are humans. As I told you yesterday, we are those who have been taken, throughout the years, by aliens. These aliens could see many hundreds...maybe even thousands... of years ago that while humanity is an intelligent race, we were dooming our planet to eventual death. Long before our sun went out, or some other natural disaster hit Earth, we would be in danger of extinction. They felt our race had promise so they decided to save what they thought were the best of us."

She paused as a group of women brought in food and drinks and put them on one of the side tables.

"Why didn't they just take everyone at once?" Bill asked.

"I'm getting there, no need to jump ahead," she chided. "They knew that those left on Earth would still need leaders, so they left some behind, knowing that we, the Taken...we call ourselves that name as well...would still flourish. They had hopes that one day those left behind would find their own way to the stars and meet up with those who had been taken."

"What about those who were taken and sent back? I've read these people spent years...some, the rest of their lives...being ridiculed for what happened to them. Why were they sent back?"

"The Takers wanted to make sure that the human race on Earth had leaders. Before they were sent back, those being returned were enhanced at the DNA level to ensure their offspring could lead the charge to send humans into space. I know it seems...because humans were enhanced... like we didn't accomplish space travel or create other groundbreaking technologies on our own." Anne looked pointedly Bill. "We did, but in less time than it would have taken without the Takers' help. We might not have made it into space before we doomed ourselves or another race doomed us. We are a good race, if we try to be. That is one of the things we have learned here over the years."

"What about this village? How long have you been here?"

"This village has been here for about one thousand years. This planet was known to have certain powers that could extend human life and give us a chance to live to our true potential," Anne answered with a tone of finality.

"Now, I don't think telling you everything at one sitting is a good idea. I've given you enough information to take back to your leaders. What I'd like to do now is give you a chance to look around and see what our community is all about. But I will tell you one more thing before you do go. Our Takers have created different communities throughout the galaxy.

Ours is a community primarily of artists. We grow our own food and fend for ourselves. We've given up the practice of eating meat protein and other foods that involve the killing or harming of animals. The animal skins we wear are from our farm animals that have died naturally. We don't kill animals ourselves, but we won't stop you if that is part of your belief system. We want that to be known."

"Will I be allowed to speak freely with the members of your community?"

"Yes, we hide nothing. We are okay if you find out something I was planning on telling you later. I just don't want to overload you with too much."

"What about the people from the Mission X expedition? Will I be allowed to see them as well? My commander will want a report on their condition."

"Of course you will be allowed to see them. I'll take you to them myself. I see you've brought an overnight bag; we have a room set up if you want to stay the night. If you have seen enough today, you'll be guided home, but if you do want to stay, you will be more than welcome."

Bill nodded, satisfied. "I'll decide later if I want to stay. May I leave my bag somewhere?"

"I'll take you to the room we set aside for you. Then we'll go to where the Mission X people are staying."

"Thank you." Bill turned to leave, then stopped. He faced Anne with a smile on his face. "One last question... Does this planet have a name?"

Anne smiled in return. "We call the planet and our village Haven...for that is what it is."

As they walked through the village, the people greeted Anne and smiled and nodded to Bill. On the surface, they seemed to be an open, honest people, but from his years in the service, Bill knew that looks could be deceiving.

The people seemed to be a mix of ethnic backgrounds—Asian, Hispanic, Anglo-American, Black. A strong mix of people, like their own group. Bill wondered how the Takers chose who to pick when visiting Earth all those years ago.

"Do you need time to refresh yourself, or would you like to go on?" Anne asked when they reached the room.

"I'd like to go on," he replied. "I was never much for relaxation."

Bill glanced briefly around the room, tossed his bag onto the bed, and returned to Anne who was waiting outside the door with a man. She led the way to the quarters where the Mission X people lived.

As they reached a building at the edge of the village, Anne took Bill's arm, "I want to warn you; going in and out of the atmosphere did a lot of mental damage to them." Pointing to the man, she said, "He will show you around when you're done." Then she left Bill standing in front of the building.

He could see that the back of the building faced the forest and the front had a large garden. He watched the man unlock the door and found that a bit odd, but he didn't say anything. Bill walked alone into the building. The first thing he noticed was the muted lighting. The decorations—paint, wall hangings, and window coverings—all seemed to serve the purpose of keeping out the light and muting the sounds of the outside world. It took a moment for his eyes to adjust to the resulting gloom. Once his eyes had become accustomed, he realized that the first floor was all one room.

Bill looked closer and saw a group of people hovering in the corner farthest from the door. He slowly walked toward them and found that the closer he got, the further they cowered into the corner. He stopped and considered what he should do next. Then he saw a table and chairs near the opposite wall. He walked over to the chairs and sat down. At first, he smiled at the group, but they only stared back at him. Finally, he decided that, if he wanted to converse with them, he had to do something nonthreatening. He patted his pants pockets and felt the field rations he'd brought with him. Slowly, he pulled out the bars and put them on the table. One by one, he unwrapped the bars and broke them into small pieces. He laid one piece in front of each chair at the table, including his own. The leftover pieces, he placed in the center of the table. Taking the piece in front of him, he slowly began to eat.

One at a time, the people in the corner came to the table and sat down in the chairs. They each picked up the food and, after a brief inspection, began to eat. When they had finished their one piece, they looked at Bill and then at the bars in the middle of the table. To show them it was okay to take more, he took one of those pieces and began to eat it.

After several minutes, Bill addressed them quietly. "My name is Bill Chow. I recently arrived from Earth. What are your names? Are they treating you well?"

They jumped at the sound of his voice and stopped eating, but they didn't leave the table.

"I am Joanna Carson, and we are being treated well," a woman across from him finally replied.

"Why are they keeping you apart?"

No one seemed to want to speak. Finally, Joanna spoke again.

"We suffer from visions and trances and can get violent when they happen. But we clearly remember what happened afterward. The others know we don't mean to hurt anyone and understand the reason we are violent, but still, for all concerned, it's best if we stay isolated. We are free to move about if someone accompanies us...and we do go out from time to time...but our trances tend to happen more often when we do go out. So we prefer to stay here."

Bill asked more questions about their daily life and if they did anything to help support the community.

"We mostly weave and create art here in this room. One of our people is a doctor and has a clinic set up in rooms by the garden. But it is best we stay secluded; we don't want to hurt anyone." She looked at Bill earnestly. "We really are happy here. The Taken have treated us well. We are free to do as we please and we have many friends. We know why we experience the trances and visions, and we accept full responsibility for our condition."

She paused, then continued, "Don't think it isn't hard, sometimes, being alone here, but all life is often hard. There is no reason for us to leave, even if we wanted to. You can take the message back that we are doing well here."

Bill silently acknowledged her words before responding.

"Anne will be able to get in touch with us. If you need us for anything, you can contact us. If nothing else, our commander will feel better just knowing you can contact us."

"Thank you, Mr. Chow. We appreciate the offer. Ever since we heard about your landing, we've been making something for your community." One of the group got up and brought a vase back to the table. "Please take this as a token of our esteem."

Taking the vase, Bill thanked the woman. Admiring it, he looked inside and noticed a piece of notepaper. He acted as if he hadn't seen it.

"This is very beautiful. Thank you again. I'd like to return to my settlement tonight; I have much to tell my commander. But I will visit again another day, and someone else will come for a visit soon."

As he was leaving, he juggled the vase and secretly removed the paper, putting it into his pocket. He met his guide and asked to take a different route back to the room and his bag. He stopped a few times as he walked and talked to people; however, he couldn't escape the feeling that there was more to the village than what he had seen.

When he reached the room, he looked for a secluded place to read the note the Mission X people had given him. Spotting a closed door, he opened it and found a bathroom. He quickly stepped inside, closed the door, and pulled out the paper. He was surprised to find that, instead of a plea for help, he was reading a plea for updated medical information and supplies. He reread the note again to make sure there was no coded message. He put the note back in his pocket then flushed the toilet to provide the reason for using the bathroom. He repacked his bag to fit in the vase and left the room.

"Would it be possible to meet with Anne Greene again?" he asked his guide outside his door.

"Just follow me, sir."

As they made their way through the streets, Bill noted scenes of the bustling community around him. People were doing laundry, grinding grain, weeding gardens, and many other work activities; it seemed to be a well-run community. Yet something still bothered him. He would make sure someone came back for a longer period of time, but with the note weighing heavily on his mind, he needed to return and report to Charlie. When they reached the building where he had met Anne before, he was ushered inside.

"I can see you are going to return today. I had hoped you would stay for the evening and spend more time with us." Anne looked disappointed.

"I would very much like to, but I'm sure you can understand that Commander Hudson is waiting to hear my preliminary report. I can guarantee we will send someone back to spend more time getting to know you better." He smiled, "I can even make a guess who that person will be."

"I understand. We still have some of the communication devices you use; we should keep a line open between our people."

Thinking quickly, Bill picked a channel that he knew wouldn't be used by his people and gave the number to Anne. He received a promise from her that if the Mission X group asked to speak with him or anyone else in his colony, they would be allowed to do so. Anne called in Chalara Dow to lead Bill back.

"I really don't need a guide," Bill protested.

"We don't want you getting lost along the way. The forest can be dense this time of year."

"I have a photographic memory and am an expert tracker," Bill smiled. "I remember perfectly how we got here. Just take me to where we entered the village and I will find my way back. Besides, I would enjoy the time alone," he laughed, "and it will do me good to get a good fast hike in."

"Well, if you're sure... We will monitor the designated channel until you signal that you are safely back. Please allow me this, or I wouldn't feel like I have been a good host."

Bill took his radio and programmed it to the agreed upon channel. He saluted Anne in farewell, turned, and walked from the room with Chalara a step ahead of him. From there, it took only minutes to reach the edge of the village where he had first entered.

"You are sure you don't need a guide?" Chalara asked.

"I'm sure," Bill replied. "Remind Anne I'll contact her when I get back to the colony. It shouldn't take me more than an hour and a half or so."

Chalara nodded his head in reply and turned back. Bill entered the wood and began the return trip. He knew it would only take him about an hour because of the markers he had placed on the way there. When he felt he was far enough from the village, he turned on the homing beacon that would lead him from marker to marker. Photographic memory or not, he felt better using the technology.

As he walked, he realized that Chalara had taken him to a different entry point into the forest than where they had entered that morning. He assumed they were testing him, but he wasn't bothered. He was sure that just as he had sized them up they were now doing the same. But he didn't fully relax until he found the first marker. As he would at each one, he picked it up and stowed it in his bag.

Once he was well on his way and had found the second and, then, the third marker, he let his mind wander back over the day and began to formulate his report for Charlie, Danielle, and Kala. By the time he had reached the colony an hour later, he was ready to report to Charlie and the rest. After his promised communication with Anne Greene, he went in search of the command staff. He found everyone at a bonfire in the main square and wondered what the special occasion was. He saw Charlie in a group of people, laughing at some joke, and headed in that direction.

"What are you doing back here?" Charlie asked surprised.

"I heard you were having a party...and you know how I hate to miss a party," Bill joked, though Charlie could see his eyes were serious. "We need to talk," he whispered into Charlie's ear.

"I'll get Danielle and Kala, and we'll meet you at your place."

Bill nodded and left for his housing unit. He heard a knock on his front door just as he pulled his shirt off.

"Come in," he called from the bedroom.

He heard Kala, Danielle, and Charlie enter the living area talking quietly.

"I'll be right out. I need to change so I'm not too stinky for you all. Look at the vase and read the paper next to it while you wait. I think it's the best place to start."

While Bill changed, Charlie silently read the note, and Danielle and

Kala examined the vase. When Charlie finished, they exchanged items. Danielle read and reread the note, then gave it to Kala.

"Do you have anything to drink around here, Bill?" Danielle called to him. "I have a feeling we're going to need it for this discussion."

"I sure do," Bill said laughing, as he came out of the bedroom and headed to the kitchen area.

Bill spent the next hour briefing the others, followed by three hours of their going over everything in detail.

"I think we need to make a tough decision," Charlie said finally.

"What's that?" asked Bill pouring himself another drink.

"Whether or not to stay here or move to another part of the continent. The feeling I get is that there's something about these people you don't quite trust but can't name at this point. I agree we need to have someone spend more time there, but I had the same feeling when we met with Anne. I don't like it. We need to decide if we should move."

"I think we've already used up too much of our resources to move anywhere. I think we need to find a way to make this work here," Kala said.

The others were silent as they each considered her view. Finally, Charlie stood up and went to the window by the door. He watched the people cleaning up after the bonfire. Bill and Danielle stared into their glasses. Kala watched Charlie.

Finally Kala spoke again. "I don't think any decisions should be made without consulting the colony. That's one of the reasons we came here, isn't it, to have a more open and democratic society? I think someone else needs to go back to the Taken community for a few days, at least, and learn more about what their village and the people are like. Only then can the question be brought to our entire colony."

"I agree," Charlie responded. "I think Bill's right in that either Kala or Danielle should be the one to go. Do I have a volunteer?"

"I'll go," said Kala. "From what Bill described, I think I'll have an easier time fitting in. I think three days ought to do it, and while I'm gone, you and Bill can brief the leadership committee about what he learned on his trip."

"I think you should wait," Charlie said. "That way if any questions come up that people want answered, you can bring them with you."

Kala agreed then got up and walked around restlessly. She got herself another drink and continued pacing around the room.

"What bug's got into you all of a sudden?" asked Danielle.

"After everything we've been through and now this, I suddenly feel a bit overwhelmed, that's all. Give me a few minutes and I'll be fine," she reassured them.

"A bit overwhelmed, she says," said Danielle jumping up from her chair. "She volunteers to go on an important mission and she feels a bit overwhelmed!"

"Oh, clam up, Danielle," Kala snapped back. "I may not be as seasoned as you are at your ripe old age, but at least, I'm admitting to my fears! Would you do the same, or would you still maintain the same cold exterior you always project?"

The two women glared at each other. Danielle dropped her eyes first and looked down at her empty glass.

"I'm sorry," Kala said softly. "I guess we're all a bit jumpy these days, finding out we're not alone after all."

Suddenly, a thought occurred to Kala and she turned to Bill.

"Did the others say if the Takers had returned recently?"

The look on Bill's face answered her question.

"You know, I didn't even think to ask," he said slightly abashed.

"Did they mention how they were able to run the machines that hid them or if it was automated?"

Bill shrugged his "no."

"Well, I guess I'd better draw up a list of questions we want answered and see if the leadership committee have their own before I leave. We'll review it before I go. Right now, I think I'd like to go home and relax. Some time alone would do me good."

Kala left for the housing unit. About halfway there, she stopped and changed direction and went back into the center of the village to pick up fresh produce. Then she went to the unit. Charlie still wasn't there when she arrived, so she started cooking. Knowing that he probably wouldn't eat right while she was gone and that he would probably stay up late drinking with Bill, she decided to leave some prepared food for him. Cooking also helped steady her nerves. While a pasta sauce was bubbling on the stove, she started making a batch of the salad dressing that Charlie liked so much. When that was done, she was about to make Charlie's favorite bean dish when he walked in the door. He came into the kitchen area, took her by the shoulders, and turned her toward him.

"So, what's really bothering you?" he asked gently, "When you should be resting, instead, you're cooking away!"

"Everything...nothing...I don't really know. I guess that I'm suddenly realizing this is all for real. It's not one of my books and it's not a dream I'll wake up from. I'm on a planet we thought was uninhabited, and now I'm going to meet with people who have lived here longer than I care to think about. On the surface they seem benign, but from Bill's report, they could be hiding a secret that could destroy us all. This is a critical assignment and I don't feel up to the job."

"If you'd rather, I can send Danielle."

"No, I need to go, if for no other reason than to prove that I can do it. But something *is* bothering me. Are they still getting intelligence about Earth? I mean, didn't Bill say Anne knew that our reason for coming here was that Earth was in trouble?"

Charlie didn't answer right away, and Kala began to wonder if she had heard Bill correctly.

"You heard him right," he said reading the look on her face. He shook his head. "I just hope that we can work with these people. I'm going to contact WASA, and I hope we'll get a response before you leave. Bill said he'd contact Anne when you're ready to leave. She'll send someone to guide you to their village. I'm authorizing you to stay for three days, but if, for any reason, you feel the need to come back early or to stay longer, go ahead. Just let me know."

Kala sighed gratefully and turned back to the stove to give the sauce a stir. She grabbed the bag of fresh beans and started preparing them to marinate.

"What's all this?" Charlie asked, taking the hint of a subject change.

"I want you to eat well while I'm gone. You'll probably stay up all night drinking with Bill on an empty stomach, so I'm making some meals for you. I figured we can also stock up the freezer unit. And I just felt like cooking. It helps calm me."

"Looks like you're making some of my favorite dishes."

"Nothing but the best for my commander."

"And for your housemate?"

"Get me some of the packaged beans from the cabinet," was her laughing reply.

They laughed and joked as he helped her finish preparing the bean dish.

"Why don't you take some of this with you?" Charlie asked suddenly.

"It had crossed my mind, but I don't want to weigh myself down. I can take the recipes. Food is always a good treaty maker. I'm hoping I will be able to learn more about their ways of preserving so we can use them here. When the colder weather hits, we can be more prepared."

"Food is always a means to common ground," Charlie said nodding his approval.

He was always amazed at Kala's ability to think on her feet. From the first day that she had agreed to join his mission, she had dealt with everything that had been thrown at her. Scared as she might be at the moment, he was sure she had been scared before, and she had made it through.

"What's different about this trip that's making you nervous?" he asked as they jarred the sauce and beans.

"I'll be totally on my own," she replied after thinking about the question.

"You were alone when you came on Sierra," he replied gently.

"That's not quite what I meant. What I'm saying is that, for the first time, I'll be the sole representative of our group. There'll be no one to back me up and no one to ask if I'm doing the right thing. When I came on Sierra, I was going away from my family and friends, yes, but there was always someone to back me up when I made a decision or gave an order. Now, I'll be alone with no backup."

"You'll always have backup. Bill knows how to get there; you'll have radio contact; and if you need to, you can turn on your tracker and get the hell out. Once you're a safe distance away, you can contact us by radio and we'll come get you."

"Yes, but that'll take time and what if I don't have time? What happens if I get put into that room with the Mission X group, and they won't let me go? I'm sure if that happens, they will have taken my radio and all my other gear. There'll be no way to get in touch with you."

"And I'm sure you know that if you're not in contact at designated times and there is no explanation from Anne or her people, we will send someone to look for you. Kala, you have to start believing in yourself at some point. The sooner you start truly believing in yourself, the sooner you will be able to accomplish what we need you to do."

Chapter 27

The rest of the afternoon, Kala finished her cooking and gathered supplies for her trip. She took three days' worth of clothes and a battery backup for her radio—just in case. Packing completed, she called to Charlie, who was out in the garden weeding, to see what he wanted for the evening meal. The next day was going to be a long one, and she wanted to relax and go to bed early.

While they were eating, they went over what might come up in the leadership committee meeting the next day. When Kala stood up to do the dishes, Charlie waived her back into her seat.

"You've done enough for today. Relax for a little bit. You have long days ahead of you."

She nodded gratefully, sitting back down in her chair.

"Do you think you'll need something to help you sleep tonight?"

"I think I'd better not. I don't want to be muddled in the morning, and I'm afraid that, if I take something, I will be."

"I wasn't thinking of giving you anything medicinal," he replied with a sly grin, and putting his hand on her thigh.

"Nice try, Romeo," she said swatting his hand away with a laugh. "I need to get a good night's sleep and that won't help!"

She stood up and gave him a kiss to soften the comment. He put his arms around her, and they stood arms entwined, just simply being in each other's embrace. When Kala finally broke the hug, she felt calmer than she had all day. She went to the cooling unit and pulled out a flask of water before going to her room to sleep.

The next morning, she awoke earlier than usual and lay in bed listening to the sounds of her world. Reluctantly, she got up and plunged into her morning routine. After showering, when she was back in her room getting dressed, she heard Charlie moving around. By the time she was dressed, her stomach was rumbling, reacting to the smells of whatever Charlie was cooking for breakfast.

"Something smells wonderful," she said as she walked out into the common room.

They sat down and ate breakfast in silence. When Kala was done, she sat quietly and looked around the room. She had a feeling, and recently, she had learned to trust her feelings. She got up and went to her room, searching for her pictures of family and friends. She had a hunch that these would be a way to break the ice and make a bridge between her and the Taken.

"Find what you were looking for?" Charlie asked when she came back.

"It's just an idea, but I think these holo pics and some recipes will be the key."

"The key to what?"

"Breaking the ice with the people in the village. Shouldn't we be on our way to the leadership committee meeting?"

Charlie looked at his watch and agreed they should, indeed, be on their way. Kala grabbed her gear and they walked to the community center. While they waited for the others to arrive, Kala contacted Anne Greene to let her know to send the guide.

The meeting was going quickly and smoothly, and Kala was relieved that they were taking so well to her idea of sharing something of Earth with the Taken, when a committee member suddenly spoke out.

"This is how you plan to root out a possible conspiracy? By sharing recipes and pictures?"

"Bill never said there was a conspiracy," Kala said. "All he said was that something didn't feel right. He seemed to think they weren't telling us everything. That could mean they are holding something back for our own good or there is something they are embarrassed to tell us. We'll just have to wait and see."

They concluded the meeting with wishes for Kala's safe journey and a successful visit. When they walked out, Kala could see that her guide was already there, talking to a few members of the community. She walked over to him to introduce herself and found that it was Chalara Dow, the same man who had guided Bill. She gave Charlie a kiss before shouldering her pack and left the camp with a straight back and butterflies in her belly.

They walked most of the way to the village in silence, and Kala relished being able to observe the nature of her new world. When they got close to the village, Chalara stopped and turned toward her.

"We have a problem in our community that we're hoping you can help us with."

"What's that?"

"We were wondering about the medical advances on Earth. Our medical technology is severely out-of-date and our people may suffer from the lack of current medical knowledge. Do you think it would be possible for you to help us?"

"I don't see why not. I'll see what you need when we get to your settlement. Is there something specific you're looking for?"

"There are many things, but Anne is reticent to ask for help, and I don't want her to know I'm asking you. It's been many years since we've had any contact with the Takers, and we fear something may have happened to them. We used to get regular shipments and updates but..." he shrugged helplessly.

"Is this what you held back from Bill when he visited you?"

Chalara nodded.

"It would help, when I talk to Commander Hudson, to have a list of what you need, but I think we should be able to help out"

Chalara sighed with relief before turning and moving forward once again. Once they entered the village, Kala was led to where she would stay.

"I'll let Anne know you're here. You are free to walk the settlement with the exception of the Mission X building. You'll need someone to go with you to visit them. It's regulation, so please don't try and see them without a guard or me to go with you."

Making a decision, Kala hesitated then spoke softly, "Chalara, they sent a message back with Bill; they were also asking for updated medical information and supplies. Do you know anything about that?"

"They didn't mention anything to me about it, and I see them almost every day. When I told them you were coming, they seemed to think they would be able to contact their families on Earth. We told them we weren't sure but that you would know. They only want to let their families know they're okay. Honestly, that's all there is to it, and if they implied anything else, they haven't told us about it. Please believe me."

"I do believe you, Chalara. I'm not here to pass judgment. I'm just here to learn more about your community and tell you a bit more about ours. You don't have any reason to lie to me. Right now, I don't think otherwise."

Chalara left her in her quarters, and Kala briefly checked in with

Charlie, deciding to wait to tell him of Chalara's request until she had more information. She settled herself, putting away her things. Soon, she heard a knock at the door. Kala called "Enter" and found herself looking at Anne. They stood taking the measure of each other before Anne spoke.

"I hope your journey to our village was a good one."

"It was very nice. Chalara is a good guide." Kala motioned to the door. "I was wondering when I might start looking around."

"You're free to start immediately, just as long as you understand the rules about seeing the Mission X people."

"I was told that I needed to contact a guard or Chalara whenever I wanted to go there...for my own protection."

Anne nodded. From Kala's observation of the woman, she wasn't much older than herself. Kala wondered if she'd have the same slight lines around her mouth and eyes and the same graying at the temples after a few years of being in a leadership position. The two women eyed each other again before Kala turned away and walked over to the window.

"This is a lovely place you have here. From my short time walking to this dwelling, I can see that everyone seems happy and well-established in their tasks."

"We try to make it so. It isn't always easy, and there have been times of strife, but we found years ago that by keeping things simple, we can keep people happier. It's worked for us. But over the past few generations, we have found that we've been having fewer and fewer babies. We don't know why."

"Maybe you need some new blood to invigorate your bloodlines."

"Maybe. There are many things we need, and I believe there are many things you will soon find you need in your settlement. We are a friendly people and truly want to be friends and allies with you and your people, Kala. We're not going to change now. I hope that, if nothing else, you take this with you from your visit."

"May I look around now and speak with the people?"

"Of course! Just remember to let someone know if you want to go to the Mission X building." Anne looked thoughtfully at Kala. "Has anyone explained the reason for this precaution to you?"

Kala shook her head.

"We think that, when they tried to go back to their mission ship, the acclimation change back to their atmosphere did something to their body chemistry. We found they now have mental powers that they can't control. They go into trances and have visions of the future. But they only go into trances when something bad is going to happen... They have saved us from disaster more than once. But they get very violent during the trance and are sick for days afterward. When they first started having these visions, they would remember the vision but not being violent. After a time, they began to remember everything." Anne's voice took a pleading tone. "If you believe nothing else, please believe that it was their idea to be kept apart. Now when one of them has a vision, the others are there to keep the one calm. Once the trance is over they report it to us, and we act to deal with the prediction." Anne stared into Kala's eyes. "Do you believe me?"

Kala said nothing, mulling over what Anne had said. Then she nodded. For now, she had no reason to doubt the woman, but she knew she would have to find out for herself. Kala had a flash of doubt that she would be able to complete her mission, but pushed it away as fast as she could. She had to start trusting herself.

She smiled at Anne. "I'm ready to start looking around now, if you don't mind."

"That's fine. Just let us know if you need anything."

"I can talk to anyone, other than the Mission X people of course, without asking permission?"

"Yes."

"Thank you for all your help."

After Anne left, Kala sat at a table and made notes of her conversation with Anne about the Mission X crew. She knew that Charlie and the others would be very interested in that information. When she was done, she got ready to go out. Taking nothing but a bottle of water, she wandered into the streets. The first thing she noticed was how friendly everyone was. No one turned away from her, and everywhere she went, people offered her food and drink. When she felt hungry, she accepted samples of the food, and when her water ran out, she accepted a refill of whatever beverage was offered.

By the end of that first day, Kala knew her way around the village fairly well. She had spoken to many of the people and was getting a handle on how things were run. She enjoyed the quiet pace of things. No money was exchanged, as the village used a barter system. Anything and everything could be gotten for a trade. At first, she didn't think she had anything worth trading, but as soon as she found that the people enjoyed her ration bars, she entered into the bartering spirit. She even brought out a few of her food recipes and traded them for food she found more palatable. Knowing that Sierra settlement hoped to build a village like this someday, she also traded for some of the crafts and ways of making dye.

When she arrived back at her quarters for the night, she found that someone had left a meal for her on the table. Just as she was sitting down to eat, she heard a timid knock on the door. Looking at the food she sighed and got up to open the door. She was surprised to find a strange woman and man standing there. The man introduced the woman as a member of the Mission X crew. Kala realized he was the obligatory guard. She opened the door wider to let the woman in and motioned for the guard to wait outside.

"Let me know if there's a problem," he said as Kala shut the door.

"What can I do for you?" Kala asked the woman quietly.

"My name is Joanna Carson. We heard you were coming and had hoped to be able to give you a gift of our own. Since you didn't come to see us, I was elected to come see you and bring this gift to you. We're not all allowed out at once.

She handed Kala a small jar. Kala inspected it and was immensely impressed.

"Thank you very much. I know just where I'll put it when I get home. Was there anything else?"

"No, just that we hope we'll see you another day."

"Don't worry. I am planning on stopping by tomorrow and spending as much of the day with you as I can."

"That sounds nice. We don't get much company, and we'll be happy to spend time with someone new."

After the woman left, Kala made more notes about her first-day activities and the impromptu meeting before contacting Charlie.

Kala first relayed Chalara's request, adding she was waiting for the list of needed information and supplies. Then, she told him of her conversation with Anne. When they were wrapping up, she asked what her priority should be with the Mission X people.

"Just make sure they're being treated properly. I think that's all we can do at this point. I've sent a message to WASA to inform them of your visit. I'm not sure yet about sending more people here, but I did put the possibility out there. I don't want an issue with these people if we can help it. How is it there...really?"

"I think we can learn a lot from these people and vice versa. They know quite a bit about this planet that they can teach us, and there have been a lot of advancements on Earth that we can teach them. I think we'll be able to work well together."

"Just make sure you stay vigilant. We need to know if they are hiding anything other than needing updated medical and technology information, and we need to know soon."

"I don't think they're hiding anything from us. They're only naturally suspicious, just like we are. After this many years on their own, who wouldn't be? If we take things slowly, we'll be okay."

After signing off, Kala ate her dinner, trying to remember when she had last eaten such good food. The Sierra settlement gardens were only just starting to produce and the labs hadn't been able to synthesize good protein replacements. As she sopped the last of a delicious sauce with a piece of freshly baked bread, she sighed contentedly. She decided to put off dessert and take another quick walk around the village to see what went on during the evening.

CHAPTER 28

As she strolled through the village, Kala saw that many people ate outside, enjoying their meal in the mild evening air. She made a note to eat breakfast the next morning at a table outside her quarters. Changing her mind about when to see the Mission X crew, she decided to visit them then instead of waiting until the next morning. She went to the village headquarters to arrange for a guard. One was available and quickly assigned to Kala. With the guard escorting her, she headed to the Mission X building. She waited as the guard first unlocked the door and, then, knocked.

"You came tonight," said Joanna Carson in a surprised voice from where she stood inside the door. "We thought you weren't going to visit until tomorrow."

"I decided to take a walk and it led me here," Kala replied with a smile. "May I come in and visit?"

"Of course," replied Joanna as Kala moved past the guard and entered the room.

The guard entered behind Kala, closed and locked the door behind him, and retreated to the corner where other guards were sitting at a round table playing cards. Joanna led Kala to a large table in center of the room where the Mission X crew was just finishing up their evening meal. They made room for Kala to join them.

"I really would like to get to know you all. Once our colony is more settled, maybe we can find a way for you to come and visit us there."

Kala paused and looked at the faces around the table. They were silent. She spoke again.

"Was there something in particular you wanted to speak to me about?" she asked.

After hesitating, Joanna, who seemed to be the leader, answered.

"We were hoping that, maybe, there had been advances in medical science that could help us with our condition. We want to be more productive members of society, and we can't do that if we must stay in this building all the time."

Kala thought carefully about the request before replying.

"This is the third time someone has expressed a concern about medical issues. Chalara Dow asked about medical equipment and processes and there was the note you sent back with Bill Chow. Anne Lasson also expressed an interest in medical advances. I do believe we plan on including medical treatment in any agreement we make between our peoples."

Joanna nodded and seemed satisfied with Kala's response.

Kala spent the next hour talking with the Mission X crew, learning about them and the other inhabitants of the village. While they talked, Kala felt comfortable that they were not hiding anything.

The crew told her about how they had tried to go back to the ship after being acclimated to the planet.

"What exactly happened to the ship?" Kala asked, curious.

"After a few people had come down and gone through the change, we wondered if we'd be able to go back to the ship. We didn't have the more advanced equipment you have now, so we couldn't get the biological readings we needed to know for sure. We had large enough shuttles to get everyone and everything down in one shot. A few crewmembers wanted to go back to the ship and try to land the ship like we had planned. We filled the shuttle air supply with planet air as insurance and Jon took the minimum complement needed to land the ship. Jon and his crew began to have trouble breathing after getting the ship on its inbound trajectory; unfortunately, the reverse change didn't take effect immediately and the ship burned up in the atmosphere because of its incoming trajectory. That was the end." Joanna looked down at her hands briefly, then continued, "A group of us tried to take one of the remaining shuttles back into space... to radio for help...but had to turn back almost immediately because of mechanical problems. Soon after we were back on the planet, we were afflicted with the trances and visions foreseeing disasters, we think, because of our brief exposure to non-planet air."

"When did you meet these people?" Kala asked after a pause.

"Shortly after the shuttle landed, but before our affliction showed up," responded Joanna. "We were welcomed into the village and free to roam at first. When we starting falling into trances, no one knew what to do with us. It was finally decided that we'd be allowed to stay, but only if we agreed to be sequestered in the manner you find us now." Joanna smiled. "We are allowed to walk outside for exercise either in the early morning or in the evening when no one else is out and about. It's as much for our safety as it is for theirs. We don't want to hurt anyone; it is a frightening thing to see when we go into a trance, even for us."

"But you aren't being mistreated?"

"Not at all. We are given all we want or need to live. We also have our own gardens in back, and we trade the excess produce we can't use for what we can't grow or make ourselves. If we see something in a vision, we always call for Anne...or someone on the ruling committee...and let her know what we have seen because it usually affects the entire community."

Kala wanted to know more about the visions, but after a little more conversation, tiredness overtook her, and she begged off and rose to leave.

"I'll come and eat the midday meal with you tomorrow, if that's okay," she promised.

"That sounds wonderful," the doctor, Larla McCoy, said. "We eat at the same time everyone else takes their breaks."

Kala left, accompanied by her guard, and leisurely made her way back to her quarters. As they passed a house, the guard bid her good night and made to break off, saying this was his house, and he would leave her to continue to her quarters alone. Kala motioned him to stop, a question on her face.

"Back at the Mission X building I saw guards were inside. Why were they there?"

The guard smiled. "Anne has decided that rather than have you request a guard to accompany you each time you go there, it would be easier for you if we just have guards stationed in the building while you are here. This way, you can go there as you please. She was going to tell you tomorrow."

Kala nodded, grateful for Anne's perception and this convenience. She waved good-bye to the guard and continued on alone to her quarters, noting how trusting the villagers were. No doors seemed to be locked, and the shutters on the windows were left open. She also noticed the lighting that was used on the exterior of each home. The lights didn't appear to be powered by electricity, but acted the same way. She wondered if the power source was something the Takers had given the villagers or something they had discovered after they had been left on the planet. She added it to her "to-ask" list.

When Kala woke up the next morning, she was sure of two things: one, that she had fallen asleep as soon as her head hit the pillow and, two, that she hadn't moved all night. She got stiffly out of bed and did a few stretches. Once dressed, she found someone had left her breakfast. Taking the food to the table outside, she ate and drank, planning her agenda for the day.

As this was going to be a full day of exploration for her, Kala intended to take advantage of it and engage as many people as she could to find out about the village.

During the morning, she found that the villagers didn't have a name for their village. They'd never had a need to distinguish it from another village before, so their ancestors had never needed to name it. They also knew that their ancestors had gone through atmosphere acclimation while in deep sleep on the ship that had brought them from Earth. Villagers were completely honest and open about where they had come from and how they had arrived on the planet.

They told Kala the Taken were stored in deep sleep until the Takers felt they had enough to seed a planet. If people were deemed not able to be part of a colony, they were sent back to Earth. Kala felt sad remembering the stories she had heard of people being ridiculed for reporting their abductions.

At midday, as promised, Kala returned to the Mission X building to eat with the crew, happy she could go there alone. Over lunch, she asked more questions about life on the planet and left, going back out into the community, with a desire to wander and learn more about what the crew had told her.

In the afternoon, she learned each adult had learned his or her trade from a master. Children weren't required to choose a trade until they were in their teens. Until then, they rotated among the trades and learned a little bit of each. Once they had chosen a trade, they worked exclusively with one of the masters in that trade. They apprenticed for a minimum of five years and, most of the time, at least ten years passed before they moved up to the position of journeyman. From there, the move to master depended on how quickly they picked up the intricacies of their chosen trade. But she also learned that those who showed an aptitude for medicine and food production were apprenticed earlier, even as young as five years old, since these fields were so important.

Kala was surprised to hear that each person knew the full story of their ancestors all the way back to their original Taken. Schooling included lessons about their history as well as reading, writing, math, and the sciences. Those who had been chosen for medical and farming work went through different schooling to prepare them from a young age for these trades. All the rest went to a generalized school that taught the basics. As these students got older, their lessons would become more specialized as they became more interested in a specific trade.

Later in the afternoon, she again returned to the Mission X crew to spend more time with them. She had heard, briefly, at lunch that they each practiced different trades and each had a member of the outside community who apprenticed with them. But one of the Mission X crew was a medical doctor, who was more advanced than the village medical people, and village people apprenticed with her. Kala was not surprised to hear the Mission X doctor was one of the more popular people to apprentice with and usually took two apprentices at a time. Even so, because of a long waiting list, those waiting to work with the Mission X doctor often apprenticed with the village medical people instead.

Back in the village, Kala was happy to confirm that the Mission X people were not being mistreated. They were, in fact, quite highly regarded; the rest of the village looked up to them. Kala found that the villagers were more upset that the Mission X crew had lost their ship and the means to receive technical and medical updates. But now that Kala's people were here, the villagers hoped the Mission X people would receive medical help, and their two peoples would be able to work well together.

At the end of the day, Anne found Kala sitting with some of the weavers and approached her with an invitation.

"Would you like to take the evening meal with the village elders?"

"I'd love to. Do I have time to wash up first?"

"Of course! Take your time. I'll pick you up in about half an hour."

"That would be perfect," Kala replied.

Anne arrived in a half hour as promised.

"So, what do you think of our little village?" she asked as they walked to dinner.

"I think you've been able to accomplish many things since you've been here," Kala replied thoughtfully. "But, you've had generations to create a working society. And you've had help in the process. I hope we can work together to create a working society of our own. I know you have much to offer us."

Anne simply smiled.

"Have you ever explored any other areas or landmasses?" Kala asked as they entered the dining area.

"Not for a long time, but Chalara is our current chief explorer.

He has all the records. He'd be able to give you all the details of areas that are dangerous or not worth exploring. You should speak with him."

"Maybe we could have an exchange of information. He could come to our settlement and speak with our people about what he's learned."

"That sounds like a wonderful idea," Anne said, smiling again, and pointed Kala to a chair.

Kala sat at the place Anne indicated and noticed that she had been placed at the opposite end of the table from Anne. Kala was immediately pulled into a conversation about what she could tell her tablemates about Earth.

As the meal continued, Kala realized she was giving more information about Earth than getting information about the planet they were on. She didn't worry; she knew giving information about Earth was one of the reasons for her visit to the village. The evening was turning out to be more of a pleasant respite than an exchange of information. After the final course had been served, Kala excused herself with thanks and went back to her quarters to make her scheduled contact with Charlie.

"I'll be heading back tomorrow."

"Have you learned all you can?" Charlie asked.

"Not everything, but that would take longer than I care to. I have learned a great deal...a lot that will help us to settle in. I do believe we will be able to make a lasting alliance with these people. I don't think they're holding anything back from us, and I also believe they'll be willing to share information as long as we're willing to share. We don't need to do everything at once. I'll make a complete report when I get back, but I think we have a good resource here."

"Okay, come back as soon as you feel is best. We'll be waiting for your return."

"I will contact you when I'm leaving."

"Okay, we'll talk then."

In the morning, once she was packed and ready to go, Kala sought out Anne to say good-bye.

"I hope we can make an agreement between our two communities to have peace." Kala held out her hand.

"I see no reason there should not be peace between our peoples," was Anne's reply. "We each have things the other wants, and I believe that if we can treat each other with respect, there shouldn't be a problem. Should I send for Chalara to lead you back?"

"That would be wonderful. Could you have him meet me at the Mission

X building? I'd like to say good-bye to them as well."

Anne nodded, and each woman turned toward her own destination. After chatting with the Mission X crew and promising that she would visit them again, she found Chalara waiting for her outside the door.

"We're sorry to see you leaving already. It was nice to have someone new in the village, even for a little while."

"It was nice to be so welcomed, but it's time I returned to my people, report in, and get back to work."

"But you are working by getting to know us," Chalara said with a laugh, taking her into the woods.

"This is true," Kala replied, "but we've been planting and the first animals should be birthing soon and..."

"No need to explain. I understand. Do you think I'd be allowed to look around your settlement today?"

"I'll ask Charlie when we get back. I don't see any reason that you shouldn't be able to."

They continued to chat as they traveled. As they got closer, Kala noticed more activity further out from the settlement. A lot had happened since she had left. She took Chalara to the main meeting hall in the center of the settlement, made Chalara comfortable, and radioed Charlie. After a few minutes, he arrived with Danielle and Bill. Kala introduced Danielle and then asked Charlie if Chalara could spend the rest of the day looking around.

"Of course. You can spend the day," Charlie said smiling. "Why don't you have the midday meal with us before looking around? Kala can be your guide, if she's not too tired."

"I think I can handle a little walkabout," Kala replied, smiling at Chalara.

At lunch, Charlie, Bill, and Danielle asked Chalara many questions. Finally, Kala stopped them, laughing, saying no one in the village had made her endure so much questioning.

When they had finished lunch, Kala asked, "What would you like to see first?"

"Do you have any medical facilities set up yet?" was the immediate response.

"We do," Kala replied. "It's not what we want it to be, but we have some basics set up. Let's go."

She led Chalara to the medical building and introduced him to the doctors on staff for the afternoon. For the moment, they were treating only minor injuries, bumps and bruises, scratches, and broken bones.

But they did have a primitive surgery set up. Chalara was impressed.

"You might think this is primitive, Kala, but we have nothing like this back in our village. I don't know if we have anything suitable to trade for anything you might have here."

"You might be surprised" came the reply from behind them.

They both turned to find that Charlie had followed them to the medical building. He smiled as he approached them.

"Don't worry, I'm not trailing you. I just needed to get medication for some overtaxed muscles."

"Be that as it may, I still doubt that we have anything you could find useful," Chalara said, still a bit downcast.

"You will find," Kala said, laughing, "that no matter what our differences, we still have many similarities between our peoples. We will find them, and we will use them to our own benefit, yes, but we will also use them to benefit each other. Don't worry, Chalara, we won't take advantage of you if you don't take advantage of us."

Chalara nodded his head solemnly in promise to Kala's request. Once Chalara had seen all the medical facility had to offer, Kala took him on a general tour of the settlement, ending back at the hall where they had eaten.

"I think once everything is done here, your village will be much bigger than ours. I hope you remember friends well."

"No fear, Chalara. If our dealings with each other are honest, then we have nothing to worry about. We will always be friends."

"I think I'd best head back. Anne will worry if I'm not back by nightfall."

Bill and Danielle came back to the hall to bid their guest good-bye and watch him leave. As he reached the edge of the settlement, Chalara turned and waved.

Now anxious to be home, Kala gathered her gear and made her way to her and Charlie's housing unit. She could see Charlie puttering around in the garden as she walked up the path.

"Hey, stranger," she said by way of a greeting. "What're you up to?"

"Just waiting for some beautiful woman to pass this way. I thought I'd see if she wanted to spend some time with a dirty old man. You game?"

"Just come inside and keep me company while I unpack," she said laughing. "I'm too tired for games right now but, maybe, once I've showered and changed, you can persuade me."

"Sounds good to me."

Charlie followed Kala, and as she unpacked her things, she told him about her trip. Charlie listened intently without interruption for the first go-round. Then he asked her to go through it again, this time peppering her with questions.

"So you really think they're on the level?"

"I do," she replied. "I think they are getting worried that the Takers haven't been here for a while, and they don't feel that they can provide for their people at a level of..." she paused, looking for the right word.

"Competence?" Charlie offered.

"No," she said, shaking her head, "but that will work for now. I believe they've grown stagnant and they need new blood. I don't think they'll do anything like kidnap one of us, but I do think they want a new influx of ideas and procedures from Earth. From what I understood, it's been a few hundred years since their last new arrivals. I think they're feeling a bit left out of the loop."

Charlie watched Kala as she placed her dirty things in a pile to take to the laundry. He thought about how things were progressing in Sierra settlement and realized that they were already breaking into social groups that would probably be the same for the next millennia.

"Charlie, are you listening to me?" he suddenly heard Kala asking him.

"I'm sorry, my mind must have wandered. What were you saying?"

"I was just asking if you had contacted Earth to send more settlers."

"No, I haven't. I was waiting until you got back to hear your report. I have the message all set to go, but I wanted to make sure you thought it would be worth it."

"I think it would be very worth it. Yes, we'll be stuck here because of the atmosphere, but maybe, if we send WASA the data on it, they'll be able to come up with a solution. I think this planet will be a very good home for the people leaving Earth."

"Okay, then, I'll make that recommendation," he sighed, glad the decision was made. "Would you like anything for an evening meal?"

"I'm still working on lunch, thank you, but I will take some of your famous tea, if you don't mind."

Chapter 29

As the weeks and months went on, Kala found she was working more and more with the artisans. Charlie was working with the scientists; Danielle was working with the electronics group; and Bill was working with the heavy machinists group. Joe Malabar was now head of security.

More visits happened between their colony and the village, and a barter system was set up. Soon, there was no distinction between them; they were simply all humans set to keep the race alive.

Charlie received a positive reply to his request for more settlers. WASA was now making ready for another thousand people. Secretly, Kala hoped that Lindsey would come, but she didn't think she'd change her mind. In her heart, Kala knew Lindsey well enough to know that she wouldn't want to leave her family.

They also received an update on the ship that was approaching Earth. It was still on course, though traveling very slowly; the experts now expected it to arrive in ten years. Mixed feelings developed among them: some wanted to be on Earth to help with whatever might happen and some felt that, at least, the human race would survive, if a disaster happened.

Almost two years to the day that Sierra Mission had arrived, the Brava Mission landed with a new group of settlers. Once they were absorbed into the daily routine, planning started to have elections for a permanent ruling council. The leadership committee of the Sierra-Brava settlement and the leaders of the Taken village decided that, together, they would create one ruling council that would work for everyone. To achieve this, at least one member from the Taken village would be on the council. There were no objections. Leaders from each place hoped that, after a few years, there would be no separation between the Sierra-Brava settlement and the village, with each area expanding until they met in the middle. But, knowing this would take years, the two communities would work together as best they could until then.

Six years later, when the Sierra-Brava settlement and the village were finally one community, dissension erupted again.

A small group of the original dissenters decided they didn't like how the merged community, now called Haven, was being run and wanted a change. Instead of going through established channels within the community, they decided to force change by taking a shuttle to the *Sierra* to contact Earth and making their demands to the Earth government. But, contact with Earth could not be established there because of disrupted communications, so they tried from the *Brava*. Not knowing why they couldn't make contact, the rebels destroyed the communications software on both ships, returned to the planet, and destroyed some of the hardware on the planet. The damage was almost beyond repair. When the ruling council heard what the rebels had done and that all communications with Earth might possibly be lost forever, they met to decide how to deal with the troublemakers. Charlie urged them to act quickly and proposed moving the dissenters to an isolated area.

"I don't see why we have to do anything," Anne Lasson Greene argued from her position as the current head of the council.

"Do you agree with what they did?" asked Jenna Hopeman, a council member.

"You know I don't agree with the destruction." She paused considering her next words carefully. "It just seems that we need to find a way to punish them without being too harsh."

"They ruined equipment that we may never be able to repair, even with the help of the hi-tech people; they wasted fuel that we can't replace, and because of what they did, we may never know the fate of Earth."

"It seems the fate of Earth was pretty clear at our last communication," said a quiet voice from the back of the room.

The room was silent as people looked around trying to identify the speaker. Anne stood up from her place at the council table and walked over to the window and gazed out.

"It might have seemed clear to you, whoever said that, but the rest of us would like to know what happened to friends and families. After all we've accomplished, to have something like this happen is very disappointing.

We've taken our two peoples and made them one, we've extended our two communities into one with many offshoots, and we've made good use of the resources that we have here at our disposal." She sighed. "But I think Charlie is correct. We need to deal with these people and we do need to act quickly."

She turned around and walked to her seat. "I think that moving the troublemakers to a place where they can have their own village and run things how they want is a perfect idea. There is an island off to the west that could serve this purpose. I propose we move these troublemakers to this island."

The other council members weighed the proposal. After minutes of discussion, Anne rapped the table for attention.

"Shall we vote on the measure before us?" she asked the group.

The vote went as Charlie and Kala thought: the dissenters would be taken to the island to live. The council also decided to let the dissenters take family with them, if they wanted.

"What if others want to go as well?" Kala asked.

"What do you mean?" Anne asked.

"Well, if others feel the same way but weren't part of what happened, do we offer them the opportunity to go too? If there are other dissenters here, we take the chance that trouble will happen again."

The council continued to debate how much fuel was available, how many shuttle trips to the island would be needed, and if trips to the ships would be needed. In the end, they decided they no longer needed anything from the ships, and they could make up to three trips to bring the dissenters to the island. After that, anyone who wished to join them would have to find their own way. Johnston Groves, Haven's law expert, was elected to write up the formal declaration and have it posted. The dissenters, families, and any followers would be moved to the island by the end of the week.

Kala and Charlie hardly talked on their way home from the meeting.

"Credit for your thoughts," Charlie said finally as they were preparing dinner.

"Just thinking about what might have happened if they had been successful."

"With the fate of Earth unknown, I don't think much. I just hope hostile aliens don't try to track the source of the transmission. That could truly mean the end of the human race."

"I hadn't thought of that."

They worked in silence before Charlie tried again.

"What's really on your mind? You've been distant for a couple of days now and I can't figure it out."

"I just think it's about time we made our situation a bit more permanent."
"Okay..." Charlie responded. "You think I'm going to leave you or something?"
"Of course not, I just think a child should have parents who are married."
Charlie stared at her in amazed silence. Then, he whooped in delight before picking her up and spinning her round and round. When he realized what he was doing, he smiled sheepishly and carefully placed her back on her feet. And at dinner, they talked only of happier times to come.

Over the next few weeks, the news spread throughout Haven until, it seemed to Kala, everyone knew.

Kala and Charlie married and started preparing for the baby. The business with the dissenters melted into the background once they were taken to the island with their families and followers. Because of the damage done to their communications, what they had done was never quite out of mind, but the worry faded.

CHAPTER 30

Two more years passed quickly and without incident. The scientists found a way to control the trances and visions the Mission X crew were experiencing, and they were able to come out and rejoin the regular population. When the next elections were held for the ruling council, two Mission X people were elected.

Even though the dissenters had damaged a major portion of the communications, they had left the sensors intact, and Haven still manned a long-range watch for any approaching ships or wayward asteroids. One day, the sensors picked up something.

"Commander Hudson, come in please," came the call over the radio in Charlie's now permanent house.

"Hudson here," Charlie replied, thinking *What's with the "Commander" business?*

"We've got a blip on the long-range sensors, sir. Need instructions."

"Is there any way to tell what it is?"

"We can try, sir, but it's pretty far off right now."

"Well, try. I want you to have something more than just a blip for me when I get there."

"Aye-aye, sir."

"Hudson out."

Charlie stood looking at the radio, trying to decide if he should notify anyone before going to the control center. He decided to tell only Kala for the moment. No point getting worried for nothing; they'd not be able to defend themselves from space, anyhow.

"Kala," he called quietly, so he wouldn't disturb the baby if she were sleeping.

"Right here," Kala whispered coming out of the baby's room.

"I just got a call from the control room. They have a blip on the long-range sensors. I'm going there to check it out and see if anything can be determined at this point."

"Let me know if you need me, and I'll take Charlene over to the nursery."

Charlie nodded and left the house. He was hoping the blip wasn't a ship, but if it was, he hoped the aliens weren't the ones who had been headed toward Earth. He preferred the aliens who had initially seeded their new home with humans. Whatever or whoever it was, because of the dissenters' destruction, they would have difficulty figuring it out. When he got to the control center, he found that Bill was already there.

"What are you doing here?" Charlie asked with a smile on his face.

"I was on duty and told them to haul your sorry ass in here to do some real work for a change," was the flippant reply.

"As opposed to what?"

"Changing dirty diapers!"

Charlie just laughed. Bill waved him over to a board in the center of the room that was quietly beeping. Charlie stared at the blip over Bill's shoulder before going to an open station.

"Frequency?" Charlie asked, slipping into commander mode.

"I just wish there was a way for us to get back up to the ships," Bill said. "We could get a much better look from up there."

"Don't the shuttles from the *Brava* still have fuel?" The quiet question came from the corner.

Bill and Charlie looked at the direction of the speaker and then at each other in amazement.

"I completely forgot about them when we took the dissenters out to the island," Charlie said. "Do you think there's enough?"

"Can't hurt to look," Bill replied.

They were in luck. The main shuttle from the *Brava* still had enough fuel for a round-trip to the ships. They could also refuel the shuttle at the ships.

"Now...who is going?" Bill asked.

"I think it should be you and me," Charlie replied. "We know what we're looking for."

"I agree. Maybe we should take someone from the *Brava*. It's the newer ship and might be slightly different from what we're used to."

Charlie agreed, choosing a senior member of the *Brava*'s crew. Bill sent someone to find Adel Cooper and bring her to the control room.

"If we left now, it would be dark by the time we got back, and we're not lit well enough for a night landing," Charlie spoke thoughtfully. "Whatever it is isn't close enough to get here overnight."

"You're right. We can leave tomorrow morning," Bill agreed.

Charlie was optimistic. "We can be up and back by dinner time. And, hopefully, the damage is only to communications and doesn't extend to Brava's radar and long-range sensors."

"Do you think it's possible we could fix the damage to the communications systems while we're up there?" The question came from Adel, the *Brava* crew member, as she entered the room.

"Unsure," replied Charlie. "It all depends on what was damaged. We've fixed all we can down here, so we'll have to see what we find while we're up there. One of us can work on that while the others try to get a fix on this thing headed toward us. I hope it will only be a matter of resetting a few things. We'll meet here at dawn and get suited up."

After making their flight plan and filling air tanks with planet-side air, Bill and Adel left. Charlie stayed for a few more minutes, watching the blip on the screen. It wasn't moving very fast; in fact, it hardly looked like it was moving at all. *I really hope this isn't what I think it is,* he thought. *If it turns out to be what was headed toward Earth, we may be in trouble.*

Charlie shook his head, pushing the thought away, and returned home to be with Kala and the baby. When he got there, though, he found a note from Kala telling him that she had taken Charlene for a walk. Hungry, he made himself a small salad, and just as he sat down, Kala arrived back home.

"Everything okay?" Charlie asked as she sat down at the table, pulling the stroller beside her.

"We're fine; we just needed some fresh air. What happened at the control center?"

Charlie brought her up-to-date and told her his plans for the following day. He noticed the look of worry on her face as he talked.

"Don't worry yet, love," he said. "We have to see what this blip is first before we start to worry."

"If you say so," she replied, not sounding convinced.

At the sound of Kala's voice, Charlene woke up and Charlie leaned over and plucked her from the stroller. He settled her in the crook of his arm and rocked her back to sleep. Once she settled, he looked at Kala.

"I mean it, Kala. Don't worry. We can't know what it is until we get up to the *Brava*. Please try and be positive."

"I know you're right, but I was hoping we'd be able to live a quiet life for more than ten years!"

Kala stood up and started clearing the table while Charlie glanced between her and Charlene. Finally, he stood up and took Charlene into her room and placed her in her crib.

"Kala, what's really bothering you?" he asked when he came back.

"It's been so long since we've been up in space. I guess I'm just worried for you. Don't forget, you have a family now." She smiled wanly.

"Kala, I have to go. I'm one of the few people who can fix what's wrong. Besides, we all have families now and I can't ask someone to go if I'm not willing to go...and you know it."

"I do know it. It's just that with the air thing...and space being unforgiving... and you have a child to think of now... It just scares me, that's all."

Charlie walked over to Kala gave her a hug.

"I promise you, it will be fine."

"Just make sure it's a promise you can keep. I love you too much to lose you."

The next morning, Kala got up with Charlie and sat with him while he ate breakfast. When he was ready, she quietly got Charlene out of bed without waking her, placing her in a buggy, and they walked together to the shuttle site.

There, they met up with Bill and Adel, who quietly fussed over the baby. Kala kissed Charlie good-bye and quickly returned to the house. Charlene was beginning to wake up and would soon want her breakfast. After feeding Charlene, Kala heard the engines of the shuttle rev up and she ran outside with Charlene to watch the departure. They followed the shuttle disappearing into the sky.

"Well, that's it, baby," Kala said. "They're off."

CHAPTER 31

In the shuttle, Charlie, Bill, and Adel were switching from takeoff mode to docking mode. The trip was a quick one but still hard work that took a lot of concentration. Upon arriving at the *Brava*, they docked in the main docking bay. Onboard, they set the shuttle to automatic fuel refill and headed for the bridge.

On the bridge, Charlie began checking the long-range sensors for the blip, while Adel and Bill started working on communications. Fortunately, all the work that had been done on the planet helped them to make repairs quickly on the ship, and they soon were able to try connecting. Charlie joined them with a satisfied smile on his face just as they were ready to try.

Using the shortwave communications devices they had brought, Charlie contacted the control room to advise they were ready to attempt to connect. After a tense fifteen minutes, Adel was able to reestablish the link with the planet below.

"Thank goodness for small favors," said Bill quietly. "It wasn't as bad as we thought."

"That's only the first part," Charlie replied in a relieved tone. "Now we see if we can link up with Earth."

Charlie nodded to Adel, who nervously stated, "This could take a bit as there's going to be a lag before they answer us back,"

"Our air tanks are doing fine, so let's give it a try."

Adel began entering the sequences needed to make the WASA connection and, then, sent a message saying they were back online and waiting for a response. She hit the send button, and they sat back to wait.

"About how long is the lag?" Bill asked.

"Probably about ten to fifteen minutes."

The time passed slowly as they waited for word that their message had been received. Finally, at the twelve-minute mark, they received a response from WASA that their message had made it through. The reply told them that the ship that had been approaching Earth had turned out to be friendly, but the government, being cautious, had not disclosed any of the Earth outposts to the aliens.

Adel informed WASA about the dissenters and the planet's communications destruction and the work they had done to make repairs from the ship. She told them there might still be problems connecting from the surface, but they would try a test when they returned to the planet. WASA again replied affirmatively and they broke off communications. Bill, Charlie, and Adel sat in silence for a few moments relieved they had been able to contact WASA and to learn that Earth was still safe. Charlie got up and paced back and forth.

"I guess we'd better make sure we have a live connection to the planet before we head back down," he said, "and we'd better check out the defense weapons and deflectors while we're here."

With a successful connection and their other checks made, the three returned to the shuttle bay and unhooked the shuttle from the fueling station.

Looking at Adel, Charlie said, "We'll have to go to *Sierra* at some point to make repairs there."

"But not today," she replied. "We don't have enough air in the tanks. Now that we know what to do, we can come back at another time."

Soon they were on their way back to the surface.

"I'll be glad to get out of this damn suit," Bill muttered as they touched down on the planet.

"That makes two of us," laughed Charlie.

"Make that three," Adel agreed, laughing as well.

Once they had changed back into their plain clothes, they hurried to the main communications building. Adel took her place at a console and began typing another message to Earth.

"The delay from here will be slightly longer because we're going through a ship. But we should know in about twenty minutes if we have a new connection to Earth."

But after fifteen minutes, the console began to beep with the incoming reply from WASA.

"We're up and running again," said Charlie. "That's a good sign. Now, to make sure nothing like this happens again."

With that, he shooed everyone out of the communications room except himself, Bill, and Adel. They worked for an hour to implement authorization codes in all the communication units. Going forward, any programming changes would require Charlie's or Bill's authorization code. When they were done, Charlie saw that it was almost dinnertime.

"I'm ready to go home. I want to spend time with Charlene and Kala tonight." He smiled in anticipation.

Charlie invited the communications staff back to their posts, and he, Bill, and Adel happily left for their homes.

"So, how did it go?" Kala asked.

"We were able to get everything fixed," Charlie replied, feeding Charlene and alternately wiping her face. "We should see an incredible meteor shower."

"Are you sure we're only going to get a shower and not a direct hit?"

Charlie nodded, then added, "Well, I can't be sure of the exact trajectory, but I'm hopeful. The other good news is that we added authorization codes to the communication units so that no one can change any programming without Bill or me inputting our code. No one should be able to make programming changes to the communications grid again."

"It's the meteors that worry me."

"Me, too, but we're monitoring. There's not much we can do at this point. I'll ask the planet old-timers if they remember any meteor showers or meteors hitting the planet before, and we'll go from there."

"Will there be anything we can do about a direct hit if we know we're in danger?"

"The ships have defensive weapons that we should be able to use to break up a meteor before it hits the atmosphere, but I don't think we'll have a problem."

"Okay, if you say so, I'll believe everything will be all right," Kala smiled. "Now, how about some dinner?"

Later, after Charlene was in bed for the night, the two of them sat up talking.

"Tell me again about the meteor shower."

"What can I tell you that I haven't already told you? There is a meteor shower headed this way. Hopefully, the meteors will pass us by and just give us some kind of show in the sky. We can't be sure, though. We made sure that the deflectors on the ships are still working, and if a meteor comes that close, we hope they'll be able to help push it out of orbit."

"What if it does hit the planet?"

"A meteor strike would probably be a life-ending event. It would probably create a nuclear-type winter if it did hit. I suppose we could go into the cave system in the far south, but it would mean living underground for many generations."

They sat in silence for a few minutes before Kala got up and walked over to the window.

"I would hate to see our wonderful community end," she said sadly.

"It wouldn't end. It would just change," Charlie replied.

"No, it would end. It would become something totally different. It scares me what we would lose if we had to move underground. The fresh air, the trees, the arts... Everything would change to be centered on survival instead of the type of life we've become used to."

Charlie didn't respond right away. Instead, he thought about what she had said and how he could respond in a way that would reassure her.

"Kala, there's nothing I can say that will change what might or might not happen. If, and I stress *if*, a meteor hits, we might not even survive in the cave systems. If we do survive, things will change. We will still have all the things we have now, but we'll do things differently. Right now, I don't see the sense in worrying about it. The meteor shower is still a long way off and a meteor will probably not even hit the planet."

"Don't you think we should develop a plan in case it looks like a meteor might hit?"

Charlie thought about her question and then nodded.

"I think that's a good idea. I'll inform the ruling council of the approaching meteor shower and call a meeting to discuss a plan of action and putting it into place. We could start storing supplies in the caves and setting them up for people to live in. We have a lot of people, though, and I'm not sure we'll have space for everyone."

"Will everyone want to go?"

"Probably not. Some of the Taken might believe the Takers will come and save them. We'll have to wait and see." A sudden thought made Charlie laugh. "Hell, there might even be some technology the Takers left that would help us prevent a meteor strike."

"I guess you're right. It really does no good to worry about something that might not happen."

"Then, again, you are right, too, in that it will be good to be prepared for something that might happen. Just believe me that it will all work out in the end."

CHAPTER 32

The next day, Charlie called an emergency meeting of the ruling council to tell them what he, Bill, and Adel had accomplished while they were aboard the ships. He told them about fixing the communications and getting back in touch with Earth, and then he told them about the approaching meteor shower and a potential meteor strike. They were silent when he was done.

"So, you really think we need to plan to move into the caves?" asked Anne Greene.

"I think it's something we should consider," replied Charlie.

"You think this meteor shower is really that much of a threat?" asked someone else.

"It might be, it might not be. We really can't be sure at this point; it's still too far out. We'll be watching to see where it goes and if the deflectors on the ships will help at all."

"But, in your opinion, you think we should get the caves ready."

"In my opinion, yes. I think we should get the caves ready. Even if only a portion of a meteor hits the planet, it will create major problems. We need to be ready."

The council members vigorously discussed what to do. In the end, they came to the decision to get the caves ready—just in case. No matter what the outcome, they decided to keep the community going as it was. Charlie passed along Kala's misgivings that going into the caves would change how they lived. The council agreed that they would need to work hard not only at saving their community but also keeping it going as before.

"Anne, as a native of this planet, do you know of any equipment that the Takers would have placed here to deflect meteors?"

Anne turned to the other council members who were original dwellers. They briefly discussed Charlie's question.

"The records go back at least a thousand years," she began. "I personally don't remember anything about a meteor deflector, but that doesn't mean there isn't one. We can search the records. Maybe something exists we can use, or even place on one of the ships, to nudge a meteor out of our orbit."

The council agreed to meet the next day to start setting up teams to plan for an evacuation to the caves. Charlie volunteered to search the records for a defense against meteors.

After the meeting ended, Anne called Charlie aside.

"You really think all this planning is necessary?"

"I do. I would hate to lose all we have built here... and especially what your people built. I believe having a plan is critical; I think we need to be ready for anything."

Charlie started with the year the Sierra mission had arrived and worked his way backward. As he went further back, he was amazed to see the detail in the records, both from the humans and the Takers, but there were often holes. When he had gone back about five hundred years, he realized he was at the beginning of the records.

He stopped, surprised, because Anne had said the records went back a thousand years when the humans had first been brought to the planet. He went in search of her.

"Do you really know when humans were first brought to this planet?" he asked when he found her.

"No. We were taught it was millennia ago, but an exact time frame was never really told us. Why do you ask?"

"The records you gave me to look through only go back five hundred years. Could there be more records stored somewhere else?"

Anne puckered her brow in thought and then went to talk to someone. After a few minutes, she came back.

"I've instructed Lorraine, my assistant, to take you to the rest of the records that we have access to. If you don't find what you're looking for there..." She shrugged her shoulders.

"Something just occurred to me," Charlie smacked his thigh. "Is there an old building or structure that you don't use or don't know its purpose?"

"I don't follow you," she replied.

"Well...a structure or building that you no longer know why it was built or what it was used for, or, maybe, even one with unusual symbols."

Anne thought about this before answering.

"There was another, older city. By the time I arrived here, our people were already living in the village you know, but the Takers had showed us another place just to keep its memory alive. We saw a building that we've always called the 'triangle' because of its shape. But we weren't told its purpose. Do you think this building could be what you are asking about?"

"You've never told us about an old city before. If this building stands out and you don't know its purpose, it could be important. I'll look at the rest of the records you have, and then someone can show me the old city and this building. Maybe there's something in the records about the building; we might be able to find out what it was for."

Once Lorraine had taken him to the second batch of records, Charlie resumed his search. He was happy to see these records continued back from where the first batch had left off. About seven hundred years back, he found his first reference to the triangle building. He learned the building had been called the metebuilding. As he read, he found that the metebuilding was the main computer room for an advanced civilization, and it had deflector technology. He wondered if it would still work.

Pleased that his search had been successful, he decided to stop for the night. He looked forward to a nice quiet evening with Kala and Charlene.

When he got home, the first thing he noticed was that Bill was playing with Charlene, and Adel was in the kitchen helping Kala with dinner.

"Did I forget that you guys were coming over to dinner tonight?"

"You've been so busy I thought you could use a nice evening hashing out what's going on," Kala said with a laugh.

"That does sound like a good idea," Charlie grinned. "Either of you want something to drink? I know I could use something after reading a thousand year's worth of musty old records!"

As it turned out, Charlie had his quiet evening. He told them about the old city and the metebuilding. All were curious about what secrets each might hold.

"I wonder why they didn't mention the city before now." Bill was puzzled.

"I don't think they were trying to hide anything," Charlie said. "It's probably not important to them after everything that's gone on. They probably hadn't even thought of for years before we showed up."

"I know, but I'd think it would be important to mention it."

"You'd think, but they never lived there so why think about it. Anyway, I'll see it tomorrow when Chalara takes me there. You guys want to come with me? Maybe we'll discover more technology that can help us than just what's in the metebuilding."

Both Bill and Adel excitedly responded "Yes!"

After Bill and Adel had left, Charlie put Charlene to bed. When she was asleep, Kala and he sat and talked.

"Do you really think the deflector technology in the metebuilding will work?" Kala asked.

"I hope so. We need something if we want to stay out of those blasted caves."

The next day, Chalara led Bill, Adel, Charlie, and a few scientists to the old city.

"What exactly are you looking for?" asked Chalara.

"We want to examine the meteor technology in the triangle building to see if it will still work," answered Adel.

Chalara nodded.

"We're also looking for a more complete history of the planet. The records you have are good, but there are holes. We may learn something important here," said Charlie.

"The ancestors seemed to leave out a lot," said Chalara. "I'm a record keeper as well as a guide, so I've examined the same records you have. They certainly leave much up to the imagination."

"And that isn't good," Bill responded. "Why do you think they did that?"

"They probably didn't mean to. The records say they relied a lot on verbal history to fill in the gaps. When outbreaks of illness decimated the population here, the Takers went back to Earth to get more people to seed. Those are probably the times when much of our history was lost. It's a shame because we probably would be in a much better situation now if we knew more."

"That's the truth," Bill said softly to Charlie only. "They should have written more down."

"If you remember your Earth history, though, a lot of history was passed down verbally. So much has been lost over the years on both planets."

Standing at the edge of the old city, they stood quietly looking at the run-down buildings around them. Many of them were covered in vines while others were just crumbled ruins. The team looked around for the triangle metebuilding. Finally, Charlie spotted it and pointed.

"While I go check out the metebuilding, why don't the rest of you check out the town? Chalara, please point out anything you might think is important."

Charlie headed straight to the triangle building, which was located in, what looked like, the center of town. As he walked, he could almost hear and see the ancient people that had once lived there. He wondered what had prompted them to move and when they had moved. The records didn't say.

How long did they live here? he wondered. *What was life like for them? Why did they leave?* He had no answers.

Once Charlie got to the triangle building, he walked around it examining all three sides. He could not see a way in. After one go-round, he studied each side. He noticed each side had words and symbols carved into them. Setting up recording equipment, he captured the words and symbols for further study back in Haven.

The words seemed to be an ancient dialect of what looked like English from Earth, but he couldn't be sure. Knowing that Adel had studied languages in preparation for her mission, he radioed her to join him at the building.

When she arrived, he asked, "Can you read any of this?"

She took her time studying each side before responding.

"I think I may be able to translate, but it'll take some time."

"Okay. I'll go see what Chalara and Bill are up to while you work on this."

Adel nodded absently, already absorbed in her new task.

Charlie found Bill and Chalara working their way through one of the larger buildings on the edge of a main square.

"Find anything?" he asked, entering the building.

"Nothing yet," Chalara replied. "But from what I remember of my history, this building was one of the main meeting halls. They may have stored records here as well. We might get lucky and find something."

"We need to bring more people here," Bill said. "There might be more here than our team can deal with. It might be worth it to bring another team here while others are preparing the caves."

Charlie considered Bill's suggestion before nodding.

"I was thinking along similar lines myself. I've got to get back for another meeting this afternoon. Why don't you all stay here, and I'll arrange for more people to return here to explore the city."

Bill and Chalara nodded their agreement. Before he left, Charlie stopped at the triangle building to see if Adel was having any luck.

"Some," she said. "It'll take me more time, but I think I'll be able to figure it out." She rubbed her neck and rolled her head to relieve the tension.

"Don't rush. I'd rather we get it right. It may be something that can help us."

At the edge of town, Charlie turned and looked again at the city he was leaving. Overgrown with weeds, trees, and vines, it was a veritable ghost town. After a final look, he turned and headed toward Haven.

CHAPTER 33

Once back, Charlie went straight to the ruling council meeting.

"Now that everyone is here, why don't we get started?" Anne, who was again leading, began the meeting.

The discussion went immediately to the impending meteor shower. Anne's assistant spoke first.

"I've talked to and heard from many people," said Lorraine. "Everyone is willing to do whatever it takes to save our community."

The talk then turned to what needed to be saved and what could be let go. They decided that a little bit of everything should be saved. The caves were so expansive that, even filled with the total population, there was no danger of running out of room.

Next, Charlie brought up the business of another exploration of the old city.

"What good would that do?" asked Don Parker, an artist and newest member of the council.

"First, the records say the triangle contains a deflector technology," Charlie replied. "We need to see if and how it works. If a meteor is headed our way, it can be the means to deflect it. Also, there are words and symbols on the triangle that are being deciphered. The translation may point us to other important information in the city. Second, I believe that the more complete history we have of this world, the better off we will be. The more we know about the past, the better we can plan the future."

All the council members did not feel as Charlie did, but, in the end, his argument won out. Charlie was given the go-ahead to assemble a volunteer team to do a complete exploration of the old city.

Word of the old city had spread quickly and Charlie found he had no trouble recruiting volunteers. Satisfied with the number and diverse skills of volunteers, he went home to Kala and Charlene. He knew Bill, Adel, Chalara, and the rest of that team would return by dark as arranged.

The next day Charlie, Bill, Adel, and Chalara found a group of about twenty people waiting for them. All were excited and prepared to spend a day exploring the old city.

"We need to be careful, people. This isn't a party. We need to go over the city with a fine-tooth comb to make sure we don't miss anything important. We're not quite sure what we're looking for, but record anything that speaks of historical events or daily living. Now let's move out."

"Were you able to figure out the words and symbols on the triangle?" he asked Adel once they were under way.

"Some, but not much."

"So there's nothing you can tell us so far?"

"I'd rather not make any guesses. The language is very familiar to me, but it's just different enough that I can't quite make it out...yet. I'm hoping one of the old-timer volunteers will be able to help."

When the group got to the old city, they split up into teams of two and three. They fanned out throughout the city and started to clear away the brush and vines. Every now and then there would be a shout for Bill or Charlie to come and look at a find.

Right before lunch, Adel and Bunny Walterson, one of the old-timers helping her, made a breakthrough. Bunny cracked the code on side one of the triangle, and from there, they were able to decipher side two.

"How did you figure it out?" asked Bill.

"I have a thing for languages," Bunny replied. "When I compared what was on the triangle to Adel's rough translation attempt, side one, then side two, came to me. Side three is a bit different, but not enough to take me a long time to decipher."

"Well, are you going to keep us guessing or are you going to tell us what it says?"

"There's an underground city right under this one," Bunny said, with a satisfied smile on her face. "When the Takers first brought people to this planet they were split into two groups: high-tech types and low-tech. The high-tech people lived underground and ran the machines. The low-tech people lived on the surface and had an agrarian society."

"You got all this from the words on the triangle?" Adel asked astonished.

"Not all of it. Some of the other old-timer volunteers found clues and brought them to me, so I'm getting this by piecing the words and the clues together."

"So, what do you think this triangle is?" Charlie impatiently asked.

"Well, from what I can gather this was the place where the two societies came together," Bunny responded.

"Aah..." Charlie interrupted, excited. "That's why it is called the metebuilding!"

Bunny smiled and went on. "Somehow, this triangle should move on its base to reveal an entrance to the underground city. I don't think the two peoples got together very often, and I'm not sure what we'll find once we figure out how to make the triangle move."

"Do you really think that's possible?" Bill was struggling to understand what this meant to them.

"How did you figure out the order in which to read the sides?" Charlie asked Bunny and Adel.

"They were numbered for us. If you look at the base you can clearly see a one, a two, and a three at the bottom," Adel replied.

Charlie looked closer at the base and saw the numbers.

"I wonder if they have anything to do with the opening sequence needed to open the doorway," he offered.

"They probably do," answered Bunny, "but for right now, we're using them to reference the sides. From a common-sense standpoint, the wording does seem to follow the numbering as well."

"When do you think you'll have side three translated?"

"Give me another hour or so and I should have it."

Charlie nodded his head, satisfied.

"I'm going to wander around and see how the other teams are doing. Take a break if you need one, but I want that structure totally translated today if you can."

Charlie began his rounds with the teams nearest the triangle and worked his way outward. He found that not much had been found so far other than items used in day-to-day living. A few teams had found faded papers and plaques.

Once again, Charlie found himself hoping that a meteor wouldn't strike so they could continue exploring the city. He was finding the history quite interesting. Just as he finished with one of the teams, he heard someone call his name. He stopped where he was and looked around to see Adel waving and running toward him.

"We figured it out. We're ready to try opening the triangle. Would you like to join us?"

"Are you kidding? I'm right behind you!"

They ran back to the triangle and helped Bunny pull their equipment away to a safe distance.

"I can't guarantee that this will work," she said. "It's probably been many centuries since the triangle has been opened."

"That would lead me to believe that no one is alive down there," Charlie said. "If people were living down there, they'd have to know we were up here, and someone would have come up to talk to us."

Bunny walked around the triangle pushing on it in a few places. Charlie began to wonder if there was any method to where and what she was pushing. Just then, the ground shuddered under their feet, and they jumped in surprise. Then they heard a squealing sound, and the triangle moved just a little bit. It moved enough to give them a glimpse of a stairway leading down, before the triangle ground to a halt. They looked into the small opening; a rank smell wafted up to them. Quickly, they all backed off, coughing.

"Should we try to open it further?" Adel asked.

"Yes," answered Charlie, quickly and firmly.

The four shouldered up to the triangle and gave it a heave. The monument moved a bit more before stopping again. They gave it another heave and it moved again. Before they tried again, the triangle began moving and, then, opened up all the way on its own. A cloud of dust flew up at them and the rank smell was even stronger. Everyone backed up and looked at the structure and the hole in the ground that was now uncovered.

"I think we should let it air out a bit," suggested Bill.

"Good idea," replied Charlie. "Did anyone think to bring rebreathers?"

"I don't think so," replied Adel. "We should send someone back to get them."

"I'll go," said a voice from the back of the crowd that had gathered.

Charlie looked around to identify the speaker. It was Don Parker, one of the volunteers. "Thanks," he said. "Get as many as you can carry, so we can send down a good-sized crew."

"You got it," Don replied.

"And bring as many plain face masks too. The kind a medic would use."

Don nodded in understanding and swiftly left for Haven. The group that had gathered around the triangle again turned to look at the hole that now loomed in front of them.

"I need a few to go down to the underground city." Charlie considered the group and picked a suitable number to stay. "Those not staying should get back to work while we wait," suggested Charlie.

Those not chosen hesitated—wanting to stay—and then slowly turned away to go back to what they had been doing. Charlie, Adel, Bill, and Bunny stood staring at the triangle and the hole in the ground.

Suddenly, the triangle started to move again. They could see that it was opening even further, and they watched even more of the hole being revealed. They stared in awe as another cloud of dust rose from the hole, then backed up as more of the rank smell filled the air.

"It's maddening to wait to find out what's in there," said Charlie.

The others nodded, smiling at his impatience. Charlie turned to Bunny.

"So, tell me what the third side said that gave you the clues on how to open this thing."

"It was a code. The whole thing was a complex code that they made even more difficult to crack by putting the third side in a dialect that must have been ancient even to them. The code told what words were the pressure points that would turn on the mechanism below to move the triangle. The high-tech types probably knew they would lose people to the surface and would have to automate their system. That's why they left instructions on the triangle. They must have known things would break down eventually. They did the best they could, but things eventually went the way they thought it would. It's sad."

She paused and sipped her water bottle. Charlie and the others looked at the open hole in front of them, and he knew they were each wondering the same thing: what was down there?

As they stood there looking at the hole, Don returned with the rebreathers and masks. He brought them to Charlie and held them out.

"That was quick," Adel said.

"I ran the whole way," he replied between gasps. "I want to know what's down there as much as everyone else."

Charlie thanked Don and was about to send him back to his team when Bill spoke up.

"Should we go down now or give it some more time?"

As soon as Bill spoke, they heard a noise coming from hole and quickly turned toward it. They noticed that inside the hole looked brighter. Bill went over to look.

"It looks like the lights came on," he said. "It seems brighter than it was when it first opened."

"I wonder if the systems were set to come on automatically when the triangle was opened," said Charlie.

Bill walked closer to the opening and, leaning over, sniffed.

"Still stinks, but I think with the masks we'll be okay."

"Do you think someone should stay topside in case there's a problem?" Adel asked.

"You volunteering?" asked Charlie.

"Heavens no!" Adel exclaimed. "I want to go down there as much as you do. I was just wondering if it might be prudent to leave someone up here with a radio just in case we need help."

Charlie turned to Don. He quickly agreed to stay with the radio. Charlie, Bill, Adel, and Bunny donned their masks and descended the steps. When they got down to the bottom, what they saw amazed them.

"Their technology is almost up to the level we had at the time we left Earth," said Adel.

The others did not disagree. They stood where they were inspecting the immediate area. After a moment, they looked at each other.

"What do we do now?" asked Bunny.

"We split up and look around," answered Charlie. "Don't touch anything until we've scoped out the area, and the place has aired out. Open any doors or windows you find. They may help to air out the complex faster. Keep in contact with your radios and...be careful."

They split up into groups, moving down the three different hallways. The technology and the size of the place amazed them. It seemed to encompass the entire space below the city above them.

Each group found doorways to the outside and opened them. There were no windows. They found a lot of different technology but couldn't comprehend what it had been used for. When they had gone through the entire complex, they met back at the stairway under the triangle.

"This place is truly amazing," said John Baker, one of the techs from the *Sierra*. "I've never seen anything like it, even on Earth."

There were murmurs of agreement.

"Where are all the bodies or remains?" asked Kiana Johnson, one of *Brava's* techs.

No one had thought of this and they realized they hadn't seen any living quarters.

"Were there any doors that we didn't open?" asked Charlie.

"We couldn't open two doors. We didn't want to force them," replied Bill.

"Same here. At least three for us," said Adel.

"Anyone else?" asked Charlie.

The others shook their heads.

Bill, and then Adel, led Charlie to each unopened door. The three pried the doors open, and within the rooms beyond, they found living quarters and more doors to other rooms. But still no bodies or even traces of bodies.

"I wonder if they all left to go topside when they realized there wasn't going to be anyone to take over for them," said Charlie.

"You know, I wonder if they lived on the surface with the others and just came down here to work," replied Kameron Good, a former computer tech.

The suggestion surprised them.

"What about the living quarters?" asked Scott Denney another computer tech.

"They're just bunks," Bill said. "There's no place for making meals... only a communal eating room...and there's no place to wash. We did find bathrooms but no showers or bathtubs. Maybe those sleeping quarters were for those who had long shifts and needed to rest. Or maybe just a place to sleep overnight if they got off work late so they wouldn't bother anyone topside by coming up late."

Everyone agreed this explanation made sense.

"I think it's time we got to the surface ourselves. It's getting late and we need to be heading back. We didn't bring anything to camp out here," Charlie said. "One person exit each door and stay there. I want to see where they all come out."

Several people left to go out the doors that had been found, while the rest of the group ascended the stairway to the surface. Charlie and Bill eventually found all the people standing outside the doors. Once all the door locations were marked, they returned to the triangle.

"I want two people posted at each door until we get back to Haven and can talk to Joe Malabar. Bill, when we get back to Haven, I want you to work with Joe and assign people to come back here immediately and guard each door for the time being... Again, two guards for each door. We don't fully know what we have here, and we don't have a lot of time to find out. I want the place to stay open tonight so that it airs out and we can work here tomorrow without having to wear masks."

Bill nodded and sped back to Haven. He quickly had Joe assemble his best people and returned with them in almost no time. The guards were posted, orders were given, and everyone else made ready to leave the old city. Charlie gave the word and they all headed back to Haven, leaving only the guards in the old city.

CHAPTER 34

Before going home to Kala and Charlene, Charlie went in search of Anne. He found her in her office, just getting ready to leave for the day.

"Did you know anything about a technology center under the old city?" he asked without preamble.

"A what?" Anne was incredulous.

"Well, I suppose that answers that question," he said. "It appears to be a fully equipped TechNet-type center under the old city. It can rival anything we had on Earth when we left ten years ago."

He let Anne digest this information.

"So you're telling me that the ancients had technology that was comparable to that of Earth in this century?"

"That's exactly what I'm telling you. It'll take us some time to get it working, but we have a few computer techs who should be able to get it up and running."

"Will we be able to have it working before the meteor shower gets here?"

"Right now, I think we'll be fine, but I think we should have people working in the old city and still preparing the caves."

Anne nodded her head in agreement. Then she walked over to the window and looked out.

"I wish we knew what the Takers were thinking when they first put humans on this planet. It was so long ago... How did they train the people of that time to work on machines of this time? It makes no sense."

"A lot of things aren't making sense right now. And I think we'll find a few more mysteries before we get to the truth. If you don't mind, I'm going to steal a few more computer techs tomorrow and see if they can get this technology center up and running. Maybe, then, we can solve some of our mysteries."

"Take whomever you need. I think we have enough to work in both places."

Charlie nodded his thanks before turning to leave Anne's office. As he reached the door, Bill came rushing in.

"We've been trying to reach you on the radio," he said between breaths.

Charlie and Anne waited for the winded man to catch his breath before continuing.

"The power has come back on in the old city! Something we did triggered the mechanism, and all the bells and whistles are ringing away."

"All right, I guess we're going back tonight. I need to go home first and tell Kala what's going on." He looked at Anne. "Do you have paper and a pen I can use?"

Anne handed him a pen and notepaper, and Charlie wrote down some names.

"Get these people and take them, along with the techs who were there today, to the city. Start them working on the computers. I want to know what they're doing by the morning. I'll meet you there later."

Bill nodded and left the room.

When Charlie got home he found Kala was just putting Charlene to bed. He went into the bedroom, took a quick shower, and changed his clothes.

"What's going on with you?" she asked when she came out of Charlene's room.

"Seems something we did today turned on the power in the underground city. All the computers are coming back on."

"Computers? Underground city?" Kala asked, confused.

"That's right! You don't know!"

Charlie told her what they had found and what appeared to be happening now.

"Wow! That is truly amazing. Are you going to be home at all tonight?"

"I don't know. I'll try to come back in a few hours. I want to see what the techs find out. It may take a while. Do you want to come with me? We can get someone to watch Charlene."

"I would like that. I can take Charlene over to the night-care facility. Can you wait for me?"

"I'll pack us some dinner and we can leave when you get back. Are you sure you want to wake her up when you just got her down?"

"Don't worry. I can do this without so much as having her hiccup!"

While Kala was taking Charlene to the night-care facility, Charlie put a light supper together and packed it up in a carry sack. Kala arrived back just as he finished getting the food together.

"She all set?"

"Good as gold."

"Let's go then. I'm anxious to see what's going on."

As they traveled to the old city, Kala asked many questions, and Charlie filled her in on the details she wanted. She was just about up to speed when they arrived at their destination.

At the triangle, Kala let Charlie descend first. As they went down the stairs, Kala noted how much light there was.

"Probably a combination of the lights and the computers," Charlie told her.

"Makes sense."

When they got to the computer section, they saw that all the people Charlie had requested were already at work.

"So what's the deal?" Charlie asked Kameron Good.

"Well, it looks like the triangle moving was the catalyst to get all this stuff going."

"Any idea what 'all this stuff' is?"

"Not yet, but seeing how familiar the software is to us, we should know soon."

"Any idea yet what time frame it came from?"

"It's obviously not as old as the city above. From the base code we've been able to access so far, it comes from about our time...maybe a year or two after we left since it's not something we were using when we left. Some of our people are running tests on the triangle to see how old that is as well."

"Any idea where the software came from?" Kala asked.

"Well, that's a bit easier. From the base code we're accessing, it seems like it came from North America. But we won't be sure until all our tests are run."

"How can that be?" Kala asked.

"We don't know," Kameron said.

Charlie and Kala moved on to talk to the other techs. They got the same answers that the first tech gave them. Looking around, they found a small room furnished with tables and chairs that looked like it could hold about twenty people. The lights were on in this room as well, so they decided to stay and eat the dinner Charlie had packed.

"Well, what do you think? They say the software came from our era in North America. How can that be? We were told this place was built a thousand years ago. Could it be that these aliens could travel through time as well as space?"

"Or maybe they landed here recently, without our knowledge, and set this place up."

"How could they do that without our knowing?" Kala asked, astonished.

"Who knows? It seems they can do a lot of things that we're unaware of. If it really is technology from our time and Earth, then maybe they set it up before we got here. Ten years would give it enough time to get as run down as it was."

"But if it is from our time and place and they brought it here before we got here, wouldn't Anne and her people have known about it?"

"Not necessarily. This place is far enough away that if they had wanted to remain unseen, they would be."

"What if they have some kind of beaming technology?" "Who knows? They seem so far ahead of us in so many other ways," Charlie shrugged.

Back in the computer section, they approached Kiana Johnson. Bill, Adel, and Bunny joined them.

"Let us know when you have the systems running," said Charlie.

"Should only be another minute or two for this station," she replied.

"Then we'll wait here."

They waited in silence while the Kiana worked. Charlie looked down the row of other techs working at other stations. As they waited, it seemed the lights were getting brighter.

"Did the lights just get brighter, or was that my imagination?" Charlie asked of no one in particular.

"They just got brighter, sir," replied John Baker. "I think I've found the primary control unit. I've accessed the system and we're into the database."

Everyone gathered around John. They watched as he accessed the primary system.

"I was right. We're in. What do you want me to do first?"

"See if you can search for when this complex was set up."

He punched a few keys and then sat back.

"This will take a..."

Before he could finish his sentence, the answer popped up on the screen.

"Seems this facility was set up twelve years ago...two years before Sierra Mission left Earth. The city above is centuries older. I doubt that the Taken people in the village knew about this complex," John continued.

"That's one mystery we still have to solve," said Charlie.

"What else have you found?" asked Adel.

"It looks like this complex was set up specifically for our use. It seems they thought we'd find it sooner."

226

"How could we have?" asked Bill.

"I guess they thought the Taken would bring us to the old city and we'd find this complex under the triangle."

"Can you find anything about a deflector of any kind?" asked Charlie.

"I'll search," John said, again punching keys.

While they waited, Bunny, Adel, Bill, and Kala looked at the activity at the other computer stations. Everything appeared to be coming on at once, and the techs were busy gathering information from the different programs that were starting up.

"Commander Hudson!" Kiana Johnson soon called out.

Charlie was about to argue the use of his title, but decided not to when Kala caught his eye and shook her head. He caught the meaning well: Let it go. This is the time for titles.

"What is it?" he asked going back to the woman's station.

"I think I've found something. A deflector doesn't exist now, but there is information, along with the schematics, on how to build one using planet material."

"Does it say how long it would take to build and deploy said deflector?" asked Kala.

"No, it doesn't. But the printers are working. If you want, I can print out a copy of these instructions and the schematics."

"*Is* there any paper?" Bill asked jokingly.

"We found plenty of usable paper sealed in plastic containers while we were searching earlier today."

"Print out one copy for now," said Charlie. "I want to see what building this deflector would entail."

With instructions and schematics in hand, the group went to the room Charlie and Kala had found earlier and sat at a table.

Bunny, Bill, Adel and Kala watched Charlie go through the documents once and, then, a second time.

"Well, building the deflector looks fairly straightforward. It should take about a week to get it up and running. Unfortunately, we don't have anything to test it on. The meteor shower won't be close enough to try it on for another three weeks. I'd hate to build this thing and find it doesn't work."

"Could we test it on one of the shuttles or ships?" asked Bunny.

"I'd rather not lose one of our means of transport or our contact with Earth."

"But I thought we were out of fuel for the shuttles," said Bill.

"We will be once the fuel on the ships runs out, but we may be able to convert them to solar power someday. Who knows? We might find information here that tells us how to manufacture fuel. We need to find something else to test the deflector on. The hookup is through the triangle, which needs to be in its closed position. We need to go over this more carefully. Why don't we take it back to Haven and go over it there? I think we can leave the restart of the complex's system in the capable hands that are here."

Reaching Haven in the growing morning light, Charlie, Bill, Adel, and Bunny returned to their homes; Kala went to the night-care facility to pick up Charlene. By the time Kala returned to the house, Charlene was awake and ready for her breakfast.

"Why don't you try and get some sleep," she said to Charlie. "I have a feeling you'll soon be pulling some late nights, and you'll need to rest when you can."

"I will. I just want to go over these documents again."

"No. You need to rest now, while you can. The next few days are going to be tough and you need to be clearheaded."

"Yes, Mother," came the facetious reply.

Kala shook her head in feigned disgust as Charlie retired to the bedroom and closed the door. She fed Charlene and then took her outside to play. As Kala watched Charlene play with her dolls, she wondered what their future was going to be like.

Would the meteor shower pass the planet without incident? Would they need to use this deflector? Would they need to move underground? Suddenly, a crying Charlene roused her out of her thoughts.

"Oh... What's the matter, baby?"

"Fall over," Charlene hiccupped.

"You poor thing."

Kala shook her head and tended to her daughter. She was glad she and Charlie had Charlene. If anything happened to either one of them, the other would have someone to hold on to.

Kala decided to take Charlene over to the day-care facility and get some sleep herself. She had a feeling the following days were going to be long and tiring for herself as well as Charlie, and she needed to take her own advice when it came to sleep. When she got back from the day-care facility, she quietly entered the bedroom and lay down next to Charlie.

After what seemed like only a few minutes, she woke up alone. She got up and dressed and went looking for Charlie. She found him at the kitchen table going over the deflector paperwork.

"Anything interesting?" she asked.

"Lots. I see now the deflector and the old city computer systems need to communicate with a ship. To repair the dissenters' damage, we had to bypass some of the systems on the ships we'll need. I don't know if the deflector or the computer systems will be able to access the ships. I hope our techs will be able to make them work."

"Do you still think we'll need the ships' deflectors?"

"I think it's time we went to the ships again and checked on the meteor shower from there. With a hookup to the old city computers, I think the ships' systems will be able to tell us more."

"When will you go?"

"After I've had time to study this more," Charlie said, holding up the papers, "and go over it with Bill and Adel."

The radio suddenly came online. It was a call from the old city.

"While you take this, I'm going to get Charlene from day care. We should spend some time with her; she's probably going to be there a lot the next few days."

Charlie nodded as he answered the call and blew Kala a kiss.

"This is Commander Hudson. What can I do for you?"

"We've found more information that we think you should see. Can you come back to the computer complex?"

"I'll be there later this evening, and I'll be spending the night. Should I bring anyone else with me?"

"You should probably bring Chief Chow and Adel Cooper. We found a document that shows us how to make the deflector work with the repairs we made to mend the damage done by the dissenters."

"I'll bring Bill and Adel. We'll plan on staying for a few days. Good work!"

"Thank you, sir. We'll see you later, and we'll call Chief Chow and Ms. Cooper."

The call ended and Charlie sat staring into space. He was wondering how those who had left the technology for them would know about the damage done to the communications systems on the ships and how they would have to fix it. He decided to talk to Anne before he went back to the old city. Almost immediately, Kala came back with a sleeping Charlene.

"Let me put her down and, then, you can tell me who called."

"It's about time we had some lunch. Do you want anything?"

"Whatever you're having is fine," Kala whispered, carrying Charlene to her room.

Over their late lunch, Charlie relayed the tech's message and their conversation and told Kala he was going to spend a couple of days in the old city.

"I feel like these aliens are still watching us, even though they haven't been to the planet in years. Maybe we should try contacting them," Kala suggested.

"I had the same thought. I'll have a tech put a message on repeat to see if we get a response. It may be that they want to make sure we succeed here, but they don't want to be known."

"Do you want me to go with you?" she asked, following Charlie into the bedroom. She watched him begin to pack.

"Not on this one, dear heart. I don't think the old city is a place for a child, so one of us should stay here with Charlene."

"I could leave her with someone from day care."

"I think it's best if I went alone on this one. I'll call you every night and keep you up-to-date."

"I guess you're right," Kala said, wistfully. "Now that we have Charlene, we both can't go running off whenever we want."

"I know you're disappointed, love, but this is something for command..."

"I was command!"

"What I meant was..."

"I know what you meant, but it still rankles a bit. Now that we're here and settled...been settled for ten years...it seems we're reverting to the old ways where the woman always stays home with the children."

"Do you want to go and I'll stay home with Charlene?"

"No. You've already studied this stuff and I'd just be trying to catch up. But I do want to go back again. I miss the technology."

"How about we both go together now? You can leave Charlene with night care for a few hours, get your fill of technology, and then come back. Would that help?"

"It would help. Thank you, love," Kala said, smiling.

Kala quietly arranged with night care that, if she didn't come back, Charlene would stay overnight. She quickly threw some clothes into a bag for herself and made up a bag for Charlene. When she was done, she joined Charlie.

"What's that?" he asked pointing at her bag.

"I thought I'd bring a bag just in case. Charlene is set up to stay overnight in night care in case I want to stay. I didn't think you'd mind."

Charlie shook his head and laughed.

"I guess one night won't hurt Charlene!"

After dropping off Charlene, Charlie and Kala headed to Bill's place. They found him just coming out the door with a bag in his hand.

"I didn't expect you to come along, Kala."

"I needed a night of light entertainment," she replied laughing. "Are we meeting Adel anywhere?"

"I called her. She said she'd meet us at the old city."

Kala, Charlie, and Bill traveled in silence to the old city, each deep in their own thoughts. When they got there, they headed straight for the triangle entrance and descended into the complex below. They made for an area that had been designated as crew quarters and dropped off their gear, then went to the computer room.

"Glad you're here," Scott Denney said, addressing Charlie and Bill. "We discovered more information after we called you."

Scott handed the print copy to Charlie. As Charlie read a page he handed it to Bill, who read it and, then, handed it on to Kala. When they were done, they looked back to the tech for an explanation.

"It looks like the aliens know about our trouble with the dissenters and the botched communication with Earth and the damage it did to our systems. They also know what we did to fix it and how it might complicate the plans to build the meteor deflector. So, they sent us this document."

"All that seems obvious," said Bill.

"Yes, it does, but there's more. Not only do they know we found this complex, but they're also monitoring our use of it. We found a signal going from this room out into space."

"Can you track where the signal is coming from and going to?" asked Kala.

"We're working on it, ma'am, but so far, we can only tell the general direction. We know they can be undetected on the planet, but they can also hide themselves in space. They may be right above the planet or light years away. We're trying everything, but not knowing how to use all these systems yet...even though it is similar to what we had when we left Earth... is holding us back."

"I wonder if they actually took the technology from Earth or if they built it themselves," said Bill.

"That's an interesting thought, sir," Scott rubbed his chin. "If they took it directly from Earth, then who made the modifications? And when were they made? If these beings created it themselves, why make it different from what we are used to? In order to slow us down? Or to make it so we can't find them?"

"How do we know these beings aren't humans?" asked Adel from the back of the room. She had entered shortly before the tech had alerted the others to the signal.

Everyone was silent as they considered Adel's question.

"We *don't*," Charlie said after a moment. "But if these beings are human, then that means humans are using time travel, and I just don't believe that's possible."

"Should we contact WASA to let them know what's going on?" one tech asked.

"Yes. Can we get a connection from here, or do we need to go back to Haven, or go up to the ships?"

"We haven't been able to make a connection from here yet," said Kameron Good from another station, "but we're working on it. This station is a communications station. We're copying the setup from the ships as fast as we can, but we're not quite there yet. We should be able to make a connection by morning."

"That gives us time," Kala smiled. "We need to plan what we want to say and not go off half-cocked."

Taking the earlier and latest documents to one of the conference rooms, Charlie, Bill, Adel, and Kala poured over the papers again. As they worked, Anne came into the room.

"Nice to see you here," said Charlie.

"I thought it was about time I got over here," she replied. "There are so many rumors going around about this place, I thought I should see it for myself. I heard you had been called back and thought I'd join you for a bit. I can't stay all night, but I'd like to know what's going on."

Anne sat down and they filled her in. They also told her Adel's theory of who the aliens were.

"I'm not sure I believe they're human. I do want to know who brought humans here in the first place, and who could build a place like this with no one knowing about it. I assure you that, although we knew about the old city, we didn't know about this complex. If we had known, we would have told you."

"Like you told us about the city?" Charlie said a little bit bitterly.

"We didn't think it was necessary. We've never had any problems in the past, so it never occurred to us that this place could be important. We've been up front with you about everything else since we've met. I would hope that would count for something."

"It counts for a lot," said Kala, putting her hand on Charlie's arm. "It's just that, since you have been so up front, we thought you would not leave anything out."

"We honestly didn't think this city could possibly have any uses for anyone anymore. That's the only reason we never said anything. And we really thought you'd eventually find it on your own. With all the exploring you've done, it's pretty surprising you *didn't* find it."

"We've probably walked right past the city numerous times," said Bill, "and never saw it. And who knows when this underground complex was installed. Could have been within the past ten years or it could have been before. There is just so much that is a mystery that we need to know.

Is there anything else you think you should tell us now?"

"Probably. With everything that's happened, we old-timers should think again what we need to tell you. I'll talk to the others and make up a list. We can schedule a meeting next week and go over anything else that we each might think is important. Does that sound fair to everyone?"

Conversation erupted as they all started talking to each other about what they thought was important to know. After a few minutes, they stopped talking and looked at each other sheepishly.

"I guess we need to figure out for ourselves what's important," said Kala. "We'll figure out what we want to know and you decide what you want to tell us. When we meet, we'll discuss."

"Sounds like a good idea to me," replied Anne.

CHAPTER 35

As the night wore on, Charlie, Kala, Bill, and Adel went over the latest information they had received. They were glad to find that the ships would play only a minor role in using the deflector, supplying the extra power boost needed.

"Well, this is an unusual plan," said Bill.

"It certainly is," replied Charlie. "Kala and Adel, what do you think?"

"It's a relief to have a defense against space-born projectiles," Kala said. Adel nodded her agreement.

"But I wonder what the payment is going to be."

"What do you mean?" asked Bill.

"What I mean is when people give you something, they usually want something in return. If I offered to give you a cure for cancer, let's say, wouldn't you think I wanted something in return?"

Looking around, Kala saw they reluctantly agreed.

"Well, I'm wondering what these 'people' want by giving us this computer complex and feeding us information," Kala continued. "It seems to me we're doing their work for them. I'm a bit suspicious."

"Can you put your finger on anything specific?" Charlie asked.

"Not yet, but give me some time. I have a bad feeling. I don't know what's causing it, but I think that Anne might be a part of it because of the way she's kept things from us over the years. Now, suddenly, she's willing to help. I wonder if even the old-timers are in with her."

Silence followed this statement, and they guiltily looked at each other. They could tell each one was thinking the same thing.

"So what do we do now?" asked Adel.

"I think we have to confront Anne," said Bunny, speaking up from the door. The four turned in their seats, startled by the words and the speaker.

"But not now. We must first make sure we're all in agreement about what we will do. And we must keep our suspicions to ourselves. We need to act like everything is normal."

"But you're one of the old-timers," said Charlie, surprised

"Yes, I am, but Anne keeps her own counsel; she always has. We knew about this city, and some of us even suspected that there was more to it than she would tell us. Now we know. I think we need to move cautiously. The safety of the entire planet and all our lives are at stake."

No one at the table disagreed with her.

"So what do we do now?" asked Kala.

"You build the deflector. For the moment, you need to act like everything is normal. But, we find out what is being hidden from us and make sure everything is out in the open."

They murmured agreement and returned to studying the papers in front of them. Suddenly, Charlie sat back in his chair.

"Bunny, are the 'old-timers' the aliens that we've been talking about?"

Bunny looked at him carefully before answering.

"Not all of them. Most of them are what Anne said, direct transplants or descendants of transplants from Earth." Bunny paused, then spoke decisively. "We who are alien have been watching Earth for eons and know that in the last hundred years, humans have gone from a violent race to a nonviolent one."

Charlie and the others stared at Bunny.

"You?" Charlie shook his head, incredulous at this revelation.

Bunny nodded.

"But I don't understand. Why have us do your dirty work? Why not build a meteor deflector yourselves?"

"There are many reasons. But the most important was...is...to push those on the planet to better themselves."

There was silence.

"I still don't think we understand." Kala spoke softly. "The Takers... you...have the technology. Why haven't they built a deflector?"

"There wasn't a need until now. We were instructed to keep watch on the skies...and we have. No other meteor shower has gotten this close."

Still skeptical, the four tried to digest Bunny's explanation.

"So what you're saying is that the Takers want us to better ourselves by building a deflector, is that correct?" Kala asked.

Bunny nodded again.

"Okay..." Charlie spoke up, deciding to accept Bunny at her word. "So is there enough time for us to build the deflector before the meteor shower arrives?"

"From what the plan and schematics show, we appear to have plenty of time. Our own people have estimated the meteor shower won't arrive for another three weeks, and the deflector can be built in one."

"I just hope it will work," Charlie responded, shaking his head.

"The Takers have told us these deflectors have worked for many generations. But they must be programmed correctly."

Charlie nodded. "Do the other old-timers know who you are and why you're here?"

Bunny once again looked at Charlie carefully. Finally, she seemed to make another decision.

"No. As far as they're concerned, my companions and I are the same as they. We find ways of inserting ourselves into the society. When we arrive on a planet, we identify ourselves as another group of taken humans."

"Will you continue to do this?"

"Not likely. Now that you know who I am and what the aliens are doing here, we'll likely be more straightforward about first contact."

"Does Anne know who are the aliens and who are the humans, or did you fool her too?" Charlie asked, his voice hard.

"She is as in the dark as everyone else." Bunny sounded apologetic. "Charlie, we really don't want to hurt anyone. Your race is the most promising one we've ever met. We want to make sure that humans continue to exist."

Suddenly tired, Charlie looked at his watch and was surprised to see morning had come.

"Okay. That'll have to do for now. The first thing we have to do is build the deflector, make sure it works, and stop worrying about a possible meteor strike."

He sounded resigned "I think we're done here." Looking pointedly at Kala, he said, "I think we should all return to Haven and rest."

Kala nodded her agreement.

Charlie continued, "We need to meet with Anne and the ruling council and bring them up to speed."

There was a murmur at the last comment.

"We need the entire council behind us," he said, "not just Anne. We must make sure that they all understand what has been and is happening here. That will make it easier to tell everyone."

Charlie, Kala, Bill, and Adel left Bunny working at a computer. On the way back to Haven, they walked in silence, once again, each deep in their own thoughts.

After picking up Charlene and eating, Kala, Charlie, and Charlene napped—a much needed rest for the parents. They were woken up by the bleep of the radio.

"Hudson here."

It was Bill.

"Charlie, we're meeting in an hour with Anne and the council. They've agreed to meet today so we can bring them up-to-date. And I've called Bunny to advise her of the meeting time."

"Where should we meet you?"

"In front of the meeting hall."

"We'll see you in an hour then. Hudson out."

Charlie and Kala didn't have to wait long after dropping off Charlene at day care for Bill, Adel, and Bunny to arrive. They entered the meeting hall.

Charlie let Bunny take the lead. She held nothing back. She explained why the Takers had taken earthlings and seeded other planets with them: her people thought that humans had promise, and they didn't want humanity dying out, either by their own hand or some other event.

"So your people, the Takers, have taken people from Earth and seeded them on other planets because of the belief humans have potential," was Anne's only response when Bunny was done. She was clearly skeptical.

"It's the truth," was Bunny's simple response.

"And the Takers placed some of their own people on the seeded planet so you could keep track of us."

Bunny acknowledged Anne's statement with a nod.

"Do you really look like us, or are you disguised," a council member asked.

"We look enough like humans that a disguise is easy to accomplish." Bunny smiled. "We never meant any harm to the human race. We just wanted you to survive your brutal past. Once it was clear that you would survive and become a peaceful people, we ceased our activities. But we continued to keep track of the planets we seeded with our own people. In this way, we were able to ensure that each community survived."

The room erupted with talk and questions. Anne let it go on for several seconds before she banged her gavel.

"I know Bunny's revelation is a shock," she said, "but we need to focus on the potential meteor strike. Should we continue to create a space in the caves or will the deflector solve our problem?"

"It is always best to have a backup plan. There were planets we seeded that had other problems we were unaware of. Only by the resourcefulness of the humans we had placed there were the inhabitants able to survive. Here on this planet, you are also proving your resourcefulness."

"So what you mean is we should continue to prepare the caves?"

"Yes."

"Okay. You say the deflector will take a week to build. Take the people you need to get it up and running, the rest of us will continue setting up the caves. Obviously, we want the deflector to work, but you're right, we also need a backup plan. I want daily reports on your progress, and I want the committee to be present when the deflector is turned on. Will it deflect continuously or will it activate only when it is needed?"

"Once it is programmed and running properly, it will only activate as needed. We will need to monitor it regularly, but turning it on will be as easy as flipping a switch."

"We'll see. I think it would be best if Bunny were in charge of this project. Are there any objections?"

There were none and she continued.

"I would like Charlie and Kala to be my contacts on the project. Are there any objections?"

Again, there were no objections.

"I will expect a full report on everything once we're out of danger. Until then, daily progress reports will suffice."

Anne ended the meeting. As everyone was leaving Anne called back Charlie, Kala, Bill, and Adel.

"I want your progress reports to be as detailed as possible. If Bunny is telling the truth, we'll have to decide what to do with this information, but not until we've dealt with the meteor shower. Please keep me updated on everything. Understood?"

"Understood," everyone replied at the same time.

Stepping into the afternoon sunlight, Kala and Charlie watched Bill and Adel head toward their homes to prepare for the week's stay in the old city.

"We need to decide which one of us goes when. We can't leave Charlene with in day care for a solid week."

"Maybe one of us takes the day shift and the other takes the night shift? That way one of us can always be home with Charlene," said Kala. "Is that a workable plan?"

"Yes," Charlie grinned, thankful for Kala's logic. "Which shift do you want?"

"Why don't I take the day shift? You go now for tonight, and I'll start tomorrow. Is everyone going to be staying in the computer complex?"

"Yes. There're places to sleep and eat, so I suppose we are."

"Well, I'm thankful for that."

Kala prepared an overnight bag for Charlie, packing something to eat and snacks.

"Well, guess I'm ready. I'll see you in the morning." Charlie was anxious to go.

"I'll see you bright and early. Love you." Kala wrapped her arms around Charlie.

"Love you too." He kissed and held her tight. Then he left.

Chapter 36

Kala stood thinking in the now silent house. Shaking herself, she remembered Charlene and left to pick up her daughter. She spent the rest of the day and into the early evening playing with Charlene. After dinner, she gave Charlene her bath and put her to bed. Just after she got her down she heard the radio beep. It was Charlie.

"Hi! What's up?"

"We'll be able to do it! We *are* going to be able to build this deflector, and it should work!" Charlie's voice was excited.

"Well, that's good news. Will you have to go up to the ships anytime soon?"

"Yes, we will, but that won't happen until later in the week, once we've gotten the basics done here on the ground. From what Bunny's shown us, it definitely should take only a week."

"That's great. How close is the meteor shower?"

"At last check, still three weeks away."

"All in all, good news."

"How are you and Charlene?"

"She's in bed and that's where I'm headed. I'm exhausted and need a few hours' sleep if I'm going to be able to function tomorrow."

"Well, we'll have made a good start tonight, so things should go well tomorrow."

"What time should I arrive in the morning?"

"Not before daybreak. Everyone here is getting ready to turn in. It's been a long day, and we're exhausted. I'll be the only one staying up all night."

"Okay, I'll get there sometime after daybreak. I'll bring Charlene to day care first, and then travel."

"Hey, why don't we just leave Charlene in day care all day so I can sleep once I get home? You can pick her up when you get home."

"Good idea. If you wait for me to arrive, we can switch shifts there."

"Even better. Then I can brief you myself," he said, his voice tinged with longing. "I'll see you in the morning."

"I love you," she said.

"I love you too," he said and signed off.

The next morning Kala was up before dawn. Soon she was on her way to the old city. When she arrived, she found Charlie, Bill, and Adel at breakfast.

"So, what are you sleepyheads up to this morning?" she asked.

"Adel and I are just about to get back to work," said Bill. "Charlie can bring you up-to-date, then join us in the computer room."

The room emptied, leaving Kala and Charlie alone.

"What happened during the night?"

"Not much. We started the programming for the deflector. I did some more digging on what we'd have to do to modify the ships, and it doesn't look like there's much work to do there. Just some changes to the ship deflectors, and that shouldn't mess with the communications."

"Can't we communicate from this location now?"

"We can, but that will take some modifications as well, and we want to finish the deflector work first. Later, when we have time, we'll update the communications array."

"That makes sense," Kala replied. "What's on the schedule for today?"

"More programming. Quite a bit is needed. Mostly, it's getting the communication link to the ships working, but I don't think there'll be any problems. Just a lot of grunt work."

"Well, I guess I'm as briefed as I'm going to be without going in there and getting my hands dirty. Time you went back to the house and get some rest. I left some food for lunch, and Charlene is scheduled to stay in day care until I get back tonight."

"That sounds wonderful. Thanks!" Charlie kissed her and left.

Kala stood in the door of the computer room, taking in the scene. There were fifteen to twenty computer stations active, and most of them were occupied. There was a bank of screens above the computer monitors, displaying different types of information.

Kala walked slowly round the room and carefully looked at the different computer monitors. Some stations were monitoring the life signs in the room, while others were monitoring the ships in space.

"How do they keep track of the ships in space?" she asked Kiana Johnson, who was sitting at a ship-monitoring station.

"Once Sierra Mission landed and was established on the planet, the aliens placed their monitors on board the ships. Then, they came here and connected the monitors to these stations. This technology is still new to us."

"That it is," Kala replied, smiling and moving on to another station.

This station didn't seem to be monitoring anything.

"What's this station for?" she asked.

"For entering and accessing information." Bill, sitting at the next station, answered her question. "It can access ship data and the ships' communications stations, anything we might be entering at the other stations here, and communicate with Haven and even Earth."

Kala sat down at the station and checked it.

"Did we put safeguards on the computers?" she quietly asked Bill.

"Yes. Everyone must create their own login with a password. Status level will determine what access each person has. The first thing we have to do today is set you up with a command level sign-in. Give me a sec and we'll set you up on that station."

"Will it be station specific?"

"No, user specific. We're going to do the same thing on the ships as well."

Kala nodded, satisfied. She sat and waited for Bill to finish her setup. While she waited, she continued to look at the other stations.

"What else can be monitored from this room?" she asked Scott Denney, who was sitting nearby.

"Everything...from the old city above us, to Haven, to most of the planet. We haven't fully accessed these systems yet."

An old question stirred in Kala's mind.

"What about those of us who wanted a low-tech society?" she asked, turning to Bill.

"We can still have it," he replied. "Who says we have to use this room for anything other than communications and meteor deflection?"

"What about the dissenters? What if there are still people in Haven who helped them or believes in what they stood for? Wouldn't they try to gain access to this room for their own purpose?"

"We will keep the complex locked up and have a regular staff who works here. Those who don't want anything to do with technology won't have to see it or even think about it. I know I'll feel safer knowing it's here, but I doubt I'll ever want to work here once this is over."

Kala smiled; she was happy with Bill's answer.

"Okay...let's get you set up with a user name and password!"

Once able to access data, Kala started reviewing the different aspects of the deflector activity. When she was satisfied that everything was going okay, she started accessing what the aliens thought were important parts of their daily life in Haven. She found the aliens were highly interested in the number of yearly births and deaths and the kinds of jobs people were doing.

She also learned the computer room had been used on and off since they had arrived on the planet. Probably by Bunny and her alien comrades, she assumed. She saw that no confidential information was ever sent to the alien home world, but information was sent nonetheless.

"Bill, did you notice that this complex was used to send information to the alien home world? I'm assuming Bunny and her comrades used it."

"Yes, we noticed. We're hoping you'll handle this. Maybe talk to Bunny about it?"

"Do you think it's that important?"

"We think it's important enough to look into. It's disturbing that aliens have been watching us to ensure we're living up to their expectations. We need to know if there are other reasons they have been watching us."

"Consider it done. I'll talk to Bunny sometime today. I want to do some more checking, just to make sure I have all the facts."

Later, Kala found Bunny helping out in the section where the deflector was being built.

"Bunny, do you have time to talk?"

"Sure. What's up?"

"Let's take a walk topside. I have a few questions for you."

"Just give me a minute to make sure things are going well here."

Out in the fresh air, they walked over to a bench and sat down.

"How long have your alien friends been keeping an eye on this planet?"

"We've had some of our people here ever since we first seeded the planet. We try to keep an eye on all the planets we seed. We want to make sure they'll succeed."

"But once you're sure, why don't you leave them alone?"

"We never interfere. We just watch."

"What happens if the planet you seed isn't successful? Do you send in help?"

"Sometimes we do. Sometimes the planet is too far away to monitor it the way we want to. We keep track of it, and if the inhabitants need help we try to supply it. If we can't, then they survive the best they can. But, mostly, we seed planets near our home world so we can monitor them easily."

"Hmmm... You said you started taking humans because you saw potential in us for good things?"

"Yes... So far, of all the races we've dealt with, the humans have had the most potential for good. We wanted to make sure you survived."

"But how did you know which people to take?"

"We didn't in the beginning. We made some grave mistakes and the Taken didn't survive on our first couple of planets past the first five years. Once we learned what our mistakes were, we started observing the people on Earth more closely. When we found people of strength and character, we took them. If we didn't get enough at one time, we placed those we took into stasis and found more. Once we had enough, we seeded a planet. And we always made sure never to overcull an area."

"Your records must be very detailed."

"Very. We always record everything; we have records for every person ever taken. Your parents, for instance. We were going to take them before the situation arose with you and Lindsey. With your mother pregnant, we couldn't risk taking her and putting her in stasis. It all turned out for the best because they raised a good daughter and a good leader."

Kala was stunned. Her parents might still be alive if her mother hadn't helped Lindsey's parents. But then, Kala would not be alive. She shivered and changed the subject.

"So tell me about this planet. When did you first seed it?"

"We didn't."

"What? I just thought you told me you did?"

"Well, in a way we did, at least, another branch of our people did. They seeded this planet about fifteen hundred years ago. They kept the same kinds of records we do, but they didn't store them the same way we do. Their records were lost. We don't know why they chose the humans they did or why they brought those humans here. We do know the other branch didn't have the same reasons to seed planets, but their reasons were never known to us."

Kala was slowly digesting this new twist in the planet's story. Seeing her reaction, Bunny paused, but Kala gestured her to continue.

"When my people found this planet, about a thousand years ago, we were surprised to find humans were already here. We kept an eye on the planet, but the others, who first seeded the planet, never showed up. So we took over."

"So the records we have only go back a thousand years?"

Bunny nodded.

"But humans were brought here long before that?"

Again Bunny nodded.

"Okay...go on."

"We found a thriving civilization. Every now and then, my people would make a drop and insert one of us into the population...at the most, our group numbered thirty. We use a covert method to contact the home world, but make contact infrequently. My people periodically returned to keep us up-to-date on the current technology. When you showed up, on your own, we thought that the human race had finally progressed far enough to not need our help. But when we saw the meteor shower on a trajectory toward this planet with a probable meteor strike, we knew that you would need our help one last time."

"How do you drop your people with no one knowing?"

"I don't have time to explain now. Let's just say that we have our ways. When the danger has passed, I'll tell you all I know."

"You'll keep your word to tell us?"

"I'll keep my word."

"And you'll answer any questions we have?"

"I promise."

"So...continue. You saw a meteor shower is approaching and realized we would need your help."

"We built the underground complex and made it to activate when the triangle was moved. We knew you would search the records and that Anne would tell you about the old city. We also knew you would ask questions, but we thought we'd have time to answer them. For now, all you need to know is that we have a way to stop a meteor strike. The home world has told us a meteor *will* strike this planet, and everyone will die unless we build the deflector."

"What about our plan to go into the caves?"

"It won't work. An impact will be deep and the devastation will be too great."

"You sound almost scared."

"I am scared. This isn't something to take lightly."

"I'm not taking it lightly, Bunny. It just seems odd that, for such an advanced race, your people can't divert a single meteor away from a planet. Why make us do it?"

"My people can divert it, but we want you to have the technology to protect yourself in the future."

"Why? Don't you think we're doing well enough without it?"

"Kala, it's not like that..."

"Then tell me what it is like," Kala said, irritated. "So far, it seems we've done everything you've wanted us to. Why should we continue without some explanation?"

"There will be an explanation, but not until after the meteor has been deflected and destroyed."

Kala didn't respond. Instead, she thought about where the discussion was going. She inhaled and exhaled deeply and looked at Bunny.

"So, for now, we do what you want and build the deflector. We use it on the meteor and save ourselves. Then what? Where do we go from there? There are those of us who came here to get away from technology. We sent people to that damned island because of technology. You've been watching us for ten years and didn't know all this?"

Bunny didn't say anything. She stared at the ground and sighed.

"I'm not saying we're not happy for your help, Bunny. It's just that... Why did your people feel the need to meddle with the human race?"

"I've already told you. Because we felt you had promise."

Kala sighed. Just then, two techs came out from the triangle. Kala stood up and Bunny followed her lead. They walked back to the triangle.

"I need to process this information, Bunny. I also must share it with Charlie and Bill as well as the ruling council."

"Of course. Just don't think we're the same as the humans who were sent to the island."

"Oh, I don't think you're anything like the people who were sent to the island. I don't know if your deception is worse or not, but at least, yours was for the common good. Their actions were for their own good."

"We really didn't mean any harm."

Kala sighed again and nodded her head. She returned to the computer station she had been working at before and sat staring at the screen organizing her thoughts before she leaned forward and began typing. She wrote up a full and detailed report of her conversation with Bunny.

"What are you working on?" asked Bill.

"A report on my conversation with Bunny for you and Charlie. It was very informative."

"What did she have to say?"

Kala told Bill everything. When she finished, he was shocked.

"I wonder why they find humans so interesting."

"I don't think that's what's important right now."

"Oh, I agree, but the reason will be something to pursue later."

"What I wonder is why they think we'd want all this technology? They knew we were looking for a place where we could get away from it."

"Right now, this technology is going to save our butts, Kala. From what she said, we wouldn't survive the impact even if we went into the caves."

"I know, but if they know a meteor is going to strike, why don't they just take care of it for us?"

"To help us be more self-sufficient? That's the only explanation I can think of. They may want us to think on our feet like they know we can."

"You may be right, but it still rankles a bit. I mean... We come all this way just to find out we've been led here all along? Doesn't that gall you just a bit?"

"Yes, it does, but I find that, sometimes, you have to let go. Things become a bit easier to deal with. Right now, we need to deal with this meteor strike. We can deal with the other stuff later. You okay with that?"

"I'll have to be, won't I? I'm just the type of person who, sometimes, lets her emotions get in the way, that's all. I'll be fine."

Later, entering the break room for lunch, Kala and Bill saw Bunny and a few techs there, eating. They sat down at the table with Bunny.

"I hope you're not too mad at me after our conversation earlier," Bunny said to Kala.

"I'm not mad, Bunny," Kala replied. "But I have questions that I'll want answered after we've dealt with the meteor. Right now... I think I understand all I need to."

"I'm glad. I consider you a friend and I wouldn't want that to change." And then they talked about inconsequential things.

"With the progress we're making," said Adel happily working at her computer station, "we might even be done before the week is out."

"If we keep going day and night like this, you may be right," said Bill. "What do you think, Bunny?"

"I agree. If we keep going like this, we'll be in very good shape."

They continued working throughout the afternoon without encountering problems. Bunny was there to answer questions, but very few popped up. Each computer had a set of detailed instructions that the programmers and techs worked from. All that was needed was data entry. It was just a matter of how fast they could accurately do this.

When Kala was ready to leave for the afternoon, she printed a copy of her report for Anne and waited for Charlie.

"Well, hello there, stranger," she said with a smile.

Kala briefly summarized her talk with Bunny and told Charlie how the rest of the day had gone.

"I emailed you a copy of the report, so you can read it at your leisure tonight. This copy is for Anne."

"Okay."

"Well, I'd better get going. They'll be expecting me to pick up Charlene, and I want to rest up tonight. I'm exhausted."

They kissed, and Kala left. In a way, she felt like she was commuting again, like she did when she was on her way home from school. In Haven, she stopped by Anne's office and gave her report to Lorraine. Then she headed to the day-care facility to pick up Charlene.

And that's how the rest of the week went for Kala. Get up early in the morning, get her and Charlene ready, take Charlene to day care. Travel to the complex, work on data entry, prepare a progress report for Anne, update Charlie, return to Haven, pick up Charlene. She talked more to Bunny, but their conversations were never as detailed as the first one. As promised, Bunny answered all Kala's questions. She was a wonderful resource.

"How many of your people are on the planet right now?" Kala asked one day at the lunch break.

"We are down to less than twenty now."

"How long has it been since someone new came?"

"The last drop was right before you arrived. We knew you were on your way here, and we wanted some fresh eyes here."

"Are they all in Haven?"

"Not all. Some of them sided with the dissenters and went to the island with them, and others died. We are not planning to drop any more now."

"Why? We could learn so much from each other."

"Because you want to be a low-tech society, and we are not that way. Those of us who dropped accepted a low-tech way of life. Each assignment we accept has its drawbacks, and, for this planet, it was the lack of technology. It is very hard for us to do without technology."

Kala thought about Bunny's admission.

"It was hard for some of us to get used to a low-tech life as well," she said finally. "As the dissenters showed, some humans are never happy unless they can have things their own way."

"The same is true with our people."

After lunch, they were to finish the programming of the computers. The next day would be the day to go to the ships to do the limited programming needed there. Charlie was taking the night off because he was going to the ships.

Kala and Bunny spent the afternoon going over the preparations for the work on the ships. Bunny was optimistic that everything would go well.

"I think we're ready," Bunny said when they finished.

"You really think this is going to work?"

"We're sure it's going to work. We've saved other planets using this method."

"I feel better. It's good to know we're using a system that's been tested."

The plan for the next day was to send up four people to the ships: Charlie and Bill and two techs. From the two computer stations on each bridge, they would do the necessary programming and communicate with Earth. Charlie had been keeping WASA up-to-date on the recent developments, but he wanted to ensure that WASA had the most current information.

Though communications with Earth had been less and less frequent over the years, it was still necessary to keep in contact. Even though they were now on their own, it was comforting to stay in contact with their home planet. Kala had talked to her family and Lindsey over the years. They had exchanged pictures of weddings and children, and all the other important events in their lives.

But this communication would not be an exchange of the mundane concerns of daily life. They would send WASA the plans and schematics of the meteor deflector. If a meteor came Earth's way, WASA would have a way to deal with it. They would also send the details Bunny had given them on the Takers.

Since Charlie, Bill, and all the techs were spending the night in Haven, Bill posted guards at all the interior and exterior doors of the computer complex and around the triangle. Charlie didn't want to take any chances that new dissenters might interfere.

Charlie gave the marching orders to Bill and Kameron Good and Kiana Johnson, the two techs chosen to go with Charlie and Bill.

"We'll meet at 6 a.m. tomorrow. I want to be in the air at 7 a.m."

On their way to pick up Charlene at day care, Kala and Charlie walked arm in arm. Kala would drop Charlene off early the next morning so she could watch the liftoff.

"I'll miss going into space," she said as they walked from the day-care facility to the house.

"I know, love, but you know our rule."

"I know. One of us stays on the planet at all times."

"I promise when she gets older, if there's enough fuel, I'll take you up again. But, now, she needs one of her parents."

"I know, love, I know. Let's talk about happier things."

They talked nonsense with Charlene while they made dinner and she played with her toys. After dinner, Kala cleaned up, and Charlie got Charlene ready for bed. Done for the night, they went into the bedroom and made love.

CHAPTER 37

The next morning, Charlie, Bill, and the techs met at the shuttles as planned. After Kala watched the shuttles lift off, she traveled with Adel, Bunny, and a group of techs to the old city and the computer complex. While Adel directed the techs, Kala busied herself consolidating reports and was glad to see Adel and the techs at the computer stations double and triple checking the data they had entered during the past week. Needing a break, she got up and went topside to get a breath of fresh air.

When she came back in, she saw emails from WASA had been placed at her station. She handled the work-related ones, and delivered the personal ones.

Meanwhile, up on the ships, the planned activity progressed quickly. The data entry had been done on each ship, and Charlie had made contact with WASA and sent the information on the meteor deflector.

On the *Brava*, Bill radioed Charlie.

"We're done here. How about you?"

"We're done as well. Time to get back down to the planet," Charlie replied. "You two head back. We'll be right behind you."

Back on the planet, they headed to the computer complex to report their success.

"Now we play the wait-and-see game," said Adel, "What did the trajectory of the meteor shower look like?" she asked Charlie. "Is there a meteor headed our way?"

"Looks like it's right on course for the planet," he responded. "After what I saw today, there's no doubt. Our first opportunity to deflect the meteor will be next Wednesday. If that doesn't work, we'll have two more shots at it."

"It'll work the first time," said Bunny.

"Only if you're correct about the programming and data we entered."

"I'm sure. Our home-world scientists used the same plan to save our planet."

"I'll accept that," said Bill. "We have to have hope in something."

"Well, even with hope, I think we still need our backup plan," said Charlie. "Let's go home and rest up. There's still plenty of things to move to the caves.

"So how was it up there?" Kala asked as they walked home from the day-care facility after picking up Charlene.

"As beautiful as you probably remember it from when we first arrived."

"Did everything go well?"

"Everything went just as planned."

"Don't feel like talking about it?"

"What's there to talk about? We went to the ships, we installed the programming, we contacted WASA, and we came home. What's this need to hear everything?"

"And what's this need not to tell me anything?"

Charlie sighed. He was tired and wanted nothing more than to have a nice hot shower and talk about something other than the deflector for a while, and he told Kala so.

"I'm sorry," Kala was a little hurt. "It's just that I feel a little left out, not being there."

"Well, all went as planned and that's all there is to it. I'm sorry I snapped at you. It's just that I'm tired and want to rest."

"I understand. I'm sorry, too."

They walked in silence with Charlene back to the house.

CHAPTER 38

The following Wednesday, Bill, Kala, Adel, Bunny, and Anne were gathered around Charlie at a computer station. Everyone was anxious, concerned that the meteor deflector would not work—except Bunny. Charlie entered the codes and his finger paused over the "Enter" key. Looking at the faces surrounding him, he pressed the key. There was a brief pause, the ground shuddered, and they heard a high-pitched squeal. Then, silence.

All eyes were on the monitors as the connection with the ships came up, the computers whirred, and data scrolled by. After what seemed like an eternity, everything stopped—no more whirring, no more data. They did not move in the ensuing silence and stared at the computer monitors.

"Well," said Charlie, "I wonder if it worked."

"Pull up this link and you'll find out," said Bunny, handing him a piece of paper.

Charlie's hands hit the keys and he typed what was written. What came up was a link to the ships' monitors, showing the meteor. There was an audible sigh of relief. They now knew the link from the surface to the ships was working. They could see the meteor and a green light heading toward it. The light reached the meteor and focused on it. The trajectory of the meteor slowly began to shift.

"Well, it seems to be working," Adel said quietly.

"Just like I told you it would," Bunny said.

"No disrespect, Bunny, but we had to see it for ourselves."

"I understand, but sometimes you have to have faith."

"True enough," Charlie said still staring at the computer monitor.

They watched as the meteor moved away from the planet. Suddenly, the meteor exploded and broke into pieces.

"What the hell just happened?" Bill asked.

"What *was* that?" Adel echoed.

"Our destruction beam activated," said Bunny.

"*What* destruction beam?" Kala asked, without taking her eyes off the monitor.

"I uploaded a destruction beam along with the deflection beam. They piggybacked to create a resonance as the meteor moved. We hoped the vibration would destroy the meteor. And it did. We didn't want this meteor to pose a threat to any other planets.

"Why didn't you tell us?" Charlie's voice was tense.

"Would it have made a difference if I had?" Bunny replied, a bit defensively.

"Charlie, why don't you lay off? She was only doing what she thought was best. Why do we need to know everything that goes on?" Kala stepped in, trying to diffuse the sudden emotion.

"You're right, Kala, I'm sorry, Bunny. It's just that I'm tired and very glad the danger is finally over."

"Don't worry. I didn't take it personally. I'm tired too. I think we all are. We need a break. Now that the meteor is destroyed, we can leave the monitoring of the meteor fragments and the rest of the meteor shower to the techs. If something happens, one of them can come and get us. Do you agree?"

Everyone agreed. Charlie assigned a few techs to keep monitoring and he and the others left. Traveling back to Haven, they spoke little, feeling drained after the past week's intense work and not in the mood to talk. When they reached Haven, they immediately went their separate ways.

The next day, Charlie and Kala met with Anne to give her their final report.

"So you think that Bunny was trying to make things easier by not telling us about the destruction beam?" Anne asked when they were done with their report.

"Yes." Charlie and Kala answered in unison.

"Okay... So what's next?"

"We monitor the fragments and make sure none of them are big enough to do any damage," Kala replied.

"And if there are?"

"Then we try the beam on them," said Charlie. "If there's still a danger, we may have to use the caves, but I don't think that will happen. The beam shattered the meteor pretty well. But I don't think the fragments will be any danger to us here or to any other planets."

"Guess we're all set, then," said Anne.

"I think so."

"What about communications to Earth? Can we accomplish that from the computer complex?"

"I believe so. We tried once and were successful, so I'll say communications will work on a regular basis."

"And what about those who don't want anything to do with technology?"

"They don't have to use the complex or go anywhere near it, if they don't want to," Kala replied. "But they'll have to understand that, now we do have it, some of us will be going there to use the technology. They'll have to accept it."

Anne nodded and sighed. She thought of all that had happened in the past week, but felt relieved the crisis was over.

"Things will be changing around here," she said, more to herself and not to Kala and Charlie.

"But most of it for the good, I believe," said Charlie.

"Do you think we'll be getting any more visits from Bunny's people, Kala?"

"I think only by our invitation. I believe we should keep that door open. If we need anything in the future, it would be nice to have friends to help us out."

"Agreed," said Anne. "I'll leave that to you two. I think you've gotten close enough to Bunny to work something out with her and her comrades."

Kala and Charlie murmured their acceptance of this new responsibility.

"And don't forget, we are changing the ruling council this spring. I want one of you to consider being on it."

"Yes...funny you should say that. We've discussed it and decided Charlie will be the one, if asked. I'm going to spend more time with Charlene, and I'd like to start working in the arts."

Meeting over, Kala and Charlie left, looking forward to the first normal day in a while.

"Let's not get Charlene yet," Kala said. "I'd like to have lunch at home... just the two of us for once."

Charlie smiled his "yes."

Over lunch, they talked of the future and what it might hold for them.

"Do you want another child?" Charlie asked.

"What brings that up all of a sudden?" Kala asked, taken aback by the question.

"I was just thinking that I've always wanted at least two kids. I was wondering how you felt about it."

Kala hesitated before answering, nibbling on her lunch while she thought.

"I guess a brother or sister for Charlene would be a good idea. She's two now, so it's probably a good time to start trying."

"Want to start trying now?" Charlie asked, his eyes finally expressing all his pent-up longing.

Kala laughed and led him into the bedroom.

CHAPTER 39

Over the next week, the techs monitored the trajectory of the meteor fragments. They confirmed no large pieces would come near the planet. Once word spread that the planet was safe, Haven held a thanksgiving celebration with much food and music. Everyone attended and the ruling council congratulated Charlie and the team for keeping the planet safe. That night, the meteor shower lit up the sky, providing a dazzling display for all to see.

Charlie and Kala soon found themselves pregnant again and started planning for the new baby.

"Do you want a boy or a girl?" Kala asked one day.

"I won't lie," Charlie said, "I'd love a boy, but I'll truly be happy with a healthy baby."

"I'd like a boy too. We'd have one of each...and we can stop."

"What! You don't want to have ten kids?" Charlie laughed.

"No, I don't want ten kids! I never thought I'd want *one*, but I'm very happy with Charlene, and I know I'll be happy with this baby. I enjoy being a mother more than I thought I would."

They began building an addition to their home, and many of their neighbors helped them, excited to be part of the new life coming. Once the addition was completed, all they had to do was wait for the baby to arrive.

In the spring, Charlie was elected to the ruling council and happily spent his days using his knowledge and experience to advise the community. Kala visited the computer complex to keep in touch with family and friends on Earth. She learned that the aliens who had traveled to Earth were the very same Takers—Bunny's people—who had seeded their planet and watched over them.

Bunny told them the name of her people was the Grondi, and that the Grondi had helped the inhabitants of Earth clean up the planet. Humans on Earth were no longer in danger of extinction. Happy that the Earth and its people had survived, the people of Haven continued building their community as they wanted it, living a low-tech life in harmony with their Grondi guides and guardians.

EPILOGUE

Kala sat in her house, looking out the windows and admiring her gardens. An old woman now, she found herself thinking more and more about Earth. She realized that, soon, probably when her generation died out, Earth would not only be a distant memory, but also a myth as well.

She had come here as a young woman, along with others, with not much more than a dream and a desire to see the human race survive. She, and other men and women, had worked hard over the years, and their dream had become a reality. There had been obstacles—some major, some minor—but they had been able to deal with them all.

She noticed the time, got up, and slowly made her way to the main square. There would be a full gathering tonight, perhaps the last for a long time, and representatives from even the most distant settlements were expected.

As the last of the Sierra mission original command staff still living, Kala held a place of honor in the leadership. She had no real authority, but she was always given a chance to express her views on any decision or issue in front of the board of governors. She enjoyed the chance to see how everyone was fairing and hear the most recent gossip.

Along her way, people greeted her. She could smell the food being prepared; she heard the laughter; she watched the children play; and she was pleased that her community had become a new Earth, as all originally hoped when she first landed.

She heard someone call her name and turned to see Jacob Patterson, one of Charlene's friends, walking quickly to catch up with her. She shooed away the children that had gathered around her with the promise of a story later and waited for Jacob to catch up with her.

"Fine weather for the gathering, isn't it?"

"Couldn't ask for better," she replied, continuing to walk toward the square.

"You'll be staying for the feast after the gathering, won't you?"

"You know I will, Jacob."

"Will you be voting on the ballot presented?"

"Jacob, what are you fishing for?" she asked, pausing and eyeing the young man. Kala had not lost any of her intuition and ability to see through innocent questions.

He looked down at his feet and scraped a piece of invisible moss from the stone under his left foot. Kala put her hand under his chin and pulled his face up so she could see into his eyes.

"What is it, Jacob? Not much happens around here that I don't hear about eventually, so if there's something I need to know, why don't you tell me."

"It's just that there's talk about going to the island again."

Kala sighed and dropped her hand. She looked up to the sky and wished, yet again, that Charlie were still alive to help her with the decision she would need to make.

"Thank you for telling me, Jacob. I'll go talk to the governors before the gathering starts. Don't worry, you've done the right thing."

When she got to the board's office, she knocked lightly on the door and waited for it to be opened for her. She knew that the governors would be there getting ready for the gathering, and she wouldn't have much time to convince them of she thought they should do. When the door opened, she entered with her head held high, and she walked to the center of the room.

"Kala, this is a surprise! We were just getting ready to convene the gathering."

"I know, but I've just heard some disturbing news."

The governors looked at each other, and Kala could see the worry in their faces.

"If it's about the trip to the island, we'll be putting it up for a vote, and we'll abide by the people's decision," the head governor responded.

"It shouldn't be put to a vote at all," Kala said. "You know that the decision made by the original ruling council was for life."

"We know quite well what that decision was, and why it was made. But, at the last regular communication, it was made clear that the original dissenters have all died and only the children are left. And if you remember correctly, the decision was made for the life of the original dissenters, not necessarily their offspring."

"And how do we know that the parents didn't poison their children to their cause? How do we know that by letting them back into our midst we won't be doing ourselves harm?"

"We don't. But don't you think there comes a time to forgive? Their parents suffered as they had to, but we feel that it's time to abide by the beliefs this colony was founded on."

Kala looked at the leaders of her community and, for a moment, was torn. Then, she looked down and sighed.

"I know I can trust that you will do the right thing for the community, but I have a bad feeling about letting these people back, even if their parents are gone. We've worked a very long time to get things where and how we want them. Can we risk having everything ruined?"

"We understand," replied the governor, "but there are circumstances that make this vote necessary. Advances have been made on the island that will infuse much needed new blood and new ideas into our community."

Seeing their minds were made up, Kala simply nodded and made her farewell. She walked out into the twilight and slowly made her way to the square. For a moment, she stood at its edge in the dark twilight, watching the hustle and bustle of the last minute preparations. Her thoughts turned to the past, as they seemed to more and more these days, and she wondered briefly if old people always began to reminisce before they died. She missed Charlie more than ever.

With a shake of her head, she walked out of the shadows and into the light to the benches in front of the dais. She watched as the governors entered the square stepped onto the dais, and settled themselves. As if by some unseen signal, all the people of Haven and the settlement representatives suddenly appeared and filled the square.

The vote went the way Kala knew it would; the people living on the island would be allowed back into the general population if they wanted to rejoin them. When the board declared the meeting over, the people gathered for the meal. Kala stayed only as long as she needed without seeming rude before returning to her home. She picked up her favorite picture of Charlie and sat down in her chair.

"Well, it's finally happened. They've done as you thought they would and the children are coming home." She stifled a sob and closed her eyes. "You were always such a rock and were able to see things more clearly then I could. Maybe they're right, but I don't think I'll ever know. I feel old, Charlie, I feel so old! I just wish I could see Earth one more time."

She sat in silence and listened to the sounds of her house and her world. She would be forever grateful that she had been chosen for the Sierra Mission and had embraced the adventures she had experienced.

At her funeral, the entire planet population gathered once again in the main square. Words of praise were spoken and love shown for the woman who had stood strong to make their world the way they wanted. Everyone was eternally grateful. As the last person filed passed her casket and the last flower had been placed, the first of the songs and poems began to be written so that she would always be remembered with love.

About the Author

Kate Roshon grew up in Philadelphia, where her parents still live in the house they have lived in for over fifty years! She currently lives in Townsend, Delaware, with Walt, her husband of more than twenty years. Though she never had children, she has raised many furry kids. The current crew includes two dogs, Piglet and Eponine; two cats, Spot and Nimby; and six unnamed chickens! After working a long day at the Dover Air Force Base, she enjoys reading, writing (of course!), and her needlepoint. The best part of her day is the time spent with her family and furry friends.

CPSIA information can be obtained
at www.ICGtesting.com
Printed in the USA
LVOW03s2109090517

533828LV00013BA/128/P